ICESPY

BY NORMAN L. MILLER

Marshall Jones Company
Manchester Center, Vermont
Publishers Since 1902

©Norman L. Miller, 1995
All Rights Reserved
Library of Congress
Catalog Card Number 95-077163
I.S.B.N. 0-8338-0224-0

PRINTED IN THE UNITED STATES OF AMERICA

Dedication

To all athletes who are pursuing their goal to win Olympic medals despite the tremendous odds!

Acknowledgement

This book would never have been created without Terry Brown and Jerome Malinowski suggesting that I write it. Jerome not only encouraged me, but also created the cover. I extend my gratitude to Jack Hume and R. Austin Healy for their faith in the story and to those who graciously provided me with technical advice. Thanks to Arliss Murray for the endless hours of helping; Jack Ricci who helped edit my rough draft; my wife, Marilyn for her support and hours of proofreading and to publishers Peggi Simmons and Craig Altschul of the Marshall Jones Co. who had faith in the book's merit.

This is a work of fiction. While the places are generally real, any resemblance to people, organizations, or events is purely coincidental and come directly from my own imagination.

Norman L. Miller, 1995
Princetown, New York

Contents

Chapter One:
Schenectady, New York 2

Chapter Two:
CIA Headquarters, Langley, Virginia 14
Riga, Latvia, USSR 16
Schenectady, New York 18

Chapter Three:
Headquarters, Andrews Air Force Base 24
Schenectady New York 25

Chapter Four:
Lake Placid, New York 32
Riga, Latvia, USSR 33
Sigulda, Latvia, USSR 39

Chapter Five:
Montreal, Canada 42
Frankfurt, West Germany 43
CIA Headquarters, Langley, Virginia 46
Winterberg, West Germany 47
Lake Placid, New York 49

Chapter Six:
Bethesda, Maryland 54
Winterberg, West Germany 55
KGB Headquarters, Riga, Latvia, USSR 57
Schenectady New York 58
Lake Placid, New York 59

Chapter Seven:
CIA Headquarters, Langley, Virginia 62
Frankfurt, West Germany 63

Chapter Eight:
Rochester, New York 70
Winterberg, West Germany 70
Syracuse, New York 73
CIA Headquarters, Langley, Virginia 76

Chapter Nine:
Winterberg, West Germany 78
Riga, Latvia, USSR 82
CIA Headquarters, Langley, Virginia 83
Neustrelitz, East Germany 84

Chapter Ten:
Winterberg, West Germany 88
Stuttgart, West Germany 90

Chapter Eleven:
McGuire Air Force Base, New Jersey .... .96
Marburg, West Germany .... .96
CIA Headquarters, Langley, Virginia .... .101

Chapter Twelve:
Winterberg, West Germany .... .104

Chapter Thirteen:
Riga, Latvia, USSR .... .112
Virginia Beach, Virginia .... .113
Winterberg, West Germany .... .115

Chapter Fourteen:
Schenectady New York .... .124
Winterberg, West Germany .... .127
Stuttgart, West Germany .... .128

Chapter Fifteen:
Winterberg, West Germany .... .132

Chapter Sixteen:
Winterberg, West Germany .... .144
Witzenhausen, East Germany .... .147

Chapter Seventeen:
Lake Placid, New York .... .154
Weimar, East Germany .... .155

Chapter Eighteen:
Riga, Latvia, USSR .... .166
Kassel, West Germany .... .171

Chapter Nineteen:
Schenectady, New York .... .176
Riga, Latvia, USSR .... .181
CIA Headquarters, Langley, Virginia .... .182

Chapter Twenty:
Lake Placid, New York .... .184

Chapter Twenty-one:
Riga, Latvia, USSR .... .198
Calgary, Canada .... .200

Chapter Twenty-two:
Montreal, Canada .... .208
Moscow, USSR .... .208
Schenectady, New York .... .209
CIA Headquarters, Langley, Virginia .... .210
Riga, Latvia, USSR .... .213
Newark, New Jersey .... .215

Chapter Twenty-three:
Riga, Latvia, USSR .... .220
Tallinn, Estonia, USSR .... .223

Chapter Twenty-four:
CIA Headquarters, Langley, Virginia .... .234
Riga, Latvia, USSR .... .235

Chapter Twenty-five:
North Atlantic .... .248
Tallinn, Estonia, USSR .... .248
CIA Headquarters, Langley, Virginia .... .249
The *Beriozka* .... .250
The *Willsboro* .... .254

Chapter Twenty-six:
CIA Headquarters, Langley, Virginia .... .260
Schenectady, New York .... .261
North Atlantic .... .262
The Pentagon .... .265
Sondrestrom Air Force Base, Greenland .... .265

Chapter Twenty-seven:
Polar Ice Cap .... .272
The Pentagon .... .272
Albany, New York .... .273

ICESPY

Chapter One

→ *Ice Spy*

Schenectady, New York

The ringing telephone took a few seconds to wake up Shawn Murphy. He fumbled for the phone on the night stand and picked up the receiver. Still half asleep, he muttered a confused greeting. The caller asked if he was Shawn Murphy.

"Who is this?" Shawn asked curiously.

"My name is Joe Sweeney. I apologize for calling you so late, but it's imperative that I speak to you as soon as possible."

Shawn glanced at the clock radio that read 1 a.m. He growled into the receiver, "Who the hell do you think you are, calling me at this hour?"

"I'm sorry, but it's very important and could be beneficial for your work with the Olympic Bobsled program. Does the name 'Rusty' mean anything to you?"

Shawn's interest piqued instantly and the mention of the name "Rusty" ran chills up and down his spine. He hadn't heard his former code name since he left the Central Intelligence Agency nearly twenty-five years ago. None of his current circle of associates knew anything about his past history with the CIA. Time stood still as the memories came rushing back.

The caller's voice broke the silence, "Shawn, are you still there?"

"Yeah, I'm still here."

Angela, Shawn's wife appeared to be sleeping throughout the conversation, but he knew better. He lowered his voice as he attempted to conceal what was taking place on the phone. It was impossible to speak freely and he knew what she was thinking.

Joe suspected there might be a problem because of the change in Shawn's voice and asked, "Is it difficult to talk because your wife is there?"

"Yes, it is."

"Can you meet me sometime tomorrow?"

"Ok, meet me at the Oxbow Tavern at 5 p.m. when I get out of work. Do you know where it is?"

"Just head me in the right direction. I'm familiar with Schenectady."

Shawn gave Joe directions to the tavern and told him to meet him in the lobby. He hung up the phone and although the bedroom was pitch black, he knew Angela was staring at him. She turned on the lamp and sat straight up in bed. She didn't have a suspicious nature, but it had taken her a long time to rid herself of the fear that came with being married to a CIA agent. The old feeling began to build inside her.

"Just who are you meeting at the Oxbow tomorrow?" she demanded.

"It's nothing for you to worry about. I'm meeting someone who wants to talk to me about bobsled business."

"Bullshit." she exclaimed in disbelief, "Don't give me that crap, I want to know who you're meeting!"

The anger in her voice made him realize that she suspected the caller was with the CIA. He told her that Joe claimed that he could help with the bobsled program. Angela made it very clear that she did not appreciate people calling at that hour in the morning to discuss bobsled business. She did not share his love for the sport. Bobsledding in her opinion was a violent and dangerous sport. His accident during the 1984 Olympic trials nearly killed her husband and the horrifying memory was still very clear in her mind. She also shared his dislike for many of the characters who controlled the sport, but understood his desire to help the athletes reach their dreams of competing in the Olympics.

"Angela, you've been around bobsled characters long enough to know what they're like. Sometimes these guys start on a project and work all night. We both know about Professor Bodynski's style. He often works all night."

She hated phone calls after they had gone to sleep. They usually meant someone was very ill or might even have died. Regardless, they always reminded her of the late night calls he got when he was an agent and generally meant she would not see or hear from him for days or even weeks. She sighed reluctantly but didn't make it an issue. Angela turned the light off and drifted back to sleep, but Shawn remained awake. Memories of when he worked for the CIA in Europe drifted back into his mind.

Shawn had barely fallen back to sleep when the alarm went off at 6 a.m. He got out of bed and went into the bathroom to shower. The hot water felt good and he thought about Joe's phone call. He wondered how the agency might be able to help him with his bobsled work. He knew they had an ulterior motive. It must be something big because the agency doesn't involve itself helping an organization like bobsledding without expecting something in return. He suspected that the agency must need his help. If he got involved, he would have to watch them very carefully to be sure the bobsled program actually benefited. He knew all too well that the CIA used people to reach their own objectives.

Shawn sat down at the table, picked up the morning paper, and hoped to avoid any discussion about Joe's phone call. He wasn't that lucky because Angela sat down directly across from him and he knew from the look in her eyes that she was still upset.

"I've never heard of a Joe Sweeney in the bobsled organization. People don't call in the middle of the night to talk about business unless they are a close friend and have a serious problem. The only group of people who do things like this would be the CIA."

He was startled that Angela put it together so quickly. He thought for a moment and quietly said, "I really don't know for sure, but I think you're right."

"You know how I feel about the Agency. How can they help you with the bobsled program?"

"I don't know, but I'm going to meet this Joe tonight and find out. Obviously, I couldn't ask him the specifics over the phone."

"Shawn, we agreed when you left the CIA that you were finished with that kind of work."

"Don't let your imagination run away with you. I'm simply meeting him to hear what he has to offer. It's not a big deal. You and I know that everyone thinks they have a solution to the bobsledding problems, but they rarely work out. I can't let any positive idea get away, regardless of the source."

→ *Ice Spy*

He looked up at the wall clock and realized he would be late for work if he didn't leave immediately. He kissed Angela good-bye and the look on her face told him that she was still uncomfortable about his meeting with Joe.

Shawn was tired when he arrived at the office one minute before eight. As soon as he walked in, his supervisor, M.Sgt. Olive Hanson, began reminding him that his monthly report was due that afternoon. Shawn told her the report would be ready on time and sat down at his desk. He closed his eyes and fervently wished she would drop dead. He hated this assignment. Olive was the supervisor for public affairs at the Schenectady Air Force Base. She was given the position as a result of pressure from her lawsuit claiming sex discrimination. Colonel David Crosby, the base commander, resolved the suit by transferring her to Public Affairs from the Personnel Department. Public Affairs is a small operation and Colonel Crosby believed her strange personality was less likely to cause problems in the smaller office. She had no experience in public affairs and the result was a miserable working environment.

Olive wasn't a morning person and usually overslept. She would call in late about twice a week and give Shawn some excuse for her not being at the office. Since she missed her breakfast, she would leave early for lunch and take extra time before returning. This consistent pattern irritated Shawn, who was punctual, making their working relationship next to impossible.

Since Olive lacked experience Shawn was forced to do additional work and was extremely frustrated whenever she claimed credit for results.

The work day dragged on and Olive's usual biting commentaries continued throughout the day until he completed his report and gave it to her. He often wished she would remarry someone who lived out of the area and would move far away. Olive had been married once, but the union lasted only seven months. Her husband obtained a divorce and Shawn often thought to himself it must have been mental cruelty. He certainly understood what her husband had gone through.

Shawn had never been a clock watcher, but today he glanced at the time every fifteen minutes until 4:30 finally arrived. He rushed out of the office and went out the back door to the parking lot. He was exhausted by the lack of sleep, but now, his adrenaline was pumping and he was eager to meet Joe. While he drove to the Oxbow, he wondered what Joe would look like. The heavy traffic was frustrating as he kept his new Corvette running at a snail's pace.

When he arrived at the tavern, the bar was crowded with the normal Friday night regulars from General Electric's local plant. He stood in the small lobby for only a couple of minutes when in walked a young red-haired man. Joe introduced himself and commented about how easy it had been to locate the tavern. They exchanged greetings and walked into the smoked-filled bar. Shawn spotted an empty booth in the dining room that was far enough away from the bar that the smoke wouldn't be so bothersome. He was a former bobsled athlete, turned coach, and the smoke always irritated him.

Shawn motioned with his hand to the waitress and when she arrived they each ordered a beer. They made small talk until the drinks arrived.

After the waitress left, he asked Joe how the Agency could help his efforts with the bobsled program.

"We have a situation that may benefit both of us, if we can work together. A Soviet bobsled coach approached one of our undercover agents working in the Soviet Union with a plea for help. Our agent, Walter Shapnek, is disguised as an American in the import-export business. Walter is convinced the coach has access to a lot of important technology that would be available to us if we help him defect."

"I don't understand how a Soviet bobsled coach would have the ability to accumulate enough technical information to make it worth while for you guys to get involved."

"Frankly, Shawn, we didn't believe a coach would have the level of technology that we could use, but the man is extremely smart and has given Walter enough information to convince us he isn't a mad scientist."

Joe reached into his attaché case and pulled out a photo. The dining room had begun to fill up so Shawn suggested they order dinner then excused himself to go to the men's room. On the way back to the table it occurred to him that the coach in the photo was Boris Yegorov.

When he returned to the table he asked Joe, "Is Boris Yegorov the coach?"

Joe smiled and asked, "How did you figure it out?"

"Boris built the Soviet bobsled program from scratch and won a bronze medal during their first Olympic competition in 1984. I don't know the reason why, but I do know from brief discussions with Soviet athletes that he had a serious falling out with their government officials."

The waitress arrived to take their dinner order, interrupting their conversation. Joe waited till she left and quietly began to tell Shawn what the CIA knew about Boris Yegorov. He explained that Boris had been a very successful Soviet luge coach and his athletes had won several Olympic medals under his direction. There hadn't been a bobsled program until 1974, when Boris went to the Soviet government with a plan to create one. He convinced his friend, Daumant Znatnajs, the Soviet Minister of Sports, to spend about two million dollars a year on the program.

Shawn thought that it was amazing, because the United States government wouldn't offer two cents to help their athletes with the Olympics. Their waitress returned with dinner and Joe waited until she left to continue his story. Shawn was amazed at the abundance of information the CIA was able to collect from their agent in the Soviet Union.

He noticed the tavern was quiet and looked at the clock on the wall. It was eight-thirty. He suddenly thought about Angela and decided to call her so she wouldn't worry. Shawn excused himself and went to the rear of the bar to use the pay phone.

A voice answered with a soft "Hello."

"Hi, hon, it's me. I thought I would give you a call and let you know I'll be home soon."

"Ok. I'm tired so I'm going to bed. Wake me when you come in and tell me about your meeting."

Shawn assured her that he would and returned to the table where Joe was reading some documents he had taken out of his attaché case. He put the documents away and picked up where he left off with the story. Walter had told them that Boris had guaranteed Daumant that his athletes would win a gold medal in bobsledding at the 1984 Olympics in Sarajevo, Yugoslavia.

"He wasn't too far from his goal," Shawn commented. "His team won the bronze and the U.S. finished in fifth place."

"Yup, and that's the start of his downfall. On his advice and promise to Daumant, the Soviets dumped over $18 million into the program for nine years and still couldn't win the gold."

Joe continued the story telling him that there was more than money involved. Boris assured the government that his program would be the envy of their competitors and the Soviets made sure that the rest of the world knew about their new bobsled program. They wanted everyone to think they built their program overnight, and its instant success would show the world that they could be leaders in any sport they chose to enter. They didn't want anyone to know they had secretly worked on it for six years before entering world cup competition in 1981.

"I don't understand how I can benefit from all this. What does the Soviet bobsled program have to do with me?"

"We believe Boris has the type of technical information that our government can use and it would be helpful to the bobsled program. We'll help Boris defect only if he provides us with the technical information we can use."

"Does he have that kind of information?"

"We believe he does. Boris was educated as a physicist at the Zalkalana Institute and he is recognized as one of the foremost metallurgists in the Soviet Union."

Shawn thought about all the unsuccessful research Americans had done in an attempt to learn what types of metals worked best on ice for bobsled runners. Joe explained that Boris had also worked at the Soviet Military Research Center in Kiev. He received his Doctorate in Materials Engineering from the prestigious Lenina Institute. He has also been recognized for his work with alloys and titanium used in their space program.

"Why is that so important?"

"You have to understand Soviet politics, Shawn. Boris Yegorov is half Latvian, not a full Russian. It is very unusual for a Latvian to be educated in a school that is as respected as Lenina."

"Why was he allowed to go there?"

"His mother is a Russian, otherwise it would have been impossible for him to receive this type of education."

"What difference does it make if you are a Russian or Latvian?" asked Shawn. "He is still a Soviet isn't he?"

"You're right, but the Russians invaded the Baltic States in 1940 at the beginning of World War II. The Russians killed, raped, and pillaged these poor people. Latvia was hit really hard. The Russians sent anyone they thought was even thinking of resisting to Siberia. Thousands of people were never heard from again. They even dug up graves and removed jewelry that had been buried with the bodies. Trainloads of jewelry and artifacts were sent back to Moscow during the early forties."

Shawn remembered some of the horrible things the Russians did when he was working in Europe and would never forget some of the sick things they had done to their own people. Joe continued his story about the Russian occupation of Latvia in 1940. The Russians believed the Germans were about to invade the Port of Riga, so they burned most of the large buildings and warehouses in the city so the Germans couldn't use them if the invasion was successful. Among the buildings burnt was the Latvian's most sacred possession, the Dome Cathedral that was built in 1209. After the war, the Latvians rebuilt the Dome Cathedral piece by piece so it looked almost the same as it did before the war. The Russians wouldn't let the Latvians rebuild the 30 altars that were inside the cathedral before the fire, but let them use the rebuilt building as a museum.

"The Latvians hate the Russians, Shawn. You can be sure that if Boris has the chance he will help *anyone* except the Russians."

"Our bobsled team might benefit from his help, but what's in it for the CIA?"

"We looked up some old articles written about his work in Soviet technical journals. He has an incredible amount of knowledge dealing with metals and their resistance to water and ice."

Shawn thought the story was crazy. If Joe was telling the truth, the Soviets might have found the right combination of metals and alloys to use for bobsled runners. Using the information for the bobsled program wouldn't be important to the government, but it would be extremely valuable to the Navy Department. Reducing water or ice friction would allow subs and ships to slip through the water faster and use less fuel.

"Why does Boris want to defect? You make it sound like he's desperate?"

"He is," replied Joe. "He committed a cardinal sin in the eyes of the Soviets. When his team didn't win the gold medal at Sarajevo, he blamed the athletes."

"Was he justified in blaming the athletes?"

"We think so. Boris kept all the bobsled technology to himself and it would appear that he had free access to all the technical information used by the Soviet Military Research Center at Kiev. Remember that Daumant Znatnajs also arranged for him to receive over $18 million to develop his program. He is certain the Russians will kill him."

"Why would they want to kill him?"

Joe motioned to the waitress to clear the table and the two men ordered another drink. They waited for her to return with the drinks and when she left Joe stretched his arms and relayed to Shawn how Boris tried to convince the Soviet officials that the program failed because the athletes didn't produce. They didn't believe him and, of course, the athletes were bitter once they learned Boris blamed them. The sport was controlled by Russians and Boris was a Latvian who was looked down upon by the Russians. Now both the government and the athletes were upset with him. The East Germans recognized his ability and took advantage of the situation by secretly hiring him to work on their bobsled program.

"We've suspected for several years that the Soviets and East Germans had discovered some type of alloy that was combined with steel and hardened just right to give them an unfair advantage with their runners."

Joe looked around the nearly empty room and lowered his voice slightly. "It's fairly obvious that Boris discovered how to make runners less resistant to ice and has used it with both country's bobsled programs."

"I would think the Russians would be quite upset if they suspected that he shared this type of information with the East Germans." Shawn wondered if Boris had really discovered the alloy. "If this is true, then why did he use the information for Olympic sports and not give it to the Soviet Navy?"

"I'll tell you what we think," replied Joe. "Nobody helps their competitors in the Soviet system even if they're the East Germans. That's a sure death sentence."

"Why haven't they killed him?"

"Boris outsmarted the Russian officials. He kept his secret from the Russian military because he knew they would use it and he would never receive any recognition for his work. He believed that if he could build a bobsled program that would dominate the sport in the Olympic Games, he would receive world recognition and be rewarded with more money from the Russian officials to continue his work. He hated the Russians and had no intention of providing the information for their military.

"After the Soviets failed to win a gold medal in 1984, the athletes refused to work with him and the Russian officials continued to pressure him. They were embarrassed for what they believed was a failed program. They didn't understand how good his program was. His equipment was superior to the rest of the competitors at Sarajevo and the East Germans understood that Boris had developed runners that enabled their sleds to have an unfair advantage. They believed the Soviet bobsled drivers were unable to control the faster sleds and it was driving skills that prevented the Soviets from winning the gold medal.

"The East Germans invited Boris to work with their technical program, but not with their athletes. They paid him an extraordinary amount of money in German marks and he stashed it in a Swiss bank account. The Russians want the money and his technology. We believe they will not kill him right away because they want the technology, but if they suspect he is planning to defect or provide the information to another country he will be killed immediately. The government keeps a constant surveillance on him."

"Does our Navy department really think the technology will reduce friction on water and ice?" asked Shawn. "How much information does the Navy have on this?"

"There is no question that this information could benefit both the Soviets' and our Navy. We believe the Soviets haven't been able to obtain the information or they would have killed him by now. Regardless, the people at the David Taylor Research Lab are very interested in obtaining this technology."

"What is the David Taylor Research Lab?" asked Shawn.

"This is the U.S. Navy's billion dollar research lab." Joe looked around the room to be sure nobody could hear their conversation and leaned close to Shawn. "There's something else you should know. Boris has been working very closely with the leaders of the Latvian's underground movement to separate Latvia from the Soviet Union."

Shawn learned the Latvian Socialist Slate Party filed papers with the international courts requesting that the papers the Russians used in 1940 to occupy their country be declared illegal. He now understood that the tension between Latvians and Russians would be extraordinarily high.

"How do I fit into the picture?"

"You've been selected to be on the United States Olympic Bobsled coaching staff so you'll be able to move freely in and out of European countries. We'll have to work on a way to get you into the Soviet Union for bobsled work so you can make contact with Boris. The military has to release you for temporary duty as an Olympic coach so you're a natural choice."

"The military should release me, but you've got to understand that I work for some very small-minded people." Shawn knew that Olive would do everything possible to prevent him from being reassigned to the Olympic coaching staff. If he was gone for any length of time Colonel Crosby would find out that he had made a terrible mistake when he put Olive in charge of public affairs at the Air Force Base. She didn't have a clue about doing the job. "There is a strong possibility that my supervisor won't release me for Olympic duty, Joe."

"Don't give it another thought. I think the Department of Defense has just a bit more power than your boss. It will be a rather simple task to get you released." Joe told him not to worry about the military giving him the time because the Agency would make all the arrangements for him in Washington. He explained that Shawn's experience as a former CIA agent, plus having Olympic credentials, would get him just about anywhere they would want him to go in Europe and the Eastern Bloc countries. The combination of the two was something they could depend upon.

The bartender walked over to their table and told them that the tavern was closing so they left and went out to the parking lot. Joe told Shawn he would call during the next week to see if he would help with the assignment and they shook hands and left. He promised not to call at 1 a.m.. and they both smiled. Shawn looked at his watch as he drove onto the street and it was close to midnight. The story still hadn't made its full impact on him. It was fascinating that Boris was in possession of such extraordinary technology and wanted to defect.

As Shawn drove home he wondered if the training he received so many years ago would still be there. Why had the CIA approached him? He worked in public affairs at the Air Force base which didn't make him a strong candidate. The CIA must have opened their records on his past employment with them and believed he could do the job. He had worked as an agent in France and was accustomed to moving around Europe. He spoke French fluently, although he seldom had a chance to use it. He thought about working again as an agent and chuckled because foreign agents wouldn't expect to have him operating there. A perfect cover, at least for several months, certainly long enough to accomplish whatever needed to be done. The setup looked perfect. As an Olympic bobsled coach for the United States he often traveled to Eastern Bloc countries and the Soviet Union. Nobody would think it was odd for him to be there now.

The idea began to build excitement in him. His first problem would be

Angela. He would have to convince her that he should take the assignment. He couldn't tell her everything or she would give him all kinds of grief. She made it clear when he left the agency that she would leave him if he ever returned. She lived on tranquilizers whenever he had to go out on assignments and it had taken years for her to rid herself of the fears.

Pulling the car into the driveway he noticed the lights were out. It was so late that he hoped she would be asleep or too tired to question him. He needed more time to think about the offer. Shawn went into the bedroom and began to undress. "I thought you were coming home soon after you called me? I was worried that something might have happened to you."

"I intended to, but the story Joe was telling me just took a lot more time than I expected. You knew I was at the Oxbow."

"Do you really think he can help?"

"If what he says is true, they might be able to obtain information on how to make the runners faster."

"How? You've tried everything. You even had some of the brightest people at the General Electric Research Lab working on the runners and they came up empty. Metallurgy students and their professors at RPI and Union were unable to improve on what the team was using."

"The Agency might be able to help us obtain some very important technical information, but I don't know the full story yet. We have to meet again to work out the details."

"You know how I feel about you working with these people."

"Don't worry, I only want to help them enough to get the information." He lied! "Lets go to bed, I'm exhausted."

Meanwhile, Joe rolled his window down at the New York Thruway toll booth and put the ticket over his visor before rolling the window up again. He dreaded the three hour drive to the City and it would be difficult for him to stay awake. He turned the air conditioner to high to help keep him alert and punched search on the radio looking for a station with a strong signal. Soft music poured from the speakers so he left the dial on 95.5 so he could relax and not have to think.

Joe set the cruise control on 62 mph as he drove south. He thought about Shawn and how he looked young for the age of fifty. He must spend a lot of time working out to stay in such physical shape and Joe hoped that when he turned fifty he looked as good. It had been years since Shawn worked with the Agency and Joe wondered if he might have become too soft mentally for this type of assignment. Maybe not. Shawn had a reputation with the military for being a tough person when needed and his records indicated that he was someone who succeeded with any assignment given to him. This dedication was apparent in Shawn's work with the Olympic bobsled team.

The next step was for the Agency to make certain the technology that Boris Yegorov had was worth all the expense and risk needed to help him defect and stay alive. He would meet with his boss, Fred Unser, Director of European Operations. Fred worked at the CIA Headquarters in Langley, Virginia. Then he needed to talk with Bob Gilmore, a research physicist at the Taylor Lab. He was confident Bob would be able to give him all the significant information he needed and hoped that he would agree with Walter Shapnek that the technology would be a major breakthrough for the Navy. Joe finally arrived at the Lincoln Tunnel at 3:30 a.m.. Twenty minutes later he entered his apartment in downtown Manhattan. Exhausted, he collapsed on the bed without undressing. He was asleep within seconds.

The sparrows chirping outside the bedroom woke Shawn. He could feel the heat from the morning sun coming through the window. That meant it would be another hot August day. He looked across the bed and noticed that Angela wasn't there. On Saturdays when it was hot, she preferred to get up early and do housework before the heat got uncomfortable. He had promised her that he would go to the landfill and get rid of the accumulating garbage in the garage. He got out of bed, stretched, and got dressed. Angela had breakfast ready, so he sat down at the table and picked up the morning paper.

"What's the plan of action for today? I hope you didn't forget about going to the landfill?"

"Nope, I'll go right after I finish eating."

Angela avoided looking at Shawn to prevent him from seeing how upset she was about him doing work for the Agency. She thought her prayers had been answered years ago when he agreed to resign from the CIA and work for the Air Force. He loved bobsledding and she knew he would do whatever he could to improve the sport. She didn't want to worry him and hoped to conceal her dreadful fear of him working behind the iron curtain again. Tears swelled in her eyes as she left the kitchen to begin her Saturday morning dusting.

Shawn finished breakfast and drove to the landfill with the trash. As he drove back to his house the proposition Joe made wouldn't leave his mind. There had been so many people in the past who were convinced that their ideas were the right answer to the bobsled technology mystery. Everyone's, except Professor Bodynski of Syracuse University had failed. By the time he reached his house Shawn had made his decision. He wasn't interested in helping either Joe or the Bobsled association, but he knew he was the only association official really interested in helping the athletes. When Joe called the following week, Shawn knew what he would tell him.

Chapter Two

→ *Ice Spy*

CIA Headquarters, Langley, Virginia

Joe Sweeney showed his identification to the receptionist. She put his code into the computer and told him that Fred Unser was expecting him. He entered the waiting elevator and rode to the fifth floor. Fred was talking on the phone and motioned with his hand to take a seat. Joe sat down and looked around the room admiring the clear view of the fighter jets circling nearby Langley Air Force Base. The huge office always impressed him. An oversized sofa, executive desk, and large conference table with ten chairs barely filled the room. A collection of photos Fred had taken during the many years he worked in Europe covered the walls. Photography was one of the few things Fred enjoyed doing outside of work and he had mastered this particular hobby. His scenic photographs of European landscapes were spectacular.

"Joe, buddy, you're looking good!" Fred exclaimed as he hung up the phone and walked over to shake his hand.

"What's with the gray hair, Fred?" Joe enjoyed kidding him about his hair since his own was still red.

"The gray doesn't bother me. I'm just happy to still have hair. My brother lost most of his before he reached forty."

"Did you look at the file Walter sent on the Soviet character who wants to defect?"

"Yes. I met with the special operations people to start working out a plan. They believe it could be done, but they need a lot more information."

"How much time would they need?" Joe asked.

"Why? Is time a serious problem?"

"This coach knows he's in serious trouble, Fred. Once the KGB gets its hands on the money the guy stashed in a Swiss bank account they might kill him without getting any technical information from him."

"How much money did the East Germans give him?"

"About $5 million."

"You're right. There's enough money involved for them to waste him. I suspect they'll start to put a lot of pressure on him to try and obtain his technical secrets. It's hard to believe these countries put so much value on winning gold medals."

Fred briefed him about whom they were sending to meet with Walter Shapnek in the Soviet Union to start the operation plan. They had to be extremely careful not to blow Walter's cover or bring attention to the Soviets that they had an interest in Boris Yegorov. The Russians would then kill him without trying to obtain either the technology or the $5 million in the Swiss account. Fred was certain Boris wouldn't give them any information until he was hidden safely in the United States. He had one other problem to deal with before the plan could be put in action. They hadn't anticipated this operation and budgets were a very sensitive issue around here. He would have to meet with the finance department upstairs to have additional money transferred into his budget.

Joe briefed Fred about his plans to visit with Bob Gilmore at the Navy Research Lab. They both agreed that Bob wasn't the only person who understood the technology, but was about the only one they knew who could explain it simply enough for the average person to understand. Joe then briefed him about his meeting with Shawn Murphy in Schenectady. He said he believed Shawn was interested and would take on the assignment, but admitted that he was also a difficult person to predict.

Fred urged him to stay in contact with Shawn, because the Agency needed him. They agreed that Shawn had the ability and determination to accomplish whatever would be required and their records indicated that he had nerves of steel when under pressure during his employment with the Agency. "He's very involved with the U.S. bobsled organization, but doesn't trust their officials and with good reason."

"Why do you say that, Fred?"

"It appears that some of the officials are helping themselves to the funding they receive from the United States Olympic Committee and private donations."

"You mean the bobsled officials are stealing money from the athlete's program?"

Fred told Joe they suspected some officials were abusing the association's credit cards with their high lifestyles and the bills were paid with funds intended to be used for athlete's training. The majority of the misused funds were spent on business trips to Europe that the athletes suspected were mainly vacations.

"Is it possible that Shawn is involved with this?"

"Rest assured. I know for sure he isn't."

"How do you know?"

Fred leaned back in his chair and began to smile. He told Joe that Shawn had gotten so upset about the association officials open practice of misusing the funds that he went to the Olympic Committee and requested their help in exposing them. The Olympic Committee didn't want to get involved because the bad publicity would have a dramatic effect on their fund raising efforts for the larger sports association. They felt that the money the bobsled officials might misuse was comparatively small to the overall Olympic budget. The jerks controlling the bobsled association kept getting more greedy and at the same time got careless. Apparently, Shawn fooled them into thinking he didn't know what they were doing and took the information to the FBI. They now have an undercover in the bobsled organization who is working on obtaining evidence to use in court.

"This information wasn't in the file. How'd you learn this?"

"I did my homework, young fellow. I called the Feds to see if they had any information about the bobsled organization and they were loaded with it. You need to know what we're working with, Joe. Some of these people operate as if they're Colombian drug lords."

Fred continued his briefing. It was apparent that Lestor Fetor, an ex-convict with Mafia connections, had taken control of the association with a very simple scheme. Anyone could join the United States Bobsled Association and receive full voting privileges by simply filling out an application and paying a $25 fee. Lester and another mob friend, Nino Casatelli, had several hundred people make out applications and they paid their membership fees for them. They held the new membership applications until the last day and then filed them with the association. At the next annual meeting when new officers were elected, they controlled the election and got themselves elected as officials.

They kept the current president, Wilbur Hippenbecker, but made it clear that he would stay in office as long as he continued to work with them. Fetor was convinced that Hippenbecker wouldn't be a problem for them, because he was on an ego trip and was obsessed with the title. He was content to take frequent trips to Europe to represent the bobsled association at international meetings and rub shoulders with other bobsled officials. The FBI wasn't sure if Hippenbecker was aware of the real reason that Fetor and Casatelli took control of the Association. The FBI suspected they had set up a money laundering system for the mob by using the association.

"Are you serious?" Joe asked in amazement. "You mean the mob launders money through the bobsled association?"

"You got it. Fetor and Casatelli are only in it for the bucks. The unsuspecting athletes are working their butts off trying to earn an Olympic medal and these characters spend their money faster than they can get it."

"This is bizarre," said Joe.

"There's more," replied Fred. "Their executive director is also a real gem. In fact, the bobsled athletes refer to him as 'Slime' when the officials aren't around. His name is Roger Ferris and he lives in the fast lane. Drugs, booze, and women. The athletes claim his hand is always in the petty cash and the Feds believe they're right."

"How can we help them?"

"We don't get involved. The FBI is in place and in time they'll put these low-life thieves away. In the meantime the officials get along well with Murphy and we don't expect them to get in our way."

Joe briefed Fred about Shawn's concern with getting released from military duty to serve as an Olympic coach. He explained how jealous his supervisor was and that she was making it very difficult for him with his job at the Air Force Base. Fred chuckled at how some people in the military think they have more power than the Pentagon. Fred assured Joe that when the time came for Shawn to leave, the Pentagon would have him released so fast their heads would spin. They spent the next few minutes discussing Joe's trip to Bethesda to meet with Bob Gilmore at the David Taylor Research Lab. After working out a few minor details with the plan to help Boris defect, Joe left CIA Headquarters and drove his rental car back to the airport to catch a shuttle to New York. He knew there was a lot of work that had to be done if the agency was going to get Boris out successfully.

Riga, Latvia USSR

As he approached the desk to register, Walter Shapnek remembered how bad the accommodations had been during his last visit. The Hotel Riga was state owned and most of the employees were Russian. They didn't hide the fact that they didn't want American business people in Latvia. The KGB suspected the Latvians were secretly trying to set up trade agreements should they be successful with their efforts to have the papers Stalin used in 1940 to occupy Latvia declared illegal. Now the Russians were putting a lot of pressure on the Latvian people to maintain control.

"*Dohbriy dyen.*" Walter greeted the young girl sitting behind the desk in Russian. Smiling, Walter gave her his name and told her he had reservations for the next two days. The girl looked at Walter with no expression on her face and asked for his passport, declaration, and visa. She took his credentials and disappeared into another room behind the registration desk. Walter knew they would keep the passport and visa for a couple of days to check him out. This always amused him. They must have checked him out a hundred times and every time he checked into a hotel they would check him out again. It amused him at how far behind the Soviets were from the free world. In the United States, a computer would have your entire life history available in seconds. The girl returned and told Walter they would have to keep his papers for a day or two.

"That's fine. May I have my room key now?" Walter asked.

"*Dah*, your room is #320 and here is your declaration."

"*Spaseeba.*" He thanked her in Russian then picked up his room key and papers. The girl sat down and resumed her work. Walter couldn't help thinking the Russian hotel employees all had faces made of stone. He picked up his luggage and walked to the elevator, which was old and slow like everything else in the hotel. Finally, it reached the third floor. He stepped out and approached the lady behind the security desk. All Soviet hotels have a desk on each floor and someone is there 24 hours a day. Just another way the Russians keep track of everyone.

"*Dohbriy dyen*," Walter said greeting her.

"*Dohbriy dyen*," she replied as Walter gave her his room key. She would have to make out another registration paper before he could go to his room. She finished the registration paper and handed the key back to Walter.

"*Spaseeba.*" He smiled and started to walk down the hall to his room.

"*Da svidahniya.*"

Surprised at her saying good-bye, Walter turned and smiled. She smiled and began to blush. Suddenly she remembered what would happen to her if someone observed her being so friendly with an American. The Russians considered this to be an improper act against the state. She abruptly regained her "stone face" appearance and sat back down at her desk.

Walter decided to keep track of her. It's nice to know who is friendly and who isn't. He thought she must be a Latvian. Entering his room he didn't bother checking for bugs the KGB would have planted. It wasn't worth the effort and sometimes it was better to have them hear the conversation. He enjoyed letting them hear erroneous information when he had the opportunity. If he needed to discuss something important with someone, it was a lot easier to leave the hotel and go for a walk. He checked his watch and decided to take a short nap before meeting his contact from Langley.

→ *Ice Spy*

Schenectady, New York

Shawn arrived at his office early to prepare for a radio talk show scheduled that afternoon to promote the Air National Guard. He enjoyed being a guest on talk shows but had to be careful because talk show hosts often try to create controversy on the air to encourage listeners to call in, which, of course, causes more controversy. He was a frequent guest and the hosts always appreciated his quick wit and ability to remain composed on the air. Audiences liked this informality and programs with large, active followings attracted sponsors.

Looking up at the clock, Shawn noticed it was after nine and Olive still hadn't arrived for work. Sergeant Bruce Monroe was sitting at his desk listening to his radio through ear phones. Monroe was a religious fanatic and listened to evangelistic messages on a Christian radio station every day for hours. Shawn shook his head in disgust. He knew both of Monroe's true personalities. On the down side, Monroe was a liar and a thief. Money and personal items had to be kept under lock and key in the office or they would mysteriously disappear. The second personality displayed a Christian attitude that was convincing enough to fool most people. "Just the kind of person you would expect Olive Hanson to hire for Public Affairs," Shawn thought.

"Monroe, did Olive call you this morning?"

"No, I haven't heard from her yet, but I'll give her a call. She probably overslept."

"She's an embarrassment. Everyone on base must be at work by seven-thirty and I don't think this broad has ever been on time five days in a row. She's always complaining that she never gets any respect. Maybe if she tried to get to work on time like everyone else, the people who work here wouldn't be down on her all the time."

"Give her a break, you know she lives alone and has nobody to help her out. It's tough for a divorced woman to maintain a house all alone."

"She doesn't really live alone, Bruce boy. She has plenty of company at night. Her problem is that she doesn't go to sleep at a decent time like normal people who have to be at work early in the morning."

"You've got a lot of nerve saying she sleeps with men every night." Bruce was outraged.

"Open your eyes, Bruce boy. I didn't say she slept with men, I said she has plenty of company and doesn't get enough sleep. Don't put words in my mouth. The bottom line is, she spends very little time actually working here. Hell, you should try working yourself. I'll bet that sometime during the day, in between the evangelist's screaming for everyone to repent, a voice on your radio whispers for Bruce to try working. Even if it's just a little work."

"I don't need this." He stood up and walked toward the door slamming it as he departed the room.

Shawn shook his head and laughed. He knew Bruce would go directly down the hall into the vacant chaplain's office and call Olive to tell her what happened. Bruce and Olive were very close friends. Olive often gave motherly advice to Bruce who had his share of problems with women. He had been married four times and was now living with another woman. He suspected that Bruce and Olive had slept together on several occasions.

Shawn left the office to get some coffee and watched Bruce slip into the chaplain's office. Bruce shut the door and dialed Olive's number. The chaplain was away on vacation so he knew nobody would hear his conversation. After the phone rang eleven times Bruce heard a faint "Hello."

"Olive, did you oversleep?"

"Oh, shit! What time is it?"

"Twenty minutes to ten," replied Bruce. "Personally, I don't care if you sleep all day, but Shawn's running his mouth about you never coming to work on time. He was bitching about you and I not pulling our share of the work load."

"Let him run his mouth, Bruce. I put the screws to him a few days ago, he won't be such hot shit in a couple of days," laughed Olive.

"What did you do to him?"

"I fixed it so he won't be going to the Olympics."

"How the hell did you do that?"

Olive told Bruce how she had gone to the communications office to send a message to Washington and was alone in the room when a message requesting that Shawn be reassigned to temporary duty as an Olympic coach came in on the computer. She deleted it in the computer so there would be no record of it at their base, but the sender would think they had received the request.

"I love it," laughed Bruce. "The lousy bastard deserves it."

"Listen, Bruce, if anyone looks for me just tell them I called and I'm at the newspaper taking care of some advertisements."

Bruce hung up and went back to the Public Affairs office. When Shawn returned to the office, Bruce told him that Olive had called and she was at the newspaper office. Shawn chuckled and dialed Olive's telephone number. She answered on the second ring and said, "Hello."

"Hi, Olive. I just called to see if you were okay," Shawn said.

Olive cursed and slammed the receiver down. She picked up her pocketbook and left for the office. Shawn looked at the clock when Olive arrived. It was ten-thirty.

"Good morning, did you get enough rest, Olive?" asked Shawn.

"Listen, you wise-ass, I've had about enough of your sarcastic comments."

"Really, Olive. You should try coming in on time occasionally, and maybe do a little work when you're here and maybe I wouldn't make sarcastic comments. Oh, by the way, I noticed in your report to the commander that you took credit for my story about Science Foundation's Airlift."

"Why do you always imply that I purposely take credit for your work? Did it ever occur to you that maybe I simply made a mistake?" she yelled.

"Oh, it has occurred to me, but you do this every month and make the changes after the commander has seen the report so he thinks you are actually doing something."

"Listen, you son of a bitch. You work for me. Do you understand that? I'll run this office anyway I want. If you have a problem with that go talk with Colonel Crosby."

→ *Ice Spy*

"No, Olive, I don't have a problem with your leadership. In fact, I'm really impressed." He put his coat on, picked up his brief case and started to leave for the radio station. "Olive, I have to leave and do another talk show, why don't you come with me and be a guest on the show?"

"I've got too much work to do," she lied.

"Shawn chuckled to himself as he walked out the door. He knew she would always have a good excuse for not going on a talk show. He thought about her being a guest and laughed thinking it would be hilarious. Colonel Crosby would have a hemorrhage because her incompetence would be obvious to everyone and he knew a lot of people at the base would tune in the talk show whenever Shawn was on the air. Olive had enough sense to realize this and avoided talk shows assiduously.

As soon as the program was over, Shawn returned to the base and went directly to the communication unit to check on the message from Washington. The clerk on duty checked the computer and shook his head. Shawn was suspicious and wondered if Olive might have intercepted the message somehow. He was sure that something was wrong and asked the clerk to please check once more. Nothing. The message was important because he was scheduled to be in West Germany with the Bobsled team in just one week. He thanked the clerk and returned to Public Affairs.

The events of the day gave Shawn a migraine headache. He took four aspirins as soon as he arrived home and laid down to take a nap. Several hours later the phone woke him. The communications clerk at the base called and said no messages for him had come in from Washington.

Angela was still at work and would probably go shopping before she came home. He listened to the telephone messages on his answering machine and his mood changed when he heard Joe Sweeney's voice. Joe left his phone number and asked Shawn to call him. He had forgotten about Joe. Maybe Joe could get word to the right people in Washington. Shawn didn't have the right connections to reach the general who could make the decision to overrule Colonel Crosby if Olive was successful in convincing him not to permit his assignment to temporary duty. He dialed Sweeney's telephone number and Joe answered on the third ring.

"Hi, Joe, this is Shawn Murphy."

"How are you doing, Shawn?"

"Not too good. I had a bad day at work and now I've got a bitch of a headache. I still haven't received a message from Washington recommending my base commander to release me for temporary duty so I can work as a coach in the Olympics. I was told the general signed the message, but it still has not arrived at our base and I'm running out of time."

"Don't worry about the message. We will take care of it tomorrow morning. Did you think about our proposal?"

"Yes, I did and I'm on board with you," he replied. "My main concern right now is my job. I can't help you if I don't get reassigned to temporary duty."

"Don't worry about getting out of work. Just get your personal affairs taken care of and we will take care of your problem at work. You must really work for a simple-minded bitch. I can't believe she wouldn't be ecstatic about you being selected as an Olympic coach. My God, she works in Public Affairs. I should think she would thrive on all the positive publicity the Air Force would receive from your work with Olympic athletes."

"You hit the nail on the head, when you described her as simple-minded. Some day I will tell you the real story about her. Do you have any more information about our man?"

"Not at the moment. We have someone working on that situation right now. I'll brief you when we meet again." Joe assured him that his reassignment problem at work would be resolved during the next day or two. Shawn suspected someone from the Department of Defense would meet with General Abbott, the Commander of the Air Force. Shortly after that meeting, Shawn's commander would be directed to complete the reassignment immediately.

Joe told him to continue with his plans to leave for Lake Placid on Monday. Shawn was scheduled to report a day early and help the athletes prepare for the Olympic Trials in West Germany. Joe assured him that he would be contacted shortly after he had arrived in Europe with the team and brought him up to date on the current status of their plan.

"Will you be going to Europe?" asked Shawn.

"I expect to, but I'm not sure just when. I'll be real busy at this end putting everything together. It's been a long time since you've been involved with espionage work, Shawn. Keep a cool head and be on guard at all times. Don't worry, we won't turn you loose without help. We will bring you up to speed while you're in West Germany."

"Joe, I want to thank you for all the help so far. I hope this works out because our athletes need a lot of help. The bastards who are running the association don't do anything to help them. The assholes make it harder, because they spend the bulk of the athletes money on their personal agendas."

Joe agreed and gave him some last minute information and instructions before they finished their phone conversation.

Shawn hung up the receiver and thought about what could happen during the next several months. He had mixed feelings, yet he knew what he needed to achieve. The down side would be Angela. Being married to her twenty-five years was long enough to know exactly what would go through her mind. He didn't need to tell her his decision, she would know. He also knew she would not attempt to stop him even though the assignment would create tremendous stress on her.

Chapter Three

Headquarters, Andrews Air Force Base

General Abbott arrived at his office just as his secretary answered the phone call from the Department of Defense. She placed the caller on hold and quickly explained to the general the purpose of the phone call. He made a motion with his hand telling her to transfer the call to his desk in the adjacent room. With his coat still on, he shut his door and picked up the phone. Nothing irritated General Abbott more than having the Department of Defense call and chew him out because a subordinate commander couldn't follow simple directions. The general assured the caller that he had sent a message to Colonel Crosby as he had requested and would send a second immediately. He would personally call Murphy's base commander to be sure he understood his message.

General Abbott hung up the receiver and pressed his intercom button. He told his secretary to get the file on Shawn Murphy and then get Colonel Crosby on the phone. He was furious and thought to himself that it was amazing that people like Crosby work themselves up into a command position. He thought about Shawn Murphy and wondered what he was doing that was so important the Department of Defense got involved. Whatever it was, it had to be big if both departments got into the picture. Regardless, he didn't want to be on the bad side of the Department of Defense. Crosby must be a fool. He would find out what happened to his first message and heads would roll. He couldn't afford a problem like this in his command.

His secretary signaled him on the intercom that Colonel Crosby was holding on the phone. General Abbott picked up the telephone and spent the next ten minutes explaining to Crosby that he wanted Murphy transferred to temporary duty as an Olympic coach effective immediately. He made sure that Crosby understood what would happen to him if there were any more problems with the transfer and that he was looking into what had happened to the original message he sent to the base. He hung up and asked his secretary to get Shawn Murphy on the telephone. She signaled moments later that Murphy was on the other line.

"Hello, Sgt. Murphy?"

"Yes, sir," replied Shawn.

"This is General Abbott and I apologize that you didn't get the message I sent out last week. I just spoke with Colonel Crosby and made it very clear to him that I wanted him to transfer you to temporary duty as an Olympic coach. I'm really pleased that you have been selected for this position. We'll give you all the support you'll need. Just go out there and make us proud at the Olympics. If you have any more problems just give me a call; understand?"

"Yes, sir!" Shawn was thrilled. "I appreciate you calling me, I know you're busy."

"I'm never too busy to make this type of call. We'll be taking care of all the details. I'll call next week before you leave for Europe. I'm thrilled that you will be representing the United States at the Olympics."

The general went into the briefing room next to his office where his staff was waiting. He spent the next twenty minutes explaining to them about

Shawn Murphy's situation and the involvement of the Defense Department. He didn't feel the need to mention Shawn working with the CIA at this time. He instructed his deputy to execute all the necessary paperwork required to complete Shawn's reassignment. The general told his staff how upset he was that the first message sent out wasn't received at the Schenectady Air Base and he wanted an investigation started immediately to find out what went wrong. He was concerned that they might have a security leak and they couldn't afford this type of a problem. He instructed his deputy to start his investigation with a phone call to Shawn Murphy. General Abbott needed to know if there was a security leak at the Schenectady base or was Murphy simply a victim of an extremely incompetent supervisor. Regardless, he was going to get answers and take care of the problem.

Schenectady, New York

General Abbott's deputy called Shawn and spoke with him for about twenty minutes, being very thorough with all the details of his problem with his supervisor, Olive Hanson and her supervisor, Lt. Col. Amos Fowlkes, the deputy base commander. The deputy reiterated how upset the general was that the message selecting Shawn as an Olympic coach hadn't been received and suspected that someone at the base had intercepted and destroyed it. He told Shawn that he was aware the Communications unit maintained a security camera and had a video of every person who entered or left their building, including the time. It wouldn't be too difficult to determine who was in the building during the time the message was sent. Shawn briefed the deputy in depth about his problems in the Public Affairs office and how Lt. Col. Fowlkes covered up for Olive to prevent Colonel Crosby, the base commander, from learning about her incompetence. Shawn knew that both Olive and Bruce were eavesdropping on his phone conversation.

Shawn hung up the phone and Olive asked suspiciously, "Who were you talking with, Shawn?"

"That was a personal call, Olive. If he wanted to talk with you he would have called you. I have a feeling that he might be calling you in the very near future." Olive's obvious discomfort amused Shawn.

Olive got up and left hurriedly, slamming the door as she walked out. She went directly to Lt. Col. Fowlke's office and told Amos about the conversation she just overheard between Shawn and General Abbott's aide in Washington. She was extremely upset that Shawn had implicated her and Amos. Olive suddenly began to cry and Amos rushed around his desk to comfort her. Sobbing, she told him that she had been in the communications office when the message from General Abbott was printed by the computer. The communications clerk wasn't at his desk, so she deleted the message from the system and destroyed the printed message. She told Amos she was certain an investigation was being conducted to learn what had happened to the message and she would be court-martialed once the general learned the truth.

"Don't worry about him. He can run his mouth all he wants, but he isn't going anywhere and I'll guarantee that he doesn't." Amos continued to hold

Ice Spy

Olive and began to gently rub her back while he consoled her. She had never been held by a black man and his muscular body began to excite her as he held her tightly and used both hands to caress her back. She thought about the rumors on base she had heard about him abusing his former wife and wondered if he really was a wife beater. Suddenly, they heard Shawn outside the office talking to Chief Curley in the hallway and Amos told Olive she should return to her office and act as if nothing had happen. He told her to stay calm and assured her that he would make sure the investigation would go nowhere.

Chief Curley closed his door and told Shawn about a phone call he had just received from General Abbott's aide. The chief was concerned about the missing message, since he was directly responsible for all base communications. Chief Curley listened to Shawn and wondered what the real story was about the reassignment. He had been in the military for over thirty years and had never known the Defense Department to get involved with something like this. He was certain that Shawn must be involved with something very big to have a four-star general personally call him. The chief chuckled to himself when Shawn explained that Olive and Amos were trying to prevent the temporary duty assignment.

"Excuse me," interrupted the chief politely. "The general told you that another message would be coming through the system?"

"That's what he said, Chief."

"This is exciting," chuckled Chief Curley. "I'll alert my people in communications to watch for it and I'll call you as soon as we get it."

"Thanks, Chief. I'll see you in the morning. I've got a lot of things to get done or Angela will be on my case. Thanks for all your help."

"My pleasure. I'm really excited that you were selected to be an Olympic coach. It's a shame these people don't support you, because it would really be to their benefit. Before you leave, let me tell you something. This morning, Amos, Olive, and I had a meeting to discuss your temporary reassignment. They were both violently opposed to your transfer. I reminded them the Department of Defense might be involved since you had been selected by the Olympic Committee to represent the United States. Amos stated that if you went, you would go over his dead body. I told him that the Department of Defense might have a bit more power to make reassignments than he did. He laughed and said, 'Not on this base. I decide when someone gets reassigned, not the Department of Defense and you can take that to the bank.' "

"What a bastard. Well it looks like I might go over his dead ass body after all. I think Olive is in with him right now telling him about my phone conversation with the general's aide. I'll see you tomorrow." Shawn got up and left, suddenly feeling much better.

He went to the bank and prepaid his mortgage and car loan so Angela wouldn't worry about them while he was gone and then went home to prepare for his role in the Olympic Trials. There was so much work to be done and a lot of pressure was on the American coaching staff since our bobsled teams had not won an Olympic medal since 1956. American bobsled teams finished fifth place during the 1980 and 1984 Winter Olympics. Shawn and the rest of the current staff were determined to produce a team that would win a medal in Calgary.

Headquarters, Andrews Air Force Base

Everyone stood at attention as General Abbott entered the conference room. He shut the door and told his staff to relax and sit down. Everyone sat down and then began to brief the general about what they had learned on the Shawn Murphy situation. One by one they told him about their conversations with Shawn and several other key people at the base. The general's aide summed it up best describing several of the people Shawn worked for as small-minded characters who were enraged about him being selected as an Olympic coach. He believed they were also very jealous over all the attention Shawn had been receiving at the base and in the newspapers. The aide commented that Shawn had done an outstanding job in public affairs and it was apparent that Monroe and Hanson didn't carry their share of the office workload.

"Did anyone find out what happened to the message?" asked General Abbott.

"Yes," replied an aide. I checked our log in the computer and it was sent, however there is no explanation about why it wasn't received by the communications people in Schenectady. Their computer shows that it was received and printed, but nobody knows what happened to it."

"This is incredible!" said Abbott. "Did you contact the OSI?" The Office of Special Investigations should have been contacted immediately he thought.

"Yes, sir." replied an aide. "They believe it would be difficult to prove who might have taken the message without a witness that actually saw someone remove it. They suspect that Master Sergeant Hanson may have been involved since she was recorded on the security camera's video tape entering the building just prior to the message being sent. They need to question her first before they can determine if she might be guilty."

"Just who the hell does Hanson think she is?" asked the general, to nobody in particular. "She must be a complete idiot. Is there anything else we should address right now?"

"Not at this point, General," replied an aide. "We should meet once again in the morning to review the file to be sure everything is in place with the reassignment papers. I assume that Murphy's base commander, Colonel Crosby, will approve the request when we send it to him?"

The general briefed them about his phone conversation with Crosby and assured them that the papers would be signed and Murphy wouldn't be harassed when he returned from the Olympics. He glanced around the room watching everyone nod their head in agreement. The staff stood at attention when he left the room. The rest of the staff remained behind for a few minutes, discussing the bizarre behavior of Olive Hanson and Amos Fowlkes. The staff agreed the next day would be unpleasant for both of them.

→ *Ice Spy*

Schenectady, New York

Olive was busy trying to get the base newspaper together when Amos called and told her to come to his office. She opened Fowlkes' door and was surprised to see Chief Curley also there waiting for her.

"Please shut the door, Sergeant" said Amos. "I just received a call from communications and apparently a message was received from General Abbott directing us to release Sergeant Murphy for temporary duty so he can work as an Olympic coach."

"General Abbott can't direct us to transfer anyone. He can only request that this be done and we don't have to approve the request," replied Olive.

"Excuse me, Sergeant Hanson," said Chief Curley, "but are you aware that the Defense Department is telling General Abbott what to do?"

"I don't care," replied Olive, unable to comprehend Chief Curley's reference to the Defense Department's powerful influence over the four-star general. "Shawn Murphy is not going to the Olympics."

"I don't think you have any say in the matter," replied the chief.

"I'm not impressed that Shawn has managed to get them involved. Lt. Col. Fowlkes will make the decision here on this base."

The chief knew that Amos had a lot of power with Colonel Crosby, the base commander, and he never let an opportunity go by when he could rat on people to Crosby. Many of the people assigned to the base referred to Amos as "The Snitch." He normally got his way whenever he asked the commander for a favor. Crosby allowed Amos to travel on government time and expense to attend an incredible number of minority-related functions throughout the country each year.

The chief suspected that Amos and Colonel Crosby had discussed the possibility of Shawn's temporary assignment and that Crosby didn't care one way or the other, but would agree with Amos. He also knew that now it really didn't matter what either of them thought because if they tried to fight the Defense Department they would not only lose the fight, but they would start the end of their careers. He suspected Amos and Olive weren't bright enough to understand this, but knew that Colonel Crosby did and wouldn't offer a fight. Shawn Murphy would be leaving on time. They just didn't know it.

"I agree that Colonel Crosby doesn't have to release him," replied the chief. "But let me explain the facts of life to you. Think about what has happened so far. The people involved here have enough power to make a four-star general pick up the phone and call Shawn to apologize. These people retire generals if they look cross-eyed at them."

"It's frustrating that Shawn is pushing us around," replied Olive.

"I don't look at it as being pushed around. I think its a great honor and the base will receive a lot of favorable publicity," replied the chief. "I know one thing, General Abbott's staff has talked to a lot of people here and I don't think we have seen anything yet."

"I spoke to his deputy yesterday," replied Olive nonchalantly. "He just wanted some general information about our reasons for not reassigning Murphy."

"Well, you should've talked with him this morning. He said the General is on a rampage over this mess. I must congratulate you, Olive. The General sure knows who you are."

"Good. It's nice to have a four-star general's attention."

"You know something, Olive, the general described you as an incredible idiot when addressing his staff, then corrected himself and said you had to be the world's biggest asshole. I don't think I would want that kind of attention. You should say a prayer that heads don't fly. One more thing; the OSI is involved. It seems that the message was sent around the time you were in the communications building. They suspect that you might have stolen the message and tampered with their computer. If you did, it was really a stupid move."

Headquarters, Andrews Air Force Base

General Abbott instructed his secretary to get Colonel Crosby on the telephone for him while he looked through Shawn Murphy's file. Moments later she called on the intercom and told him that Colonel Crosby was waiting on the phone. The general spent the next ten minutes briefing Crosby on the status of Murphy and the OSI's investigation regarding the missing message. The General made it very clear that he expected the person to be court-martialed if the OSI could determine who had destroyed the message . Crosby assured the general that he would file charges if the mystery was solved and that Murphy wouldn't have any more problems.

"I certainly hope so, because I don't enjoy having the Defense Department calling me and reaming my ass out because some idiots who work for you don't have enough brains to come in out of the rain. And if that's not enough, I had phone calls from Associated Press inquiring as to why the Air Force wasn't supporting the Olympics. The Public Relations people with the bobsled organization sent out a press release. You need to get a handle on Hanson and Fowlkes and either get rid of them or hide them in some out-of-the-way closet where nobody ever sees them. If you don't comprehend what I'm telling you, let me say it a bit more directly so you will understand. You get your base under control and manage it the way you should or I will get someone up there who can," stated the general angrily. "Do you understand what I'm telling you?"

"Yes, sir, I understand and I apologize, because I surely didn't realize Sergeant Murphy was having a problem," lied Crosby. Hoping the general would hang up.

"Well, you'd better wake up! My staff related the rumors about the way Fowlkes bullshits you all the time and you never question him or the trips he takes. I also understand that your people have been complaining to you about him for years and yet you still let him do as he pleases. You'd better open your eyes real quick and get a handle on who you're relying on for information, because this guy is an idiot."

"Yes, sir," replied Crosby.

"You better give some thought to what I said about running that base properly, I meant what I said about replacing you and I can do that in a heart beat."

→ *Ice Spy*

The General hung up without saying good-bye. This in itself was a message to Colonel Crosby.

Colonel Crosby put the receiver back on the phone and cursed. It didn't take a rocket scientist to figure out his future in the military was seriously threatened. He knew his days as a base commander were numbered, because Abbott didn't forget or forgive and would use the first opportunity to shift him out of his command. His career could be ruined because of Fowlkes. He should never have listen to him. A cold chill crept over his body.

Chapter Four

→ *Ice Spy*

Lake Placid, New York

Shawn felt Angela's body tremble as he held her one last time before leaving. She smiled, pretending she wasn't worried about him working for the CIA, but he knew the truth. They had avoided talking about the risk he might be taking by working on the assignment. He kissed her one last time and left his wife behind, promising himself to call her when he arrived in Lake Placid.

Leaving Interstate 87, Shawn drove his Corvette west onto Route 73 in the direction of Lake Placid. He noticed the leaves on the trees were changing colors early. Regardless of the season, he always enjoyed driving through the age-old Adirondack Mountains. As a child he often roamed them with his Uncle Irvin, who lived in the small town of Wadams, located in the foothills east of Lake Placid.

Irvin, a full-blooded Mohawk Indian, had worked as a hunting and fishing guide until his failing eyesight had forced his retirement in 1975. During summer vacations he shared his unique knowledge of nature and taught Shawn the art of survival. The training was invaluable when Shawn was in the military and working for the Agency in Europe. Irvin never knew how often those skills had saved his nephew's life.

Shawn's past jobs with the Agency and in the military required him to travel to several different countries in the world and nothing ever compared to the mystique the Adirondacks held for him. The mountains seemed to create both excitement and calmness within him, simultaneously.

He noticed the familiar sign on the side of the road, "Welcome to Lake Placid, home of the 1932 and 1980 Winter Olympic Games." The sign brought his thoughts back to his present task, which was getting ready to leave for Europe and preparing athletes for the 1988 Olympics.

The bobsled association's office was over-crowded with athletes and their families checking passports and papers needed during the six-week stay in Europe. Shawn entered the building and found Roger Ferris, executive director of the bobsled association, in his office. He greeted Roger as he picked up the documents he needed for the trip.

"Shawn, Jason Pierce will be back in about an hour," said Roger. "He went to the hardware store to pick up some items that will be needed for the trip."

"Thanks, I talked to Jason last night to get things squared away between us. What time does our flight leave Montreal tomorrow?"

"Seven-twenty in the evening." He replied. "The bus will be here picking everybody up at 8 a.m. and will meet up with the equipment truck at the airport."

"When Jason comes back tell him that I went to the bobsled track to make sure the sleds are securely packed in the crates. The airlines damaged several sleds on our last trip because they weren't packed properly."

"I'll tell him. Call me before you leave the track in case there is something else we might need."

Shawn got into his car and drove to the track. On the way he thought about Jason Pierce who would be managing the Olympic trials. Jason was a very difficult person to work with and the athletes didn't have a lot of confidence in him. He belonged to the 'Good-old-boy' network that had controlled American bobsledding for many years. Shawn thought that Roger and Jason made a good pair because both lacked honesty and integrity. Athletes often said, if their lips were moving they were lying.

He arrived at the track and noticed the sleds were already in the crates and loaded on the trucks. He would have to wait until they unloaded them in Germany to learn if they were packed securely. This irritated him, because he knew that neither Roger nor Jason really cared if the equipment got damaged during the trip. Their interest in the sport was a long way away from athletes and winning at the Olympic Games.

He called the bobsled office and told Roger that the equipment was already on the truck and asked if anyone had inspected the crates prior to loading them on the trucks. As he suspected, Roger had left this to the athletes. He drove back to the office and thought about the bobsled trials. He tried to imagine what the unfolding scenario would be when he met Boris in East Germany.

Riga, Latvia, USSR

Walter placed a call to Fred Unser in the United States. The CIA was well-aware that the KGB was monitoring the call and used a code to communicate with their agents. In addition to the code they had a special phone line used only by Walter and the CIA operators. They were given instructions to answer with a company name that had been set up for the cover. Walter moved around the Soviet Union as an American import-exporter who specialized in medical supplies and prosthetics.

Walter told Unser that he had a meeting with a Latvian company that might be interested in exporting artificial limbs to the United States. He asked Fred to make arrangements for a specialist to meet him in Riga to evaluate the quality of the Latvian prosthetics. Fred interpreted Walter's hidden meaning and knew that Walter needed an expert to evaluate Boris's technical information. He told Walter that he would send Jamie Suriano, a prosthetist, who spoke fluent Russian. Fred hung up the phone knowing exactly what was needed and Suriano would be perfect for the assignment.

Suriano worked at the Massachusetts Orthopedic Institute in Boston and the CIA had used his services in the past to evaluate foreign products. He was also a research metallurgist specializing in "physical metallurgy" which is the branch of metallurgy that adapts metals to human uses. His past work with the agency on highly technical assignments had been very successful. In addition to his technical expertise, he spoke fluent German, French, and Russian.

Fred contacted Jamie and arranged for him to meet with Walter the next day. He hung up and made arrangements for Jamie to take the next available flight from Boston to Moscow. American Airlines left late in the day for London/Heathrow then on to Moscow. He would continue his trip from Moscow to Riga on an *Aeroflot* flight and stay at the Hotel Riga until Walter contacted him. He then sent a coded message to Walter so he could arrange to meet with Jamie in Riga.

Jamie registered at the Hotel Riga and waited until he heard from Walter

→ *Ice Spy*

Shapnek as Fred instructed him. Fred had reminded him that the hotel rooms and the phone were bugged, but Jamie knew this from past assignments with the Agency. The phone rang while he was unpacking his luggage and when he answered, there was silence on the line so he hung up and continued unpacking. Within minutes someone knocked quietly, then slipped a piece of paper under the door. He opened the door and looked into the hallway. It was empty. He closed the door and picked up the paper containing instructions that directed him from the hotel to a subway entrance eight blocks east, near the waterfront, at 5 p.m. He flushed the instructions down the toilet and finished unpacking.

Walter stood in the hotel entrance for several minutes observing everyone to determine if any agents from the KGB were in the lobby. It was normal procedure for the KGB to place several agents in hotel lobbies where foreigners were staying to maintain a surveillance on them. He knew it wouldn't be long before they would arrive to shadow Suriano whenever he left the hotel. Confident that they weren't in the lobby yet, he quickly left the hotel walking in the direction of the waterfront where he would meet Jamie.

The cool air hit him immediately as he stepped out onto the sidewalk and he wished he had put on a light jacket. As the sun disappeared behind tall buildings the temperature dropped dramatically. There wouldn't be enough time to go back. This was his penalty for an extended nap.

Jamie gazed across the Daugavu River at the Zakusals TV center's huge tower as he waited for Walter. The TV center was about the only building in Riga that wasn't plain concrete. Turning in the opposite direction, he could see the famed Dome Cathedral. Scaffolding reached up to the base of the belfry that stood high above the ancient decaying brick buildings surrounding the cathedral. Riga had a rich historical background and the city's origin dated back to 1209 A.D.

Walter assumed that Jamie would be followed by the KGB and was prepared. He stepped into a fish market on the way to the waterfront to evade the KGB just in case they were following without him seeing them. This was a simple way to determine if an agent was on his trail. Every store had long lines of people waiting to purchase food and nobody ever went to the head of the line to look at what was available. Window shopping was a waste of time in the Soviet Union because food was so scarce that shoppers purchased whatever was available.

The KGB wouldn't follow Walter into the store since it would be too obvious they were following. On previous trips to Riga, he had cased out several stores in the area to determine which had rear doors that would allow him to slip out without being observed, leaving the KGB waiting on the street. Walter chuckled as he slipped out the back door unnoticed by anyone in the fish market. He walked quickly on the narrow cobblestone street in the direction of the *Metpo* where he had instructed Jamie to meet him.

The subway entrance came into view and Walter slipped into the doorway of a vacant building. He wanted to check one last time to be sure nobody was following him. From the doorway, he had an excellent view to observe Jamie and the area around the subway entrance. He had to be dead certain that nobody was observing them. The building entrance he stood inside had the appearance of centuries-old decay. The wooden shutters were hanging on broken hinges that were now a single piece of rust. Strong, moisture-laden winds blowing across the Daugavu River for centuries had removed any vestiges of paint on the shutters. Although the building was vacant and located near the waterfront, the accepted filth normally found in buildings along New York City's waterfront, was noticeably missing.

From his vantage point, Walter noticed a man dressed in a wrinkled suit that made him look out of place for this poverty-stricken area. Walter suspected that Jamie was unaware he was being followed, so his plan changed immediately. He decided to wait for the opportunity to give him a signal before he started down the stairway into the long tunnel leading to the ticket booth.

Walter's chance came when he noticed the KGB agent turn his back and took several steps away to purchase a pack of Russian cigarettes. Moving quickly, he approached the stairway and quietly told Jamie, "You're being followed. We've got to ditch this guy. Don't get on the subway until the last possible minute when the doors are closing."

Walter walked to the ticket booth and purchased his token. Jamie followed a few moments later with the agent close behind him. The arriving *Metpo* screeched and rattled as it came to a stop. The doors slid open and Walter casually stepped into the car and took a seat near the rear. No more than forty-five seconds passed before the *Metpo* doors started to close. Jamie entered at the last moment just like a professional agent. Walter was greatly amused when the subway car pulled away, leaving the KGB agent standing alone on the platform. He studied Suriano as the subway rattled along the tracks. He was about five foot nine and Walter guessed that he must weigh about one eighty with no fat. Walter had the same build except he stood at six foot and was about twenty pounds heavier.

They rode the subway for a short time before Shapnek moved to the seat next to Suriano. The loud noise of the subway would cover their conversation, allowing them to talk quietly without being overheard.

"You look good, Jamie," Walter smiled as he greeted him. It was good to be with someone he knew from the States and Jamie was a sight for sore eyes. Working alone behind the Iron Curtain for long periods of time was a lonely part of the job.

"You look good yourself, Walter. Before I forget, Fred Unser sends his regards and asked me to remind you to be careful."

"Fred is funny. He worries about us as if we're his own children. I shouldn't kid about him. There have been times when I was glad he worried about me."

It had been two years since the two men worked together on another assignment in West Germany. Walter suddenly noticed that Jamie was nearly bald at thirty-seven. The change in his appearance was so dramatic that he just had to comment on it, saying politely, "I don't mean to offend you, but I'm astonished that you've lost so much hair in such a short period of time. Your hairline was just starting to recede the last time we worked together."

"Yeah, I guess there's nothing I can do to slow down the process. It's strange because the rest of the men in my family have a full head of hair. I guess it wasn't meant for me to have a lot of hair," replied Jamie ruefully.

He unconsciously slid his hand over the top of his head.

"It'll work well for the spy business," said Walter teasingly. "How do you like the Riga Hotel?"

"I think the Soviet clock stopped in the year 1917. I anticipated it to be old, but I never expected it to be this outdated. It's clean and has nice furniture, but everything is extraordinarily old."

They carried on a casual conversation for the next thirty minutes, observing other passengers as they got on and off the subway. Walter was extremely careful, wanting to be sure that nobody was following them. Both men thought about how the Soviet subway compared to New York City's. Each had the same thought. This subway system was exceptionally clean and free of gang members.

Walter finally decided it was safe to speak openly since the car wasn't full and nobody was sitting within four rows of them. He began discussing the information he had gleaned from Boris Yegorov. He shared all the technical information he accumulated while Jamie listened intently, nodding his head indicating he understood.

Walter told him about the meeting he had arranged with Boris for the next day. He would slip a piece of paper, with instructions as to where he should meet them, under his hotel door. He reminded Jamie they should not be seen together at the hotel or on the streets until after the meeting. Walter finished his briefing and the two men sat silently until the subway reached the center of Riga near the hotel. To keep a low profile, Jamie left the subway without shaking hands or saying good-bye. Walter was familiar with Riga and continued riding until he had reached the opposite side of the city. He got off the subway and took a bus back to the plaza near the Hotel Riga.

He entered the hotel lobby and chuckled at the sight of three KGB agents who were sitting and waiting patiently. They stared at him as he walked across the lobby floor to the elevator. Walter went up to his room and relaxed for an hour before he left the hotel to make arrangements for the meeting between Boris and Jamie. He left by the side door of the hotel to avoid alerting the three agents.

He walked the seven blocks to where Boris lived with his wife on the first floor in a former horse stable that he had converted into a one-bedroom apartment. Walter stood in the shadows to be sure nobody had followed, then walked past the apartment knocking once on the door as he kept moving toward the cemetery located a short distance away. Darkness had created a blanket over the city and a single knock on Boris's door was the prearranged signal to meet Walter in the cemetery. He had glanced quickly through the window and saw Boris sitting at the kitchen table and knew he would meet him in just a few minutes.

Walter looked around to determine if anyone else was in the cemetery. It was difficult to see anything because the large number of trees had grown up so close together. When his eyes adjusted, he could see the enormous amount of damage the Russians had done to the graves. He recalled what Joe had told him about Russian soldiers robbing the Latvian people of everything they had of value when Russia occupied Latvia in 1940. Latvians could visit the cemetery, but photos or repairs to the exposed caskets or headstones weren't allowed. The darkness in the cemetery led to a feeling of uneasiness for anyone passing through at night.

"You appear to be lost in thought," Boris said, startling Walter who had not heard the Soviet coach approaching.

"You scared the hell out of me," replied Walter shakily. "Each time I come here I get depressed. I just can't imagine how bad it was in 1940. I see scenes like this and when I return to the United States I get frustrated when Americans bitch about how difficult it is to live there. They should come over here and see what real government abuse is all about."

"I suspect they still wouldn't understand, Walter. The Latvian people suffered for centuries and we still don't give in. Some day we will take down the Russian flag and raise ours in its place. The day will come when we will speak Latvian freely instead of Russian. There is a serious movement in place now that will some day break up the Soviet Union. Enough of this! Why did you come?"

"I have someone from the States who must talk with you to determine if your technical information is authentic."

"You do not trust me?" asked Boris in a quiet, but angry tone.

"I trust you, but my government will have to spend an incredible amount of money to help you and your wife defect. They must be certain the information is worth the expense."

"My technology is worth much more than what your people will spend," he replied with confidence.

"I believe you. But, I need to have an expert verify that the technology is authentic, since I really don't understand metallurgy or friction between metals or anything related to this. Please understand that I'm just an agent who is trying to help you. I must have an expert assist me so I can convince my government."

"Yes, you are right, I'm very nervous, Walter. I lose much sleep. If I don't leave the Soviet Union soon I'm afraid that there will be a knock on my door in the middle of the night. They will arrest me and within days I will be killed. I will do what you ask. When should we meet?"

"Let's meet tomorrow afternoon at the Mez Park, in Siguida. You know, near the sandstone cave where we met last summer."

"I remember the place."

"Good. I will bring a man who will talk with you. He will understand when you explain the technology to him."

"I will meet you," replied Boris curtly. He turned and disappeared into the darkness.

Walter had a lot to think about as he walked back to the hotel. He stepped out of the elevator when he reached his floor and walked over to the desk to pick up his key from the attendant. Looking around, he didn't see anyone, so he decided to find out just how friendly the attendant might be. As he walked toward her, she began to smile.

"Dohbriy dyen," said Walter with a flirtatious smile. "Are there any messages for me?"

She returned his greeting and said, "There are none, Mr. Shapnek."

"Please call me Walter. What's your name?"

"Natasha."

Walter looked around the room again to be sure nobody was observing them. Seeing nobody, he gave her a single American dollar bill. One American dollar in hard currency was worth more than all the rubles she would earn in two days working there.

"*Pazhahlasta.*" (Thank you very much) she replied gratefully. Her friendly smile indicated that she liked him and was grateful to receive the American currency.

The next morning he woke up early and wrote out detailed instructions on a sheet of paper for Suriano. He instructed him to pack his suitcase and check out of the hotel late in the morning. He should take the subway to the city limits and then walk three blocks to School #5 and wait for Walter to pick him up with a car. On his way out of the hotel, he slipped the note under Jamie's door and knocked softly. He continued down the hall. The woman currently working at the reception desk sat there with no facial expression as he placed his room key on the desk in front of her. She filled out a receipt and handed it to him without looking up from her desk. Walter chuckled as he rode down in the elevator thinking about her stone-faced expression, so common. Russian people had no hope for the future, except to survive the desperate conditions created by a socialist system that obviously was not working. The longer he thought about this, the more compassion he had for their sad situation.

Georgi Pasevs sat at his desk in the KGB Headquarters staring out the window. He was thinking about the punishment he would receive if his commander, Ivan Liepinsh, discovered that the two Americans had slipped away from the agents he stationed at the Hotel Riga. Georgi was the Vice Commander and had a lot of power in the KGB, but knew the commander would not accept any excuses. Liepinsh was known for his brutal treatment of prisoners as well as his own agents when they failed. The KGB understood that American CIA agents were highly skilled at being evasive, but there was no way he could ever explain how his agents allowed two businessmen to disappear.

Georgi yelled to his assistant in the next room, "Viktor come in here immediately!"

Viktor Assitons rushed into Georgi's large office which had not been cleaned in months. It overlooked the market square in central Riga, giving an excellent view of whatever might be happening outside. He responded in a frightened voice, "Yes, Vice Commandant."

"Send four people down to the Hotel Riga. Leave two who can do the simple job of following the Americans once they return to the hotel, and have the other two bring the imbeciles to me at once. Do it now! Do you understand me?" screamed Georgi, spraying him with saliva. He was infuriated and was getting angrier by the minute.

"I will go right away," said Viktor as he moved swiftly out the door.

"You make sure that whoever you send can stick to the Americans or you will join the two imbeciles."

Georgi began to get an uneasy feeling in the pit of his stomach. He was caught in the middle because the commander would not stand for any more mistakes with his staff. If Liepinsh did find out what happened and that he covered up the incident, he was dead. The only thing Georgi could do would be to make certain the two agents never talked again.

Thirty minutes later, Viktor knocked on his door and said, "Vice Commandant, I have Sergejs and Auseklis secured in the van parked in the courtyard."

"Very good, Viktor, take them downstairs at once and get rid of them."

"What shall I tell them downstairs?"

"They took bribe money from the Americans," lied Georgi, knowing nobody would believe him, but would never question him either. "You know how to handle this. Yes?"

"Yes, I will take care of them at once as you wish." Viktor knew full well that Georgi was protecting his own ass. He also knew better than to question him or else he would join the two agents downstairs. He started to leave, but stopped at the door, saying, "The Americans have disappeared once again. I found Sergejs and Auseklis in the lobby and sent one of the other agents upstairs to check on the Americans. They were gone. They checked their keys at the desk which means they went down the fire escape at the rear of the hotel and not the main entrance. I left two agents in the lobby and sent someone else to watch the rear of the building.

"Get rid of Sergejs and Auseklis, the greedy bastards. Perhaps this will convince others who might think about taking hard currency in exchange for turning their heads."

Viktor took the two agents to the basement handcuffed and at gun point. A single shot to the back of their heads ended Georgi's immediate problem. Nobody ever left the basement of the KGB's *corner house* alive unless they were sent to Siberia.

The Latvians had nicknamed the KGB headquarters building the *corner house*. Despite the suffering and difficult times as a result of being occupied for so many years by the Russians, the Latvians never lost their sense of humor. They believed that humor helped them endure the difficult times and joked about "the corner house," saying "It was the tallest building in Riga and from the fifth floor one can see Siberia." In reality, everyone feared the corner house and avoided looking at the building as they passed by on their way to work or to shop. Steel bars covered frosted windows and the wire mesh inside the glass was a constant reminder that the Russians still used the torture chamber downstairs. The corner house's beautiful architecture outside masked the horror taking place inside. Most Latvian people had vivid memories of relatives or friends taken there and were not seen for years. Some were never seen again.

Sigulda, Latvia, USSR

Walter saw Jamie up ahead on the street corner near the school and looked in his rearview mirror once again to see if any KGB agents were following him. Satisfied that he wasn't being followed, he eased the car over to the curb and motioned for Jamie to get in. The trip to the sand caves in Sigulda only took an hour and they discussed what they should say when they met with Boris. Satisfied that they were ready for the meeting, both men became quiet. Walter thought about his plan to get the Soviet coach and his wife out of the USSR while Jamie enjoyed the Latvian countryside. The sun was out, adding an unusual warmth for the late fall day.

When they arrived at the park, Walter spotted Boris waiting for them near the large sand cave. He looked quickly around the area for anything unusual before parking the auto a short distance from him. The three men walked around the Mez Park talking for the next two hours. Walter didn't understand the technical information that was being discussed and stayed a short distance away from the two men, watching for any signs that the KGB might have tailed them. Boris finished giving Jamie the information he asked for and then reminded Walter forcefully he must work out something in the near future or he and his wife would be killed. He then gave Walter another twist to the situation and said his wife would not leave the country without her parents. Now they had to help four people leave the country. Walter assured him that he would be back in touch with him quickly and the men departed.

Jamie waited until Walter pulled the car out on the highway to explain that the information Boris gave him was authentic. He was convinced that Boris knew the proper mathematical combination to integrate an alloy composite with steel that would reduce friction on both water and ice. Jamie was ecstatic and told Walter that Boris was right. If they didn't get him and his wife out soon they would indeed be killed. They would lose the information because he would never be able to accurately recall the formula Boris gave him.

Walter drove Jamie to Pytalovo, an hour's ride east of Riga to catch the train. He was certain that the KGB would be watching for them at the train station in Riga. The ride gave them extra time to talk freely about the new information. Walter said he was going to West Germany the next day and would call Fred Unser from there where the phone line would be safe. He dropped Jamie off at the train station and waited until he left on his way to Moscow where he would catch a flight back home.

He drove back to Riga thinking about how he would help Boris and his wife defect to the States. He had to be sure there were no mistakes.

CHAPTER FIVE

→ *Ice Spy*

Montreal, Canada

Shawn Murphy sat in section D-12 at the airport in Montreal waiting for the flight to Frankfurt, West Germany. Thoughts of the vast number of preparations he made for the trip were going through his mind. He smiled when he thought about the six dozen roses and pre-signed cards he had purchased for his wife. The florist would deliver a dozen and a card to Angela at her office at the insurance company every Thursday morning. He knew she loved flowers and it would help ease the stress he created for her by taking the assignment. The people she supervised enjoyed kidding her whenever they had the opportunity and this would give them something to kid her about, not that they didn't have enough already.

He got up and went to a pay phone and called Angela to talk with her for a few minutes before he had to board the plane. The pre-boarding announcement came over the speaker so he said good-bye and gathered his luggage and walked to the boarding ramp with the rest of the group. He hoped he could catch some sleep on the flight to Frankfurt.

"Hi, Shawn. Is everything together for the trials?"

Shawn turned and was shocked and puzzled to see Roger Ferris standing behind him. "Roger, what are you doing here? I didn't know that you were going with us!"

"It was a last minute thing," replied Roger sarcastically. "There really isn't a lot of work that needs to be done at the bobsled office. It's about time Sandra did something herself without me telling her how to do everything. Besides, if I'm with the team I can help with the translation since nobody can speak fluent German."

"I really don't care. I was under the impression that Wilbur Hippenbecker was expecting you to help him with the association's insurance and the new budget."

"Done deal. I took care of them before I left yesterday."

"You secured a new insurance binder for the athletes?"

"Done. In fact, as we speak, the policy is being typed. Don't be so concerned, Shawn. Relax, man. Jesus, I should think that you'd be happy that I'm going with you to help out."

"I'm concerned with the problems we went through with the insurance last year."

"What're you talking about?"

"You know what the hell I'm talking about. Don't tell me you forgot when we returned from the first world cup race in Europe last year, it was discovered that you hadn't taken care of the insurance? Thank God nobody was injured in an accident."

"Don't give me that shit again. I had everything ready to go on time. Wilbur forgot to take the paperwork and give it to the insurance company. I did what I was supposed to do."

Shawn wondered if Ferris ever told the truth. Sandra Wilson, the association's secretary, had found the package under a pile of work on Roger's desk and gave it to Wilbur. There was no point in arguing with him because Roger was never 'wrong.' He was a pro at covering his mistakes and shoving work onto Sandra. Shawn knew the athletes would not be happy that "Slime" was going to Winterberg with them. Ferris would be useless to the team in Europe, Shawn thought. He had a serious drinking problem and was known to use drugs. He would be out every night drinking and chasing women. He always arrived at the bobsled track about noontime when practice was finishing and had a reason for not being there in the morning. The excuses he normally gave were that he had to do something for the athlete's accommodations, which, of course, everyone knew was bullshit. He looked like death warmed over as a result of drug and alcohol abuse. He always had a cigarette in his mouth which didn't help either.

The final boarding announcement interrupted their conversation and Shawn followed the athletes onto the boarding ramp and slid into his seat next to the window. He closed his eyes to rest and shortly after the plane took off he was sound asleep. He slept during most of the flight and was surprised when he heard the flight attendant make an announcement over the intercom.

"Please fasten your seat belts and return your seat to the upright position. We will be landing in Frankfurt, our final destination, in about 15 minutes. Our pilot advises us that the temperature at Frankfurt is thirty-eight degrees with a heavy overcast. We thank you for flying on Lufthansa Airlines and sincerely hope we can serve you again in the near future."

He could feel the plane descending during the final approach to the runway. Soon the plane landed and taxied into its final parking spot and everyone stood up to begin taking their carry-on luggage down from the overhead compartments. Shawn was amused at the confusion created by the passengers rushing to get off the plane. It was typical of the 'hurry up and wait' syndrome experienced by everyone who ever served in the military.

Frankfurt, West Germany

Several minutes passed and Shawn realized that nobody was leaving the plane. The impatient passengers waited for the doors to open and suddenly a voice on the intercom explained that there was a minor delay and all passengers except the American bobsled group could leave the plane. The departing passengers were startled to see several German police officers, armed with assault rifles and dressed completely in black uniforms, waiting to board the plane.

The police boarded and informed the bobsled group that they had received a terrorist threat against all Americans traveling to Europe. They advised the group to remove anything on their clothing that would identify them as Americans before leaving the plane.

Jason Pierce approached the person in charge of the German security unit and asked, "Would you arrange to have the customs people check our credentials and luggage in a private room?"

"Yes, this has already been arranged," replied the police officer. "I notice several athletes still have USA labels on their clothing. These labels must be covered or removed for their own protection before you will be permitted to leave the plane."

Shawn and Jason lined all the athletes up along the aisle and checked for anything that might identify them as an American. When the group had finally done this, they were allowed to leave. They were led to a private room where the German customs representatives quickly checked their credentials and luggage. The police led them outside where a tour bus and three trucks were waiting for them and the crated bobsleds.

The large number of German police in their black uniforms startled Shawn. They seemed to be everywhere in the airport and outside in the street and on the rooftops. The police officers were armed with AK-47 assault rifles and appeared ready for any problem that might arise. The sight was both frightening and reassuring.

It took nearly two hours for the athletes to load all the equipment and luggage on the three trucks. Everyone got on the bus and Jason waited until all were in their seats before he took a roll call to be sure nobody was missing. Everyone was on the bus, except Ferris. This was no surprise to Shawn.

"Has anyone seen Roger in the past thirty minutes?" asked Jason.

"He left with a foxy lady in a sports car," replied a voice from the rear of the bus.

"What did you expect?" yelled another athlete in disgust. "Anyone with part of a brain knew he was only coming with us to party on the association's money."

"There you go, Jason. Now you know why they call him 'Slime.' The bastard never does anything to help us and comes along just for the free ride," replied Shawn. "You don't have to be a rocket scientist to figure out what he's doing."

"That's enough," yelled Jason. He appeared quite irritated and Shawn knew he was too stupid to know how to keep Roger under control. There was only one way to do it and that was to put him on the next plane back to the States.

Jason told the bus driver to leave and they began their long bus ride to Winterberg. It would be late in the night when they arrived and everyone would be exhausted. It didn't take long for the athletes to settle down and most went to sleep. Shawn thought about Roger and the money the association would be wasting on his expenses. Money they didn't have and this meant that the athletes will have to go without some things so that Roger could simply take a vacation at their expense. Unfortunately, Shawn and Jason had no control over the situation, since Roger was well liked by the new people who had taken control. Shawn suspected they liked Roger because he was in a position to help them without anyone knowing what they were doing.

Shawn looked at Jason and asked, "Why did Roger come over here with us?"

Jason shrugged his shoulders and said, "I've no idea why and furthermore I didn't know he was coming until I saw him at the airport. I intend to call Wilbur and find out as soon as we get to the Hotel Zur Sonne."

"Are we staying at the Zur Sonne again? I thought everyone agreed that we would stay at a different hotel this time?"

"That's where Roger made the arrangements. He said that their price was best."

"I bet he never got other quotes. I think Roger prefers it there because all he has to do is make a phone call and tell them how many people are coming and what the dates will be."

"Roger told me that he had checked with other hotels and they were too expensive."

"The hotel owner knows a good thing when he sees it. He caters to Roger because he wants the lucrative business we give him in the off season." Shawn suspected that Roger never sought other less expensive accommodations for the bobsled team because he was receiving a kickback. The bobsled group generally has about 40 athletes and several coaches who stay for six weeks at a time when the hotel is normally empty. The hotel makes a lot of money each year from the association and would not want to lose the business.

"That's not really true, Shawn. I talked to him about checking with some other hotels. A lot of problems would arise if we changed hotels and the small amount of money we might save isn't worth it," Shawn shook his head at Jason's stupidity.

"The board of directors instructed Roger to check out other hotels to see if we could get better prices and a better menu for the athletes. The food we get at the Zur Sonne is really lousy for Olympic athletes."

"What're you talking about?" replied Jason in a huff, "I've stayed there for years and the food is excellent." Shawn knew that Jason didn't care about what he ate as long as there was plenty of it.

"I'm not complaining about the quality of their food. It's the type of food they serve. The athletes need food that is more nutritious for training. The food they serve tastes great, but it is full of fat."

"There's nothing wrong with the food."

"Let's ask the athletes what they think about the food. The last time we stayed there they served us pork products at least once a day for twenty-eight days in a row. Maybe you don't care, but the athletes were really pissed. They are in training and shouldn't eat food with a high content of fat. We need to start feeding the athletes better or forget about medals."

"I'll talk with the chef and see if he can make some changes. The problem is that a better menu costs more."

"I've got the solution, Jason. We charge Roger for his own expenses and what it costs us to fly him over here. We won't even ask him to pay back what he steals and there will be plenty of money to pay for a better menu."

"Just worry about your job and I will take care of the rest," snipped Jason.

Shawn smiled. He knew Jason was a close friend of Roger's because of their mutual business connections. Roger always covered for Jason and the others who controlled the association. It frustrated Shawn that Jason was in charge of this trip. He wasn't very intelligent and his lack of understanding about the menu was about par for him. Anyone with the slightest bit of knowledge about nutrition would know that athletes in serious training should not eat pork products every day. Shawn thought about a quote attributed to Adlai Stevenson, "There is nothing more horrifying than stupidity in action." Stevenson must have known Jason Pierce.

Jet lag and the tense situation at the airport had exhausted everyone. The bus ride from the Frankfurt airport to the hotel in Winterberg would take about three hours, allowing plenty of time to settle down. The bus left the autobahn and began traveling along the narrow and steep mountain roads leading to Winterberg. The bus slowed down notably as it snaked its way around the tortuous road creeping closer to the Zur Sonne. The only sound inside the bus now was the faint music coming from a small portable radio the driver had on the dashboard.

CIA Headquarters, Langley, Virginia

Joe Sweeney was admiring a newly framed photograph of the unfinished cathedral in Cologne, West Germany. He turned when he heard someone enter Fred Unser's office and smiled when he recognized Jamie Suriano. Joe walked over to meet him. They shook hands and exchanged friendly greetings. Joe had worked with Jamie on a project several years ago when the Agency needed his professional expertise on metallurgy. Joe was impressed with him as a person and as a professional.

"How have you been, Joe?" asked Jamie.

"I've been fine and, like everyone else, I'm busy. You look good. Fred will be right back. He was just called down the hall for something and said he wouldn't be gone long." "I didn't realize you were working on this deal. I was surprised to find out that Walter Shapnek is working on it also. I've worked with him on some other projects in the past. If you guys keep calling me for help I'll probably get to meet everyone in the Agency."

Joe explained that he became involved with the case after Walter gave them the initial information. He was working it in the States to determine if the government could arrange for Boris Yegorov to defect if the technology he claimed he possessed was legitimate. "Did you learn enough to determine its value and authenticity?"

"There's no question, he has contrived a formula to reduce friction on water and ice. I prepared a detailed report for Fred and sent it to him by courier from Boston yesterday. He called last night and asked me to fly in this morning to discuss it with him. Fortunately, I was able to get on an early flight."

The door opened interrupting their conversation and three men walked in with Fred. Joe recognized Gary Circe, the CIA's Director, although he had never met him. He didn't have a clue about the other two men. Fred introduced them to the CIA Director and the other two who were attorneys with the Agency and the Justice Department.

The men took seats around the large conference table on the other side of Fred's office. Circe reminded everyone that the meeting was 'Top Secret' and the case should not be discussed with anyone not presently in the room. He told them that the decision had been made to get Boris Yegorov and his wife out of the Soviet Union. They would arrange to give them a new identity and let them live in the States. He explained that the scientific technology he had developed was too valuable for the CIA not to help him. He agreed with Jamie that Boris's discovery was too valuable to ignore or leave to the Soviets. Earlier in the day, the director met with Naval Intelligence and they were impressed with the report. Navy Intelligence was certain that the Soviets have not applied the technology. They assumed that Boris was withholding from them to keep himself alive and suspected that the Soviets would be keeping a very close watch on him.

"Gentlemen," said the gray-haired director, "The code name for this secret mission will be *IceSpy.* Fred Unser will be the coordinator for the mission. Fred and his staff have been working for several weeks to verify the information and have a good handle on the project."

The attorney from the Justice Department gave a short briefing on the legal problems that might surface should information about the *IceSpy* mission leak out. The group chatted for a short time about the benefits of the technology to the navy if the project was successful until Circe stood up to leave and said good-bye. As an afterthought, he looked back at Fred and asked him to call when his report was ready for the President.

"I will be there to answer any questions the president may have," he said, as he turned and walked out the door.

Winterberg, West Germany

It was past noon and everyone was exhausted when the bus finally arrived at the Zur Sonne Hotel. Ferris was there waiting and explained that he forgot to tell them he had made arrangements to have someone drive him to the hotel ahead of the bus to finalize the details. Shawn knew better than this and suspected that Roger simply didn't care for the long bus ride.

Roger and his attractive female companion greeted the group heartily and said, "There's beer and snacks in the dining room for everyone, courtesy of the hotel." Shawn assumed that the hotel would either bill the association later or would somehow charge them without their knowing.

A small number of athletes took advantage of the beer and snacks, but most went directly to their rooms. Jason followed the athletes into the dining room and suggested that they sleep late the next morning. He asked everyone to meet him in the dining room after lunch for a short meeting.

The next morning, traffic outside the hotel woke Shawn. He reached over to the bed stand and looked at his watch. It was after 9:00 a.m. He got out of bed and walked over to the window and opened the curtain to look at the view from his window. It was a familiar sight since he had stayed at the hotel several times in the past during trips to the Winterberg bobsled track.

The contrast these mountains made with those of upstate New York always impressed him. The Bavarian Alps were breathtakingly beautiful, but in his opinion they could not compare to the Adirondacks. Nevertheless, the German mountains had an individual beauty of their own that appealed to Shawn's profound love for nature. A knock on the door interrupted his mountain gazing. It was Jim Bogdan, the bobsled association's trainer.

"Good morning. Do you want to take a walk with me and check the condition of the ice on the track?"

"Sure, I just need a couple of minutes to get ready. I just got out of bed and need to shower first. I'll meet you in the dining room in ten minutes if you can wait?"

"That's fine. I'll chat with some of the guys and we can leave whenever you arrive." Jim started down the hall then turned to remind Shawn that Jason was planning to have a meeting with the athletes at noon.

Shawn was pleased that Jim had been selected to work the Olympic trials with him. He was very talented and the athletes liked and respected him. Jim was also extremely honest and that was a quality the majority of the people, who controlled the bobsled association, seemed to lack. A former jet pilot in the Air Force, stationed at Plattsburgh AFB, Jim became interested in the sport and was a member of the 1980 Olympic team that placed fifth at Lake Placid. He was an excellent trainer and was the association's only full-time employee that Shawn or the athletes trusted.

Shawn finished his shower and got dressed in his team warm-up suit and grabbed a light jacket before leaving his room. He had felt the warmth of the mid-morning sun when he looked out the window earlier. Jim was in the lobby chatting with Skip Reynolds and his teammates when Shawn got downstairs. Skip and Shawn raced together during the 1984 season and Shawn was pleased he was competing in the '88 trials. Maybe this time Skip would make the Olympic team. At forty-three he was the oldest driver in the trials, which, would be his last.

Shawn and Jim left the hotel. They discussed Jason and Roger while they walked to the track.

"I called Wilbur last week and asked if we could have another person help us with the coaching. I had someone who was willing to volunteer his time. We just needed to pay his travel and expenses," said Jim. "The lying bastard told me that there was no money to even pay someone's expenses and then Roger jumps on the plane at the last minute."

"The day before we left I was at the bobsled office all day and nobody mentioned that Roger was going to Europe," said Shawn. "Suddenly he shows up at the airport and has the attitude that he was part of the program from the start."

"I have a feeling that it's going to get worse. I really suspect that this new group of people will spend a lot of time and association money over here."

"I think you're right, Jim. I can't put my finger on it, but something isn't right with this new group. I've heard rumors that Lester Fetor has strong ties and might be directly connected to a mafia family in New York. I had a friend in the FBI check out his criminal record and this guy has a rap sheet that goes from stolen cars to murder. He got off the murder rap because the only witness died in an auto accident a week before the trial."

"He doesn't move an inch without that other character, Nino Casatelli, at his side. Did you check him out also?"

"Yeah, but there is nothing really. He just seems to be a thug who makes a living by sucking up to Lester and his friends."

Jim and Shawn walked inside the main gate at the start area and down the track to the finish, checking the condition of the ice at different places along the way. As they walked down the path, they noticed the warm sun had melted the ice on the refrigerated concrete track in several places. They arrived back at the start and went into the office to greet the German workers, they remembered from previous trips to Winterberg.

Jim questioned the supervisor about the poor ice conditions and was assured that the track's refrigeration system would be powerful enough to overcome the unseasonably warm conditions. Jim and Shawn left the office and visited a couple of small gift shops located near the track. After browsing for nearly an hour without purchasing anything, they returned to the Zur Sonne Hotel for the noon meeting.

Jason was waiting for them when they arrived. "Where have you guys been? I've been looking for both of you for the past hour."

"Shawn and I took a walk to the bobrun to check the ice," replied Jim.

"How is it?"

"It's really soft," replied Shawn. We talked with the track supervisor and he said the refrigeration system is large enough to overcome the sun's warmth. Apparently, the average temperature had been well below freezing every night until a couple of days ago. I guess it takes a few days for the refrigeration system to reach its full capacity. They said not to worry and the ice will be ready in two days when we're scheduled to start training."

"Good. I appreciate you guys going up to check on the track. Take a look at the training schedule I put together. Check it over and pencil in any changes either of you might have before it gets typed. I intend to post the schedule on the bulletin board so the athletes have a chance to study it before practice."

Jason's meeting lasted about twenty minutes. He spent most of the time advising the athletes on how to properly unpack and prepare their sleds. Skip Reynolds and Bob Carver complained that the cold cuts served for lunch had too much fat. Jason promised them that he would talk to the hotel staff about changing the menu. Shawn knew this would never happen. When the meeting ended, the athletes left to unpack their sleds. It was a beautiful afternoon, unseasonably warm again, and the athletes enjoyed working outside wearing shorts and T-shirts. Shawn laughed to see them working in shorts and thought they might as well enjoy the warm weather. In a day or two it will be bitter cold again.

Lake Placid, New York

Sandra Wilson was unlocking the bobsled association's office door when the phone began to ring. It was Jason Pierce calling from West Germany trying to get in touch with Wilbur Hippenbecker. She told him that Wilbur was in Rochester. Frustrated, Jason asked her to have Wilbur call him in Winterberg right away to discuss the purpose of Roger being with the team. Sandra assured him that she would contact Wilbur immediately and give him the message. She could tell by the tone of Jason's voice that he was extremely upset with Roger. His unexpected and unwelcome arrival in Montreal with the vague excuse that he was needed as an interpreter had inflamed Jason to no end.

John Chapadeau, the association's treasurer, walked into the office just as Sandra hung up the phone. The position of president and treasurer were voluntary and did not have a salary, but they were provided with a generous expense account that they kept very confidential. John wielded a tremendous amount of power over the athletes and coaching staff as the association's treasurer and never missed an opportunity to remind them. His abrasive personality and misuse of power were the main reasons that he was despised by most people who came in contact with him. He took great pleasure in being sarcastic to anyone he believed was below his social standing. The athletes resented him because they saw how he used his expense account in Europe to support his flashy life style. Money was no object for John, yet the athletes received a scanty amount of financial support from the association. When their equipment needed repairs, John told them to make do with what they had because there just wasn't any extra money. His only interest in people were those who could benefit him, those who had wealth and influence. People directly involved with the Mob were especially lucrative to his accounting business. The New York City underworld was eager to conduct business with John because he was brilliant in creating money laundering schemes.

"Good morning, John. I didn't realize you were coming to Lake Placid today."

"I have some things to do before I go to Winterberg."

"You're going to Winterberg, too?" asked Sandra in dismay.

"Your job is to answer the phone and not run the association," His tone of voice implied that this was none of her business.

"Where is the association going to get the money to pay for all the extra airline tickets everyone is using?" Her caustic tone of voice matching John's.

"What do you mean by 'everyone'?"

"I just got off the phone with Jason and found out why Roger didn't show for work today. Good old Roger went to Winterberg and told nobody he was going. Lester called yesterday and said he was going over to make sure everything was done right. You know what that means."

"No, Sandra, I don't know what that means," he replied sarcastically.

"Well, if Lester goes, then Nino will have to go. Sometimes I think they sleep together."

"Who the hell is telling everyone that it's okay for them to go to Europe? Get Wilbur on the phone so I can talk to him."

"Help yourself! You know his number, my job is to answer the phone," replied Sandra. "Tell him that Jason wants him to call. Use the phone in Roger's office."

She waited for him to close the door before calling her husband at his law office. Chester Wilson was a respected attorney in Lake Placid and the bobsled association was one of his main accounts. He had been successful in using his influence to secure a job with the association for his wife. As the association's secretary, Sandra was able to keep Chester informed of the daily business.

Sandra quietly related to her husband the story about Roger going to Winterberg without telling anybody and that John, Lester, and Nino were making plans to join Roger in Europe. Chester was furious about the money they were wasting since the association was almost bankrupt and would be if they did not obtain some serious sponsorship in the very near future. She heard

John hang up Roger's phone so she told Chester she would call him at noon and hung up abruptly so John wouldn't know she had called him.

John walked out of the office and began to question Sandra to find out if she had any indication that Roger was going to Winterberg. He was visibly upset that nobody was aware of Roger's plans to attend the trials. John was the association's treasurer and was well aware of their meager financial situation. This was not a good time to let Roger loose in Europe with an association credit card in his possession.

"Did Wilbur have any indication that Roger was going to Winterberg?" she asked.

"No. He talked to Roger last week and the guy never said a thing about going."

"So what else is new around here? Everyone who thinks they are important has an association credit card and does whatever they want. Why are you going to Winterberg, John?" she asked with an acerbic smile.

"That's none of your business, but I'll tell you why. I have to go and make sure the bank accounts are set up right and that there are no other fiscal problems."

"I thought that's why the board of directors selected Jason. He's experienced in that type of work."

"He's a pinhead," replied John in disgust. "The board doesn't decide anything unless Lester and Nino tell them what to do. They pressured Wilbur into selecting Jason because they wanted someone stupid managing the trials. Jason is perfect because they can easily manipulate him when they go over there."

They both knew that Lester and Nino only went to entertain their friends. During the short period of time since they took control of the association, Lester always invited several of his business buddies along on trips to impress them. "Where's all this money coming from?" asked Sandra.

"They won't use association money if I have anything to say about it," said John. "Do you have a key to Roger's desk?"

"Nope. Roger keeps everything locked and he's the only person with a key. I guess he's afraid I might see something," She replied with a snicker.

John turned without saying good-bye and left the office leaving Sandra staring at his back.

Chapter Six

→ *Ice Spy*

Bethesda, Maryland

Fred Unser's flight from Norfolk was on time, but the early morning rush hour traffic into Washington was a nightmare. Unser was on his way to the David Taylor Research Lab to see Dr. Robert Gilmore. The heavy rain, responsible for several auto accidents, slowed traffic on Interstate 495 to a crawl. He knew it would be impossible to make his appointment on time and he hated being late. He knew that Gilmore wouldn't get upset, but it would frustrate him all day.

The receptionist smiled sympathetically as Fred approached her desk. He was dripping wet after the long walk from the parking lot. He showed the receptionist his identification card and told her that Dr. Gilmore was expecting him. She called the doctor's number and told him that Fred was at the reception area. Gilmore asked her to give him a visitor's pass and said he would send an escort to meet him. Fred was well aware that the tight security required for the Navy Research Lab was the same as the CIA Headquarters in Langley. Work done at this laboratory is treated as top secret by Naval Intelligence. The sensitive research conducted for the navy here was a desired resource that many foreign countries attempted to infiltrate, hence the heavy security.

His escort arrived, a young woman who was startlingly beautiful, to accompany him to Gilmore's office. They got off the elevator on the fifth floor and walked down the long hallway. The young escort opened the doctor's door and then excused herself and left. Fred was sorry to see her leave. Gilmore was sitting at his desk waiting.

"I apologize for being so late."

"Don't worry about it. I was late getting to the office myself. The rain slowed everyone down," Gilmore replied. "Fred, I've asked another triboligist to sit in on the meeting, I hope you don't mind."

"Not at all, but please keep in mind that *IceSpy* is top secret."

"Everything we work on here is top secret. This fellow is a tribologist and an expert on water and ice friction. He'll provide some significant technical insights for us. I would feel more comfortable with him here since he's also an expert on Soviet Naval technology.

Gilmore went to his desk and called the tribologist. Fred recalled what Joe Sweeney had said about Gilmore. He was the only person who could explain metallurgy in laymen's terms. Fred studied Gilmore's mannerisms as he spoke on the phone. Years of CIA training and working as an agent in the field caused Fred to naturally study everyone he contacted. Although there was no need to study Gilmore, Fred did so unconsciously. It was second nature to him.

"He will be with us in just a moment." Seconds later the door opened and Gilmore introduced the two men. The discussion about the *IceSpy* project took several hours and Fred agreed with Gilmore's analysis of the tribologist; he was indeed an expert on Soviet Naval equipment. He was extremely interested in Jamie Suriano's report that included a brief description about the technology Yegorov had shared with Jamie and Walter.

The tribologist told Fred he was not surprised Yegorov had discovered a composite material that could reduce water or ice friction on metal. He said the Soviets had some brilliant scientists who were capable of discovering and developing theories like this one and suspected that this type of research was primarily for their sports programs.

"It's a well know fact that the Soviets spent about one percent of their Gross National Product on sports," Gilmore said. "A few years ago I was privileged to represent the United States at an International Seminar for Metallurgists held in Vienna. Several Soviet scientists were also in attendance, which surprised everyone. They declined to discuss their research in any depth, however, it was quite evident they were unhappy with their system. From time to time they implied their dissatisfaction because Soviet research was focused more on sports than industry."

"That's interesting," said Fred absent-mindedly, still thinking about what Gilmore said about the attitude of the Soviet scientists.

"Fred, do the Soviets know that Boris Yegorov has this kind of technology?"

"They must suspect it, I'm sure. The Agency is reasonably sure that he used the technology to build bobsled runners for the Soviets and the East Germans."

"Will he sell us the information?" asked Gilmore.

"No. He wants to leave the Soviet Union with his family. We really can't be certain that the Soviets know, but as I said, we think they might suspect he has developed something of importance. We don't believe they understand the full impact of his new technology. Once they discover we're interested in him, they'll figure it out in a hurry. You can be certain they would rather kill him than take a chance on our government getting the information. It's crucial the *IceSpy* project be kept top secret. The Agency will be extremely careful to be certain that the preliminary work is done properly, because once we make our move, time will be critical. Yegorov has all the information in his head, so he's no good to us dead."

Fred thanked both men for their help and promised to call them should he obtain any more information. He left the Taylor Research Lab and walked to the parking lot where he had left his rental car. He was pleased the rain had stopped and the sun was working its way through the clouds. On the way to the airport he thought about the Soviet coach. Time was going to be a major problem. He would call Joe Sweeney when he got back to his office and have him go to Europe to meet with Walter and Shawn.

Winterberg, West Germany

Shawn looked up and noticed Roger Ferris walking up the trail next to the bobsled track. He looked like shit and Shawn assumed he had been out all night.

"Where's Jason?" asked Roger, unfocused.

"He's at the start of the bobrun with Jim Bogdan. You'd better hurry if you want to catch him because he said he had to meet with the bank manager," replied Shawn. This woke up Ferris in a hurry.

"Why is he meeting with him? I have everything set up with the bank. Jesus, I hope he doesn't screw things up with them. I can never figure why people don't just mind their business and do their own jobs. Give me your portable radio so I can call Jason and have him pick me up."

Roger walked off to the side of the path just out of Shawn's hearing range and called Jason on the radio to find out what was distressing him. A couple of minutes later he returned the radio and told Shawn he was going to the bank with Jason to establish a separate account to take care of the daily business of the trials.

"You look like death warmed over, Roger. What happened to you last night?" asked Shawn with a grin.

"I had a killer of a night. Some German friends took me to a private party and I didn't get back to the hotel until six this morning. What time is it now?"

"Ten minutes to noon. You're getting here earlier and earlier, Roger. Hell, if you keep this trend up you might make it by eleven tomorrow. That would be before we finish with the morning's practice."

"You know something, Shawn. You're a wise bastard."

"Oh, really! Did I say something that wasn't true or did I hit a nerve?"

Roger walked away sputtering under his breath and went down the road to meet Jason who was driving up the hill. He got into the car and asked, "What's the problem with the bank?"

"You've deposited all my operating money into the association's account."

"I don't see a problem with that. We've always done it that way," replied Roger.

"Well, having all the money in a single bank account might work for you and the officials, but it's difficult for me to manage when everyone has access to the money except me." Jason's hostility was obvious.

"Why don't you tell me about the real problem?" asked Roger angrily. He thought about what an idiot Jason was and wished he could go back to the hotel. His hangover was killing him and he desperately needed a nap.

"Last year you put my operating money in the bank and everyone withdrew money for their own use and never accounted for any of it to me. I didn't have enough money left over to pay the association expenses. This year I want an account that only I have access to and not everyone and their brother."

"Only association officials have access to this money."

Jason laughed sarcastically. "Is that a joke? Not all those guys are association officials."

"Who are you referring to when you say 'those guys'?"

"Do you want a list?"

"Yeah. Tell me who you're talking about because I've never taken money out of that account unless I used it for training expenses."

"You have no business taking money out without asking me. You should have given me the receipts showing where you spent the money," yelled Jason in a frenzy. "You people take money without asking and we don't have any left to pay expenses at the end of the trip."

"Jesus, Jason relax. You're getting wound up like a rabid dog! I haven't done anything different than anyone else. Who are you referring to when you say the 'other guys'?"

"I'll tell ya. Lester is the worst. He thinks the money in that account is for his own personal use. You can add John Chapadeau, Wilbur, and Nino. Lester sucks up the association's money, but he brags about having millions available to him from the mob. He should use their money."

"What the hell are you talking about?"

"Everyone of them suck up the association's money and then I run short at the end of the season."

Jason pulled the car into the bank parking lot and Roger agreed to set up another account to cover Jason's operating expenses. It took only thirty minutes to make the transfer and set up a new account that only Jason and Roger could access. Satisfied, Jason left the bank with Roger and returned to the car.

"Jason, let me give you some good advice. Don't ever repeat to anyone what we talked about earlier in the car. Do you understand?"

"I guess I don't." He replied with a confused look on his face.

"Jason, Jason. You must sleep under a rock. The guys on your 'list' are connected to the mob. Look, I don't want to get into their backgrounds, but you should know something," replied Roger. "Lester Fetor was arrested for murder in New York several years ago and the police suspected it was mob related. The only witness was killed in a suspicious auto accident a week before the trial. No witness, no case. They had to drop charges against Fetor. If you're smart, you'll keep your mouth shut because these guys are nobody to fool around with."

Roger's story startled Jason and he thought about Lester and his friends on the way back to the hotel. Jason got out of the car immediately when Roger parked without saying good-bye and went to his room still upset about this disturbing information.

KGB Headquarters, Riga, Latvia, USSR

Ivan Liepinsh returned to his office in the KGB *corner house* and began to catch up on reports that had been left on his desk while he was in Moscow. He read Georgi Pasevs' report on executing two of his agents and called the deputy commander into his office.

"Yes, Commandant Liepinsh. You wished to see me?" Georgi felt drops of cold sweat sliding down his back.

"What happened to Auseklis and Sergejs? Why didn't you wait for me to return from Moscow?" demanded Ivan furiously.

"I thought about waiting, Commandant, but I seized the moment. Let it be a lesson for others who might think of taking bribes," lied Georgi.

"What made you think they took bribes?"

"I had them brought here as soon as it was discovered that the two Americans had disappeared. I searched them and found American hard currency in their pockets. I arrested them and had them executed for treason. I have the money locked in my desk for you," lied Georgi. The American cash hidden in his desk was from a black market deal he made several months ago.

→ *Ice Spy*

Ivan told him to get the American cash and bring it to him. He suspected Georgi was lying, but wasn't going to push the issue. Georgi rushed out of the office and retrieved the five hundred dollars that was worth thirty times more in Russian rubles. Regardless of its value it wasn't worth his life. He thought about leaving some in his drawer then quickly changed his mind.

"Commandant, here is all the hard currency I collected from them."

"Good, Georgi. You will be rewarded for what you did. Next time you check with me first, do you understand?"

"Yes, Commandant. Thank you for being so understanding. Will that be all?"

"Yes, you may leave now."

Georgi left the commander's office and breathed a sign of relief. That was too close. The next time Americans were in Riga he would make sure his people stuck to them like glue.

Schenectady, New York

Colonel Fowlkes called Olive Hanson on the phone and asked her to come to his office. He asked her to enter and shut the door. His lips were pressed together and his facial expressions told her that he was about to explode. He handed her an envelope containing a card and said it had come in the morning mail. She removed the card and began reading it. The front of the card had a religious scene; a stained-glass window with small words scrolled at the bottom, 'Jesus loves you.' When she opened the card she almost fell off her chair. On the inside of the card in large print was another message, 'everyone else thinks you are an asshole.' The card was unsigned and the envelope was postmarked, Frankfort, West Germany.

"Maybe, Shawn Murphy sent this. If he did, can you do something about it?"

"I don't know what to do," replied Amos. "I called Security Police and they said there's nothing they can do since it's unsigned. I won't let Murphy get away with this. Somehow I'll find a way to make him pay for this crap and for making us look foolish when he got the government involved in letting him attend the Olympic trials."

"Rumors are going around that he is involved in something that is very high in the government circles, otherwise the general would never have instantly reassigned him. Nobody at this base has ever seen an overnight transfer like this and everyone believes that he is involved in something on the national security level."

"There's no question that he's involved with some very powerful government officials," replied Amos. "Give me some time and I'll burn him. I would appreciate it if you didn't tell anyone about the card."

"I won't, but you might as well figure that everyone on base knows about it anyway, because you told Security Police."

"You're right, I should never have called them."

She got up and left him staring out the window.

Lake Placid, New York

Sandra Wilson put on her coat and left the office to get the mail. The Post Office was only one block away and she walked there every day, regardless of the weather. She loved the view of the snow-capped Whiteface mountain peak as well as the crisp, clean air. The air this morning was decidedly cooler and she knew winter would not be very far away.

As she turned the combination on the bobsled association's mail box she could see a notice for a registered letter. She went to the Customer Service desk and signed for the letter. She opened it immediately and her heart sank when she read the notice of cancellation from the association's accident and liability insurance carrier. Ferris lied again, she thought. She distinctly recalled hearing him tell Wilbur, "As we speak, the new policy is being typed."

She walked hurriedly back and called her husband at his law office. Chester asked her for the cancellation date and told her he would take care of it. He dialed Wilbur Hippenbecker's telephone number at the Credit Company in Rochester where he worked. When Wilbur answered, Chester said, "Sandra just called me and said the insurance company sent the association a cancellation notice in this morning's mail. I was told that Roger took care of this. We went through this same bullshit last year for Christ's' sake. You should follow up on these things."

"I shouldn't have to check up on everything he's supposed to be doing," replied Hippenbecker defensively. "We pay him thirty grand a year to do these things. I'm only a part-time president, not a baby sitter."

"Well, maybe you should get rid of him if he's incompetent. Why did you let him go to Europe when there is a ton of work that needs to be done here?"

"I didn't. He decided for himself. Sandra called me a short time ago and said Jason was upset and wants me to call him. It's not a bad idea that he went to help them set up as long as he doesn't stay more than a few days. I will take care of the liability insurance problem and get in touch with Roger to get him straightened out." Wilbur was furious that Roger didn't tell him he was going to Europe. He had a habit of making Wilbur look foolish.

"You always say that, Wilbur, and then never do anything about him. You should've fired him when you caught him stealing from the petty cash last year. That was the perfect opportunity for you to get rid of him. Instead, you just yelled at him and then covered up the whole thing. That's why he walks all over you."

"We don't have the money to hire someone who is qualified to replace him."

"What can I tell you, Wilbur. Add all the unnecessary money he spends to his salary and legal expenses and that's what the association is paying for incompetent work. Forget him for now and find a way to come up with five thousand during the next twenty days to take care of the insurance."

"The association is broke. We sent the rest of our funds to Winterberg to pay for the Olympic trials."

"That's your problem, Wilbur. Maybe you should think about hiring a reliable business director to manage the operation."

Wilbur slammed the phone down and cursed. He did nothing but go around

→ *Ice Spy*

picking up behind people. Chester was right. He should get rid of Roger. He called the airlines and charged an airline ticket for Frankfurt on the association's credit card. He would have to go to Winterberg and clean up the mess Roger had created, after he borrowed on the association's line of credit to pay for the liability insurance.

CHAPTER SEVEN

→ *Ice Spy*

CIA Headquarters, Langley, Virginia

Gary Circe sat at his desk waiting for his staff to brief him on the *IceSpy* project. Although he had been CIA Director for three months, he still wasn't comfortable with the position. This would be the first time he officially briefed the president and it was all the more difficult because this briefing was on a covert operation. Gary had thirty-five years with the Agency and was very comfortable with covert operations and, in fact, enjoyed them. However, giving the president of the United States a briefing of any capacity was nerve-wracking and he didn't look forward to this part of the job.

Gary's secretary, stepped into his office interrupting his thoughts. "Mr. Circe, the President's staff has arrived and everyone is waiting for you in the conference room."

"Thanks. I don't know why having to give the president's staff a briefing is so intimidating, but my stomach is in knots."

"Don't worry. You're the third director I've worked for and the others were the same way. You'll do just fine just like they did."

"I hope so. Hold my calls until the staff briefing is finished. What time do I have to be at the White House tomorrow?"

"The meeting is scheduled for nine-thirty."

Gary walked down the hall to the conference room where Fred Unser and the others were waiting for him. He nodded to the group and sat down at the end of the conference table. He asked Fred to bring everyone up to date on the *IceSpy* project. The briefing included information they had received in the past twenty-four hours. The undercover agent working in Riga informed them about the KGB executing two of their own agents. Fred believed they did this because Walter and Jamie had been successful in their efforts to evade the KGB surveillance. He told the staff there was a strong possibility the KGB suspected they were CIA agents and not American businessmen working for a medical import-export firm in Boston.

The KGB's ruthless execution of its own agents made it extremely risky for Walter to return to Riga. Future meetings with Boris Yegorov would have to be with another agent. Walter had suggested in his report to Fred that another agent should attempt to meet with Yegorov outside the Soviet Union. Fred suggested that a meeting between Boris and Shawn Murphy could take place in Altenburg, since the Soviet coach could still travel to East Germany. Any meeting there between the two men could be cleverly disguised as bobsled business. The Altenburg bobsled track would be an excellent cover for them to exchange information.

Fred Unser discussed Joe Sweeney's mission to Germany to work with the group. Fred believed it was critical that Boris not be connected with Walter, because the KGB would rather kill Boris than lose the technical information to the United States. He made several suggestions that he though would make the *IceSpy* project more favorable to the president's staff.

The briefing lasted several hours and after it ended everyone departed but Gary, who returned to his office to prepare his final report to the president. He was still apprehensive about the meeting with the president and wanted the briefing to be flawless.

Frankfurt, West Germany

John Chapadeau handed the German auto dealer his bobsled association credit card to pay for the rental car. His flight from Newark exhausted him and he was eager to be on his way to Winterberg. The dealer thanked him for his business as he turned to walk out the door but John didn't bother to reply. He got into the car and raced out of the parking lot onto the highway. John loved the excitement of driving a Porsche at high speeds on the autobahn.

Bobsled association members could not understand why he took on the extra burden of working as a volunteer treasurer. It was obvious to everyone that he had a lucrative source of income from his CPA firm in Queens. John traveled extensively back and forth to Europe and flagrantly used his association expense account to the maximum. John never traveled with the team because he preferred the athletes, in the economy section, not see him flying first-class. When questioned about his lavish travel expenses at an association board meeting, he simply shrugged off the question. He gave a vague reply about wining and dining executives from foreign companies to encourage their financial sponsorship for the association. Nobody had the courage to make an issue of it and the matter was dropped.

John parked in the Zur Sonne Hotel parking lot and went inside to register. He noticed Ron Harrison and Skip Reynolds in the hotel dining room when he walked by on his way to his room. Jason was eating alone, so John walked in ignoring the two athletes and sat across from Jason, surprising him.

"Did you just get here, John?" asked Jason delightedly. He normally ate alone because the athletes distrusted him and believed he was an inappropriate choice as their team manager.

"I just pulled in and registered. The girl at the desk said you made arrangements for me to stay in your suite. Why?"

"I had no choice. The hotel is filled up and I had to double up everyone."

"Did you make reservations here for Lester and Nino?"

"They made their own reservations here and so did Wilbur. I know you always want to be alone, but I had no choice."

"Where's all the money coming from to pay their travel expenses?" asked John, annoyed. "If everyone keeps spending the association's Olympic funds, there won't be any left for Calgary in February."

"I think you'll be happy with the accommodations in our suite. It was originally the owner's and it's got the best of everything."

"It's not so great. I've stayed in it several times when I've been here on business. I might as well eat now and unload the car later."

"Give me your car keys, John, and I'll put your luggage in the suite."

"I don't want anyone touching my luggage. I'll do it myself, do you understand?"

"Relax, John, I was just trying to help."

"I don't need any help. I need some time to myself so I can think. Why don't you see what you can do to get Lester and Nino another hotel so I can have their suite."

"They have a room with two beds, not a suite."

→ Ice Spy

"Whatever. Try to arrange for a separate room for me."

Jason left abruptly without saying good-bye. On the way out of the dinning room, he reminded Jim and Shawn to come to his suite after dinner to finish the athletes' practice schedule. He walked across the hotel's front porch and noticed a red Porsche in the parking lot and knew it had to be John's rental.

The wind had picked up and the temperature had dropped noticeably, forcing him to pull up the zipper on his jacket. The weather change would improve the bobsled track's conditions for training in the morning. The warm ice prevented the bobsleds from going fast, which made it difficult for the athletes to train for Olympic conditions. This is the reason the association spent the enormous amount of money to send the athletes to Germany.

The short walk to the suite seemed to take forever in the bitter cold wind. He quickly entered the room and left his jacket on for several minutes until he felt warm. A short time later John arrived, carrying his luggage into the bedroom he would be sharing with Jason. To avoid him, Jason stayed in the kitchen area and placed his paperwork on the table for the meeting with Jim and Shawn.

A short time later, John came out of the bedroom and told him he was going to the hotel sauna to relax. Jason nodded and watched as he left the suite. Moments later Jim and Shawn arrived for their meeting. The kitchen area was tiny, but functional. The three men felt crowded in the confined area. Jason began looking for his note pad and remembered it was inside his attaché case in the bedroom. He asked Shawn to get it since it was impossible for him to get around the table without the two men moving for him. Shawn went into the bedroom and didn't see Jason's attaché case on the bed, but noticed another one under John's coat. He opened the unlocked case and was stunned to see neat stacks of American cash. Shawn picked up one bundle and thumbed through it and quickly estimated there was about $300,000 in used one-hundred dollar bills. He closed the case and carefully placed the coat back as he found it.

"Jason, I don't see any attaché case except John's. Are you sure it's in here?"

"Jesus, don't touch John's or he will have a fit," replied Jason. "I'm sorry, I must have left it in my car." Shawn took Jason's keys and went out to the parking lot to get his attaché case. He thought about the enormous amount of cash and wondered how John got it through the German customs. He knew it wasn't legal to carry over $10,000 in cash out of the United States. It puzzled him as to why John had the cash and suddenly it occurred to him that customs seldom, if ever, checked the luggage of officials with Olympic credentials. Maybe John wasn't really interested in securing sponsors as he claimed and was using his position as the treasurer to launder money for his mafia clients. This would also explain why he took so many trips to Europe.

Shawn remembered Joe telling him the FBI had someone working undercover in the association, but he had no idea who the agent might be. He wished he knew so he could share the information about the cash with him. Shawn returned to the kitchen with the attaché case and they continued working on the practice schedule.

Twenty minutes later John returned from the sauna and took a shower.

He then got dressed and left the suite. Shawn noticed he was carrying the attaché case and he suspected that he would not let the cash get out of his sight for very long. He assumed that by the end of the next day the cash would end up in a Swiss bank account.

The rest of the meeting lasted thirty minutes and when it was over Shawn and Jim left the suite. On the way out, Shawn said, "Jim, let's take a walk, I need to tell you something, but I want your word that you won't discuss it with anyone else."

"I should think you could trust me by now."

"When I went into the bedroom to get Jason's note pad from his attaché case, I opened John's by mistake. There must have been at least $300,000 in one-hundred dollar bills in it. He must have left in a hurry and forgot to lock it."

"No shit! What the hell is he doing with that kind of cash over here?"

"Jim, he's got to be laundering money for some of his mafia clients. The association has never seen that amount of cash at one time. I believe he's using his Olympic credentials to slip the cash through customs and then he deposits it into a Swiss account."

"What a miserable low-life bastard! Whenever we need money for association expenses, he makes everyone feel guilty like they are wasting money. Yet, for his personal expenses, money is no problem. I wonder what he would say if one of us rented a Porsche like he does? He even complained that Jason rented the Volkswagen bus to transport the athletes and their gear from the hotel to the bobsled track."

"The money deal really frustrates me. He spends the association's money as if it were water and at the same time he's making a bundle from the mob using the association's credentials," replied Shawn, still visibly upset over his discovery.

"Well, the next few days should prove to be very interesting."

"Why do you say that?"

"All the self-appointed Big Shots will be arriving," replied Jim, chuckling. "I wonder what excuse they will use this time for being here.?"

"I'm sure they're here to make sure the trials are conducted properly. Those phony bastards will come out to the track every day when we're about finished with practice. They'll offer semi-intelligent advice on what they think we are doing and then disappear until the next morning. I'm sure they were all trained by Roger."

They returned to the hotel and went upstairs to their room. Shawn went out on the veranda and stood in the clear, cool air to collect his thoughts. The cold air finally forced him inside and he decided to call Angela and find out how she was doing without him. They talked for only a few minutes to keep the cost down and he promised to call her again at the end of the week. He wasn't tired yet he knew he needed his rest for the next morning. He went into his room and fell asleep shortly after his head hit the pillow.

Early the next morning Shawn went outside to walk and give himself some time to think about John and the enormous amount of cash he brought to Germany. His gut feeling told him that John's involvement with the mafia would be a disaster to the bobsled association and the Olympic Committee if the information ever leaked to the media. It would severely hamper their efforts to raise money. Shawn returned to the hotel from his run and saw Jason leaving with the Volkswagen bus to pick up the bobsled officials at the airport in Frankfort. This meant the athletes would have to carry their heavy gear on the long walk to the bobsled track.

Training at the track went smoothly and the condition of the ice improved, making the sleds faster much to the delight of the athletes. That was short-lived, however, as the hotel served pork for lunch. They were becoming exasperated with Jason's lack of understanding of their nutritional needs. Shawn listened to their angry discussions about how Jason lied just like the other officials and really didn't have any interest in their attempt to qualify for the upcoming Olympic Games.

The athletes spent the afternoon with Shawn repairing and realigning their sleds and preparing for the next day's practice. Shawn received a phone call from an old friend, Professor Ray Bodynski, from Syracuse University. Shawn took several Graduate courses in design at Syracuse that Professor Bodynski taught and the two had become close friends. The professor took a personal interest in Shawn's work because one of his hobbies was designing Grand Prix Race cars. The professor designed a new bobsled with his students as a class project at Syracuse and they worked hard to complete it in time for the Olympic Games.

Ray told Shawn the prototype sled was ready for the track and he would bring it to Winterberg the following week for Shawn to test. Ray shared his concern about the strange attitude Lester and Nino had exhibited toward his sled-building project at a recent association board meeting. Strangely enough, it was Wilbur Hippenbecker who kept the project alive. The professor and his students invested a tremendous amount of time and effort toward researching aerodynamics to build a faster sled. The project didn't cost the association any money since the United States Olympic Committee and private donors provided all the funding.

Lester and Nino's lack of enthusiasm for the association's ability to solicit private help in designing new equipment only confirmed Shawn's belief that these officials had no interest in the athletes. It was obvious that their priorities were to vacation on the association's funds and not to help the athletes prepare for the Olympics. Shawn felt relief that Ray was able to complete the project without Lester and Nino interfering. He looked forward to testing the sled and hoped the new aerodynamic design would be faster than the older models the association provided the athletes.

Shawn suspected that Lester and Nino's lack of interest might be jealousy regarding the large amount of publicity the project created in the media. The project was managed by the professor and not association's officials. Ray made it clear at the start of the project that Syracuse University would manage the funding. He was concerned because of the abundant rumors about association officials using previous donations for their personal use.

Shawn and Jim were eating dinner when Jason slid into the booth and asked, "How did training go this morning?"

"It was perfect," replied Jim. "Roger must have overslept, because he didn't make it to the track until we were finishing."

"Did you have any problems picking up our distinguished guests?" asked Shawn. He and Jim had a difficult time keeping a straight face.

"What a bunch of bastards." Jason was furious, his face a blistering red. "Lester called me yesterday and instructed me to meet him and his friends at the Frankfurt Airport with the Volkswagen bus. I drove three hours and found out he changed his mind. He rented a Mercedes, so he could have a 'nice' car to drive his friends around Winterberg. The bastard would have rented a Jaguar if he could have found one. I wasted the entire day, driving to Frankfurt and back."

"What difference does it make if Lester rents a Mercedes as long as he pays for it himself?" asked Jim, trying to conceal his amusement.

"Do you really think he pays for anything over here?" snapped Jason. His sudden open display of anger surprised both Shawn and Jim. Normally he never complained about Lester or Nino, because they kept him on the association's payroll.

"How does Lester get away with charging his personal expenses to the association?" asked Jim.

Jason reacted to Jim's loaded question with obvious frustration and stared at Jim with his dark narrow beady eyes. Professor Bodynski once remarked to Shawn that Jason's very narrow, recessed eyes were probably a result of inbreeding. Jason replied through clenched teeth, "Why do you think John Chapadeau is here?" They didn't reply to his question, so Jason continued in his usual twangy voice. "I'll tell you why. Lester has a business in New York that is tied to the Gambino family. Chapadeau does the accounting for both of them. You didn't really think they had an interest in bobsledding, did you?"

"Frankly, Jason, I don't know what to believe about these people," replied Shawn.

"Well, I'll tell you one thing for sure. They won't get their goddamn greedy fingers on the money the association allotted for me to fund the Olympic trials here in Winterberg," said Jason, still agitated. "Roger went to the bank with me and transferred money into a separate account."

"Why did you do that?" asked Jim.

"Because last year, Lester, Nino, and Roger had access to the account and the money kept disappearing until it was nearly gone. Now I'm the only one who can make withdrawals."

"What happens if you get sick and we need money for the trials?" asked Shawn.

"Don't worry, I left Roger's name on the card." Jason excused himself and left to do some work in his suite. Once he was out of ear shot, Jim and Shawn began to laugh at how stupid he was to leave Roger's name on the bank account. They couldn't believe that Jason was really that imbecilic since Roger was the largest money abuser in the association.

"You should have told him the story about Lester getting off the murder rap because the only witness got mysteriously killed in an auto accident," laughed Jim. "He wouldn't sleep for a week if he knew the truth about Lester and his friends' backgrounds."

→ *Ice Spy*

"I know. When Lester finds out what Jason did, he will make him switch the bank account around so fast his head will spin."

The hotel clerk interrupted their conversation to tell Shawn he had a phone call at the front desk. He was surprised to hear Joe's voice. They chatted for a couple of minutes until Joe suggested Shawn meet him outside in the parking lot in a few minutes where it would be more private. He excused himself to Jim and walked outside to wait. Within minutes Joe arrived in a rental car. He left the car running to keep warm and to prevent any one outside from hearing them and explained to Shawn what happened to Walter and Jamie when they met with Boris in Riga.

He reminded Shawn that they must take precautions to be sure nobody would know he was involved with the CIA. He suggested that Shawn introduce him as a friend who had been stationed with him in the States and now was stationed in West Germany. This story would avoid questions or suspicions anybody might have about Joe whenever he came to visit with Shawn. The two men returned to the hotel dining room and Shawn introduced Joe to Jim Bogdan.

After dinner, Shawn told Jim they were leaving to visit a German pub and reminisce about old times over a few beers. They drove aimlessly on the highway for the next hour while Joe briefed Shawn about *IceSpy* before they returned to the hotel. They talked for a short time and then Joe left after telling Shawn that he would prepare him for the mission when he returned. Shawn went to bed, but was too excited to fall asleep. He stayed awake most of the night trying to visualize what would be in the future for him and Boris Yegorov.

Chapter Eight

→ *Ice Spy*

Rochester, New York

Wilbur Hippenbecker rushed out to his car located in the credit company's parking lot where he worked. He drove as fast as he could in the heavy noontime traffic, hoping to fix the association's cash flow problem and return back to work within his one-hour lunch time. He hoped it would not take more time than he had to obtain an advance against the association's line of credit. He had called earlier to secure an appointment with the branch manager who was now waiting for him.

"Good afternoon. I appreciate you taking the time to meet with me." It irritated Wilbur that he had to take time to finish up work that Roger should have done in Lake Placid. His supervisor at the credit company was unhappy with all the extra time he had been using for bobsled business during the past year. On several occasions she had clearly indicated her displeasure to him about his abuse of company time. When he had first been elected president of the association, the company was excited to have an employee hold such a prestigious position. The excitement began to dissolve as the position of president of the bobsled association required him to travel for weeks at a time. He used company time to conduct association business and his supervisor soon resented the arrangement.

"Wilbur, I have some bad news for you," the branch manager said discreetly. "I thought it would be a simple transaction to move funds from your line of credit to your operating account. I checked the balance after you called, and the association has overdrawn the line of credit we provided last summer. Our branch in Lake Placid should never have made the last transfer."

This sounded unbelievable to Wilbur. "Could you tell me how much money was transferred and the date?" The manager looked at the computer printout and told him that the amount was $10,000 and the date was September twenty-sixth. Just two days before the team left for Winterberg.

"Would you call Lake Placid and find out who signed for the money?" Wilbur had a gut feeling it was Roger.

The manager called the branch in Lake Placid and after a few minutes of conversation, he hung up and told Wilbur that Roger Ferris, the association's business director, signed the transfer request. Wilbur thanked the manager for his help and returned back to work. He was now ten minutes late. He would have to charge the flight to Frankfurt on the association's credit card. He hoped the line of credit on their visa account wasn't over extended. When I get to Winterberg, thought Wilbur, Roger is going to have the surprise of a lifetime. Chester was right, I'm too easy on Roger and he walks all over me.

Winterberg, West Germany

Jason arrived early at the bobsled track and became irritated that the ice was soft. He located the track supervisor and complained that the association was paying an enormous amount of money to conduct the trials there because the Germans assured them the warm weather wouldn't be a problem. "The ice is still too soft and we need to have the refrigeration turned up higher."

"The refrigeration is turned up to the highest level it can go. We can't control the abnormally warm weather," replied the track supervisor sarcastically. "We cautioned Mr. Ferris that this might happen and he said, 'not to worry.'"

Jason left the track office, slamming the door behind him. As he walked towards the athletes standing on the equipment platform he noticed the thick fog was still hanging in the tree tops. The dampness seemed to reach his bones and he felt chilled. He could barely see the white car driving up the access road next to the track. As it came into view he wondered who was visiting the track so early in the morning. Suddenly he realized it was Lester in his rented Mercedes. Nino Casatelli and Roger Ferris were with him. He thought something must be wrong to get these three out of bed so early.

Lester began blowing the car horn, when he saw Jason, to get his attention. Jason was strongly inclined to ignore him but looked in the direction of the car. Lester pointed his finger at Jason and then pointed to the rear seat of the car. The athletes watched curiously as Jason nodded and walked reluctantly over to the car. The emotional expression on Lester's chubby face was enough to tell them that Jason was in serious trouble.

Lester opened his window and demanded Jason to get into the back seat. He opened the rear door and slid in next to Nino, asking, "What's up."

"I'll tell you what's up, you simple son-of-a-bitch," screamed Lester. Jason was startled and began squirming as cold chills crept down his back. "I just came from the bank and they informed me that you switched money from the association's account to another account and that only you and 'sticky fingers' Ferris here can make withdrawals. You've got to be the dumbest son of a bitch I've ever known."

"I don't have to sit here and listen to you insult me. I'm tired of you and your friends using the association's money as if it was your own," replied Jason, irritated.

"Oh yeah? How'd you like to have a tire iron shoved down your fucking throat?" threatened Lester, whose dumpy face was now purple. "You work for me. If you don't like it, I'll arrange for your replacement. Do you want me to replace you, asshole?"

"No," whimpered Jason. His shirt was soaking wet from sweat.

"You screw up once more and by the time they find your body, nobody will be able to identify who the hell you are. Do you understand what I'm telling you?"

"I understand," replied Jason terrified at Lester's threat. "I'll transfer the money back this afternoon after practice."

"I don't think you got my message, you asshole," screamed Lester, his saliva hit Jason in the face. "You're going for a ride with us and make the transfer right now. I don't want to hear your shit about doing it later. Do you think I was born yesterday? You-son-of-a-bitch, you'd better not do anything like this ever again or I'll bury you alive." Jason was terrified and knew Lester meant every word.

Nino, who had been sitting silently throughout Lester's hysterical outburst, glanced out the window and noticed the athletes had stopped training and were staring at the car.

"Lester," he remarked. "Calm down! The athletes can hear you."

"Screw the athletes! I don't give a shit if they can hear me. This stupid bastard really upsets me." Lester started the car and continued, "There should be a law against people being as stupid as you are, Jason."

He drove towards the bank in downtown Winterberg. Nino, who was sitting next to Jason, placed his arm on the back of the seat behind him. Jason really didn't know him but feared him as much as Lester. He had heard rumors about him and believed everyone. He was convinced that Nino was as ruthless as Lester and suspected that he did Lester's dirty work. While Lester was yelling at him, Nino stared at Jason with stone-cold black eyes.

Lester parked the car and told Jason to get out. They walked into the bank with Roger and Nino going directly to the manager's desk. Jason completed the transfer back into the association's account and closed the new account. The manager looked at Jason curiously, who stood there silently, embarrassed about his situation. Lester politely reminded Jason that he would not be moving any more money.

"If you ever get out of line again, it'll be your last time. Do you understand, shit head?"

"Don't worry, I won't do anything to upset you," stammered Jason. "I didn't mean to irritate you. I was only trying to manage the money for the trials."

"Jason, I'm not the kind of a man who holds grudges against anyone," smiled Lester. His sudden change of character frightened Jason further. "Let's say you made a mistake. I shouldn't have gotten so upset with you. You just do what I ask and we'll get along fine. Do you want me to take you back to the bobsled track?"

"No. Just drop me off at the hotel." Jason wasn't ready to face the athletes after Lester's tantrum in front of them.

Lester drove into the hotel parking lot and left Jason at the sidewalk. When Jason was out of hearing distance Lester turned to Roger. "You little slime ball, if you ever pull a stunt like this again, you'll sleep in a hole next to Jason. Now get your ass out of here and don't you ever forget what I told you."

Nino got into the front seat when Roger left the car and once Lester drove back out onto the highway, they both broke out in spontaneous laughter. "The stupid bastard got so scared that he pissed his pants," laughed Nino hysterically. "Look! The back seat's all wet. Maybe he shit in his pants too."

"How do you know he didn't?" asked Lester laughing. "We need to keep an eye on him. Guys like him are so stupid that they might talk to the wrong people. If he becomes a problem we'll take his identification papers and just waste him. I know a place in a remote part of the forest where we can dump him and the Germans will never figure out who he is or what happened to him."

"How about a little lunch?" It thrilled Lester to frighten Jason. He enjoyed terrifying people. "I'm starving." Lester drove to a restaurant north of Winterberg that was a favorite of the jet-set crowd.

Shawn looked at the calendar on the wall and noticed it was the third Thursday since he left the States. Angela would be getting another dozen roses today. A knock on his door interrupted thoughts of Angela. He went to the door and was shocked to see Jason standing there shaking uncontrollably.

His narrow beady eyes seemed to be focused on something in the far distance and not on Shawn standing in front of him.

"Come in, Jason. What's wrong with you?" Jason rushed into the room and with no hesitation began telling Shawn about his nightmare ride to the bank with Lester and Nino. He had a difficult time speaking and Shawn felt sorry for him. Jason spent the next twenty minutes relating to Shawn about his morning's experience. His greatest fear was the rapid increase of association officials who appeared to be connected to the mafia.

Shawn studied Jason while he rambled on about his nerve-wracking experience. He was a pitiful sight, shaking, pale, and terrified beyond words. In a way, Shawn thought it couldn't have happened to a better guy. Jason was a compulsive liar and not very reliable to those who worked with him. He couldn't help feeling sorry for him, but suspected that Jason's experience with the two mobsters wouldn't be his last. Shawn was concerned about the bobsled association's future. Lester's strong-arm influence would destroy years of the their hard work to develop athletes and in time his grotesque take over and behavior would reach the media. This would have a major impact on their financial ability to manage an Olympic training program for future athletes.

Syracuse, New York

Professor Ray Bodynski looked around his congested studio at the university making sure he packed all the equipment he would need while he was in Winterberg. The professor's new two-man sled had gone through extensive indoor wind-tunnel testing during their pursuit to develop a fiberglass cowling that would be less wind resistant than any other sleds in the 1988 Olympics. He was eager to take the sled to Winterberg and have Shawn Murphy test drive it so they could complete the final adjustment needed before the Olympic team would use it for training.

Satisfied that he had everything he needed, Ray locked the studio and drove to the airport to catch his flight from Syracuse to Newark, where he would meet a connecting Continental Airlines flight to Frankfurt. The one hour layover in Newark gave him time to eat a sandwich and look quickly at a newspaper he picked up on a seat. He didn't look forward to the nine hour flight over the Atlantic and brought some work along to keep his mind occupied.

Ray was unable to focus on his work because his mind kept drifting to the problems the bobsled association had given him with his research project. He attended two of the association's board of directors meetings in Lake Placid and Jason Pierce spoke very negatively on both occasions. Jason tried to convince the board members that it was impossible to develop better equipment to make bobsleds go faster. He believed the association needed to improve the drivers' skills if they were to be competitive in the Olympics.

The professor was baffled at Jason's narrow thinking since the association had nothing to lose, because all the research was paid with private or Olympic funding. Ray suspected that Jason incorrectly assumed that funding for research could be used for the association's general operation. He tried on one occasion to explain to Jason that money designated for research couldn't legally be used for other association expenses, a common practice in the past.

He had a lot of confidence in Shawn Murphy and knew the coach would test the sled and give him accurate feedback on its performance. He closed his eyes and thought about his project and tried to envision what would happen in Winterberg. Within minutes he was in a deep sleep.

Winterberg, West Germany

Shawn told Jim the story about Lester and Jason during their customary early morning walk to the bobsled track. The incident didn't surprise Jim, but he was amused at Shawn's picturesque description of Jason's terror.

"I've been watching Lester and his cronies ever since they took control of the association," said Jim. "I was shocked when Nino walked into my office one day and asked to see my training program for the athletes. I reluctantly showed it to him and assumed he was familiar with training athletes since he wanted to see the program."

"Was he?"

"He completely baffled me. I was totally confused about what he was doing. He never asked why I had athletes doing certain things or what the reason was for doing some of the exercises. Suddenly, he began telling me how he wanted the training program changed. I asked him why he was telling me to make changes in my program since I'm paid to be the association's trainer. He then informed me that he was selected by the board to be the association's vice-president in charge of training, or some wild title like that."

"I went through the same thing with him. That's why we don't have any other coaches over here helping with the trials. He informed all the coaches that he's running the program and they answer to him. One by one they dropped out of the picture because nobody wanted to put up with his stupidity."

"It would be all right if he had a little knowledge about either training or coaching, but you only need to talk with him for about three minutes to figure out that he's a total idiot."

"Did you ever look at Nino's famous 'whiteout workout' he gave the athletes?"

"No! What's a 'whiteout workout'?" asked Jim, clearly puzzled.

"Wait till you hear this." Shawn laughed. "He gave me a new workout program and said that he wrote it specifically for our bobsled athletes. I was shocked when I read it. He took a high school football workout program and went through it using whiteout to cover up the word 'football' and then typed in 'bobsled.' Then he made photo copies."

"No. You've gotten to be kidding. Nobody is that stupid. Are you pulling my leg?"

"I'm serious, Jim. Listen to this." Continued Shawn, unable to control his laughter. "When he typed in the word 'bobsled' the type size and style was different, plus in some places it was crooked."

"Oh, my God. I can't believe he's that stupid. Yes, I can. The athletes must really be impressed with Nino."

"Oh, yeah. They were hysterical when they read it," laughed Shawn. "The workout wasn't a bad program. It was too superficial for Olympic level athletes, but Nino wouldn't understand." Shawn shook his head in disgust and said sarcastically, "Nino's a real asset."

"I bet he wouldn't understand what plagiarism is either."

The two men reached the gate to the bobsled track and agreed to meet later for lunch, then parted direction. Shawn turned to walk along the track to do his daily check on the condition of the ice. Moments later, Ron Harrison stopped him and asked if he could discuss the hotel menu with him.

Harrison was an unseasoned athlete from Detroit, Michigan who was trying to qualify as a brakeman with the team. He said the athletes were frustrated that the hotel was still serving them food that was very high in fat content.

"I'll talk to Jason again, Ron, but you should have the other athletes complain also, so he doesn't think I'm the only person who is unhappy with the hotel's lousy selection."

"These are supposed to be the Olympic trials. How the hell do they expect us to perform our best when we eat this kind of shit everyday?"

"They don't give a damn. Have the guys tell Jason to talk with the hotel owner and see if he can help out. Maybe he can give us fish or just plain old hamburg. I'll let you know tomorrow how I make out with him. I have to be careful because Lester and Nino don't like any changes."

"You know what Lester and Nino can do, don't you? Those bastards come over here and suck up our expense money, eating in expensive restaurants and partying every night. Do you know, that yesterday one of the guys asked Lester for a ride to the machine shop to get a part repaired for his sled. Lester told him to walk, the exercise would be good for him. By the way, the only people the athletes have any respect for are you and Jim."

"Thanks, Ron. We appreciate the confidence. Sometimes we get so frustrated with the association officials we would like to tell them to just shove it, but we don't because you guys would have no help at all. I'll talk with you tomorrow." Ron left to prepare for practice and Shawn continued his inspection of the track, thinking about the athletes' difficult situation.

After the practice session was over, Shawn and Jim walked back to the hotel discussing the results of the morning's training. Shawn told him about his conversation with Ron. When he finished relating the story, Jim said he had a similar talk with Dave Leon and Skip Reynolds. They agreed that they should talk with Jason and try to convince him to work out a different menu with the hotel. When they saw Wilbur Hippenbecker checking in at the front desk they looked at each other and smiled. Jim commented sarcastically about how well the trials would be managed now that Wilbur was there helping. Shawn thought that Wilbur had about as much chance of keeping Lester and his group under control as a snowball had in hell. They both chuckled and joked about the situation, but sadly realized that the Olympic trials were rapidly becoming a third rate circus act.

→ *Ice Spy*

CIA Headquarters, Langley, Virginia

Gary Circe sat at his desk thinking about the previous week's meeting with the president. The meeting had been extremely productive. The president gave his approval of the *IceSpy* mission, without any objection. This surprised him. Fred Unser and his staff were working overtime to put all the pieces together and they could not afford to make any mistakes. There would be a lot riding on this mission. The lives of Boris Yegorov and Shawn Murphy, as well as several other agents were at great risk. He believed the new technology Yegorov had created was worth the tremendous risk his agents would take.

Any country having this technology would have the ability to move faster on or under water and use less fuel at the same time. Fred Unser was right when he said it was just as important the Soviets not obtain Boris' technology, if their mission failed. Boris was in an extremely difficult situation. The Soviets would kill him if they discovered he was defecting to the United States to exchange the technology for freedom. The CIA would have to kill him if he stayed in the Soviet Union, to prevent the Russians from obtaining the information.

The agency would need to have all the pieces of the puzzle in place and then move swiftly, because the KGB would kill Boris instantly if they uncover the *IceSpy* mission. He shuddered to think about the impact from the media if the mission failed and became public. His future with the Agency would be tied directly to both the secrecy and the success of *IceSpy*. He closed his eyes and tried unsuccessfully to think about something different.

CHAPTER NINE

→ *Ice Spy*

Winterberg, West Germany

The next morning the air temperature was down considerably. It had continued to drop each day as the winter season rapidly approached Winterberg. It was the last week of October and the Bavarian Alps surrounding the tiny city sparkled in the crisp air. The cold weather improved ice conditions which were a positive morale boost for the athletes. Each was trying his best to win at the trials so he would be selected to represent the United States in February at the Winter Olympics in Calgary, Canada.

The morning walks to the bobsled track now forced Shawn and Jim to wear heavy jackets and thick wool socks. The air was crisp and much colder, yet very clear giving a breathtaking view of the Alps from the bobsled track. On mornings when there was no fog, U.S. Air Force pilots stationed near Munich would fly their F-15s north, training around the mountain peaks and up through the valleys that encompassed Winterberg.

The F-15's seemed to come out of nowhere. Suddenly, someone would see a plane and yell, "Here's the Air Force." The jets would streak up the valley at low altitude making a sharp left bank and shoot straight up the mountainside at unbelievable speeds, about one thousand feet above the bobsled track. Normally, there would be six training together in the early morning missions. After they buzzed the bobsled track they would bank sharply and return for a second pass. This pass would be much slower and pilots would dip the F-15's wings to signal a greeting to the Americans. It was thrilling each time the planes flew over the track and the excitement of the training missions stayed with the athletes throughout the entire day. The private air show became a morning ritual. On days when the fog lingered beyond midmorning, the athletes would grumble because the pilots couldn't make the low level training flights.

The cold air that moved ahead of the approaching winter season now kept the morning fog to a minimum. Shawn thought about the weather and how the air might be getting colder, but the storm that was brewing among the bobsled officials was getting hotter. He waited at the track entrance for Jim to meet him for their walk back to the hotel for lunch. The morning practice session had been tense and he noticed the athletes were beginning to feel the strain. The Olympic selection race was now only a week away.

When Jim arrived, he smiled and asked, "Were you invited to the big meeting that's scheduled for this afternoon?"

"No. I didn't know there was one."

"Something is in the works. I overheard Wilbur telling John about it. Roger made lunch arrangements at another hotel, so you and I probably won't know what's going on."

"What do you think it's about?"

"I really don't have any idea. They are always fighting over money or who's in charge. It's a safe bet those two topics will be on the top of their agenda."

Roger had made arrangements for the bobsled officials to meet at the Bernkastel-Kues, a prestigious resort hotel that was in vogue with the jet-set crowd. When the lavish luncheon was finished, the group relaxed over French champagne.

Wilbur looked at Roger and asked, "Why was the association's medical insurance policy allowed to lapse for non-payment?"

"Don't look at me. That's not my responsibility. I sent all the information the insurance company requested for the renewal and instructed them to renew the coverage. I also advised them to increase our personal liability another twenty-five thousand just as the board approved."

"I'm not talking about them renewing the policy. They need to be paid! No payment, no insurance," replied Wilbur, annoyed at how Roger managed to avoid the question.

"That's John's responsibility, not mine. I always do what I'm supposed to do."

"You never sent me a bill," snapped John. "I'm not a mind reader. You send me a bill and I'll cut a check and put it in the mail."

"Where were you going to get the money to pay the insurance?" asked Wilbur, nodding his head, in anticipation of John's reply.

"I have the money set aside in the Lake Placid account we use for operating expenses. I can make a quick transfer and send the check."

"Well, there's less than three-hundred in that account right now. I checked with the bank and not only is the bulk of the account missing, but Roger borrowed more against our line of credit and that money was withdrawn. For your information, Roger, the bank made a mistake and exceeded our approved limit. Your little friend that you run around with at night may lose her job for approving your loan request."

"I only did what I was instructed to do," Roger's face and neck suddenly became pale and his collar was soaked with sweat. "Don't accuse me of doing something wrong with the association's money."

"What the hell is going on here? Who instructed you to make the transfer and request more from our line of credit? asked John.

"I told him to do what he did," interrupted Lester. His voice exulted a distinct tone of authority. "We need to have extra funds here for our marketing program."

"You don't have any legitimate authorization to move the association's money around like this," Wilbur was visibly enraged at Lester's statement. "I'm responsible for the money and nothing gets used without the executive board's approval."

"Open your eyes, asshole," bellowed Lester. "Don't tell me you're as stupid as Jason. We are the executive board, for Christ sakes. In case you forgot about who put you in office, let me remind you. Without me, pal, you're nothing. Get off your grandstand and do what I tell you. If you get out of line again, we'll have an executive board meeting and call a vote on keeping you as the 'so-called president.' I'll put you out on your ass so fast your head will spin." Wilbur stared at Lester, without expressing any emotion throughout his intense outburst. This infuriated Lester and pushed him to a greater level of hostility. "Don't stare at me like that! I might have you dumped just to teach you a lesson."

Lester turned away from Wilbur, knowing full well that he would just sit there and take his abuse. He glanced across the long table at John. He was clearly shaken by Lester's enraged outburst and thankful Wilbur was in the hot seat and not himself.

Lester looked over at John and asked, "What do we have to do to get the cash for the insurance?"

"We'll need more than just the insurance money. We need to send advance money to prepay rent and other expenses for the Olympics."

"What about the money we have coming from the Olympic Committee?"

"We won't see that in time to use before the Olympic expenses need to be paid," replied John. "I can take care of money we will need for the Olympics."

"How can you get money?" asked Lester. "Our credit rating is shot."

"Don't worry about it. I'll borrow the cash from my firm's escrow account and when the money from the Olympic Committee comes in, it will be replaced."

"Isn't that illegal?' asked Wilbur.

"Who gives a shit," Lester was annoyed that the creative loan scheme was being questioned by Wilbur. "Those clients will never know. Right, John?"

"I move money all the time for my clients who are having cash flow problems and nobody can follow what I do," replied John snickering at how clever he was at manipulating his clients' funds. "You let me worry about it."

"How much money are we talking about?" asked Lester.

"We'll need about sixty grand to cover our Olympic expenses."

"Does that include the expenses for the athletes?" asked Wilbur.

"No. Their expenses will run another twenty grand," replied John, looking through some notes he took out of his attaché case.

"Why are your expenses more than three times those for the athletes and coaches?" asked Wilbur. "My God, the reason we're going to the Olympics is to compete."

"You let us worry about how the money is spent. You just do your job and keep your mouth shut," answered Lester. He thought that Wilbur was one of the dumbest asses he'd ever met. "Maybe today is your lucky day, because I'm going to tell you why we need the extra money. It's for marketing. I need to entertain potential sponsors. You're too stupid to figure this out, so I will explain to you how to raise money from sponsors. They don't just walk out of the woodwork and offer to make large donations from the kindness of their heart, you know. If you think that's how the other associations get their sponsors, you live in a real dream world. The name of the game is: you have to spend money to make money."

"You've got me convinced," mumbled Wilbur, quietly.

"What did you say?" demanded Lester.

"You've got me convinced," repeated Wilbur louder so Lester could hear him.

"Don't get smart with me, you stupid asshole. Thank God we don't depend on you to raise the money, because we wouldn't have shit. You're too stupid to understand how much I'm worth to the association. I could get big bucks for my services and I don't take nothin' but some lousy expense money."

"I think you owe Lester an apology," demanded Nino. Staring noxiously at

Wilbur. "Lester has done a hell of a job for the association."

"Yeah, I know. He reminds me every time I see him," said Wilbur simple-mindedly.

Everyone turned their glaze from Wilbur and looked at Lester, waiting for the eruption that would now take place. Lester stood up and rushed over and put his face inches from Wilbur's. He screamed, "Being stupid is one thing, you asshole! Don't you ever show disrespect to me in public again." Lester pushed his finger into the side of Wilbur's face, implying it was a pistol and said, "You make that mistake one more time and you'll be history."

"I didn't mean to question what you do for us," replied Wilbur. "I was only concerned about having enough money for the athletes. I'm sorry, I didn't mean to upset you."

"Are we all set with the money problem?" Roger asked, trying to diffuse the situation. "When I get back to Lake Placid next week, I'll get the statement in the mail for you, John."

"Don't waste time sending me the statement, just call and give me the exact amount and I'll express mail them a check."

"Good. Let's talk about something more pleasant," said Roger, smiling. "John and I arranged for all of you to have dinner tomorrow night at the Hotel Schlob Gevelinghausen. The mayor of Winterberg and several other dignitaries will also be there." Roger then explained that the hotel was a fourteenth-century castle that had been converted into a jet-set hotel. The dining room and bar were remodeled to resemble how it was in the fourteenth century. The dinner would be served just as it would have been for King Arthur and his knights at the round table.

"Are we taking the athletes?" asked Wilbur.

"What? You are really stupid," said Nino. "We don't want them at something like this. They wouldn't know how to act. I don't think Shawn or Jim should come either."

"It's kind of difficult not to invite them," replied Wilbur. "They're really putting in a lot of hours working and this would be a nice way of showing them we appreciate what they have done for the athletes."

"Screw them. Nino's right, let's not spend the extra money," replied John.

"How much money per person are we talking about?" asked Wilbur.

"It's about a hundred and twenty bucks and that's a bargain for what we're getting," replied Roger nonchalantly. "Wilbur is right, we should include Jason, Jim and Shawn."

"Holy shit!" exclaimed Wilbur, without thinking. The price shocked him.

The officials relaxed for another hour, sipping on champagne, while Roger described the hotel and dinner in greater detail. They returned to the hotel they were staying at just as the athletes finished preparing their equipment for the next morning's practice. Wilbur went into the dining room and sat down, waiting for the athletes to arrive for dinner. He wasn't sure if he really wanted to be with the athletes. He knew that he needed to get away from Lester and his friends. He was uncomfortable with both groups.

→ *Ice Spy*

Riga, Latvia

Boris Yegorov left his apartment and went for a walk around the city he loved dearly. His situation and what the future might be for his wife, Anita, and himself, troubled him. He wondered if his life was cursed. He was once recognized throughout the Soviet Union as a brilliant physicist and recognized internationally for his Olympic success. Fate had worked against him, making his destiny very unpredictable. He built an Olympic bobsled program that should have been the envy of the entire international sports world. He had successfully utilized his military space technology to enhance the Soviet bobsled program, putting the Soviet's technology years ahead of their competition. He used centrifuge training from the space program to help the athletes adapt to the stress created by the g-forces they endured while racing bobsleds. He built a full-size, enclosed bobsled track out of wood, with indoor lights to secretly train his athletes how to drive bobsleds. They trained year around on the track with sleds fitted with wheels. These drivers began learning as young teenagers and were highly skilled at manipulating sleds down the track at incredible speeds by the time they were in their late teens. Their competition was often years older before they were ready for international racing. No other country in the world had a bobsled training program that could even come close to what he had assembled, and furthermore, nobody in any other country knew what he had created.

He was truly convinced his athletes would earn an Olympic gold medal when they raced at Sarajevo. Unfortunately, they placed third for a bronze medal, which meant failure to his superiors. Russian officials in Moscow were extremely unhappy with what they considered to be inferior results, since they provided him with everything he requested. His program was perfect. The only thing he had not expected was his inability to predict and control the athletes' attitudes. Everything must be perfect to have a chance of winning a gold medal.

He retraced his steps of failure back to the political turbulence that was widespread within the Soviet Union. Latvian athletes on the Olympic team were superior to their Russian team members. Russian officials in Moscow refused to allow a team of Latvians to represent the Soviet Union and forced him to include a Russian, with less ability, on every sled team. This political mandate decreased the Soviet's chances of winning a gold medal. The Latvian athletes knew they would have won an gold medal at Sarajevo if they competed with an all-Latvian team. They became embittered toward him for giving in to the official's demands to include Russian athletes with less qualified skills. The Latvians suspected he sold them out to the Russians. Finally, he and the Latvian athletes could no longer work together.

He knew the biggest mistake of his career happened when he sold his coaching techniques and two sets of his high-tech bobsled runners to the East Germans. He knew the runners had no equal in the bobsled world and the team using them would have an unfair advantage without anyone suspecting. He was determined to get revenge against the Russians for destroying his life.

He deposited the enormous amount of money the East Germans paid him into a Swiss bank account to prevent the KGB from grabbing it. Keeping the money away from the Russians would be his only way to stay alive. If the KGB got the money from the Swiss account, he would instantaneously receive the death penalty. It was very clear that the only chance of survival for his wife and him would be to trade his technology with the Americans for freedom. Boris knew he was racing against time.

Tears came to his eyes as he thought about the years of pain and suffering his father-in-law endured when he was exiled to Siberia. Soon the tears were replaced with anger and he became more determined to seek revenge against the Russians. He would never forgive them for what they did to him and the Latvians since they occupied his country.

CIA Headquarters, Langley, Virginia

Fred Unser was walking out of his office to meet with Director Circe when his phone rang. He rushed back and picked up the receiver. It was Walter Shapnek. "Hi, Walter. Where are you calling from?"

"I'm at a friendly location in the East." Walter's reply told him that he was calling from the CIA's secretly controlled location in East Germany and he was confident the line had no wire taps.

"How are things going with you?"

"I'm getting by, but we have some serious problems in Riga."

"I'm aware that the KGB suspects you're an agent. Maybe you shouldn't go back there for a while until things cool down."

"It's not that, Fred. There's a big movement within the Latvian underground to lead a revolt against the Russians. The Latvians are determined to have the legal papers that Stalin and the Russians used to occupy them in 1940 be ruled illegal in the international courts."

"Are you sure?" asked Fred, alarmed by this new information. "How do you know this is accurate?"

"I just finished meeting with our informant in Riga and he just returned from a very secret Latvian Underground meeting. The Latvian Socialist Slate will file the papers very soon."

"Walter, I want you to come in to the Agency for a few days and give us a detailed briefing. Can you get across the border to West Germany in the next few days without any problems?"

"I've had no problems so far. What do you want me to do?"

"I don't want you flying commercial, in case the KGB is trying to track you. Go to Stuttgart and hop on a military flight to McGuire Air Force in New Jersey. They will never suspect you left Europe. Call before you leave and tell me what time you will arrive in McGuire so I can have an Agency helicopter pick you up."

"I should be able to catch a flight tomorrow. I think they have a C-5 that goes to McGuire every morning. I'll talk to you tomorrow."

Fred hung up the phone and thought about the Latvian Socialist Slate's movement. The political situation could become a serious problem for the *IceSpy* mission. He went down the hall to the director's office and shared

Walter's information with him. Gary agreed. They could have a potential disaster in progress. The Russians will move in quickly to subdue any attempt by the Latvians to revolt, making their plan to smuggle Boris and his wife out of the Soviet Union next to impossible. Fred told him that Walter was on his way to the Agency to give them a detailed briefing on the situation in Riga.

Fred returned to his office thinking about the new circumstances they had to deal with in Latvia. He was worried about his agents who were working in or near the Baltic area and wondered if they would ever be successful in getting Boris out alive. He spent the next couple of hours meditating about what to do next to keep *IceSpy* alive.

Neustrelitz, East Germany

Walter hung up the phone and packed his suitcase. He would drive his Porsche to Witzenhausen and cross the border into West Germany. The drive to Stuttgart would take about six hours providing the guards didn't detain him too long at the border. Looking at his watch, he saw the time was three-fifteen which would give him about three hours of driving time before dark.

He eased his Porsche out onto the highway and drove in the direction of the border crossing at Witzenhausen. He was careful not to exceed the speed limit because the East German police were ruthless whenever they arrested anyone for speeding. It was impossible to outrun them because they had special cameras in their police cars that made a photo of the license plate of the speeder. It was just a matter of them calling each border crossing and waiting for the offender to arrive.

The traffic was sparse when Walter approached the border. He crept up to the area where the signs directed everyone, and watched as a guard approached. He put his window down and waited for the guard to give him instructions.

"Your papers," stated the guard somberly.

Walter gave him his passport and visa. He carefully watched the guard to anticipate what else he might request. The guard directed him to park the Porsche in a section next to the building and go inside so they could inspect the papers further. Walter knew the guard would not give him a reason for checking his papers, but asked anyway.

"What's the problem with my papers? Everything should be in proper order. I cross your border several times a month on business. Why is there a problem now?"

"I did not say there is a problem. I want to give a closer check to your papers. Park your car to the side and get out." The guard pointed to where he wanted Walter to park.

Walter eased his car to where the guard directed and got out. He opened the trunk so the guard could look at his luggage. He knew his life was on the line if anyone behind the Iron Curtain discovered anything linking him with the CIA. Walter was confident they wouldn't find anything and the search would help to remove any suspicions the border guards might have about him. He had never crossed the border at Witzenhausen so if he was checked thoroughly, it would help the next time he returned.

Walter suspected the guard would be less likely to give him a difficult time if he displayed an attitude of confidence and gave the impression of having powerful political connections. He always dressed neatly in expensive suits when he traveled, which made him stand out. He did this so that everyone who came in contact with him would assume he was a very successful American businessman. Nobody would suspect that he worked for the CIA. KGB and CIA agents normally dressed neatly, but quite modestly, allowing them to blend in with ordinary citizens.

Walter watched as the guard looked through his luggage. "If there's a problem, just tell me now. I'm in a hurry because I have to meet my employer by early tomorrow and I need to stop and get some rest. I'll be happy to show you anything you want."

"Where do you have to meet your employer, Mr. Shapnek?" ask the guard, still looking at his luggage.

"We're meeting in Stuttgart tomorrow morning."

"Your name is on our list as someone who crosses the border often. Why?"

"I just told you that I cross your border several times each month. I work for an American company that manufactures orthopedic equipment and supplies. I furnish many orthopedic sport braces for East German athletes, in fact, my company is the only one that makes many of the devices your athletes use."

"Do you have something that will confirm this?"

Walter gave the guard several brochures from the supply that he carried with him. The brochures were printed for a small company the CIA owned and used as a cover for their agents. The Rivette Company operated a small import-export business in Hartford, Connecticut. The company manufactured orthopedic appliances, artificial limbs and braces. They specialized in sport braces.

The guard cautiously looked around the area then quietly asked Walter if he had any samples. Walter apologized and explained that he didn't have any and slipped the guard two American twenty-dollar bills. The guard smiled and thanked him and took his papers into the building to have them stamped. Minutes later he returned with the papers and waved him through the border gate.

Walter smiled at the guards at the gate as he drove past their gate house onto the small steel frame bridge that separated East and West Germany. He reminded himself to drive carefully because the narrow winding roads that went over the mountains were very dangerous. Once he got further south and away from the mountains he would reach the autobahn to Stuttgart.

The sun had disappeared behind the mountain peaks and the brisk air forced Walter to turn up the heat in the car. He glanced into the rearview mirror often to see if anyone was following him. It was difficult on the mountain roads to drive fast, but there was a benefit to going slow. It was next to impossible for anyone to follow him without being seen. He could change routes at several locations and if KGB agents were following him, they would have a difficult task staying with him.

→ *Ice Spy*

Walter suspected the border guards had been directed to notify the KGB every time he passed the border because his name was on the list. He thought about how he crossed this time without any real difficulty. The Rivette Company actually didn't manufacture orthopedic equipment. They purchased it from a manufacturing firm, installed their label and sold it to the Soviets and East Germans at low prices so they would give him preferential treatment. The CIA was well aware that sports programs in these countries are more important to government officials than food for their people.

Border guards were next to impossible to deal with when East or West German citizens attempted to cross. They instilled fear into everyone who approached their gates. Walter knew the fear also worked in reverse with these guards. Every border guard was aware of what would happen to them if someone with powerful political connections was given a difficult time at a crossing. A mistake could send them to another location where working conditions would be worse than hell. The alternative might also be death, if the political connection was to someone very high in government.

CHAPTER TEN

→ *Ice Spy*

Winterberg, West Germany

The powerful winds howled outside the hotel waking Shawn Murphy earlier than usual. He didn't sleep well after talking with Angela the previous evening. She was upset that an unseasonal storm dropped nearly two feet of snow in the Albany area preventing her from leaving the house for two days. He pulled the curtain aside to look out the window. Dark clouds covered the entire sky over the distant mountain tops suggesting an approaching storm. The weather during the past four weeks had been very difficult to predict accurately. Bobsled practice took place in nearly any type of weather conditions: from warm to bitter cold air temperatures; bright sunny to gloomy days; and from rain to snow conditions. The work went on unless the weather conditions obscured the vision of the drivers. Today looked like another bitter cold day with snow. Shawn took a shower and went to the hotel dining room to get a cup of coffee. He sat alone at a table until Jim joined him a short time later.

"Good morning, Shawn. You're up early."

"The wind woke me up and I couldn't get back to sleep so I came over to get some coffee."

"Guess where we're going tonight?" asked Jim, snickering.

"I can't imagine."

"Jason just told me that the Mayor of Winterberg has invited the association officials to a dinner tonight."

"I wonder why?"

"I guess they want to thank us for the business we've brought to the city," replied Jim. "I can't really think of any other reason why they would invite us."

"It's a nice gesture of them. Are the athletes invited?"

"No! Jason said that we're to keep this quiet so they don't find out," replied Jim. "I don't know about you but I feel uncomfortable going without them. He said we wouldn't be going either if Wilbur hadn't insisted."

"I feel the same way. The athletes would be upset if they knew they weren't invited and I wouldn't blame them."

They finished breakfast and left for the bobsled track. Snow was falling and it was deep enough that they could barely see the footprints of the someone who had walked up the road just ahead of them. Both were wearing insulated underwear under their team jackets attempting to keep the unrelenting cold wind away from their body. This would be the last two days of practice. The races for Olympic berths would begin on Saturday.

Shawn knew that Joe Sweeney would be arriving soon to begin preparing him for his part of the *IceSpy* mission. He was tired of the Olympic trials and was ready for some excitement. He wondered what Boris was doing to prepare for leaving his country.

"What's today's date?" asked Jim, interrupting his thoughts.

"The last day in October. It doesn't seem possible that we've been here since the end of September."

"Wow! The time really flew by. There's so much to do each day that after a while the days begin to run together for me. I lost track of the days."

"I've been the same way. Do you call your wife from time to time?"

"I try to call her at least once a week. How about you?"

Shawn enlightened him about the snow storm that crippled the Albany area for two days. He laughed quietly and told Jim the story about him ordering six dozen roses and having a dozen delivered to Angela every Thursday morning with a pre-written note. His thoughts drifted to the Air Force base in Schenectady. He wondered how Olive Hanson was surviving without him. He suspected that she was swamped with work and would be having a difficult time. If this was the situation, it would be great, because Colonel Crosby would discover her incompetence.

They reached the track and Shawn made a quick check of the ice and went to the start to help clean the snow away for the athletes. The athletes were getting their sleds out of the storage shed and were putting on the runners. Shawn noticed a definite change in their temperament. Their moods had changed from jovial to a more serious subdued tone. There were no conversations between the athletes as each worked quietly, thinking about the trials that would determine their Olympic fate. It was something most had worked four years or longer for. Olympic pressure became very obvious and the tension would now begin to separate the athletes. Those who could handle pressure well would excel and those who couldn't would slip further back in the standings.

Shawn looked around the start area noticing that none of the bobsled officials had arrived to help. During the past four weeks, not one official had been to the track until practice was nearly finished. Helping the athletes was something that never entered their minds. He knew that when these same officials returned to the States they would tell stories about how hard they worked at helping the athletes prepare for the Olympics. His stomach turned every time he thought about the way they abused the association and spent its money. It was always the athletes who suffered for the official's incredible greed and abuse.

He thought about the professor's new sled design and tried to imagine how it would look different than the Italian sleds currently being used at the trials. American bobsled athletes were frustrated that bobsleds were only built and sold in Italy. They suspected that the Italian sled builders kept the best designs for their teams. The athletes hoped the professor's new design would enable them to compete with a faster sled.

The snow continued falling for the rest of the morning and now was beginning to accumulate in the track. The wind picked up and swept the snow around the track viciously. Eventually the drivers' visibility became affected by the blowing snow and practice was stopped to prevent the athletes from getting injured or damaging their equipment. It was too close to the selection races to take a chance on their having an accident. Jason assembled the athletes together for a quick explanation and told them there would be a meeting in the hotel at six p.m. He suggested that they take the time to relax.

"You guys are wound up like a cork screws," said Shawn. "Stopping early will benefit you a lot more than another day of practice."

→ *Ice Spy*

"Shawn's right," agreed Jim. "Most of you guys have been pushing yourselves right to the edge of exhaustion the past few days. A day of rest will help your bodies get ready for the race on Saturday. I think that tomorrow's practice shouldn't be mandatory. Unless there is something you want to test on your sled, you should either rest or work on your equipment."

The athletes agreed and began putting their equipment away after Jason reminded them there would be a very short meeting before dinner. When the athletes were out of hearing distance he told Jim and Shawn the meeting had to be short because they had to attend the dinner with the Mayor of Winterberg.

"What time do we have to leave?" asked Shawn.

"I guess Roger wants us to meet him outside the hotel at seven-thirty. He'll be driving us to the restaurant."

"This will be interesting," remarked Shawn. "Will Lester and Nino be riding with the peasants? I suppose we should be honored if they let us go with them."

"You know better than that. They'll go by themselves in the Mercedes that Lester rented."

The three men walked back to the hotel as the snow continued to fall. Nearly eight inches had accumulated since it began during the night. When they reached the hotel Shawn went to his room to write a letter to Angela. He knew she would appreciate some mail from him after the difficult time she had with the snow.

Stuttgart, West Germany

Walter woke up early and drove to the U.S. Air Force base to arrange for a flight to McGuire. He had arrived in Stuttgart just before midnight and got a room in a guest house. He reached the gate and showed the security policeman his passport. The policeman directed him to park his car and come into the gate house to fill out a visitor's pass.

Once inside the gate house, Walter asked him to call the base commander and tell him that Walter Shapnek was there. He didn't want the guard to know he was with the CIA and knew it would be quicker to simply call Colonel DiCocco, who knew his real identification. Having any identification other than his phony passport would be fatal if found by the Soviets or East Germans. It was much simpler to have the military use the phone and check him out if there was ever a problem.

"You're cleared to leave, Mr. Shapnek," said the security policeman. "Colonel DiCocco asks that you meet him at his office."

"Thanks," replied Walter. He drove over to Tony DiCocco's office and went inside. The colonel had helped him several times in the past with flight arrangements and when he needed to use their communications to send classified messages to Langley. Colonel DiCocco stood in his window and watched Walter get out of his car.

"What brings you here this morning, Walter?" The colonel smiled and gestured for Walter to take a seat.

"I need a ride to the States this morning, if possible. A serious problem has come up and the Agency wants me there today to give a briefing. I couldn't risk going on a commercial flight because the KGB might be tipped off about my work. At McGuire, the Agency will pick me up with their helicopter."

"Today's flight already left here and went to Frankfurt to pick up some cargo. I'll call and see if it's still there. If it is, then I can have the plane come back and pick you up."

"Thanks, Colonel."

The colonel called the base outside of Frankfurt and was told the plane was still being loaded. He hung up the phone and relayed the information to Walter as he dialed another number to make a priority code-one call. Walter was impressed that the colonel was using the national security emergency system to reach the commander in Frankfurt.

He hung up the phone and said, "The C-5 is scheduled to leave there shortly and the commander will direct the crew to swing back here and pick you up."

"Thanks! I was worried when you said they were leaving there shortly."

"Let's put your car in the back parking lot, out of sight and I'll drive you out onto the flight line to meet the plane. They will land and leave the engines running. Stay in the car until the loadmaster lowers the rear ramp and signals for you to go on board."

"May I use your phone to call the Agency to tell them when to pick me up?"

"Help yourself. Tell the operator you have to make a classified call to the States."

Walter called Fred Unser and told him the estimated time of his arrival. He hung up the phone and went outside to move his car. He got into the colonel's car with his suitcase and they drove out to meet the plane. When they arrived at the flight line the colonel told the security policeman on guard duty that Walter was cleared. He used the radio in his sedan to call the base operations office and tell them the C-5 was returning shortly to pick up a passenger. The voice on the radio replied that they had radio contact with the plane and it was already on its final approach.

They chatted for the next ten minutes and suddenly the C-5 appeared in the distance. Within minutes the enormous plane seemed to fill the entire sky as it approached the runway. Walter was always amazed at how these huge cargo planes always appeared to be flying through the air in slow motion whenever they took off or made their final approach to land.

They could feel the vibrations from the mammoth plane as it touched the runway and passed by them much faster than Walter expected. The C-5 continued to the end of the runway before it turned and came back in their direction. The colonel waited until the plane stopped and then slowly drove out onto the runway toward the rear cargo door. Once the door opened and the ramp could be seen, he drove up to within a short distance of the ramp and stopped when the loadmaster gave him the signal. Walter thanked him and said he would be back in the next day or two. He grabbed his suitcase and walked toward the ramp. The loadmaster handed him a set of ear protectors to shut out the deafening sound of the huge engines that were still running and pointed to a web seat in the plane. Within minutes they took off. Walter settled into the webbed netting and was asleep before the plane reached its cruising altitude.

Winterberg, West Germany

A loud knock on the door woke Shawn from a short nap. He opened the door, surprised to see his friend, Professor Ray Bodynski, standing in the doorway. "Ray, please come in." Shawn was delighted to see his good friend. Ray wore his tweed jacket with leather pads on the elbows and a green felt hat with a feather jauntily perched inside the band. Ray was taller than Shawn and his graying beard made him look much older but, they were close in age. His distinguished appearance gave away the fact that he was a professor.

"Why didn't you call me when you arrived at Frankfurt?"

"I didn't want to bother you so I rented a car and drove up."

"Where's your prototype sled?"

"It will be here shortly. I thought it would be easier to hire a trucking company to transport it. How are the trials coming along?"

"They've been going okay. We've had the typical problems from time to time but nothing major. Where are you staying?"

"I've got a room down the street so I wouldn't have to be around the association's higher echelon," replied Ray, laughing.

"Hell, if you don't want to be around them, this is the place to stay. We only see them for about twenty minutes a day. I've never seen a bunch of characters like this group, Ray. They only come here to vacation and impress their friends."

"Do they do anything to help?"

"You've got to be kidding. I was serious when I said they never spend more than twenty minutes a day with us. They're gone day and night. Last week Lester and Nino went to Switzerland for a couple of days. Lester said they were there to do some marketing."

"I'll bet Lester can't even spell 'marketing'," said Ray, roaring. "Oh, my God! What a cast of characters. You could write a book about them, but who would believe it."

"I have to laugh every time I see them walking around the bobsled track, said Shawn, chuckling. "Nino and Lester are so paranoid about people talking about them. If a couple of athletes are talking to each other and one of the guys looks at them, Nino will walk over and ask what they are talking about."

"They didn't make it easy for me to bring the sled over to test," said Ray, seriously. "You wouldn't believe the number of obstacles I've encountered because of them and I can't understand why. This project hasn't cost the association a nickel and could help the Olympic team win a medal. It's mind-boggling."

'I couldn't understand it either, until I thought about another reason. I think it's greed."

"Why? It's free."

"I think I've figured it out. The association has always purchased their new sleds from one or two Italian sled builders. I suspect that Lester and Nino are getting a kickback and that's why they don't want any other sleds being built even if they are donated."

"I think you have something," replied Ray, deep in thought. "You must be right. That's about the only thing that makes sense. What a greedy bunch of bastards."

"Don't worry about testing your sled, Ray. Jim and I have been telling the athletes about your research project and they're delighted. They can't wait to see how it does when we test it tomorrow. A couple of drivers would like to try driving, once Jim and I have tested it a few times to make sure it is safe."

"I'm thankful that you're over here, because if you weren't, I know the entire project would be scrapped. Jason Pierce made it very clear that he would have no part in the program. The stupid jerk thinks that the association can use the Olympic R & D funding to purchase new equipment. What an imbecile."

"I hate to run out on you, Ray, but I've got to get ready for a short meeting with the athletes and then get dressed for dinner. The mayor of Winterberg has invited the Association officials and the coaches to dinner at some fancy hotel. Let me check, maybe you can come along with us."

"No thanks. I'll pass on this one. I can't get too excited about eating with Lester and his cast of characters. Besides, I'm really over-tired. I've been traveling for nearly twenty hours now and I need to get some sleep."

The professor and Shawn talked for a few more minutes and made plans to meet early in the morning to get the sled prepared to be tested. Ray returned to his hotel and Shawn went to the dining room to attend Jason's nightly meeting. Jim was sitting with Ron Harrison who was reviewing the proper technique for a brakeman to use when getting into a sled. This was Ron's first year racing bobsleds. He was extremely fast and that was good for starting sleds. However, his lack of experience for entering the sled often prevented the team from utilizing his speed. A brakeman is the last athlete to enter a sled after it starts down the track. Bobsled races are often determined by less than a thousandth of a second, so the brakeman's technique for entering a sled is critical.

"I understand you did very well on the track team at Penn State," said Shawn. "When did you graduate?"

"I got my degree there in 1982 and went on to law school," replied Ron. "I was admitted to the bar in 1984."

"Where do you practice law?"

"I don't practice law, coach. I work for the federal government. Why do you ask?"

"Just curious. I like to know where you guys are from and your occupations." Shawn was searching for information about Ron's background, because he suspected he might be the FBI's undercover agent. He wanted to share with him the information about John Chapadeau's attaché case, but was too uncertain of Ron's background to take the risk of passing it on to him at this point.

"I'm just one of thousands of attorneys who work for the government." Ron studied Shawn's face as he spoke. "I'd like to chat more with you Shawn when we can be alone, if you don't mind?"

"I look forward to that. Practice keeps us busy, as you know, but I have a lot of free time the rest of the day. Tomorrow's schedule is very light. Perhaps we can meet after Jim and I test the Syracuse sled."

"I would like that. I'll get together with you in the morning to set a time and place."

Ron excused himself and joined a group of athletes who were in the dining room waiting for Jason. Shawn studied Ron who was nearly six feet tall and quite powerful. A good looking man who appeared to have a gentle personality and was genuinely interested in people. He thought about Ron's answer to his question regarding employment. He'd been very evasive and simply skipped over the question with a vague explanation.

Ron had to be the undercover FBI agent, he thought. Shawn decided not to say anything to him even if they were alone. He would confide in Ron about some problems he and Jim had seen, and see how Ron responded. One problem would be the official's abuse of the association's funding and how they seemed to regard it as their personal cash. This would give Ron the opportunity to identify himself.

Jason arrived to start the meeting and interrupted Shawn's thoughts. He talked for a few minutes about the next day's schedule and suggested the athletes rest and get their equipment ready for the race on Saturday. He passed around a sheet of paper outlining the rules for the Olympic selection race. When the meeting ended, Jason, Shawn, and Jim left immediately to get dressed for the mayor's dinner.

Roger Ferris was waiting for the three men when they walked outside the hotel. The snow had stopped, but the restless wind made the air feel as if it were thirty below zero. Shawn hadn't brought a heavy top coat and was chilled by the time he got into the Volkswagen bus. As Roger drove out of the hotel parking lot, Shawn's thoughts went back to Ron Harrison.

CHAPTER ELEVEN

McGuire AFB, New Jersey

The turbulence outside the huge C-5 shook the plane and jarred Walter's body into the steel frame encompassing the seat's webbing, waking him abruptly. Walter assumed that the C-5 must be on its final approach because of the strong winds that were buffeting the enormous plane. Gusty winds generally occurred at low altitudes. Walter looked out the porthole-style window and smiled when he saw the New Jersey shoreline. He unfastened his seat belt and swung his feet around onto the floor, stood up and stretched his muscles.

Looking at his watch he realized that he had slept nearly seven hours. Traveling for days without proper sleep had finally caught up with him. He must have been over-tired. He looked up and saw the loadmaster walking toward him. "We're on final approach to McGuire, Mr. Shapnek. Be sure to re-fasten your seat belt."

Walter nodded affirmatively and sat back down on the webbed seating that lined the side of the mammoth cargo compartment. Several gigantic pallets, loaded with boxes and covered with a large camouflage netting to prevent the boxes from shifting during the flight, filled the center of the plane's cargo area.

"Thanks for reminding me," replied Walter, not fully alert after sleeping so long. "How long before we touch down?"

"Our wheels should touch the ground in just about fifteen minutes, sir."

"Thanks."

Walter wondered if the helicopter would be waiting for him, then thought, why should I be worried. Regardless of how complicated the arrangements might be, Fred Unser is a master at making them work.

He looked out the window and could see the buildings below and knew the plane wasn't far from the base. Within minutes the C-5's wheels made contact. The enormous engines reversed direction and slowed the plane as the pilot turned the C-5 and headed back to the parking ramp. When the plane stopped, the loadmaster opened the rear cargo door and motioned to Walter, indicating that he could get up and leave. Walter spotted the agency helicopter parked about a hundred feet away as he walked down the ramp. The helicopter was still running and the co-pilot got out to assist Walter inside.

Minutes later they were cleared for take-off and Walter was back in the air, this time, in the direction of Langley. He was glad he was able to sleep on the C-5 because the helicopter was far too noisy to ever think about sleeping. He enjoyed the scenery below as they flew at a much lower altitude than the flight from Europe. Walter was deep in thought about how he should brief his superiors when he arrived. He was oblivious to the bouncing of the helicopter as the events from the past few days raced through his mind.

Marburg, West Germany

The sky suddenly began to illuminate in the distance and Shawn got a good look at the Hotel Schlob Gevelinghausen as they drove down the highway. It was one of the most impressive sights he had ever seen. Several hundred white lights reflecting off the recent snow storm made the large white building stand out brilliantly. The entire area glowed from the hotel's reflection, reminding him of a famous scene from the Bing Crosby movie *White Christmas*. Roger parked the Volkswagen bus and everyone immediately got out to admire the hotel's extraordinary front entrance. The owner had renovated the fourteenth-century castle into a modern hotel, preserving the magnificent elegance and dignity of the former castle. It was simply breathtaking.

Once inside the hotel, a staff member led them into a private bar where Lester and the other bobsled officials were drinking with several other people. Moments later, the mayor of Winterberg and two members of his council entered. Roger rushed over to welcome the mayor's party the moment he saw him walk into the room. He chatted with them for a couple of minutes and then introduced the mayor and council members to everyone in the bar.

Lester introduced a garishly attractive young woman sitting next to him, explaining that she was recently appointed to the bobsled association's board of directors. Lester said the board needed the input from a woman and she would make an excellent director. Shawn recognized her and recalled that she worked as an employee for Lester and often traveled as his companion. He suspected that they would see a lot of her with the Olympics only a few months away. Shawn just shook his head when he thought about her serving as a member of the board of directors. Lester was slowly removing experienced bobsled members from the board and was replacing them with his friends or associates. The newest director left no doubt that Lester would maintain complete control of the association. A rather convenient way for Lester to let her travel and shack up with him at the association's expense.

He studied Lester's companion. She wore heavy makeup and a sleazy, low-cut dress, intentionally designed to show off her large breasts. She had a smooth, come-hither look on her face and she reminded him of a typical New York City prostitute. Shawn was positive that nobody would ever have the nerve to question Lester's decision to place her on the board of directors. Even the formidable John Chapadeau knew better than question him about spending association funds on his female companion.

Cocktails and champagne were readily available to everyone in the group while they sat at the bar waiting for dinner. After listening to their muddled conversation, Shawn was certain that Lester and his companions had been drinking at the bar for some time. The booze flowed freely, but the mayor and his associates appeared to display a more professional image by elegantly sipping their drinks.

Shawn nursed a tall glass of dark German beer while he studied the attractive, interesting room encompassing the bar. Centuries-old wooden beams over the bar held the personal pewter beer steins of frequent visitors. The outside walls of the room were built of stone, quarried locally he suspected, while the inside walls were made of highly glossed wood that had darkened with age. The floor was laid with gray flat-stone.

The sound of trumpets suddenly filled the room with music. Two large, thick, wooden doors separating the bar from the dining room opened slowly and standing in the center of the doorway was a rather small robust German dressed in fourteenth-century clothing. He peered through his antique reading glasses and began reciting loudly in German from a large scroll, while Roger translated his message in English to the group. Roger explained that the arrangement of the dining room would be the same as it would have been in the fourteenth century. The guests would be treated as if they were a knights representing another country and taking part in a round-table ceremony. Each person was given a mini-scroll that provided background about the country they represented.

The long wooden table was hand-carved with a top about four inches thick. A thick coat of clear varnish protected the wood and gave it a high gloss finish. Shawn noticed the dark room contained many symbols on the walls representing the era. The solid mahogany walls were covered with layers of varnish to give them a mirror-like finish, matching the magnificent table. He thought the extraordinarily picturesque room harmonized with the outside of the hotel. Ancient metal helmets, swords, shields and a variety of other beautiful artifacts were on exhibit throughout the room. Among the antiques were several complete suits of armor. Each suit also had a long lance and gave the impression that they were protecting the guests from any hostile enemy who might dare to attack them during dinner.

Each person received a small flat slab of wood for a dinner plate and two hand-carved wooden cups. A single knife for each guest was the only eating utensil provided. The meal included soup, salmon marinated in fine wine, and fresh venison covered with gravy and a special blackberry seasoning. The moment the wooden cups became empty, they were refilled with dark German beer or wine. This was the kind of service Shawn thought the association officials could do without.

"Hey, you! Come here and sit your ass on my lap," yelled Nino to a young girl who was a waitress. She twisted to avoid his hand when he reached out to grab her and ran back to the kitchen looking frightened. Shawn was disturbed with his ill-mannered action and told Jim the young girl appeared to be about fifteen years old. He glanced at the mayor and two councilmen who looked visibly embarrassed.

"Nino, show a little class," scolded Lester. "This is a first class joint, so act right."

Nino laughed drunkenly, "Girls in Europe start sleeping around when they turn fifteen. I'm just trying to help her."

"What's gotten into you, Lester?" teased Roger. "I think she has the hots for Nino. Let him have some fun! Hell, I wouldn't mind 'tapping' her myself."

"Nino! Roger! If you guys can't act rational, then get out of here right now," reprimanded Lester loudly. "This is embarrassing. We have the mayor and part of his council here as guests and you act as if you're in one of your dumps back in Placid. Enough is enough."

Shawn looked at Jim who was trying desperately not to laugh. Lester obviously possessed the power of a mafia "Don". Roger and Nino instantly shut up and avoided looking at him, fearing another verbal chastisement. Jason and Wilbur both stared at Nino and Roger indicating they did not appreciate their embarrassing crude actions.

"Roger," uttered Lester, with speech slurred by the large consumption of alcohol. "Go into the kitchen and apologize to her and then I want you to apologize to our guests."

"It's done. We didn't mean any harm." Roger went into the kitchen and when he returned, he apologized in German to the mayor and the two councilmen. They nodded and the mayor told Roger that the incident was forgotten. The strange look on their faces indicated to Shawn that the incident wasn't forgotten and they were extremely disturbed. He thought that Lester and his friends were the typical low-life characters someone would encounter in the slums of any major city where sleazy racketeers flourish. He suspected that the mayor and his associates must be disgusted with the association officials who, except John Chapadeau, were completely intoxicated when dinner came to an end.

"Shawn, it's really embarrassing when you think about our officials," said Jim, quietly. "These jerks represent the bobsled association this way and get away with it." He nudged Shawn and looked in the direction of Lester and his companion who were caressing each other at the table, obviously unconcerned about being observed by others in the room. He looked around and saw that Roger had cornered an older waitress and was talking softly to her in German

Wilbur, John and Jason, who could not speak German, were attempting to have a conversation with the mayor and his associates, who could not speak English. They were trying, without much success, to convince the mayor about how much the American Olympic Bobsled Trials were boosting Winterberg's economy. Suddenly a loud thump attracted Shawn and Jim's attention. Nino had passed out and his head had fallen sideways onto his plate of gravy and scraps. His mouth was wide open and he was snoring loudly, although nobody seemed to hear him.

Shawn and Jim got up and went into the hotel's reception area to get away from the repulsive scene in the dining room. They left the hotel and took a stroll around the courtyard enjoying the many statues that surrounded the hotel. The frigid air forced them back into the main lobby where they sat next to a blazing fireplace. A short time later John Chapadeau walked up to the front desk and asked for the dinner bill.

Shawn quietly stood up and went over and stood behind a large souvenir rack to see if John paid the bill. He recalled Jason telling him the mayor had invited them to dinner and he wondered why John would asked for the bill. "What's the total?" asked John, who couldn't read German. The cashier said in English, "One thousand-three-hundred and seventy-five dollars, without a tip."

"Add a fifteen percent tip," replied John, handing the cashier an association credit card. "I need to register some guests for the evening."

"How many rooms will you need?"

"One double and four singles. How much are they?"

"The double is two-hundred and forty and the single rooms are one-hundred and eighty."

John registered the association officials as Shawn observed him from behind the souvenir rack. Suddenly he turned and stared at Shawn who was

→ *Ice Spy*

picking up a postcard. "What are you standing there for?" demanded John, startled to see Shawn.

"I'm shopping for postcards to send home," replied Shawn, amused at John's discomfort. "Is there something wrong with me being here?"

"You're too nosy for your own good. Just be happy we let you come to the dinner, now get back into the dining room where you belong."

"Oh, really? I don't belong in the dining room with those drunken assholes," replied Shawn, angrily. "I'm not part of your group of sleaze-ball officials. I don't have to jump whenever you bark. That's one of the benefits of being a volunteer who hasn't quit the association.

"We should never have invited you. We do something nice for you and it's not appreciated."

"What are you talking about, John? Let's see if I understand this right. You're upset that I discovered that you guys lied about the mayor inviting us to dinner and that you charged over twenty-five hundred dollars for dinner and your rooms because they're too drunk to ride back to Winterberg! Do I understand you correctly?"

John picked up the room keys and walked away without answering him. Shawn watched him walk into the bar and then went over to where Jim was waiting. "I can't believe what just happened," said Jim. "Not only is he a thief but he's arrogant about it."

"What a bunch of liars. They made up the entire story about the mayor inviting all of us to dinner so we wouldn't know how flagrantly they're misusing the association's money."

John entered the dining room and interrupted Roger's conversation with the waitress. "Get your coat on and drive Shawn back to Winterberg. Make sure you take Jason and Jim with you." The waitress left instantly and Roger began searching slowly for his coat. He was extremely intoxicated and moved at a snail's pace, frustrating John who picked up Roger's coat and threw it at him. "You get Shawn's ass out of here now." John shoved Roger toward the door leading into the bar where Jason was sitting with Wilbur and the mayor.

"Get your coat, we're leaving right now," garbled Roger drunkenly, "per John's orders. Don't waste any time 'cause he is pissed."

Jason put on his coat and followed Roger into the main reception area. Roger repeated John's message to Shawn and Jim, then went out to the parking lot to get the Volkswagen bus warmed up. Shawn and Jim went into the dining room to get their coats. They looked around the room and noticed John standing in the corner, staring at them. Shawn walked over and thanked him for inviting them to the 'mayor's prestigious dinner.' John simply ignored him and walked away.

They left the hotel and when they reached the bus, Roger was sitting in the driver's seat. Jim knocked on the window and told Roger, "You're not driving this vehicle back to Winterberg."

"Don't worry about me, I do this all the time," replied Roger. His words interspersed with hiccups.

"I'm sure you do, but you're not driving tonight," Jim was becoming impatient.

"Get in the back, Roger, and don't be a bigger asshole than you've already been," demanded Shawn. "Either get into the back or I will call the German police. We won't see you again for a year."

Reluctantly, Roger got out of the driver's seat and sat in the rear of the mini-bus. A short time after Jim started driving back to Winterberg, Roger and Jason were fast asleep. Shawn thought about Joe Sweeney and wondered why he hadn't heard from him. The Olympic trials would be finished at the end of the following week and Shawn needed to know what the CIA expected of him. Joe Sweeney mentioned that he might have to go into East Germany to meet with Boris. He needed to know so he could call Angela and tell her about his change in plans. Besides telling Angela, he would have to make sure the Agency made arrangements with the Air Force to extend his temporary duty assignment in Europe. Extending his assignment would enrage Olive Hanson and she would make his life miserable after he returned to work.

Jim broke into Shawn's thoughts by asking, "Are we still going to test the sled your friend from Syracuse University built?"

"I would like to test it in the morning, if that's all right with you?"

"That's fine. I wasn't sure if the plans were definite yet."

"Tomorrow is about the only day we can really get an unlimited number of test runs," replied Shawn. "The Olympic trial races begin on Saturday and it'll be difficult to take a lot of test runs next week when the athletes are preparing for their final race."

"I'm really excited about testing a new sled," said Jim. "I still can't understand why these simple-minded jerks in the association don't want anyone doing research on sled technology. All they want to do is spend money and have a good time."

The two men discussed the association officials' lack of support until they reached the hotel. Jim parked the mini-bus in the hotel parking lot and woke Jason and Roger up before going upstairs to their small studio apartments. Shawn undressed and got into bed, still thinking about Joe Sweeney and the East German trip. He was curious and wanted to get more specific information about the dates from him so he could break the news to his wife. He began to think about Angela again and within minutes he was sound asleep.

CIA Headquarters, Langley, Virginia

The helicopter's altitude fell rapidly as the pilot headed toward a landing pad, barely visible to Walter. He checked his watch and saw that the time was nearly 7 p.m. explaining why his body felt like a piece of rubber. The C-5 had picked him up at the Air Base in Stuttgart just before ten in the morning and the time difference on the east coast of the United States was five hours.

The pilot's voice in his radio headset informed him that a car was waiting for him next to the landing pad. Walter hoped he would have time to take a shower and get something to eat before the briefing started. The moment the helicopter landed Fred Unser opened the door of the car and rushed over to help Walter with his suitcase.

→ *Ice Spy*

"Thanks for coming, Walter," said Fred, shaking his hand. Fred took his suitcase and the two men got into the car, shutting the doors to keep out the noise from the helicopter. Fred started the car and drove off toward his office.

"I feel terrible making you rush over here from Germany, Walter, but this situation is so sensitive that I couldn't risk getting the information over the phone."

"I understand. I slept most of the way over on the plane, but I still feel tired. Who are we meeting?"

"Gary Circe and several people on the White House staff who have been a part of the *IceSpy* project."

"What's the *IceSpy* project?" asked Walter.

"Sorry. I forgot that you've been gone. *IceSpy* is the code name we've assigned to the mission to help Boris Yegorov defect. We're also working on a deal to let him and his wife disappear into the protection program."

"I only hope he can stay alive long enough for us to get him out of there," replied Walter. "What time are we supposed to meet these people?"

"They're waiting for us right now. Why?"

"I wanted to take a shower and eat something first," said Walter. "I only had a cup of coffee with a small pastry in Germany and the flight crew gave me a box lunch on the C-5."

"We've ordered a small buffet for all of us and you can take a quick shower in my office when we get there," replied Fred. "You can sleep in a spare bedroom in my condominium tonight. I don't want you registering at a hotel, just in case someone from the other side observes you."

"Thanks. The C-5 returns to Europe tomorrow morning at ten."

"I know. We have to get you back to McGuire by nine-thirty. They promised not to leave without you."

Fred eased the car into his parking spot in front of the building. They walked up the steps to the front entrance and Fred inserted his Agency identification card into the slot unlocking the door. They walked through the front reception area and took the elevator to the fifth floor.

Fred showed Walter where the shower was and told him to come next door when he was finished. Fred went next door and explained to Gary and the others that Walter would be there as soon as he finished taking a shower.

The shower and fresh clothing recharged Walter's energy. During the next two hours, Walter briefed everyone about the current Latvian movement to rebel against the Russians. He explained that the information came from their undercover CIA agent in Riga. Fred taped the entire conversation and when Circe indicated that he had enough information, the group left.

During the drive to Fred's condominium, the two men discussed the *IceSpy* project. They arrived at the condo and Fred showed Walter to the spare bedroom. Walter wasted no time getting undressed and into bed. Within moments he was asleep.

CHAPTER TWELVE

→ *Ice Spy*

Winterberg, West Germany

Early morning traffic outside the apartment woke Shawn and he looked at the alarm clock on the stand next to his bed. The time was 6:20. He slid out of bed and stretched before getting into the shower. He dried himself off and had just finished dressing when someone knocked on the apartment door.

"Come on in. It's unlocked," called Shawn. Looking around, he saw Professor Ray Bodynski walk into the room.

"I hope I'm not too early?"

"Not at all."

"I'm convinced that if you and Wilbur didn't help with this project, the association wouldn't have any technology program. I find it mind-boggling that these officials are so resistant to any effort to improve equipment technology and safety."

"I spent the evening talking with the athletes last night and I heard some incredible stories. I surmised that they believe that Lester and his group use the association's money for their own personal use." Ray shook his head in disbelief.

"I think it might be worse than that, Ray. Take your coat off and I'll try to fill you in about these bastards. I don't have to meet Jim until eight so we have a few minutes. There's a few things you should know about what's going on here."

Shawn elaborated on Lester's shady take-over of the association. The two men trusted each other completely since Ray had worked for the CIA during the same time period as Shawn although they had not collaborated on any assignments. Shawn described the part about their suspected mafia connection and the cash in John Chapadeau's attaché case. Ray's eyebrows rose considerably and he looked disgusted with the whole affair.

"Has anyone gone to the police?" asked Ray.

"The FBI is working on it right now. They have an undercover agent located in the organization," Confided Shawn to his friend.

"Do you know who?"

"No. I suspect it might be one of the athletes competing here in the Olympic trials."

"Sorry, I didn't mean to interrupt. Tell me the rest."

Shawn described the FBI's record of Lester's criminal activities and then shared the story about the mayor's dinner Roger and John arranged the previous evening. Ray's shocked reaction was written all over his expressive face as he digested the story.

Shawn stood up, reached for his coat, and said, "We'd better get going, Ray."

They left the apartment and walked down the hall to the stairway. As they went past the closed doors of the other apartments, Ray was reminded of what Shawn had just told him. He thought, those creeps spent the night at an expensive hotel while we're up at dawn heading for the track. It's no wonder the athletes are upset. It's also inconceivable that no one has caught up with them yet.

On the walk over to the hotel's dining room, Ray asked if Jim was aware of the corruption within the association? Shawn assured him that he was, and stressed that Jim was the only person other than himself, whom Ray should trust.

"What about Wilbur Hippenbecker? I have the impression he's honest."

"He is, but it appears that he'll do whatever it takes to stay as the president of the association. It's very obvious that Lester and his cohorts keep Wilbur under control."

They reached the dining room and it was already filled with athletes eating breakfast. Looking around the room, Shawn noticed Jim sitting in a booth alone. They walked across the room and Shawn introduced Jim to Professor Bodynski. Ray walked over to the buffet serving table and looked at the food provided by the hotel. He observed the choice of pastry, greasy eggs, and sausage. Shawn was amused at Ray's comments. His obvious distaste for the fat-laden selection of food was the same as the athletes and coaches.

"Join the club. Thanks to our intrepid leaders, we've been eating this type of garbage every day." The professor smiled at Shawn's comments. He decided to stick with the pastries and coffee.

Jim was intensely interested in the various changes Ray and his students at Syracuse University made to the test sled. Shawn was also paying close attention to the conversation, but was diverted by several athletes who came over to greet the professor. He was a popular figure and the athletes were enthused to see him. He was always suggesting excellent ways to improve their bobsleds. Most of the athletes were openly frustrated with the association's lack of support and the professor's sound advice was a positive change of pace.

After the athletes drifted away, Jim commented, "I'm getting the impression that Lester and Nino have provided a special set of bobsled runners for a driver that they want to be in the Olympics." Jim lowered his voice. "Rumor has it that the runners were purchased in Europe with association money. These two will do whatever it takes to improve the chances of the drivers they want to win the Olympic trials."

Shawn wasn't surprised. He knew the association had a history of conducting business that way.

Jim looked at his watch, "We'd better get going or the athletes will start practice without us."

"How many are practicing today?" asked Shawn.

"I'm not sure. I don't think there'll be too many. I suspect that most of them will spend the day making repairs and adjustments to their sleds to get ready for the first race tomorrow."

"How are the trials going to be conducted?" asked Ray.

"There'll be a two-heat race tomorrow and another one on Sunday for the two-man bobsled teams," Jim told him. "The three teams with the fastest combined times will be selected for the Olympics. Next weekend there'll be another race to select the three best 4-man teams."

"Does this mean the two fastest teams of both events will become the Olympic teams and the third team will be the alternate team?" asked Ray.

"Sort of," Shawn laughed, rolling his hazel eyes.

Ray looked confused. Shawn leaned forward and lowered his voice, "If Lester and Nino's favorite team doesn't make the Olympics, you can be sure they'll have another race to allow them to qualify."

"Oh, come on." Ray was disgruntled.

"I know, but this is the way these bastards operate. They'll do just about anything to accomplish what they want."

Shawn suggested it was time to leave for the bobsled track. He felt uncomfortable discussing the association's problems in the hotel dining room where the athletes might overhear. They left the hotel and walked up the steep pathway leading to the bobsled run. It was seasonably cold and the bright sun plus the lack of wind made it a perfect day for training.

They walked at a fast pace, continuing their conversation. Shawn told Jim that he shared the story with Ray about the "mayor's" dinner.

"This is unbelievable," commented Ray. If anyone other than Shawn told me, I wouldn't have believed them. It's amazing what these characters do."

"Here's something that Shawn might not have told you!" said Jim. "We both suspect Roger Ferris and Nino Casatelli are involved with drugs."

Ray wasn't surprised. He had heard the same rumor from several bobsled athletes when he last visited Lake Placid. On this same visit, rumors had reached him about Roger's apparent abuse of the association's money. However, they suspected that Roger's mishandling of funds was on a much smaller scale than Lester Fetor or John Chapadeau. This did not make it right, though, thought Ray. His concern stemmed from the fact that if the press ever got wind of what was going on they would all be guilty by association. His professional reputation also would be on the line.

"I don't know for sure if they have a drug habit, but I do know that Roger goes out every night and stays in the bars until early in the morning," Shawn added. "I've seen him in night clubs when his eyes were glazed and he was completely out of it. I'd be amazed if he didn't have a drug problem."

"Having a drug habit is only half of the problem," interjected Jim. "I suspect that he often pays for his habit with association funds."

"How could the association allow such a group of seedy characters to take control?" Ray was puzzled over the depressing situation.

"It's a long story, Ray," replied Jim. "Let's go out to dinner tonight and we'll tell you about it."

"By the way, I'd like to hear more about the mayor's dinner," laughed Ray.

They reached the track in about fifteen minutes enjoying the brisk early morning walk. Jim left and went to prepare the start area of the track while Shawn and Ray went to prepare the test sled. They spent an hour making adjustments and installing the runners. Finally, the sled was ready and they pushed it to the start line.

Jason had just arrived at the track and quickly walked over to the start area when he noticed the test sled and the Professor.

"I don't want you guys taking up too much track time to test this sled," ordered Jason imperiously. "Do you understand?"

"What do you consider as 'too much time'?" Jason's attitude annoyed Shawn.

"Make a couple of trips and you should have a good idea about how the sled works."

"I guess that would be all right. The Swiss and Germans must really be stupid because they normally test a sled about five-hundred times to determine how well it works," remarked Shawn, ridiculing Jason's brainless reasoning.

Shawn recalled the professor commenting that Jason's narrow eyes were the result of inbreeding. He knew one thing for sure, there could never be any question about Jason's stupidity. He seemed to go out of his way to prove his ignorance.

Shawn and Jim waited in line with the other athletes in the cold air for their turn to drive the experimental sled down the bobsled run. Shawn grew anxious about the upcoming test ride. Normally, experimental sleds were tested from the half-way point the first few trips to keep their speed down in the event there was a problem. Shawn knew that Jason would limit the number of times they could test it and decided to start at the top. He was well aware that this move was very risky, but was forced to take the gamble by Jason's penurious attitude. It cost money every time a sled went down the run.

Finally, it was their turn. Shawn envisioned the ride before him. The sled would reach speeds above ninety miles per hour leaving very little time to readjust or make corrections once they started.

Jim and Shawn eased their sled to the start line. Ray and Ron Harrison held the brakes on to prevent the sled from starting while they got into it and adjusted the seats. Shawn closed his eyes and mentally rehearsed what to do once he started down the race track. He leaned from side to side inside the sled with his eyes still closed as he visualized going around each turn. Satisfied he was ready, Shawn slipped his goggles into place and twisted around to look at Jim in the rear seat.

Jim nodded and said quietly, "I'm set back here."

They shook hands to wish each other luck. Shawn knew that Jim was well aware of the risk involved but, like all bobsledders, it was never discussed. They both knew there would be no turning back once they started down the track. He turned around and picked up the driving ropes that controlled the steering. Looking straight ahead, he asked Ron to push them off.

The sled crept slowly down the track headed for the first turn. Shawn instantly began to test the steering system by pulling the ropes left and right getting accustomed to how the sled's steering reacted on the ice. He then released the tension on the steering ropes and allowed the sled to go on its own. He needed to know whether the sled pulled left or right as it slid down the track to develop a feel for the steering tension. This would be critical if he made a driving error and had to make an instant readjustment.

The sled went perfectly straight giving Shawn a confident feeling. They quickly picked up speed as the sled approached the first corner. Shawn pulled slightly on the right rope easing the sled into the approach area for the turn. The sled responded quickly and headed for the turn's entrance without any difficulty. They slipped through the turn and continued down the track, gaining speed rapidly.

The next turn was to the left so Shawn pulled the steering rope, once again easing the sled into the approach area. He estimated their speed was now up to about fifty miles per hour and was steadily increasing. The sled seemed to respond perfectly while they slipped through the next eight turns without any difficulty.

Shawn estimated their speed was now over eighty miles per hour and was escalating rapidly. Suddenly, as they approached the next turn, the sled

→ *Ice Spy*

responded sluggishly when he tugged on the steering rope. This unanticipated problem with the steering startled him. The sluggish response of the steering forced him to enter the approach area late. He over-corrected for the sled's sluggish behavior and entered the next turn at the wrong angle hitting the side of the wall. The violent blow launched them into the direction of the opposite wall. Shawn attempted without success to compensate and they bounced off the wall so violently he could see stars for a moment.

Desperately trying to re-evaluate what was wrong with the sled before he reached the next turn, he relaxed the steering ropes slightly, hoping the sled would adjust itself. It didn't. He began to tug on the left rope to force the sled into the approach area of the next turn. Again the sled reacted sluggishly and he was forced to steer into the direction of the wall. Anticipating that the sled would hit the wall brutally again, he pulled the right steering rope hoping to avoid bouncing off the wall. This maneuver didn't work and they hit the right wall so hard that Shawn felt Jim's helmet slam against his back.

Shawn suspected their speed to be over ninety miles per hour which would make it even more difficult to maneuver the sled with damaged steering. The wind rushed past his head at an incredible speed, but he could not hear a thing. His mind raced frantically trying to analyze how to correct the steering problem.

His adrenaline was pumping furiously. The most difficult turn of the entire track was in his view. This turn was nicknamed by the Germans as the 'Kreisel' because of its odd shape. The turn was a complete 360 degree circle. The entrance of each turn is sharply angled so that when a sled begins to turn, all four runners are on the ice track. Centrifugal force will pull the sled onto the side walls as they ride around the turn. The midpoint of the huge turn was sixteen-feet high, enough room for a tragic accident if an error was made.

His heart pounded and his mind searched desperately for a way to correct the steering problem. Suddenly he was out of time and the sled slammed into the upper section of the wall and began sliding around the 'Kreisel' turn at a dangerous angle. A safety lip at the top of the turn prevented the sled from flying out of the track which could have killed both of them when they hit the ground. The screeching sound of the sled's fiberglass scraping against the track wall pierced Shawn's ears as they went around the turn like a rocket.

The sled shot around the 360 degree turn in only a matter of seconds yet it seemed as if they were maneuvering it in slow motion. The g-forces on his head created so much pressure that Shawn thought it would explode. He could feel a sharp pain inside his eye sockets as his eye balls pressed against the inside of his skull. The turn's exit appeared abruptly and once again he attempted to turn the sled in the right direction. The sled vaulted off the wall out of control into the opposite side striking the right side of the sled. The impact's violent force sent another painful shock through their bodies.

This was the first time in his life that he wanted a bobsled to slow down. The next and final turn would be difficult to maneuver. It was similar to the 'Kreisel' but only fourteen-feet high. The sled continued down the long straightway leading to the one-hundred and eighty degree turn. Shawn managed to maneuver the sled once again so that it would rub along the side wall. The sled raced around the steeply banked turn and once again they could feel the punishing pressure from the g-forces. The sound of the fiberglass scraping along the safety lip was deafening and Shawn thought the vibration would shatter his eyes like eggs being dropped on concrete.

His concentration was so intense that everything was happening in slow motion although they were taking the turn at over ninety miles per hour. When the turn's exit appeared, Shawn attempted to guide the sled in that direction. Still stubborn, the sled shot down into the opposite wall and hit with the force of a ton of bricks. The sled entered the finish area and sped up the ramp. Shawn was alarmed that Jim might not be able to apply the brakes after they had crossed the finish line. He was relieved when he felt Jim apply pressure and the sled began to slow down. They drove off the track onto the finish platform and a group of worried athletes rushed over to the sled.

Shawn had a flashback of a serious accident he had in Lake Placid when he was competing during the 1984 Olympic trials. That accident nearly killed him and left him with several broken bones and a variety of internal injuries. An athlete near the sled spoke and brought him back to the present.

"Are you guys Okay?" asked the first athlete to arrive.

"I'm okay. Check Jim. He must have taken one hell of a beating."

The athletes helped Jim out of the sled and then Shawn climbed out. Jim was able to walk around although he had pain in just about every part of his body. Shawn looked at the sled and was surprised that it wasn't damaged nearly as bad as he expected. The professor had built a strong sled. A standard sled would never have survived that kind of punishment.

"Coach, do you want the sled taken back to the start area?" asked an athlete.

"No. The steering is broken. That's why we had so much trouble. Would you please put it back inside the repair shed?" asked Shawn. "I'll have the professor fix it. I don't think I'll be ready to test it again for another day or two."

Shawn and Jim laughed at each other as they walked away. "I guess we cheated death again, Shawn." Jim was hurting but he was exuberant. "I couldn't imagine what was wrong but knew you were having serious problems controlling the sled."

Shawn explained the sled's steering problem to Jim making a see-saw motion with his hands to describe the experience. "I didn't know what to expect as we approached each turn. I finally decided to just try and slow the sled by letting it rub on the walls."

"I'm amazed that you could keep the sled on its runners and that we didn't flip over. Once I could feel it going over and managed to apply enough pressure to force it back down on all four runners."

They got on the equipment truck and returned to the start area where the professor was waiting impatiently for them. He was visibly alarmed at their condition. Shawn briefly explained the steering problem and his efforts to prevent an accident. The professor was horrified as he realized the physical punishment the sled had inflicted on his two friends. They walked to the repair shed to examine the damage and determine what happened to the steering.

Ray suggested that Shawn and Jim go back to the hotel to rest while he repaired the sled. Shawn was relieved because the last thing he wanted to do was work on the sled. All he wanted to do was go some place and collapse on

→ *Ice Spy*

a bed. They left the professor and walked down the pathway that runs parallel to the bobsled track. At the 'Kreisel' turn, Shawn saw Joe Sweeney standing there watching him.

"Are you guys all right?" Joe seemed very concerned.

"We're okay. I suspect that we'll really be stiff tomorrow," replied Shawn, starting to feel every bruise on his body. "I didn't realize you were coming today."

"I made plans to spend the weekend in Winterberg."

"Jim, do you remember Joe Sweeney? We used to be stationed in the air force together and now Joe is stationed in the southern part of Germany."

"Hi, Joe. We met a few weeks ago in the hotel dining room. How have you been?"

"I've been okay. Real busy at work, but I don't mind as it helps to pass the time."

"What kind of work do you do in the air force?" Jim inquired curiously.

"I have a classified job with intelligence and, unfortunately, I can't talk about my work, or else I'll have to shoot you. Just kidding. I work in Public Affairs."

"I didn't mean to sound as if I was quizzing you," said Jim, which is exactly what he was doing.

Shawn was amused at how well Joe had covered his background. He was certain that if anyone ever contacted the air force they would find Joe listed on their manning document, a confidential military list of all the people assigned to that particular base. The CIA was extremely meticulous when they built a background for their agents. They left nothing to chance because even a minor mistake could be fatal.

Joe accompanied Shawn and Jim to their hotel and Jim excused himself and went upstairs. "Are you really okay, Shawn?" Joe was truly concerned.

"I just got the wind knocked out of me. Tomorrow will be difficult because we'll be stiff and every bruise on our bodies will remind us of what happened."

"I'd like to get together with you tonight if you're up to it," said Joe. "If you're too sore just tell me and we can let my briefing go for a few days."

"No, I don't mind. There'll be a meeting tonight in the hotel dining room to prepare for the race tomorrow. I have to attend it and then I can leave."

"Why don't you come down and get me at my hotel when you finish?" asked Joe.

"That's fine with me. The meeting should wind up around seven and I'll come right down. Which hotel are you staying at?"

"I'm at the Bavarian, Room 210. Take your time and we can go out for dinner later."

Joe left and Shawn climbed the stairs slowly up to his room, hoping his pain would disappear if he took a nap. He unlocked his room and crawled onto the bed after struggling to remove his jacket and boots. The room began to spin as he closed his eyes and drifted off to a restless sleep. He dreamt that once again he was racing down the bobsled course in the broken sled. He was reliving the traumatic plunge down the ice-cold track that nearly killed him less then an hour ago. In his dreams Angela was there, telling him "I told you so."

CHAPTER THIRTEEN

Riga, Latvia, USSR

A cold rain fell on Boris Yegorov as he stood outside his small apartment, getting a breath of fresh air. He heard his wife, Anita, calling that supper was ready. Boris wiped his feet before entering the apartment and went into the tiny kitchen to join his family. He sat down and everyone silently bowed their heads in prayer while he asked for God's blessing. He asked God to watch over his wife and her parents who lived with them. He finished praying, looked up and smiled at the three people around him hoping his prayers would protect them.

Anita's parents lived a life of horror because of the Russians. Her father was a world renowned concert pianist during his youth. His fame had brought him nothing but difficulties after the Russian's successful invasion of Latvia. Shortly after the invasion, Russian soldiers took him to their military commanders in Latvia and demanded that he give them a performance. He refused to comply as long as he was living in occupation. He was arrested and the soldiers beat him, breaking all of his fingers. He spent the next fifteen years imprisoned in Siberia.

The Russians treated Anita and her mother as parasites during the time he was in prison. Boris met Anita during the last year of her father's imprisonment. He had used his influence as an extremely successful Soviet Olympic Luge coach to get his father in-law released from prison. However, there were conditions for his release. He was forbidden to ever own property, a car, or have a telephone, so Boris, at Anita's request, invited her parents to live with them.

They were nearly finished with dinner when a single loud knock on their door interrupted them. Boris recognized the pre-arranged secret signal that meant that the CIA wanted to meet him. The CIA agent would wait for him down the street inside the dark cemetery. Anita and her parents were visibly alarmed as they watched him slip into his dark heavy jacket and walk out the door without any explanation.

Boris arrived at the cemetery and studied the enveloping darkness to locate the CIA agent, but couldn't see him. Suddenly, a voice from behind spoke quietly to him. Boris jumped, startled, but was immediately relieved to recognize the agent. They exchanged greetings and the agent apologized for startling him. He had hidden to observe if the KGB was following him. Boris nodded his understanding.

The agent informed Boris that Walter Shapnek and Shawn Murphy wanted to meet with him in East Germany. Boris recalled meeting Shawn several years earlier on a world cup tour. The agent told Boris that he would stop back in a few days to advise him when and where the meeting would take place. The agent nodded and walked away briskly into the darkness. He simply vanished into thin air, disappearing into the dark fold of the century-old cemetery. Boris stood in the cold, damp air, and thought, "I've met with this man several times, yet I know absolutely nothing about him, not even his name."

When he returned to his apartment Anita rushed over and asked, "What did they want, Boris?"

"I must take a trip to East Germany to make arrangements for the defection," he told her quietly.

"I'm worried for you." Anita looked very concerned.

Putting his finger to his lips he quietly cautioned her, "Keep your voice down. We don't know if the KGB has installed bugs in the apartment. Don't worry my dear, I'll be fine. Soon, we will live far away from the Russians, in America."

"I hope so, Boris. I'm so afraid that they will kill you."

"Have faith, my love. The CIA will get us out of Latvia and away from the Russians. We can't rush this," said Boris trying to reassured her.

"I know. I worry so much that my nerves are just about gone. I hope they take us to America soon." Boris sat in his favorite chair and attempted to nap. His thoughts were on their future. He tried to relax, but his mind refused to let him forget his horrendous situation.

Virginia Beach, Virginia

A sharp knock on the bedroom door startled Walter Shapnek. "Sorry to wake you but we have to leave soon and get you over to the helicopter at Langley," said Fred Unser.

"Thanks. I'll be ready in just a few minutes." He looked at his watch. It was 6 a.m.

Walter showered and got dressed then packed the few belongings he brought with him. Amused, he thought about the clothing he had scattered all over Europe. Some at an apartment in East Germany and some in the apartment he kept in Cologne, West Germany.

Fred had breakfast ready for him when he went into the kitchen. The aroma from the percolator was terrific and what he needed most right now was coffee.

"I miss American coffee more than anything else when I'm in Europe."

Fred agreed, "I know the feeling. They make it too strong over there."

"I like your condo," Walter said, looking around the brightly colored kitchen. He thought to himself about settling down and living a more normal life.

It had occurred to Walter more than once that he lived a lonely life. He looked at his boss, "I've been on the run now for about seven years and it's starting to get old, Fred. If I decide to come out from undercover work will the agency have something for me?"

"Walter, when you're ready, I'll have a job for you. I don't want you worrying about it because you might get careless and make a mistake. Mistakes in our work can be fatal. If you're really considering 'coming out' we need to talk about it."

"I think about switching jobs from time to time so that I can relax, but I still get thrills out of what I do."

"When the thrills stop we need to sit and talk."

"Don't worry. You'll be the first to know. For whatever it's worth, Fred, it's nice to know that you're really concerned about our safety over there."

"I know what it's like. Remember, I worked undercover in Europe for nearly 20 years. When my nerves started to get the best of me, my chief of operations in Europe yanked me out. Three years later I replaced him when he retired."

"How long before you plan to retire, Fred?" Walter smirked knowing he would get a rise out of Fred who was too young to retire.

"I've got a few years left, my friend, so don't get too eager," laughed Fred. "Don't worry. I'll always have a job for you. Your primary job now is to take care of yourself so you can fill mine when the time comes." Fred unplugged the coffee pot and looked at the wall clock, saying, "We'd better get going or we'll be late."

They left the condominium and Fred drove to the CIA headquarters where the helicopter crew was scheduled to fly Walter back to McGuire to meet the C-5. During the drive they chatted about the *IceSpy* project and how work was progressing so far.

The helicopter was running and the crew was waiting for Walter when they arrived at CIA headquarters,. The noise from the helicopter was so loud that they were unable to speak so they shook hands and Walter climbed into the helicopter. Moments after he fastened his seat belt, the pilot went through his check list and within minutes they lifted off the ground. Walter caught a glimpse of Fred waving from his car.

A short time later the helicopter approached McGuire Air Force base. The control tower cleared them for landing and instructed them to park about one hundred feet from the C-5 preparing for its flight to Germany. The rear ramp door was open and Walter could see the loadmaster waving to him. He thanked the helicopter crew and boarded the C-5 with his suitcase.

He slid his suitcase behind the webbing of his seat then sat down and fastened his seat belt. The rear door closed and he felt the powerful jet engines start up. Suddenly the enormous plane began moving down the runway, quickly accelerating to lift the C-5 off the pavement. Moments later he could feel the landing gear being pulled up into its flight position and he looked out the window watching the ground disappear below him.

His thoughts returned to Fred and how he appeared to be very mellow but Walter remembered a different Fred when they worked undercover together in Leningrad. On one assignment they were on a train going to Moscow. At three in the morning a KGB agent startled them when he burst into their compartment pointing a gun at them. The agent explained in English that he knew they were CIA agents and was willing to keep their identity a secret, for a price. He demanded two-hundred thousand American dollars or he would expose them to his superiors.

Fred agreed to pay the outrageous amount demanded by the KGB agent then told him it would take a week to get the money together. They agreed to meet in Leningrad a week later and the agent reached his hand behind him feeling for the compartment door handle. Walter remembered that the KGB agent made the deadly mistake of turning his head for a split second to locate the door handle. When his head turned, Fred leaped up from his seat and struck him on the back on his neck with an unbelievable blow. The force broke his neck instantly killing him.

Walter got cold chills thinking about the sound of the KGB agent's neck bones rubbing together when the body collapsed on the floor. They picked him up under his armpits and set him up in the seat leaning against the wall. Fred wiped up the blood that had trickled out of his nose and instructed Walter to check outside the compartment to see if anyone else was around.

He hurriedly checked the hallway up and down and was convinced that the weaving motion of the slow moving train had put everyone to sleep. It appeared that the KGB agent had been alone so he returned to help Fred. They hoisted the body up between them so it would look as if he were drunk and they were helping him return to his own compartment. They carried the dead agent out of the compartment into the empty passage way and through the door leading outside to the platform separating the two train cars.

Satisfied that no one had seen them, Fred shoved the body over the railing onto the stone railroad bed beneath the train. Both men returned to the compartment confident that their true identity was protected. The bizarre incident rattled Walter, and Fred lectured him to never let his guard down. The incident was simply a hazard of the job. The simple mistake of turning his head for only a split second, cost the KGB agent his life. They never spoke about it again, but it was a lesson that Walter never forgot.

Walter smiled when he thought about Fred, knowing he could be tough as nails when he had to be. He reached over and opened the morning newspaper lying next to him on the seat; something he hadn't done in a long time.

Winterberg, West Germany

Professor Bodynski went to Shawn's hotel to check on his friend. Hearing a mumbled reply, he opened the door and walked into the studio apartment. He looked into the bedroom where Shawn was still lying with his clothes on.

"Are you okay?"

"I hurt everywhere, but I'll survive. This isn't the first time I've been through this and it probably won't be the last time."

"I feel responsible about the steering problem, Shawn." Ray was visibly upset.

Shawn reassured his friend, "There was nothing you could've predicted, Ray. What happened to the steering?"

The professor explained that a weak spring in the steering was responsible for the loss of control and then assured him that he had installed a new one to correct the problem. Shawn listened intently to him and then sat up on the bed, saying, "When it happened I couldn't understand what went wrong. No matter what I did, nothing seemed to correct the problem. It was like a nightmare."

"It *was* a nightmare and I feel terrible about it."

"Ray, like I told you, don't worry about it. This is to be expected with an experimental sled. Thankfully you were able to fix it?"

"I have it all ready to be tested whenever you and Jim are ready." The professor got up to leave but Shawn stopped him.

"Great, but not today!" Shawn groaned.

→ *Ice Spy*

The professor laughed, catching Shawn's meaning. "We made Jason's day. When I left the bobsled track he was all smiles."

"You have to wonder if he was happy that your test sled broke or if he was happy that Jim and I got the hell beat out of us," said Shawn, sarcastically. "He's something else."

"Do you feel up to going out to dinner tonight?"

"I can't, Ray. I've got to meet a friend of mine who's here on business. I'm sorry, but maybe tomorrow night if you want to."

"That's fine with me. I'll leave so you can get some more rest."

Shawn shook his head and struggled to sit up, "I have to get up anyway to get ready for Jason's meeting. You don't have to be in a hurry."

"The athletes were very concerned about you and Jim. I've got the feeling that they have a great deal of confidence in you two guys. It's a shame that Jason and the rest of those characters are so dishonest. I really feel sorry for the athletes."

"They're a great bunch of guys and you're right about Jason and the rest of them. None of the athletes trust the officials. They've been cheated and lied to for years. They can see how these characters are spending their money and they're furious about it."

"Why don't they do something?"

"Who do they go to?" Shawn changed positions on the bed and felt a pain stab his side that reminded him to move slowly.

"The United States Olympic Committee should do something to help them."

"Lots of luck in that department." Shawn didn't want to sound sarcastic but he knew the idea was a waste of time. "They're only interested in what has a direct effect on their fund raising. I hope that the FBI will be able to expose the corrupt people who are controlling the association. Then the USOC will step forward and say they had been quietly investigating the association's activities to correct the problem."

"Did you find out who the FBI's undercover agent is?" asked Ray, curiously.

"No. I have a suspicion, but I really don't know for sure. I'm just thankful that they're attempting to get enough evidence to convict them. For your own protection, you shouldn't talk about this to the athletes." Shawn turned serious so abruptly that Ray stared at him.

"Why?"

"As I told you, Lester and some of his friends are tied to organized crime in New York City. We suspect that he and Nino are doing special favors for a driver to help his team qualify for the Olympics. I really don't know for sure, but we heard that one of the drivers is the son of a mafia member who does business with Lester. You can be sure that if this is true the driver will inform Lester or Nino about any rumors pertaining to them or the FBI. I wouldn't be surprised if they had someone whacked because they interfered with what they are doing in the association. They won't take a chance on being exposed to the FBI."

"Don't worry. I would never say anything to the athletes." The professor was very reliable and Shawn respected this about him.

"I trust you. That's why I confided in you."

"I'm going to leave and let you get ready for your meeting with Jason. I'll visit with you tomorrow at the bobsled track. I hope you feel better in the morning."

Ray said goodnight and left. Shawn smiled as his friend shut the door behind him. Looking at his watch he decided to change his clothes and get ready for the meeting. He got dressed slowly because of his aching muscles. He thought about the information Joe would share with him later when they went to dinner. Shawn left the apartment and stopped on his way downstairs to get Jim. They stepped outside and immediately zipped up their coats. The wind was brisk and the temperature had dropped several degrees since they had returned to their apartments that morning.

Both limped noticeably as they walked across the hotel's parking lot. When they entered the dining room several athletes rushed over to question them about their injuries. They laughed and joked about how they were just feeling old.

Jason started the meeting and reviewed the rules for the Olympic qualification race with the athletes. The meeting was interrupted suddenly when Wilbur Hippenbecker, John Chapadeau, and Roger Ferris walked into the room and sat down at an empty table. Jason politely thanked the three men for joining them. They nodded and acknowledged everyone in the room.

Scott Miller, who was normally very quiet, spoke loudly and said, "The association must be paying them overtime to attend this meeting, poor babies."

"I don't want to hear anymore talk like that," snapped Jason, nervously glancing at the three association officials sitting at the corner table. Wilbur, John, and Roger stared back at the group of athletes with obvious animosity.

"What's... the matter, Jason? Does the truth hurt?" drawled Skip Reynolds.

"This is an official meeting to make the selections for your start positions," replied Jason, loftily. "If you fellas want to bitch about something to these officials, do it after the meeting."

"Is this a joke?" mocked Dave Leon. "They'll be gone right after the meeting. We should feel honored that they came to visit us. Are we supposed to take up a collection and give them money?"

"Where's Lester and his 'gang', Jason?" interrupted another athlete.

"I saw them downtown in one of the bars just before the meeting started," came a snickering voice.

Blood rushed to Jason's face and he began to pound on the table with his clipboard. He yelled with his loud nasal voice, "The next person who interrupts me will be eliminated from the race tomorrow." He looked around the room staring at the athletes with his narrow eyes. Several athletes looked down so Jason wouldn't see them smirking but most of them were openly laughing.

Jason continued with the meeting, reading rules and giving his comments. Finally, he put numbers on pieces of paper and dropped them into a hat. Jason mixed them up and each driver took turns at picking a number. The number a driver drew would determine his start position for the race.

When the meeting was nearly finished, Wilbur stood up and thanked all the athletes for the hard work they had done to prepare for the Olympic trials. He wished everyone the best of luck and quickly left with John and Roger. No one made a sound while he was talking. After they left the athletes broke out in spontaneous cheering.

Shawn felt sorry for Wilbur because he was sincere about the athletes and was the only association official who attempted to help them. Yet Shawn was also frustrated with Wilbur because he refused to do anything about all the corruption running rampant throughout the association. Shawn thought Wilbur must have decided that it was more important and less dangerous to be a presidential figurehead than expose the corruption. There was no mistake about how the athletes felt about the association officials. After the meeting they were extremely vocal about association money being wasted on the lifestyle of the corrupt officials.

Shawn and Jim chatted about the following day's events for a few minutes until Shawn excused himself so he could go and secretly meet with Joe Sweeney. On his way out he noticed Professor Bodynski sitting alone in the corner of the dining room near the door.

"Hi, Ray. I didn't see you come in."

"I came in while Jason was yelling at the athletes," laughed Ray. "These guys are ready to revolt."

"I wish they would. Those creeps should be dropped out of an airplane at 20,000 feet without a parachute." He smiled at the thought.

"Shawn, I always said you're diabolical, but I love it," roared Ray.

"I've got to run, Ray. I'll see you in the morning.

Shawn left the hotel's dining room and went out into the bitter cold wind that was sweeping through the dark parking lot. He decided to jog down the street hoping it would help him stay warm. After a couple of steps the bruises he'd received from the test ride convinced him to walk and suffer the cold. Arriving at the Bavarian hotel he looked at the directory to see where Room 210 was located. The heat felt good as he walked down the hallway to Joe's room.

"How do you feel, Shawn?" They shook hands and Joe gestured for Shawn to take a seat. The hotel room was small but comfortable and Shawn sat down in one of the available chairs.

"Stiff and very old, otherwise I'll survive," joked Shawn, wincing with pain.

"There are a few things I'd like to discuss with you before we go to dinner."

"I'd feel more comfortable discussing the deal with Boris Yegorov where no one is apt to overhear our conversation," replied Shawn.

Joe told Shawn about the current status of the Latvians in the Soviet Union, explaining the seriousness of the situation and how quickly it was becoming a threat to their plan. The CIA was very concerned that the Russians might kill Boris before they had a chance to get him and his family out.

"Why don't we help him escape when he's in East Germany?" asked Shawn.

"That's no good. He will not leave without his family. It would be easy for us to get him out of East Germany if he was alone but his family is very important to him and he won't risk their safety. Otherwise, he could go anytime. Frankly, that's our main problem right now.

"Our undercover man is meeting with Boris either today or tomorrow to make arrangements for him to meet with you and Walter in East Germany."

"Won't the KGB follow him wherever he goes?"

"That they will." Joe knew all too well what life was like for people like Boris living in the Soviet Union and in trouble with the Russians. "Walter is the best there is at this type of intrigue."

"What's our cover for being there?"

"Walter represents a company that sells sport braces. He's taking you along so you and Boris can share your experiences at using Walter's products. Walter will imply that he's trying to get both of you guys to endorse his products. We want the KGB to think Walter is doing this so that the International Olympic Committee will approve his company's products for Olympic competition."

"Do you think the KGB will believe a story like that?"

"Walter has spent years building his background in the Soviet Union," replied Joe, seriously. "In general, the KGB suspects everyone. They're not aware of Walter's real purpose for being in the Soviet Union, otherwise, they would have killed him. Walter has been giving both the East Germans and the Soviets high tech sports braces for their athletes. They might not completely trust him, but they leave him alone because they can't get his products from any country behind the Iron Curtain."

"Can't the KGB buy these products in the United States themselves?" Shawn changed his position carefully, feeling every ache and pain.

"It's not worth it for them to take a chance of blowing their cover there. Whatever you do, don't ever forget and let your guard down," Joe stressed. "I don't mean just when you're behind the Iron Curtain but all the time. How you conduct yourself here in Europe, in the United States, no matter where you are, you can't ever let your guard down. It'll be fatal to someone if you do. Maybe yourself, maybe not. Could be Walter, Boris, or even his family." Joe stood up and paced back and forth in the small room. Shawn watched him intently, temporarily forgetting his sore muscles.

"From now on you have to be on top of everything. If you drink alcohol, no more than two and watch to be sure nothing is slipped into the drink. It's best not to drink any."

"I'm not concerned, Joe. I'm always careful and a very private person by nature."

"I know you are. Let's get some dinner. I'm starved."

They put their coats on and left the hotel. The street was empty of people, a typical scene in most European cities right after the dinner hour and Shawn noticed that Winterberg's Himmel Street was no exception. They turned right walking slowly down the cobbled stones. The bitter cold wind subsided making their walk more enjoyable. They continued their conversation about the *IceSpy* until they reached the restaurant Joe selected for dinner.

The restaurant was located in the basement of a centuries-old building. It was tiny in size compared to the large bar area. Germans liked to drink. Shawn and Joe went to the bar to have a drink and warm up before they went into the dining room.

"How well do you know Professor Bodynski?" asked Joe. They stood at the end of the crowded, smoke-filled bar.

"I've gotten to know him very well. He's one of the most amusing and intelligent men I've ever met," stated Shawn. "Why do you ask?"

At this moment the bartender approached and took their order for two Heinekens. Joe waited for him to leave before answering. "I'm just curious about how much you know about him," said Joe. "In this business you can't be too careful."

"He's about as trustworthy as you can get." Shawn was adamant. "In fact, he used to go out on assignments for the Agency when he was younger."

"You're kidding." Joe looked at Shawn in surprise at what he was hearing. "How did you find that out?"

"We've become close friends over the years. Once we were comparing stories about our backgrounds and we were shocked to learn that we had similar experiences," replied Shawn. "He wasn't employed as an agent but was hired from time to time to go out on assignments where his particular expertise was needed."

"I guess it's a small world some times." Joe made a mental note to check out the story. "Do you think he would be receptive to helping if we needed him on the *IceSpy* Project?"

"I'm sure he would. Do you want me to ask him?"

"No. Don't say anything to let him suspect what you're doing. If the need comes up then we'll approach him."

Their beer arrived and Joe paid the bartender. He suggested that they take the beer steins and sit at a quiet table beneath the curtained window. Shawn realized it would be easier to talk there since no one was sitting near the table.

They sat down and Joe continued, "I can't emphasize enough the importance that no one finds out what you're doing with us. In fact we don't want you to even tell anyone that you're staying here a little longer, until the morning the team leaves."

"I need to call work and tell my wife sometime, Joe"

"Don't tell anyone, not even your wife, until the morning the association packs up to leave. We don't want anyone talking or wondering why you're staying on a little longer." Joe sipped his beer slowly. "As for work, we'll take care of that." He smiled, putting down his stein. "You call the bitch you work for and simply tell her that you're staying a little longer. She'll have a fit and will try to get you in trouble. Don't worry about her. We've already made arrangements with the military in Washington to have your temporary duty extended." Joe dismissed Shawn's boss with a wave of his hand.

"Maybe I'll have you call my wife, Angela, and break the news to her," laughed Shawn.

"No, thanks," replied Joe, smiling. "There are limits to what we are capable of doing. Breaking that kind of news to your wife isn't one of them."

"I knew you didn't have the guts, Joe."

"Seriously, when you call her, be sure to tell her that from now on she should be very careful about what she says on the phone. There is always the possibility that your phone will be tapped. Be sure that she never talks to any of her friends about where you're going."

"She knows. She still remembers when I worked for the Agency. To be on the safe side, I prefer not to tell her that I'll be going to East Germany."

The waitress approached and Joe watched with amusement as Shawn struggled to order Wiener Schnitzel, a breaded veal cutlet, for both of them. The waitress listened patiently, nodding her understanding. She left and Shawn laughed, "It's anyone's guess what I just ordered. It should be veal. I just hope it isn't pork." Joe looked confused so Shawn explained how much pork he had eaten recently.

Their meal arrived in a few minutes and Shawn looked triumphantly at the veal dish in front of him. Joe continued to discuss what Walter and Shawn would be doing when they went to East Germany. After dinner they walked back up Himmel Street to Joe's hotel. They shook hands and went in separate directions.

Shawn noticed that the wind was picking up again and his walk back to the apartment was almost unbearable as the cold blistering wind seemed to blow him most of the way. His body felt numb by the time he reached the building and got inside the small studio apartment.

He went to bed and mused about his trip to East Germany. He recalled some of the trips he had taken behind the Iron Curtain during the sixties when he worked as an agent for the CIA. He fell asleep trying to imagine how much the country had changed over the years.

Chapter Fourteen

→ *Ice Spy*

Schenectady, New York

Master Sergeant Olive Hanson slammed the receiver down and sputtered a volley of vulgarities. She quickly dialed Lt. Colonel Amos Fowlke's telephone number.

"Colonel Fowlkes. May I help you?" came the reply on the other end.

"Colonel. This is Olive." She spoke, bitingly. "I just got a phone call from Colonel Crosby and he told me that the State Department is keeping Shawn Murphy in Europe for another week or so. This is bullshit and something needs to be done about it."

"Calm down, Olive," placated Amos. "I'll call the Colonel right now and find out what's going on."

Bruce Monroe took the radio earphones off his ears. He had heard the vulgarities right through his religious music. He got up from his desk and walked over to Olive, who was still visibly fuming. "What's Shawn trying to get away with now?"

"That son-of-a-bitch! He's finagled a way to have the State Department extend his temporary duty."

Blood had rushed to Olive's face making her cheeks bright red. Her mouth was clenched so tight that Bruce thought she might bite right through her lips. He had never seen her this mad. "Can we do anything to stop him?" he asked, knowing it was futile.

"I don't know. Colonel Fowlkes is calling the 'Old Man' right now. That's probably a waste of time, too. I think they're all afraid of him. Well, I'm not and I'll fix his ass when he gets back to work."

Bruce suspected Olive was suffering from an extreme PMS attack but said, "He needs to be taught a lesson. I know of an easy way to repay him for what he's done."

"How?" Her eyes looked right through Bruce as she contemplated several obscure ways she would like to destroy Murphy's career.

Bruce looked at her and smiled. "We can destroy his marriage."

"How can we do that?" The expression on her face changed from furious anger to a look of interest.

Bruce closed the door to the Public Affairs office and sat down in the chair next to Olive's desk. He grinned from ear to ear feeling wonderful about his plan to destroy Shawn's marriage.

"Revenge will be so sweet." He smiled and told Olive, "When Shawn returns to work, I'll have my girlfriend call Angela and confess to having an affair with him."

"Are you sure she'll do it?"

"She will do whatever I ask of her," said Bruce, confidently. "The Lord will help us. He knows that Shawn was wrong to leave us alone when there was an unbelievable amount of work to be done."

"Okay, do it, but make sure nobody knows what you're up to."

"Don't worry. No one will know."

Lt. Colonel Fowlkes's phone call interrupted their conversation. "Olive, Colonel Crosby wants us to come down to his office to discuss Shawn

Murphy's situation."

Olive agreed and hung up. She hurriedly got up from her desk and abruptly explained the phone call to Bruce while she left the office. Lt. Colonel Fowlkes and Olive stood outside Colonel Crosby's door waiting for him to finish a phone conversation. They stood silently, not looking at each other, until the colonel opened his office door.

The colonel was a rather tall, good-looking man with a slim build. His ever-changing personality made it very difficult to predict his current mood. He leaned back in his soft leather chair, tapping a pencil in the palm of his left hand. He tossed the pencil onto his desk and leaned forward, glaring at them.

"Apparently, both of you are upset that Sgt. Murphy has been asked to stay in Europe a little longer," The colonel hesitated a moment to see if they would respond to his opening remark. Neither spoke, knowing what would happen if they did say something. "If you can't figure out what's going on here, let me make it very simple so there'll be no misunderstanding."

They had no problem trying to figure out what his personality was this morning. He stood up and started walking around the room speaking as he circled behind them,

"I want to make it very clear that neither of you will do anything to make Sgt. Murphy's life difficult." It was obvious from the expression on his face he was upset and not in a mood to listen to their opinions.

"Apparently he is doing something for the State Department. This means that we don't interfere. I hope you can understand this? Are there any questions?"

"Yes, sir. I have a question." Olive was enraged, thinking the colonel was a real patsy and had allowed the State Department to walk all over him. "How do you expect Bruce and I to get the public affairs work done with Sgt. Murphy gone for so long?"

Colonel Crosby sat down in his chair and picked up his pencil again. He looked at Olive in disbelief that she was stupid enough to ask that question. Fowlkes looked at her in astonishment.

"Are you serious?"

"Yes, I'm serious. Bruce and I are behind schedule in our work and with Sgt. Murphy being away longer now, it means we'll have trouble meeting deadlines on a lot of work that needs to be done." Olive was petulant and this annoyed the colonel immensely.

The colonel's eyes widened as he leaned forward. He looked Olive straight in the eye and said slowly, "Maybe we should talk about your work. I've been getting feedback from other people that you've been taking credit for Sgt. Murphy's work. I've received several complaints about what you and Monroe have been writing for news releases. One paper called and said to stop sending information because they didn't have time to correct the mistakes. Whenever they receive a release from your office they no longer take the time to read them. Perhaps you should try getting up in the morning and getting to work on time. You might also try taking only thirty minutes for lunch like everyone else and then you will have the time to do your job the way it should be done."

Olive couldn't contain her anger, which was a weakness for her. She was known for speaking out when she was upset and usually her sharp tongue got her into trouble. This time was no different.

She yelled, "I don't know what you've been told, but Bruce and I work our butts off trying to make you and the rest of the people on this base look good. I don't appreciate being told that I don't put in a full day's work."

Colonel Crosby stood up and looked down at Olive. He said ominously, "The only time I ever saw Monroe stay late was when he had a flat tire. He left as soon as he could change it and I don't recall you ever working past quitting time. Explain how you make everyone look good when newspaper editors throw away your news releases."

Crosby spun around and glared at Olive. "Don't you ever answer me like that again or I will have you charged with insubordination. You had better think about losing your job if you don't start managing your office the way it should be managed. Let me reiterate what I said about Sgt. Murphy." He repeated what he had told them when they first came into his office. He abruptly dismissed Olive and told Lt. Colonel Fowlkes to stay. Amos got up and shut the office door after she left, then reluctantly sat back down in the chair.

"I want to know why you've been taking so many trips to the west coast." Colonel Crosby picked up a record of the trips Amos had taken and waved it back and forth in the air.

"I've been going out to Travis Air Force Base to study their personnel system. I'm putting together a plan to re-organize our system here, to make it more efficient." Amos was confident that the colonel would believe him.

"When you go to Travis, where do you stay?"

"I get a room at the officers' quarters. Why?"

"When the comptroller informed me about your unusual number of trips, I decided to call Travis and check up on you. Guess what, Amos?" The colonel smiled as he leaned forward.

"What?"

"They didn't even know who you were. We know that you registered and got receipts for the officers' quarters but nobody at that base knew you. Their personnel officer thought perhaps I was calling the wrong base."

"I don't know why they couldn't remember me because I was there."

"For what it's worth, Amos. I had someone at Travis call several hotels at Lake Tahoe to see if you'd been registered at one of them during the dates you were out there. Guess what?"

Amos did not have to guess what Colonel Crosby was going to tell him. He would deny everything. Let them prove that it was him and not someone else with the same name.

"You were registered at the Heavenly Ski Resort on each of the dates."

"You can't prove that it was me. Someone with the same name was there. It wasn't me. Why are you trying to make me look bad?" Amos began feeling uneasy and suspected Colonel Crosby might take some form of disciplinary action against him.

"I'm not trying to make you look like anything. You're doing a great job at making yourself look ridiculous. From now on Amos, you don't take any business trips without my personal approval. Now get out of here."

"Yes, sir," Amos got up and slammed the door behind him as he left the commander's office.

Colonel Crosby leaned back in his chair and thought about the scene that had just taken place. He wondered why he had been blessed with them. He would now have to keep a very close eye on them or he would be in trouble because of what they might do. He had very little patience for stupid people and he had been given a double dose.

Winterberg, West Germany

A sharp pain stabbed Shawn in his back and forced him to awaken. He tried not to move but it was useless. He forced himself to get out of bed and opened the bottle of aspirin. He took four, hoping they would reduce the pain. He looked out the window and noticed the storm clouds had left Winterberg. The sun was starting to work itself over the mountain top. The window was partially covered with frost so he assumed it must be cold outside. He showered and got dressed. The pain was beginning to go away and he actually felt better.

He left the apartment and walked slowly down the flight of stairs leading to the front door. When he reached the door he remembered that he had forgotten Jim and turned around and went back up the stairs to get him.

Shawn knocked on Jim's door and a voice called, "Come in."

He opened the door and had to laugh when he saw Jim walking around as stiff as a board. Jim glared at Shawn's laughter and that made him laugh harder than ever. Jim said, "It isn't funny."

"Did you take any aspirin?" Shawn's sides ached.

"I just wolfed some down. How do you feel?"

"About the same as you do. I took four as soon as I got out of bed."

"Be careful. They'll eat a hole in your stomach if you take too many." Jim tried to grin but the pain made his face twist when he put on his jacket. They looked at each other and laughed as they walked out into the hallway.

Lester's rented Mercedes was back in the parking lot. "I'd guess that all the officials will be at the track, on time this morning," laughed Shawn pointing at the Mercedes.

"Why's that?"

"Today's the first race day for the Olympic trials. The press will be there and so will the officials. Nino will be explaining all about his famous 'whiteout workout' and how it made the American athletes much faster. Wilbur, John, and Roger will tell everyone how they've been busy managing the trials." Shawn grinned widely at Jim.

"Go on. You forgot to tell me what Lester will be doing?"

"Lester will walk around telling everyone how wonderful they are. The Germans won't understand but they'll smile and nod their heads and Lester will feel like a king."

They walked into the dining room and sat down with Professor Bodynski who was already eating pastry and drinking coffee.

"You two guys look as if you survived the night. How do you feel?" Ray made a sympathetic face knowing that both of them had to be extremely sore.

"I'm a bit younger than Shawn so I'm not as sore," laughed Jim.

"I checked the alignment of the sled and need to spend some time to re-align it. I will have it ready to test by Tuesday," said Ray, smiling.

"I hope we're still alive by Tuesday," groaned Jim. They all laughed.

Shawn and Jim struggled to their feet and went to get some food. They returned to the table and sat down to eat their breakfast. The pastries were mouth-watering and they were hungry enough to eat several apiece. They finished eating and left for the bobsled track to get ready for the race. There were only a few athletes in the dining room, indicating that they were nervous about the race and were at the track preparing their equipment.

It was a clear, cold, and sunny day, perfect weather for the big race. When they arrived at the track, Jim laughed and pointed out to Ray and Shawn that both Lester and John's rental cars were at the restaurant located on the hill overlooking the track.

"You were right on the money with your prediction, Shawn." Jim told Ray what Shawn had said when they walked through the parking lot on the way to breakfast. Ray appreciated their humor.

"These guys are as predictable as a young dog that hadn't eaten for three days would be if you put a piece of raw meat in front of it," Shawn grinned and added. "That's a bit of upstate New York folklore."

"Shawn, I swear you're diabolical, but I love it." Ray often made this remark to him. He was amused with Shawn's description of the officials. "Is there something I can do to help you and Jim?"

"There's something you could do," replied Jim. "When the athletes are getting ready you might give them some help with last minute adjustments to their sleds. We'll be too busy and none of the association officials will offer to help them."

The Olympic trial race went on without any problems. Shawn eventually discovered that Vince Capobianco was the driver who was the son of Lester's mafia friend. Lester and Nino were openly helping Vince trying to give him an unfair advantage. Shawn was pleased when Vince's team was in fifth place at the end of the first two heats. They were so far behind in time it would be nearly impossible to move up in the standings. The final two heats would be the next day and the winners would represent the United States in the two-man bobsled competition at Calgary, Canada.

Stuttgart, West Germany

Colonel Tony DiCocco was sitting in his office reading the morning *Stars and Stripes* when he received a phone call from base operations. The caller informed him that a C-5 was coming in on final approach and a passenger by the name of Walter Shapnek, had requested that the colonel pick him up on the flight line. Tony assured the caller he would leave right away and would be waiting for the plane.

The C-5 came into view far in the distance and looked like a small blemish on Tony's windshield. Within minutes, the huge green-camouflaged plane began descending onto the runway in front of his car. The plane roared past him and continued to the far end of the runway before it turned around and taxied back onto the flight-line in front of operations.

The airman in the control tower called the colonel on the radio and told him to approach the rear of the plane when the ramp door opened. Within a couple of minutes the door opened and he saw Walter walking down the ramp. He drove to a short distance from the plane to wait for Walter.

"You must be exhausted," commented Tony. Better you than me, he thought. He never wanted a job like Walter's. "Would you like me to arrange for a room here on the base so you can sleep for a few hours?"

"No, thanks. I slept on the plane a bit. I need to drive up to Winterberg and meet a couple of people there." Tony noticed Walter's rumpled appearance.

"Let me at least get you some breakfast. You're like the wind. Every time you visit the base you skip in and out and never spend any time here." Tony was only half-kidding and really wanted to spend some time with Walter. He was infatuated with Walter's lifestyle although he would never think of doing that kind of work himself.

"I have time to eat and visit with you for a couple of hours. Maybe I will take you up on your offer to get a room and take a nap. I prefer to drive at night anyway."

"Great. I'll call the Visiting Officers' Quarters right now and make arrangements. You can stay as long as you want."

"Thanks," Walter said, gratefully. The jet lag was catching up with him.

Tony made arrangements for Walter to stay at the VOQ and drove him to the Officers' Club. They had a light breakfast and visited for an hour. Tony could see how tired Walter really was and drove him to the VOQ so he could get some sleep. He hated to let him go because he was intrigued. Walter shared with Tony some of the countries he had visited and some spine-tingling events that happened early in his career. Walter was careful not to tell him anything that might be damaging if he decided to share the stories with some of his close friends some night over a couple of beers. Conversation with people like Tony is very risky for anyone in Walter's line of work. Everyone agrees not to repeat what they heard but they can not resist telling a close friend who promises not to tell anyone. The friend tells his wife that night and the next day she confides in her friend and so on. Walter was always amused and generally made up stories for people like Tony just to protect himself.

He lay on the bed thinking about meeting with Joe Sweeney and Shawn Murphy. They needed to finalize their plans to meet with Boris Yegorov in East Germany after the American bobsled trial races were finished. Walter attempted to close his eyes and rest, but his mind wouldn't allow him to sleep. He thought about Boris and tried to anticipate what type of action the KGB would take to maintain a close surveillance on him when he went to East Germany. Walter knew the KGB scrutinized everything he did in the Soviet Union and would prefer not to let him leave the country.

He suspected they would allow him to travel into other Eastern Bloc countries, find out more about why he was involved with American businessmen, and perhaps learn where he stashed the money the East German bobsled officials paid him. Walter wasn't sure if they knew it was hidden away in a Swiss bank account. The KGB would make it difficult for Walter and Shawn Murphy to spend very much quality time with Boris but they would have to do the best they could under the circumstances.

He thought about his plan to meet with Boris under the premise of promoting his company's sport braces for Soviet athletes and having Shawn Murphy provide support for the product. Walter would have to wait until they met in East Germany to determine just exactly how and where he would be able to discuss the plan with Boris. Smuggling him, his wife and her parents out of the Soviet Union would be difficult at best. Regardless of the greatest prepared plans, he would have to expect any number of things to go wrong. The main objective of the *IceSpy* mission would be to get Boris into the United States without the Soviets obtaining his technical information. Failure would be death for Boris.

Chapter Fifteen

→ *Ice Spy*

Winterberg. West Germany

The Olympic trials were in their final week and everyone felt the pressure. Professor Bodynski invited Shawn and Jim to join him for a few drinks and dinner. They drove to Berleburg, a small city near Winterberg where they could spend some time alone and away from the athletes who were becoming stressed out from the tension of the trials.

Ray took them to a small German restaurant he had eaten at several times during his visit to Winterberg. The bar was typical of the area. Highly polished wood was everywhere. The decor and beer steins belonging to regulars hung from a beam overhead. They sat down in an empty booth and ordered beers from the waitress.

"I enjoy going around to different restaurants in Europe and studying their designs." Ray's eyes roamed around the room as he spoke. "Look over to the far wall next to the bar. There's a crest on the shelf that was once used as a heraldic device that went on top of a helmet. I bet it's three hundred years old or maybe more."

"You would have enjoyed going to dinner with us last week. If it wasn't so expensive, Jim and I would take you there to eat. It was beautiful, Ray. Everything was from the fourteenth century and had been refurbished to look brand new."

"The only part that wasn't clean was our bobsled officials," Jim laughed as he retold parts of the story about the dinner. Before he had finished they were all roaring with laughter. Jim and Ray drank two more steins of beer before going to the dining room. The beer relaxed them, something they had not done for several weeks. Shawn thought about Joe Sweeney's advice about not drinking too much alcohol and switched to coffee.

This was one night they would not have to eat pork. The roast beef, when it arrived, was rare and succulent. Oven-roasted potatoes were an excellent side-dish. They took their time and enjoyed a glass of sherry after dinner. They all wanted dessert but decided to pass. They divided the bill three ways and paid the waitress before leaving.

The air felt even colder after spending several hours in the warm restaurant. They could see their breath as they walked to the parking lot. Ray unlocked the car and everyone got in while he started the engine hoping to rush heat inside his small rental vehicle. While they waited for the engine to warm up, a Volkswagen bus pulled into the parking lot across the street.

"That looks like Jason," Jim said. Shawn turned to look.

"It is! I wonder what he's doing here. He probably can't stand eating pork again," laughed Shawn.

"I don't think he came here to eat," chuckled Ray. "That's a house of prostitution."

"You're kidding. How can you tell?" Shawn was staring at the building wondering how anyone would know.

"If you look over the door you will see a small blue light. Prostitution is legal in Germany and the blue light indicates where they are located." Ray grinned as he watched Jason disappear inside the building."

They drove back to Winterberg laughing about Jason. They agreed not to mention his visit to the prostitutes to anybody. Shawn enjoyed the evening with his friends away from the tension that filled the hotel. He was excited about his new venture and it was difficult for him not to share the information with Ray and Jim. He rode quietly in the car thinking about Boris and the trip to East Germany.

Bright sun and crisp, cold air made it a perfect day for bobsled practice. Their final practice day was a low-key experience. The athletes were visibly nervous and Shawn felt their apprehension keenly. The coaches deliberately allowed the athletes to slack off because rest was crucial to allow them time to recuperate from the strenuous practice schedule. It also improved their state of mind and allowed them to peak mentally for the upcoming race.

Practice was winding down when Shawn saw Joe Sweeney and another man standing next to the track. He hadn't noticed their arrival. As usual, the only people from the association were Jim, Jason, and himself. Professor Bodynski had been helping but left to prepare his sled so Jim and Shawn could take a couple more test rides when practice was over.

Shawn walked down the path next to the track to greet Joe and the stranger. "Good morning, Joe. I hope you're enjoying the bobsleds." Shawn looked closely at the other man, suspecting he might be another CIA agent.

"I'm amazed at how fast they really go. I've seen them on television and they look fast, but seeing them up close is breathtaking." Joe was visibly impressed.

"I have to test drive the Syracuse University sled. Would you like to take a ride?"

"No way!" Joe shook his head. "I'm very happy to just watch. Oh, by the way, let me introduce you to an associate of mine. Walter Shapnek."

Shawn reached out to shake Walter's hand. "I'm pleased to meet you."

"Likewise. Joe has told me a lot about your background and I'm impressed"

"I hope he only told you the good things," laughed Shawn.

"They were all good," reassured Walter, smiling. "Joe spoke very well of you and your work. What's your schedule like for tonight?"

Shawn realized immediately that Walter was, indeed, the CIA agent Joe had discussed with him. "I don't have any plans. I can meet you whenever it's convenient for both of you."

Joe turned his head in thought for a moment before replying, "Let's take a ride to Marburg and have dinner. The hour and a half ride each way will give us plenty of time to talk without worrying about anyone overhearing us."

"Do you want me to meet you some place downtown so the athletes won't see you pick me up at the hotel?"

"That's a good idea. I'm at the same hotel but in Room 315. Do you remember where you met me the last time at the Bavarian?"

"Yea. I know the Bavarian. What time is good?"

"You tell me?"

"How about seven o'clock?"

"That's good. Just come up to my room, Walter, and I'll be already."

They said good-bye and Shawn returned to the bobsled's start area.

He looked down the track and both men were gone.

Shawn finished his work at the start area and walked over to the equipment shed to check on the Syracuse sled. Professor Bodynski was going over the sled once more to be sure everything was working properly. He didn't want another problem with the steering.

"How's the sled looking, Ray?" Shawn looked at the sled curiously.

"I think everything is adjusted correctly. You shouldn't have any trouble today. Having a brand new spring collapse the way this one did is really a freak thing."

"I hope so. Jim and I can't take too many more rides like that one. Man, I'll never forget that as long as I live."

"How long before you and Jim will be ready for another test run?"

"We can go now if you're ready?"

"I'm ready. Could you give me a hand pushing the sled to the start area?" Ray and Shawn easily pushed the sled over to the start area. It was loaded on a small flat-bed cart with wheels that made the effort much smoother. When they reached the start line they lifted the sled off the cart and placed it into line with other sleds that were still being used for practice

. Jason Pierce watched everything carefully although he did not interfere or make any comments. It was obvious from the expression on his face that he was not in favor of them testing the research sled. He had made it very clear to anyone who would listen that it was a waste of time and money to try and improve bobsled equipment. He quietly muttered something under his breath and turned to walk down the wooded path that connected the bobsled track to the hotel.

"That's a sign of confidence!" laughed Shawn pointing at Jason's disappearing back.

"Why do you say that?" Jim was laughing, anticipating that Shawn was going to say something funny about Jason.

"Jason must assume we won't have a problem that would cause an accident otherwise he would stay to watch."

"You've got that right." Jim got serious. "It's people like him in the association that prevent us from winning Olympic medals."

"You should work with me in the military," chuckled Shawn. "We've got more than our fair share. The military simply moves people who are really stupid from job to job. Officers are often promoted and transferred just to get rid of them. These jerks develop incredible records because their former superiors give them excellent job reviews to encourage them to move on to another position someplace else." Jim knew Shawn was deadly serious but he still felt incredulous.

"I guess that's life in general," laughed Ray, the eternal optimist. "I see the same thing at the university."

Suddenly, it was their turn. Shawn and Jim put their helmets on and began sliding the sled to the start line. They did not mention the initial test ride although it was on both their minds. Once the sled was placed on the ice, Ron Harrison came over to help them. He held the brake and Shawn climbed into the driver's seat. Once he was adjusted in the sled, Jim got in behind him.

They wished each other good-luck and put their goggles into place. Feeling confident that the steering problem would not arise again, Shawn asked Ron to give them a good push to enable the sled to go faster this time.

He felt Ron's powerful push as the sled started down the run. His adrenaline began pumping as they moved along the slick ice in the direction of the first turn. Once they were past the first timing light Shawn tugged slightly on the steering ropes, first to the right and then to the left. The sled responded normally so he relaxed the tension on the steering ropes to be sure the sled would track in a straight line. The sled reacted properly, so he put tension back on the lines as he got near the first turn.

He maneuvered the sled into the turn's approach area and passed through the first turn with no problem, just as they had in the test run. As the sled snaked its way down the track, successfully manipulating each turn, they rapidly approached full speed. Shawn estimated they were going about eighty-five mph as the sled neared the twelfth turn. Responding perfectly, the sled slipped through the turn and Shawn could feel the pressure as the speed increased. He smiled, confident, knowing that he had complete control of the sled, something he did not have on this part of the track on their last trip.

Just ahead was the entrance to the famous 'Kreisel' turn. Shawn directed the sled into a different angle than it had taken on its first trip. He wanted to see if the sled would continue to build speed if he drove on what is called 'the edge.' This is an imaginary position on each turn that will produce the optimum speed. Many drivers stay away from this because of the high risk. Should they go beyond the edge the sled will instantly tip over and crash.

Riding the edge produced incredible pressure from the G-forces on Shawn but he maintained complete control. As they shot out of the "Kreisel" he estimated their speed was well into the nineties and gaining as they continued through the remaining turns. They passed the finish line and Shawn knew the sled was a winner. Athletes lined the finish ramp and waved their hands in triumph to congratulate them. Jim applied pressure on the brakes and the sled slowed as it went up the finish ramp. Once Shawn drove out of the track onto the finish platform Jim stopped the sled. They eagerly climbed out of the sled and began giving high-fives to the athletes who had surrounded them. Shawn and Jim looked at each other and smiled in triumph.

They returned the sled to the start area where Ray was waiting. He was thrilled with the sled's success. Shawn and Jim took turns excitedly recounting each inch of the trip. They were convinced that the professor had created a dynamic, competitive sled with definite Olympic possibilities. Now came the difficult problem. How would they ever convince the association officials to use the sled and not purchase new Italian sleds from Nino Casatelli's friends? Friends that Shawn suspected were giving Nino and Lester kick-backs.

Shawn and Jim decided to take another test ride since the track was still open for another thirty minutes. Ray took a few minutes and checked the sled just to make sure everything was still in proper adjustment. The second ride down the bobsled track was just as successful as the first. They returned to the start area and put the test sled back into the air cargo crate so it could be shipped back to the United States. On the way back to the hotel, Ray and Jim made plans to go out to dinner and celebrate the sled's success. Shawn reluctantly excused himself. He had to meet with Joe Sweeney and Walter Shapnek. He explained that he had made previous plans for dinner with Joe Sweeny but that he could eat lunch with them.

After a lunch of cold cuts and the everlasting pork, Shawn took a walk downtown to release some of the excitement that had built up inside him as a result of the two good bobsled rides. He was thrilled that Ray's work had been so successful, and relaxed by spending several hours shopping for a gift for Angela. He couldn't find anything that he thought his wife might like so he returned to the apartment to get ready for dinner.

The sun disappeared behind the mountains that encompassed Winterberg and the temperature dropped considerably. Shawn put a heavy sweater on under his jacket and left the apartment. He walked across the parking lot and noticed all the rental cars were gone. He assumed the officials were off to another fancy restaurant courtesy of the bobsled association. Ron Harrison came out of the hotel and waved to him.

"Hi, Coach." Ron was friendly but tended to be distant at times. A characteristic that was also one of Shawn's.

"How's it going, Ron?" Shawn admired the blue Gortex running suit that Ron wore.

"I'm going to take a short run to get rid of some of the tension. I get this way the night before competition."

"A slow jog will help. Don't run too hard or too long. You need to rest up for the morning. Better yet, why not take a walk to the bobsled track and back?"

"That sounds better," Ron agreed. "I'll walk up to the track and maybe take a walk downtown."

"Tell you what, Ron. Take your walk downtown now and I'll go with you since that's where I'm headed."

They walked down the street and Shawn gave some tips to Ron about how to relax before competition. They reached the Bavarian Hotel and Shawn said good-night. He went upstairs to Room 315 where Walter and Joe were waiting for him.

They were dressed as casually as Shawn was, in sweaters and pants. Joe and Walter put their overcoats on and they left the hotel and walked across the parking lot to Joe's rental car. During the drive to Marburg, Walter frequently turned toward the back seat where Shawn was sitting and asked him a lot of personal questions. He wanted to learn as much about Shawn as possible. As an experienced CIA agent, Walter knew they would take many risks during the next few months. It was crucial for him to know how Shawn would think and react under pressure. Their lives would depend on it.

Shawn recounted some of his experiences in Europe while he had worked for the agency. Walter was impressed when he heard some of the incidents that Shawn was involved in during the Berlin crisis. Walter thought it was interesting that they would be working behind the famed Berlin Wall, built in 1961 when Shawn was working in Europe.

"When will the Olympic trials be over?" asked Walter.

"The final race to select the 4-man teams will take place tomorrow and

Sunday. Everyone is scheduled to leave on Tuesday for the United States."

"Does anyone know you're not leaving with the group?"

"Not yet. Joe told me not to say anything. I haven't told my wife or my people at work."

"Don't worry about work. Joe took care of the military." Walter smiled. "I guess you work for quite a witch. When I talked to our people who made arrangements with the Department of Defense they were laughing about her."

"Walter, you have no idea what it's like working for someone like her."

"Is her supervisor the character that the general said would never become a rocket scientist?"

"Yup. Our Colonel Fowlkes will never make it as a rocket scientist. What's frightful is that someday he'll be promoted to a full colonel. They'll keep moving him around just to get rid of him and the easiest way is to promote him into another job."

"I guess he made quite an impression with your commanding general. He remarked to our contact in the Department of Defense that Fowlkes is a real dork."

"He sure is. I miss Fowlkes, but not much," laughed Shawn, sarcastically.

The dark sky gradually became illuminated by city lights and they knew Marburg was close. Snow began to fall as they approached the large city. They located the restaurant without any difficulty and Joe eased the car into a parking spot.

During dinner their conversation stayed away from the *IceSpy* project and they talked about casual events. Joe and Walter were both very interested in the bobsled association officials. Shawn amused them with outrageous stories that were true.

They studied the menu but Shawn was determined to order roast beef, no matter what else was offered. He really did not care what type or how it was prepared as long as it was not pork. The meal was excellent and when they were finished with dinner all three had a cup of coffee. They decided not to have dessert and left before the snow had a chance to accumulate too deep on the highway.

Joe drove out of the parking lot and Walter turned to continue his conversation with Shawn in the back seat. "I want you to pack all the belongings that you won't need and send them back with the team. What type of suitcase do you have?"

"I have my military B-4 bag and a couple of large bobsled equipment bags."

"Send everything back that even remotely looks military. You only need the one equipment bag and make sure it has bobsled written all over it." Walter thought for a moment and asked, "Can you keep your apartment for another week?"

"I'm sure I can. Why?"

"While we're in East Germany we can use that address and leave some of our belongings behind so the KGB will find them. It'll help us to have a place for them to check and it will back up our story about being there on bobsled business."

"How will the KGB know we're in East Germany?"

"When we go through the check point at the border we'll have to list an address. The East Germans will give the KGB our address in Winterberg before we leave the check point."

"Make sure that any identification from the military is sent back with your personal belongings," added Joe. "When you get to the border crossing you'll only need your passport to apply for a visa to enter their country."

The snow continued to fall for the rest of the way back to Winterberg. They diligently discussed their trip to East Germany and the meeting with Boris. They agreed that time would be their greatest problem in helping Boris and his wife plus her parents to escape. Walter shared some of the proposed plans that were being considered to get Boris out of the Soviet Union.

It was well past midnight when Joe and Walter dropped Shawn off at the hotel. Shawn noticed that the only rental car in the parking lot was the Volkswagen bus. Shawn thought about Jason, however thick-headed he might be, he had enough sense not to stay out drinking all night. Since the press would be at the bobsled track in the morning he knew the officials would also be there, nursing hangovers, as usual.

Shawn stood by the front door for a few minutes before entering. He enjoyed the midnight quiet. He pulled back into the shadows when a car approached and parked next to Jason's. Lester and Nino climbed drunkenly out of the Mercedes. Shawn quickly hid behind large evergreen shrubs planted in front of the apartment building. The two officials were laughing and bragging about the evening's conquests with some young German girls. They passed by Shawn's hiding place and never looked in his direction as they disappeared inside the building.

Shawn waited a few minutes before walking over to Lester's rental car. The overhead street light let off enough glow to enable Shawn to see clearly. He peered into the car and saw a couple of shopping bags in the rear seat. They were from a store in Switzerland. Lester and Nino usually spent a lot of time in Switzerland whenever they came to Europe to watch the team practice or compete. Lester always said the trips to St. Moritz and Zurich were strictly for business, looking for possible marketing opportunities.

He went upstairs to the apartment and went to bed. The next two days would be busy and stress-filled. As he drifted off to sleep he thought about Ron Harrison and wondered again if he was the FBI undercover agent. He liked Ron and hoped that he would make the Olympic team.

The next morning Shawn was awakened by the alarm clock buzzing in his ear. Normally he was up before the alarm rang but this morning he was still tired from staying out so late with Joe and Walter. He climbed out of bed and entered the bathroom. He turned the shower on and when the water was steaming hot he stepped into the stall, letting it wake him. It always took a few minutes for the temperature to reach its peak. Closing his eyes he stood under the head and let the warm stream of water soothe his back while he thought about his trip to East Germany with Walter.

Shawn finished getting dressed and put on his team jacket. He left to meet Jim Bogdan for their usual breakfast get together. It had become a pleasant morning ritual for them to eat with the athletes and chat with them about the day's training. The dining room was busy as most of the athletes were up earlier than usual. Shawn knew they were tense about the race that would begin later in the morning. This would be their last chance to make the Olympic team. He knew who should be selected for the 4-man teams if the trials were conducted properly. Vince Capobianco placed fifth in the 2-man finals and his chances for winning in the 4-man race were even less likely unless Lester and Nino did something shady.

They sat down with Professor Bodynski who was eating his breakfast alone. "How was your dinner last night, Shawn?" The professor was smiling and Shawn wondered if he suspected that Joe and Walter were with the CIA.

"It was great. We took a ride to Marburg which gave us a lot of time to get caught up on old times." Shawn knew that Ray had done some work for the agency many years ago and might be aware of what they were doing. "You missed the parade last night."

"What parade?"

"Lester and Nino returning from their shopping binge in Switzerland," Shawn grinned and continued. "This was their last chance to shop and do some sightseeing before they go back to the States."

"You know why they came back from Switzerland?" Jim stated, wrinkling his nose. "The press will be here again. They're such a bunch of phony bastards."

"They went out drinking after they finished shopping. I know because I saw them when they came in at midnight," said Shawn.

"We saw Roger, Wilbur, and John sitting at a bar in downtown Winterberg last night," replied Jim.

The professor laughed, "Roger's eyes were so glazed over he almost didn't recognize us. What a cast of characters! For all we know they all might have been on drugs."

Shawn looked around the dining room and noticed Jason was missing. "Ray, did you see Jason this morning?"

"Not yet."

"I think he's still in his apartment going over the schedule for today," Jim suggested. "You never know what's going on with these characters. John Chapadeau might be going over Jason's expenses looking for extra money for the officials to use."

While they were talking about the officials, Jason came into the dining room and sat at their table. "Here's the schedule for the weekend's race. Everything's all set. I've just got to brief the athletes once again on the rules and what has to be done with their equipment after the race."

"What's going on with their equipment?" asked Shawn.

"They have to get it ready for shipping on Monday."

"Why tell them now? The only thing they should have on their minds right now is qualifying. Give them the shipping instructions on Monday morning." Shawn was getting tired of Jason's stupidity and would be glad when the trials were over.

"That's a good idea, Shawn. I'll do it Monday morning."

Jason got up and walked around the room chatting with the athletes.

→ *Ice Spy*

Shawn, Jim and Ray finished their breakfast and left for the track. On the way they discussed the various officials and the corruption within the organization.

German spectators were already in the bleachers to watch the Americans select their Olympic team when they reached the track. Though bobsledding remains a relatively unknown sport in North America it is very popular in Europe and attracts large crowds of spectators. Jim and Shawn went to the start area to prepare the ice and Ray went to help the athletes.

Shawn noticed Roger Ferris, the association's director, had arrived at the track with John Chapadeau, the treasurer. He realized that he had not seen either for over a week and wondered why they were still hanging around in Germany. The press arrived at the track and the rest of the association officials seemed to come out of the woodwork to make themselves available to reporters.

Shawn and Jim walked to the start area where Jason was talking with Nino Casatelli and Lester Fetor. Jason saw them and rushed over immediately. He took them to the parking area where he could speak in private. "We're having a small change in the 4-man race this weekend." Jason looked down at his clipboard as if reading from something written there and avoided eye contact with either of them. "Nino and Lester have volunteered to help us at the start area."

"In other words, you're ditching me and Jim?" Shawn was astounded, then furious. "No shit, Jason. What do you want us to do?" Shawn was having a difficult time controlling his emotions.

"We really need to have you guys give the athletes a hand?" Jason was flippant, nervous about Shawn's obvious anger.

"Let me guess, Jason." Shawn glared at Jason as his anger continued to build. "Nino and Lester want to be at the start area so they may chat with reporters throughout the morning?"

"No. That's not true. They simply want to help."

"Where have these assholes been for the past six weeks?" Jim asked, staring at Jason intently, waiting for his reply.

"What do you expect me to do? I'm no different than you guys. They run the organization."

"Well, I'll tell you what, Jason. I guess we should be happy that these bastards are actually doing something besides spending the association's money. Don't forget to tell them that it takes about an hour after the race to pick up all the equipment. And don't look for me to do it." Shawn turned abruptly and walked away.

He needed to get away from the entire group for a few minutes just to calm down so he took a walk back to the hotel. The walk helped calm him down and as he went through the parking lot, John Chapadeau and Wilbur Hippenbecker were driving in with John's rental car. He walked past them without even looking up.

He went back to the apartment and laid down on his bed to think about what was taking place. There was no reason for Nino and Lester to do what they did unless they did not want the press talking to Jim or himself. That must be it! They were both jealous because the press had quoted him and Jim after the previous weekend's race when they selected the 2-man teams for the

Olympics. Both Nino and Lester had followed the press around during the race like small puppy dogs offering information, yet none of the papers quoted them.

Shawn lay in bed, deep in thought, and was staring at the ceiling when a knock on his door startled him. He went to the door and when he opened it, Professor Bodynski was standing there, looking concerned.

"Come in, Ray."

"What are you doing here?"

"I'm so pissed at these bastards that I don't even want to be around them."

"Don't let them get away with what they are trying to do. You and Jim are the only hope these athletes have that these trials will be conducted fairly."

"What are you talking about?"

"Come on, Shawn. These two characters are taking over for two reasons. One is to get their names in the paper and the other is an attempt to control the race to give an unfair advantage to their favorite team."

Shawn had not thought about them trying to fix the race to make it possible for a team they favored to win. "I was so pissed at them that I didn't think about them cheating. You're right, Ray. Let's go back up and watch them."

When they arrived at the track, the race was about to begin. Shawn noticed Jim talking with Lester and the German track officials so he walked over to listen to what was going on. Jim had complained that the start lines were unsafe. Each morning before a race or practice, small crevices must be cut in the ice to guide the sleds in a straight line until the athletes are in the sled. Lester and Nino had not prepared the track. Jim stopped working on the groves when Jason called him over to the parking lot. He was so mad that he never returned to the start area to finish making the groves.

"The race will not start until the groves are properly made according to the International Bobsled regulations." The German official looked at Lester and pointed to the tool used to make the start groves. "Grab the start line tool and get going or we will not have a race today."

Jim walked away with a satisfied grin on his face. A reporter walked up and asked him what was going on? Jim explained what Nino and Lester had done and that it might be a while since neither of them knew how to make the groves. They would have to learn the hard way in front of reporters and a crowd of spectators. It appeared that the athletes were also amused.

Shawn located Ron Harrison and went over to help him. Ron greeted him cheerfully and pointed at the runners on the sled next to them. "Coach, make sure that Nino wipes the runners of all sleds each time they go down the track with the same cloth."

Shawn knew that Nino and Lester were behind Vince Capobianco's team. Ron said, "I suspect he'll wipe everyone's runners with a cloth that has acetone on it but will use another identical cloth that has no chemicals on it when he wipes Vince's runners? He'll do whatever it takes to get his team to win."

The runners on each sled must be carefully wiped with acetone to remove any substance that someone might put on the runners to make them slippery and give the team an unfair advantage. Shawn knew what Lester and Nino would do to help Vince.

→ *Ice Spy*

"You're right and this doesn't surprise me at all. Don't worry. I'll fix that right now."

Shawn went to the equipment garage and got a clean cloth and hurried back to the start area. Nino and Lester were still down below the track's start area desperately trying to make the start groves in the ice. Two German track officials were watching them carefully to make sure the groves were done properly. He could not help laughing at the new situation.

Nino's can of acetone was sitting in an equipment bag. The bag also held a cloth, soaked in acetone, and a second cloth in a plastic bag. Shawn opened the plastic bag and smelled the strange smell of chemicals on the cloth, just as Ron suspected. Shawn soaked the new cloth with acetone and replaced the cloth soaked with the unknown chemical with the new cloth. He put the tainted cloth into a trash barrel behind the equipment garage.

He walked up to Ron who was still polishing his sled. "Don't worry about the runners." Shawn nodded his head in the direction of Vince Capobianco's sled that was next to them.

"What did you do, Coach?" Ron grinned as he waited for the answer.

"Nino had a cloth soaked with some chemical and I replaced it with another identical cloth soaked with acetone."

They laughed so hard that the professor came over to find out what was so funny. Shawn repeated the story and they roared with laughter then he and the professor went to the start area where the race was finally getting ready to begin.

"Must every sled have all the runners wiped with acetone?" Shawn asked the German official in front of Nino and several reporters.

"Of course." The official looked at Shawn, wondering why he was asking such a stupid question. He smiled with disdain and said, "They must be wiped while I watch."

Shawn smiled and walked away. He turned and noticed Nino and Lester whispering to each other. Good, he thought to himself. They got beat at their own game, thanks to the professor urging him to come back to the track.

The weekend racing went on without any more problems. Ron's team placed second in the 4-man just as he did in the 2-man race and would represent the United States in the Olympics as USA II. Vince Capobianco's team finished seventh.

Jim and Shawn made plans to go out to dinner that night with the professor to celebrate the completion of the Olympic trials. It had been a long six weeks for everyone. Now Shawn had another venture to prepare for and he thought about Boris and their trip into East Germany.

Chapter Sixteen

→ *Ice Spy*

Winterberg, West Germany

Shawn bid an emotional and fond farewell to the athletes Tuesday morning as they boarded the bus that would take them to the airport in Frankfurt. He talked briefly with Jim Bogdan and Professor Bodynski before they got on board. He watched the bus driver shut the door and slowly ease the bus out of the Hotel Zur Sonne parking lot. They were fun to be with and he would sorely miss them. The association officials were visibly upset because Vince Capobianco did not win an Olympic berth with the bobsled team and they had left Winterberg a day earlier.

He suddenly felt very alone as he walked through the cold morning air back up to his apartment. The fact that he was not very popular with his wife added to his depression. He had called Angela the evening before and, just as he expected, she was not happy about his decision to stay longer. Although Shawn had never given her exact details about the mission, Angela knew what he was involved in and was worried.

On Monday evening, Ron Harrison went to dinner with Shawn and told him that he was the undercover agent the FBI used to infiltrate the association. Ron told him that Vince Capobianco's father owned a very large corporation in the United States. Lester and Nino were trying to help Vince make the team so his father would donate a large amount of money to sponsor his son's Olympic efforts.

Shawn told Ron the story about the suitcase full of cash that John Chapadeau had in the apartment the night he arrived in Winterberg. Ron agreed that he also suspected some of the association officials used their Olympic status to smuggle cash into Europe to deposit into Swiss bank accounts. They compared notes about the Swiss bank accounts and Jason's problems with Lester and his cronies.

Ron's investigation developed some significant information involving a Swiss bank account. He overheard a discussion between Lester and John while wearing a special listening device in his ear enabling him to hear their private conversation while he was out of normal hearing distance. This took place in the hotel dining room during breakfast when they were discussing their money laundering operation for several businesses owned by organized crime members. Murphy and Harrison agreed to talk more about the misuse of associations funds when they were at the Olympics in Calgary.

He glanced at his watch. It was ten-fifteen. Joe Sweeney and Walter Shapnek were coming to his apartment at noon to begin making plans for the trip to East Germany to meet with Boris Yegorov. Shawn looked around the apartment to make sure he sent everything home that might connect him with the military. He understood the importance of not allowing the East Germans or the KGB to discover that association. If he was caught and identified as military personnel he could be imprisoned as a spy or even worse, shot. Getting caught as a spy would create extremely negative and embarrassing publicity.

Sitting at the kitchen table, he thought about some assignments he worked on as a CIA agent nearly thirty years ago. He remembered Joe Sweeney's concerns about him being away from the espionage business too long and allowing his guard to drop. He would have to stay focused all the time and not trust his instincts to do it for him.

Shawn knew the hotel's wing was entirely empty so it would be a quiet place to meet the two CIA agents. They arrived promptly at noon. They removed their coats and sat down at the kitchen table with Shawn. Walter looked at Shawn and said, "Give us a couple of minutes to inspect your apartment. While we're in East Germany it's very possible that the KGB will search this place. We'll go through everything just as they would."

They thoroughly searched the entire apartment, including under the rug and mattress, "Let's see your wallet." Walter was all business and did not give any indication that he was simply testing Shawn.

He looked through Shawn's wallet and pulled out a receipt for clothing Shawn had purchased at the military clothing store.

"What's this?" Walter handed Shawn the receipt.

"A receipt for some clothing I have on lay-away at the base."

"Put it in the mail."

Joe looked at Shawn and grinned. "All in all, I'm impressed, Shawn. You did an excellent job otherwise."

Walter extended his hand to Shawn. "Welcome aboard, partner. We'll make *IceSpy* one of the agency's most successful espionage ventures in years."

"Let's take a ride so we can talk without worrying about anyone overhearing us." Shawn looked at him curiously. Walter explained, "I don't want to take any chances, even with the cleaning people." Without waiting for an answer, Walter picked up his coat and walked toward the door. Joe and Shawn grabbed their coats and quickly followed him down the hall and stairs to the parking lot.

"This building feels like a morgue with everyone gone." Shawn looked back at the apartment doors that were still ajar. "I won't miss the rowdiness of Roger Ferris and his pals, though. The peace and quiet will be great."

"You won't be here long enough to get used to it. We leave in the morning," commented Walter shortly.

They got into Joe's rental car and drove away from Winterberg. Walter continued talking to Shawn about what the trip to East Germany would entail and what they had to accomplish.

"Where do we cross the border?" Shawn wondered if it might be one of the border crossings he had gone through when he had worked for the agency.

"I plan to cross at Witzenhausen. I went through that particular border my last time and they should still remember me."

Shawn nodded. "I crossed there years ago. It's probably all changed now."

"Don't bet on it. About the only changes these people have made are higher and stronger fences. They don't put any money into the buildings at the borders."

"Have the arrangements with Boris been confirmed?" interrupted Joe.

"I talked with Fred Unser two days ago. Our agent in Riga sent word to him that Boris would meet us at the Verzuckung Tavern in Altenburg Wednesday evening at eight."

"How did he know which tavern to select?" Shawn wondered if the tavern was near the bobsled track in Altenburg. Bobsledding seemed to be a great cover for working behind the iron curtain.

"I told him when I was in Riga."

Joe drove them back to the apartment at the Hotel Zur Sonne. He parked in the parking lot, giving Walter and Shawn more time to discuss their plan to meet with Boris.

"Shawn, if you remember nothing else, remember this. Don't ever let your guard down and you'll be all right. You're working with our best. They don't get any sharper than Walter. I'll see you when you get back to the States."

"I'll pick you up around eight in the morning. Bring along enough clothing for two or three days in case we need to stay." Walter reached out and shook Shawn's hand. "Get a good night's sleep."

Shawn went inside and packed a few items he would need the next morning. It seemed strange for him to have nothing to do. For the past six weeks, he and Jim had been swamped with work, and suddenly, he was bored. He walked over to the chair next to the window and stared out at the mountains. He folded his arms on his chest and thought about the weekend events.

Shawn smiled as he thought about how they had intervened to prevent Nino and Lester's scheme to help Vince Capobianco win. He wondered how many other times these characters had fixed races. He knew Lester and Nino would be working to get him removed from his position as a volunteer coach the moment they got off the plane in Canada. He chuckled, it had been worth it to expose the bastards for what they are. It might take time, but the day would come when the FBI completed their investigation. At that moment, all the athletes would become winners.

Shawn spent the rest of the day lolling around the apartment. He decided to go out for dinner at a small restaurant that he had discovered during his many walks around Winterberg. He enjoyed eating at the Gerwitscher restaurant whenever he was alone during the past six weeks, which was not often. The dark bread, knockwurst, sauerkraut, and German-style potato salad were delicious and he savored each bite. He took his time eating while he thought about some of the events that took place during the Olympic trials. He took a long walk after dinner to work off the calories before returning and going to bed.

Shawn was ready to leave long before Walter arrived. He was pleasantly surprised to see Walter driving a new black Porsche. Walter eased the car out of the parking lot and onto the highway leading away from Winterberg.

"Do you have your passport and Olympic credentials?" Walter did not want any last minute problems at the border.

"I have everything, including a supply of Olympic bobsled pins we can give away."

"Good deal. The border guards are always looking for gifts. They'll love the pins."

"Do you have a way to contact the agent in Riga to be sure Boris is still coming?"

"No. He can contact us outside of the Soviet Union, but there's no way for us to reach him."

Shawn nodded, "I checked around one more time to be sure there wasn't anything we might have overlooked. I don't like this, Walter." His tone was worried.

"What are you talking about?"

"If they find out that I'm on active duty in the military, they can shoot me as a spy."

"Give me a break. What do you think they'll do if they find out we're working for the CIA?" Walter knew Shawn was on edge about getting started with the mission. "Get your mind set. You are here to conduct bobsled business." He was confident that Shawn's apprehension would disappear when they reached the border.

"I know," Shawn replied. "It's been a long time for me and I'll get into the swing of things soon. How long before we get to the border?"

"We're about forty minutes away. The last time I came through, one of the guards tried to shake me down for samples of orthopedic sport braces that the company I represent sells."

"How do you give out samples of orthopedic braces?"

"I don't. There are no such samples," laughed Walter.

The Porsche seemed to be flying and when Shawn looked at the speedometer, it was reading 150 kilometers per hour. He was startled at how little he felt the speed, silently calculating that they were traveling over ninety mph.

Walter continued, "I told him that I was out and gave him an American twenty dollar bill. That's more than all the German marks he earns in three weeks. I hope he's at the border because he'll remember me."

They rode in silence the rest of the way to the border. Shawn enjoyed the countryside and the great view they were getting on the mountain road. He loved riding in the Porsche because it reminded him of his Corvette.

Witzenhausen, East Germany

"The crossing is just ahead." Walter pointed to the large sign on the side of the road.

Shawn looked straight ahead of him and, in the distance, he could see the fence and the guard building. "How long do you think it will take for us to pass through the check- point?"

"I normally figure at least two hours. Sometimes it might take a little longer. When I gave the twenty bucks to the border guard it only took about an hour and a half."

"Should we offer them money again?"

"No. Not unless they ask for something like samples. Otherwise they might arrest us. We have to let them make the first move to be sure the guard is crooked. Don't ever take a chance because the wrong guard can make your life a world of hell."

"I won't say anything. If you want the Olympic pins just tell me."

"Good. I suspect they'll come in handy because they should be considered a gift and not a bribe. The guards should want the pins, especially since we're involved with the Olympics."

Ice Spy

"What will they look for?"

"Who knows?" Walter shrugged. "The majority of the time spent here will be to make out the visa which will allow us into the country. Remember, no matter what happens, we are only meeting Boris because I'm trying to sell both of you orthopedic sport braces. The guards might try to separate us. They'll tell each of us that the other person has confessed to doing something different than we've claimed." Walter looked very serious and said quietly, "I'd die before I did that, so don't let them try and fool you."

"I won't. I remember the goodguy/badguy routine."

Walter was pleased with Shawn's intuitiveness. "You'll be all right."

Shawn was still absorbing all that Walter had just told him as he slowed the Porsche down to twenty mph. He eased the car up to the guards standing in the road. There were a few cars and Shawn hoped it might not take too long to get the visa. The guard raised his hand and gestured for Walter to stop. Walter rolled down his window and greeted the guard in German. The guard was a young man in his mid twenties. He had a strong German face with bright blue eyes and neatly trimmed blonde hair. He instructed Walter to pull the car into a parking spot next to the guard building.

Walter drove into the parking spot and shut the engine off. He waited for the guard to come over and give them further instructions. Shawn was a bit startled when a second guard knocked on his window told them to get out of the car and go inside with their passports.

Inside the stone building, a wood-burning, metal-barreled stove overheated the room. Walter and Shawn, escorted by the two unfriendly guards, walked up to the counter and placed their passports in front of the guard who was sitting behind the counter.

Walter glanced around the hot room looking for the familiar guard but did not see him. Shawn noticed that mirrors were located overhead and on the inside walls. He assumed the mirrors were two-way and that there were more guards observing them from the other side. The guard looked at the passports and a second guard came out of a room next to the counter. He told Walter to follow him and they exited through a side door.

Shawn waited silently for a few minutes until another guard came to get him. Shawn stood up and followed him into what appeared to be an interrogation room.

"Why do you wish to enter East Germany?" The guard stared at Shawn. He was eerily formal.

"I'm a coach with the American Olympic bobsled team and I've been asked to accompany Mr. Shapnek to meet with a Soviet coach who has been working with the East German team." Shawn spoke slowly and as formally as his interrogator.

"Who is the Soviet coach?"

"Boris Yegorov."

"What will you discuss with this man?"

"I'm going to share my experience using the orthopedic sport braces. If he buys these braces, Walter's company will donate some to the American team. I also hope that by helping the East German team, they will sell us bobsleds."

"Why do you expect them to sell you sleds?"

"Nobody in America builds sleds and the Italian sleds are inferior to the ones made in East Germany and the Soviet Union. The East German officials have told us that money is presently needed to help keep their team competitive."

"That doesn't mean that they will help their competitors."

"Equipment is becoming more and more standardized in Olympic and world cup competition. Soon, no single country will have an advantage because of equipment. Your superior methods of training athletes will become more important if your athletes are to continue winning."

"How do you compare your methods of training athletes to the East Germans?"

"There's no question that we're far behind your country's ability to train athletes." Shawn grinned at the serious guard. "I suspect your officials will not share any training secrets with me. Do you collect Olympic pins?"

"I have never seen an Olympic pin. Do you have any?"

"Yes." Shawn pulled out a handful of small, plastic-wrapped pins and gave the guard one. "Would the other guards like to have one also?"

"Perhaps. Could I have two? I have a son who dreams of being in the Olympics someday." Suddenly the guard was relaxed and friendly. A marked change from his first appearance.

"Of course," Shawn relaxed, too. "Here are several that you may share with whomever you wish."

"Thank you. Come with me. I will approve the visa for you and your friend."

The guard escorted Shawn out into the main room and pointed to a chair for him. The guard knocked on the door where Walter had been taken and went inside. Shawn worried that there might be a problem with Walter when suddenly the door opened and the two guards walked out with Walter. All three were smiling, which was a relief.

The guard behind the counter called them over and handed each their visa. He motioned to the front door. Shawn and Walter walked out to the Porsche and got into the car. They noticed that everything inside the car had been opened and was in disarray. The guards waved at them enthusiastically as they backed out of the parking lot.

Walter drove down the narrow road away from the crossing, very careful to keep his speed under the limit.

"You did just fine." Walter smiled and sighed with evident relief. "The guards were impressed with the Olympic bobsled pins."

"The guard started asking questions that were related to the sport. I felt that he would be excited about getting one."

"You were right and you used good judgment, Shawn. We'll be fine over here." Walter looked into his rearview mirror. "We have to watch for the KGB because I'm sure the guards have already reported to them that we've crossed the border."

Shawn fell asleep as Walter eased the Porsche along the twisting mountain road. It amazed Walter that his companion could fall asleep so quickly after all the excitement of the past few hours. Walter wished that he had the same ability as he pressed the throttle down abruptly thrusting the sports car up the mountain road over eighty miles an hour. The unexpected surge of power woke Shawn abruptly.

"What's wrong?"

"I'm not sure there's anything wrong, but another car has been following us for the past 20 kilometers. It looks like a red BMW. The KGB likes to drive BMWs in Europe, especially red ones. It apparently gives them a feeling of power since they don't have access to luxury cars in the Soviet Union that are worth anything."

"How far back are they?"

"Not too far. It may be nothing but we can't take a chance. In a few minutes we'll be in Weimar and I'll change directions to confuse them. We can double back and they'll think we went to Dresden. Boris will be followed also, but I would rather have to worry about one or two agents and not a group."

Walter slowed the car down and for the next few minutes expertly maneuvered the vehicle around the tight turns as they neared the top of the mountain. The road straighten out and Walter pressed the throttle to the floor and let the turbos thrust the Porsche down the highway at an incredible speed. Shawn gripped the over-head leather handle just above the passenger's window. His left hand tightly held on to the contoured side of his seat. Despite the extreme tension, he was thoroughly enjoying the ride.

A road sign up ahead told them that they were approaching Weimar. Walter slowed the car down to the posted speed limit and immediately turned off onto a side street. He drove down a few blocks and suddenly made a U-turn and parked against the curb. They silently watched the main street and within a few minutes a red BMW with two men raced through the small village in the direction of Dresden.

"I was pretty sure that they were KGB. Lets hope they continue on to Dresden."

Shawn was definitely impressed. He recalled Joe Sweeney's statement that Walter was the best. He was right. He had complete confidence in Walter and his anxiety was gone.

Walter waited for a few more minutes and started the car and drove up to the main street. They looked in the direction the BMW had gone. The street was empty so Walter pulled out into the opposite direction. He drove back up the mountain for about ten miles and turned onto a smaller road.

"We won't make good time on this road, but they'll never figure out where we went. I'm glad we had a head start, otherwise, it would have been difficult to lose them."

Walter drove for several miles until they reached Apolda, a typical small German village tucked away in the mountains. He pulled into a small restaurant's parking lot.

"I don't know about you, but I'm starved." Walter looked at Shawn and then his watch. "Let's get lunch and waste a little time since we don't have to meet Boris until eight and I don't want to be there too early."

"I'm so hungry I could eat a horse." Shawn almost said pork, but knew Walter would not get the reference.

They got out of the car and went inside the small pub to order lunch. Inside, it resembled a typical, small-town German pub. However, up close, Shawn realized that it was much less expensive and a neighborhood bar that rarely had outside visitors. The two Americans immediately attracted attention and even rude stares from the locals as they sipped their dark German beer.

Walter looked at his watch. "It's only two-thirty. We can stay here for about two hours and then take our time driving to Altenburg."

They relaxed and ate lunch. After the meal they enjoyed some coffee and chatted about the work Shawn had been doing as a bobsled coach. They were in no hurry. Finally, Walter looked up at the Black Forest coo-coo clock on the wall behind the bar. He motioned to Shawn that it was time to leave. He paid the waitress and within minutes they were back on the highway again. Walter drove slowly along the twisty mountain roads.

CHAPTER SEVENTEEN

→ *Ice Spy*

Lake Placid, New York

Sandra Wilson heard a loud commotion outside the bobsled office and got up from her desk to look out the window. Wilbur Hippenbecker and John Chapadeau were having an argument with Roger Ferris in front of the office. She shook her head in disgust and thought, "The troops are back." Now the office will switch from being an efficient operation back to the typical bobsled way. Work under Roger's direction was seldom productive. It frustrated her that she managed to complete the backlog of work Roger left unfinished and the office was now running smoothly. She also hated Roger fiercely because he was such a liar.

Sandra returned to her desk and when the trio walked into the office she looked up at them and said, "Welcome back. The association must be broke if you guys left Europe." The sarcasm in her voice left no doubt how she felt about them.

"Maybe you need a job change, Sandra," John remarked indifferently and walked past without even looking at her. Roger and Wilbur followed him into Roger's office.

"Why do you keep that old bitch working here?" John couldn't stand Sandra.

"We don't have any choice." Roger shut his office door and threw her a bird. "You know how much we owe Chester for legal services. As long as we owe him money we'll be stuck with his wife working in the office."

"She's all right. Her personality leaves a lot to be desired, but she's a good office manager." Wilbur nodded his head as if the gesture gave more credence to his statement.

"I wouldn't give a damn how much money I owed her husband. I wouldn't put up with her shit in my office for a minute." John stared at the wall separating them. Roger and Wilbur knew how much John hated Sandra.

"What time should I set up the board meeting for on Saturday, Wilbur?" Roger was hoping that Wilbur and John would leave so he could go to his apartment and get some rest. The jet-lag and lack of sleep in Europe had worn him down to near exhaustion.

"What board meeting?" Wilbur looked at him with a confused expression. "I don't want to drive back up here on Saturday."

"I thought Lester and Nino wanted a board meeting to evaluate Shawn's performance during the Olympic trials?"

"They're just blowing smoke because they're pissed that they got caught cheating. If we changed the manager and coaches this close to the Olympics, the athletes would hang all of us." Wilbur nodded his head again amusing Roger. Wilbur is always nodding his head he thought. "Just let it rest and they'll forget it until the Olympics."

"I don't like Shawn. He's nothing but trouble," John remarked as he put on his coat. "Wilbur, you should get rid of him and his professor friend, what's his name?"

"Ray Bodynski."

"Whatever. I'm out of here. I still have a five-hour drive before I get to New

York." John walked out of the office without saying good-bye to them.

"He's a pip." Roger laughed at John's rudeness and walked over to shut the door. "So typical of a New York City accountant. He wondered if the rumors about John and the mafia were true. They must be, otherwise, he wouldn't hang around Lester and Nino.

Wilbur picked up the phone receiver and dialed his office in Rochester. Roger left to give him privacy and decided to go over his backlog of work with Sandra. He did not look forward to reviewing with her all the business transactions that had taken place while he was away.

Weimar, East Germany

"You can be sure our KGB friends will be waiting for us in Altenburg." Walter glanced quickly over at Shawn and turned back to the road snaking up the mountain in front of them. The high-powered Porsche took the curves easily. "They'll go there to try and pick up our trail since it will be their only lead. They'll know our visas are for Altenburg."

"How do we avoid them?"

"We have to keep them confused and off track. There's an East German army camp at the extreme southern part of the village," Walter said quietly. "We'll park in a hotel parking lot near there and then walk down the street to meet Boris at the pub."

"You've never told me what we have to discuss with Boris," Shawn said, suddenly realizing that he really didn't know very much about why they were meeting with Boris.

"You understand the technology that he developed, don't you?"

"Joe Sweeney told me all about the alloy composite he is using in the bobsled runners," Shawn replied. He hesitated for a second before asking, "Why is it so difficult to get him out of the Soviet Union?"

"Getting him out isn't that big of a problem. The problem is getting his wife and her parents out. He won't give us the formula unless we get all of them out and into a protection program."

"Can the CIA do this?"

"It's all in place. Our mission today is to reassure Boris that we can change their identity and they can live out the rest of their lives in obscurity."

"Our trip seems to be such a high-risk. Wouldn't it be better to have the undercover agent in Riga explain this to him?"

"No," Walter shook his head. "The political situation in Latvia is very bad. Besides, I've built up a trusting relationship with Boris and he's uneasy with other people. That's another reason why we need you here. He knows you and there's a chance you may have to go to the Soviet Union alone to help him."

Shawn thought about what Walter had just said. He was getting into this much deeper than he had ever expected. "Exactly what do we want to accomplish today?"

"We'll only need a few minutes. I'll explain to him how the witness protection program works. He'll be paid enough for his technology so they can live the rest of their lives without being discovered. That's all he wants. I'll give

155

him some orthopedic sports braces to take to the East Germans just to make it look good." Walter pointed to a road sign giving the distance to Altenburg.

"If the KGB should come into the pub when we're with Boris we need to separate them."

"How?"

"If I signal you that it's time, I want you to leave by the back door. They'll assume you have something we don't want them to get and they'll follow you. I'll leave with Boris out the front after they've left. I can finish talking to him while we're walking back to the car."

"Seems simple enough," said Shawn and then asked, as an afterthought, "Where do I go after I go out the back door?"

"Go down the wooden steps and you'll come to the path I told you about. When you reach it, bear to the right. You must be very careful because the path is dug out of the hillside and it's very steep on the left side. The trees are very thick so it'll be completely dark. The path snakes along the side of the hill for about three miles."

"Thanks a lot. What do I do after three miles?"

"You only go about half of that distance. You'll see a break in the tree tops. By then, your eyes will be adjusted to the dark enough so that you'll notice a clearing. You'll see the power lines that go through the woods. When you reach this spot, start counting your steps. When you've gone about a hundred, hold out your right hand as far as you can reach while you're walking until you feel a wooden hand rail. This will lead up a long flight of stairs." Walter cautioned him, "Be very careful, the darkness will make your footing along the path difficult and dangerous."

"Then what?" Shawn asked anxiously.

"The stairs will lead you up and out of the woods onto a street corner. You'll be on the opposite end from where we left the car. Remember there's an East German army camp located on that corner so you'll have to move quietly. Go around the encampment and meet me at the car."

Shawn was listening intently to all these intricate instructions. He worried that he could get completely lost.

They soon reached Altenburg and drove through the small city looking for the red BMW. When Walter was confident the KGB agents hadn't arrived yet, he drove to the hotel where he had planned to park the car. He pointed out to Shawn where the stairs came up out of the woods from the path.

They watched the East German army camp for the next twenty minutes to see what kind of activity was taking place. It appeared to be quiet with very little movement within the camp. Walter explained that the army camp was a school to train army intelligence officers.

Looking at his watch Walter said, "It's nearly seven-thirty so let's start walking down to the pub. We're a little early and Boris will arrive at eight but that's all right. This will give the regulars some time to get used to our being there."

They got out of the car and walked quietly down the empty street. The sun had disappeared behind the mountains and the night's darkness was closing in very quickly. They passed by the army camp in the shadows and saw only one guard walking back and forth in front of the closed gate. Shawn noticed that the main street was parallel to the edge of the thick forest just as Walter had briefed him. He wondered how far below the top of the hillside the path ran along the forest.

They reached the pub and went inside to the back room. Walter sat in a booth facing the front so he could watch the bar and the entrance. Shawn sat down across from him and gazed around the room of the century-old pub. It was typical of old German pubs, dark and reeking of cigarette smoke. He looked at the rear door that Walter said he should leave by if the KGB agents located them and came to the pub. He resisted the temptation to get up and open the door to look out.

An old German man working as a waiter came over to get their order. Walter ordered two beers and turned to Shawn. "Make sure this one drink lasts you for the evening. We can't sit here without buying something and I don't want to let the alcohol influence us. One drink will be all right."

"Here he is," Walter motioned toward the door with his head.

Boris stood in the bar area of the pub and looked around until he saw Walter in the rear booth. He continued to glance around the room while he walked to the back room to join them. They stood up and shook hands with Boris. Shawn motioned for Boris to take the seat he had just vacated. Boris nodded his agreement and sat down. Shawn then moved into the empty spot next to Walter. He noticed the worried look on Boris's somber face.

The waiter came over and got Boris's order. While they waited, they talked about the trip to East Germany and deliberately made no mention about the purpose of this visit. Walter was attempting to relax Boris and allow the local patrons in the bar some time to get adjusted to having foreigners in the pub. Their conversation switched to bobsledding and Walter interpreted since Shawn couldn't speak German. Boris could speak some English but it was easier for him to speak in German.

Shawn studied Boris and thought about Joe Sweeney's statement that Boris looked and acted like a mad scientist. He was a very intense man with black piercing eyes and his medium yet strong build was typical of a Soviet. The stress lines on his face were so deep that Shawn thought sympathetically about the difficult past Boris and his family had endured. Latvians under Russian control had suffered unspeakably since their country was occupied.

After a while the German patrons in the bar area were more relaxed about the foreigners in the back room and ignored them. Walter felt confident that they could not be overheard and spoke quietly and slowly in English to Boris. Shawn listened very carefully to the conversation.

"We have made all the necessary arrangements to help you and your family live in obscurity after you arrive in America." Walter studied Boris's face to make sure he didn't appear to be confused about the English. Shawn noticed that Walter wasn't using contractions while speaking to Boris. He was enunciating very clearly for Boris' benefit.

Walter continued, "Our government has been doing this for several years with great success."

Yegorov questioned, "Your government has many others who defect? Yes?"

"No. We use this program to protect people who have helped our government convict gangsters who have committed very violent crimes. We call it the witness protection program."

Walter took his time explaining how the program worked and why the KGB wouldn't find out where they had relocated. Boris was pleased with the amount of monthly income the government would provide him for the technical information.

"When will your people come to get my family?" Boris looked around nervously. "We are still working on how to get you and your family out of the country. We want to get everyone out sometime during the next few months." Shapnek knew it would be very difficult to accomplish the mission during the next few months, but he didn't want to discourage Boris.

"The Russians would rather see me and my family dead than take a chance that your government would get this information."

Shawn watched Boris very intently. He was extremely nervous, yet determined to be successful in his personal fight with the Soviet government. Years of Russian control and mistreatment of the Latvian people had made them very bitter. Their facial expressions and sour personalities reflected years of Russian abuse. Boris was no exception.

"You must make this happen soon or we will be killed." Boris was having a difficult time controlling his emotions. "The money in the Swiss bank account is keeping us alive right now, but soon the KGB will get frustrated and start killing my family."

"We understand, Boris. My people are working very hard to make this happen." Walter knew the Soviet coach was under a lot of strain but was correct with his concerns. Time was running out. "We must be extremely careful when we do this. My government cannot afford to have this turn into an international incident. If we get caught in the process of secretly moving you and your family to America, the Russians would make it known to the world."

"I know, but I beg of you to move as fast as you can."

"We will, Boris," said Walter with confidence. "You must be patient and very careful. By early spring we will have all of you in America."

Walter knew the next few months would bring incredible pressure on Boris from the Russians. The KGB would watch him day and night. They might even physically harm his family. The KGB would continue to pressure Boris until they got the money.

Shawn noticed two men walking in the front door and nudged Walter's knee with his to get his attention. The men stood near the bar and looked carefully around the room. Soon one of the men nudged his partner and nodded his head in the direction of where they were sitting with Boris.

"Our KGB friends just found us so we should split up and leave," said Walter. Shawn recognized the signal and his heart began to pound. Walter told Boris, "Our undercover agent in Riga will contact you when we are ready to come for you. Shawn will be in Riga to help you."

"I hope it will be in time." Boris resisted the temptation to turn and look at them.

"They may question you about why we are here together." Walter pulled out some promotional brochures and samples from his briefcase and handed them to Boris. "Show them one of these. Do not forget to say that I am trying to sell these to the Soviet and East German bobsled associations."

"I know, I know. They might believe that is what you are doing, but they know what I am trying to do too," Boris's eyes looked like black hardened steel. "Time is short. You must hurry if your government wants the technical information. If they kill me, nobody gets it."

"I understand, Boris. We will continue to work very hard." Walter turned to Shawn. "I think we should confuse them. You know what to do, Shawn. One of them will follow you. I will sit with Boris for a while and then I will leave. I do not think the other will follow me and leave Boris alone. If he does I will try to lose him and will meet you at the car. Boris, you stay here for a few minutes and then leave."

"Good luck, Boris. I will see you in Riga." Shawn shook Boris' hand and slid out of the booth.

He walked out the back door of the restaurant taking one last look at the two KGB agents standing at the bar. They stood out like sore thumbs in the small German bar. He opened the door and stepped out into a foggy, damp night. The night air was heavy with moisture and he pulled his dark jacket close to his body. The steps leading to the path were made out of old, rickety wood and he wondered how many years the Germans had been using them.

Once he reached the path at the bottom of the steps he turned to the right and started walking briskly. The street lights and the taverns cast enough light onto the path to enable him to see where he was going. The left side of the walkway was very steep and when he stepped too close to the edge he could feel the ground give away. He stopped to let his eyes adjust to the darkness that totally engulfed the forest surrounding him. The darkness prevented him from calculating approximately how far and steep the embankment went. He was curious to know how far he would go if he fell? Thirty feet or three hundred feet. It did not matter now.

Looking back he could see the faint glimmer of light where the stairs leaving the tavern met the pathway. He slowed down to prevent slipping over the edge and to avoid brushing the undergrowth on his right side. Shawn couldn't tell if he was being followed and knew that if he was, noise from rubbing against the brush next to the path would alert them to how far he was ahead of them.

He picked up his pace once his eyes adjusted to the darkness and he gained more confidence walking on the mystical winding path. The darkness increased his confidence and he knew the agent couldn't see to shoot at him if he was following him. While he walked, he thought about other dangerous possibilities. Suddenly it occurred to him that the KGB agents may know about the path. He hoped not, but if they did and had seen Walter's car parked behind the hotel, they would know where he was going. They might wait for him near the East German army camp and not risk following him on the path.

His pace picked up as anxiety built inside him. Suddenly the ground under his left foot gave away and he slid over the edge of the path. He reached out, grasping the soil in an attempt to prevent him from going to the bottom of the steep embankment. His hands gripped the underbrush growing next to the path and stopped him from sliding any further. He paused for a minute to catch his breath before he tried to crawl back up onto the path. He reached the top and waited a moment to hear if anyone was nearby. Unable to hear anyone, he began walking.

The path continued to drop in elevation as it wound its way through the dark forest. The path made a long continual turn to the right and then it went to the left again. Suddenly he heard a loud noise in the darkness behind him. Whoever was following him must have also slid off the path behind him. He quickened his pace and kept his right hand out searching for brush so he wouldn't drift again too close to the edge.

Shawn lost all perception of the distance he had gone. He remembered Walter telling him to look for an opening in the forest where the trees had been cleared to make room for power lines. He sincerely hoped they would not be too far away. Stopping for a moment, he listened intently for footsteps coming along the path behind him. Hearing nothing, he suspected the agent had become more careful, like himself, and was moving more cautiously to prevent falling over the edge again. Maybe he was lucky and the agent went to the bottom of the steep hillside.

A short distance from where he stopped, Shawn saw the clearing in the sky where the power lines went through the forest. He was relieved to know he was traveling in the right direction. He reached out with his right hand and began to count his footsteps as Walter had instructed him. He thought that he might have missed the handrail when suddenly his hand touched the frail old wooden railing, Walter had described to him. Slowly and cautiously he proceeded up the stairs, trying to avoid making any noise in case the KGB agent was still following him. Shawn knew that his natural ability to travel silently through the forest helped him and was confident the agent would not locate the stairs.

Shawn had gone approximately twenty steps when he heard brush move below him past the stair entrance. He was certain the agent had passed by the stairs continuing along the path. He froze in his tracks to avoid making any noise. Shawn waited for about three minutes to let the agent walk farther down the path before he continued up the stairway.

When he reached the top of the stairs his heart nearly stopped. Street lights made a faint attempt to shine through the heavy fog. The murky light allowed him to survey the street and study the back of the East German army camp that he needed to walk around first to reach the car. The thick fog, faint lights, and deserted street looked like a scene from one of Humphrey Bogart's waterfront movies. He was apprehensive about moving from the dark shadows of the forest which provided a reassuring sense of security.

Shawn strained his eyes to see if someone might be waiting for him. There were several buildings across the street from the fence that surrounded the army camp. The buildings were shrouded by the dense fog and Shawn could not identify them. They appeared to be concrete warehouses used for storage. He recalled Walter telling him to turn right when he reached the street and then walk to the next corner. He should turn left at the corner and walk past the army camp's front entrance and meet him at the car parked in the hotel parking lot across the street. Shawn believed that if someone was waiting for him, they would expect him to take that route because it was the shortest distance.

He felt the urgent need to move because he suspected the agent who was following him may have turned around and could be coming up the stairs behind him. He decided to cross the street slowly. The odds were that if someone was there watching for him, the fog would partially conceal his movements if he could move slowly. Shawn remembered this camouflage trick from hunting with his Uncle Irvin.

He wasn't comfortable with the idea of going where someone would expect him to go so he changed course abruptly. He moved straight ahead into the fog toward the direction of the street behind the army camp. The adrenaline was flowing throughout his body as anxiety played with his subconscious. The street was terrifying. Moving at a snail's pace, he listened intently trying to pick up any sound no matter how faint. Nothing moved except the fog which was drifting at the same pace he was moving across the street.

At any moment Shawn expected to hear the muffled sound of a luger with a silencer being fired. After what seemed an eternity, he reached the other side of the street. He estimated the crossing had taken him about five minutes. His clothing was damp both inside and out, a combination of his own sweat and the fog's moisture.

He stood still and continued looking at the buildings to see if someone might be waiting or watching. Unable to detect anyone he walked very slowly up the street behind the army camp. He was close enough to see the chain-link fencing encompassing the camp. As he moved farther along the street he was surprised at the incredible darkness. Several large trees lined the street and their leaves prevented the lights from shining through the black night.

The enveloping darkness restored the confident feeling he had earlier while on the path. Halfway up the street Shawn reached the end of the camp's fencing and noticed a small park next to the camp.

Confident that nobody was watching him, Shawn moved slowly across the street into the dark shadows surrounding the park. He stood for a moment getting his bearings. Peering through the darkness, he could see a faint light from the street on the opposite end of the park. After his eyes had adjusted to the darkness, he saw a sidewalk leading into the park. He started walking very slowly in the direction of the faint light, being very careful not to make any noise.

He looked through the chain-link fence into the army camp and saw nothing, but shadowed buildings. The walkway was slippery because of the maple and oak leaves which had fallen to the ground. Moisture from the fog had dampened their rustling noise. After he had walked halfway through the park, his worst fears came true. Shawn stepped on a small branch. The crack was so loud that guard dogs inside the camp suddenly began to bark. He froze for an instant until lights inside the camp came on illuminating the fenced area inside the camp. Panic gripped him and he started running through the park hoping to avoid the guards who would soon be out with their dogs. As he ran he could not avoid the slushy noise the wet leaves were making underfoot. He reached the end of the park and could see the hotel just down the street across from the main entrance of the camp. The entire camp was now alive with soldiers running around and a warning siren was blaring through the night.

He ran across the street and hustled down the cobblestones looking for the car. He saw the car and glanced over his shoulder to see guards walking with dogs toward the park with flashlights. He knew the dogs would pick up his scent soon and lead them to the car. Seconds later he reached the car hoping that Walter was there waiting for him. His chest heaved as his lungs gasped for oxygen. He rushed up to the car and grabbed the door handle, yanking it open and startling Walter. He was sitting in the driver's seat with a gun pointed right at Shawn. Walter put the gun down and told Shawn to get in. He started the Porsche and backed out of the parking lot.

"Jesus Christ," Walter yelled as he drove down the fog-laden street. "Did you have to tell everyone in East Germany that you were in the area?"

"Look, you asshole," Shawn yelled back. "I nearly got killed and you're only worried about lights coming on."

"You should've done what I told you to do," Walter replied tensely as he drove slowly down the street through the thick fog. "You walked through the park, didn't you?"

"Yeah. It was dark and I didn't know if the other agent was waiting on the street. The dogs heard me step on a damn tree branch in the park, otherwise, I would've made it through without them knowing." Shawn's heart was now beating at a normal pace and he was breathing easier.

"No way, Shawn. You triggered an alarm. That park is located between the camp and some army administration buildings. Regardless, you done good." Walter smiled as he locked at Shawn. "Did you have any problems on the path?"

"I'm sure someone was following me." Shawn gave Walter a detailed report on his trip through the forest.

"Our plan worked perfectly." Walter made a thumbs up gesture. "You went out the back door and they bought it, hook, line, and sinker. One of the agents followed and the other stayed to watch us." Walter continued as they drove slowly toward the border, "We waited for about ten minutes to give you enough time to get up the path, then Boris and I left together. When we reached the street Boris went to the right and walked back to his hotel and I went in the opposite direction."

"Did the agent follow Boris?" Shawn asked. He was becoming more relaxed as Walter drove away from Altenburg.

"He followed him just as if we wrote a script for him," Walter chuckled, thinking about how they had fooled the KGB agents. "We'll be through the border before they know what hit 'em!"

"Where did you get the gun?"

"After I walked up the street for a short distance I doubled back to the bar and told the bartender the two men were KGB agents. He sold me the pistol for twenty bucks."

"What are you going to do with it?" Shawn thought about how the East

German border guards would react if they found the gun in the car. It would not be pretty.

"I'll get rid of it before we get to the crossing. I really don't want to cross at the same place where we came in, but it might be faster because they should remember us."

"What are the chances that the KGB agents will call the border guards to warn them about us?"

"Low. Pride will prevent them from admitting that we outsmarted them," replied Walter, smugly. "They won't let on that they suspect us of anything. They really don't want to look foolish since they have no proof that we've done anything wrong. You can be sure that we'll be followed in West Germany for the next few days unless we can lose them."

"I'm curious, Walter. How far down is the embankment on the left side of the pathway?"

"I'm not sure exactly. When I walked on it one afternoon last summer I estimated that it was about two or three-hundred feet. Why?"

"I nearly fell over the edge and so did the guy following me. If I knew how far down it went I would have filled my pants."

Walter laughed, "Shawn, you were super. I'm impressed at how well you handled yourself under the pressure. Joe Sweeney gave me a big buildup about you and I thought he might have over-estimated your ability. He was right on the money."

"I don't mind telling you that at times I was scared shitless."

"That's normal. How you react is what counts."

"At one point I thought about moving off the path just a bit and when the guy who was following me came by, push him over the edge of the bank. If I had known how steep it was I might have tried."

"It's better that you didn't. They would know for sure that we were up to something. Now they still aren't sure why we met with Boris."

Shawn thought about Boris. "Do you think we can get him out?"

"I hope so. It'll be a real race to get him and his family out before the Soviets figure out what's happened."

Walter continued driving for the next hour while Shawn drifted off to sleep. It was four in the morning when they reached the border crossing at Witzenhausen. Walter shook Shawn as they approached the armed guard at the gate.

"Where are we?" asked Shawn struggling to wake up.

"We're at the border crossing in Witzenhausen."

"Where's the gun?"

"Relax. I threw it out the window about ten miles back. It went over a bank along the road side."

The crossing area was brightly lit. The fog was nearly gone and Shawn could see trees being blown by a brisk wind. The guard was bundled up in a heavy jacket so he assumed the temperature had dropped since the fog lifted. Walter waved to the guard and pulled into a parking spot before the guard had a chance to direct him.

The guard used his radio to call inside the building to have another guard

→ *Ice Spy*

come out and check their papers. Shawn assumed that security was just a bit more relaxed because of the late hour and the cold brisk weather. They were both pleasantly surprised that the guards only took about thirty minutes to approve their papers and let them cross back into West Germany. Walter waited until they crossed the bridge at the border and then told Shawn he had given the guard another twenty dollars in American money. Walter drove in the direction of Winterberg and for the first time in nearly twenty-four hours, Shawn really felt relaxed.

Chapter Eighteen

→ *Ice Spy*

Riga, Latvia, USSR

Ivan Liepinsh sat in his office, studying the long line of Latvians at the store across the street waiting to purchase food. Since 1940, thousands of Latvian citizens had been arrested and questioned at the *Corner House*. Nobody really knew how many victims had been tortured and killed in its dankly dark cellar. No statistics were kept. The first two floors had frosted windows with wire mesh and steel bars to prevent anyone from escaping. A large courtyard encompassed a small parking lot hidden by a twenty-foot concrete wall. Latvians were reminded of the Russian persecution whenever the KGB drove through the huge steel gates into the courtyard with a prisoner. It was frightening to witness the gates open, permitting the KGB mini-van to drive in with yet another victim.

The KGB controlled Latvians with an iron fist and Ivan had no intentions of relaxing Russian dominance as long as he was the KGB Commandant in Riga. In fact, he felt strong personal pride in the way he maintained absolute control over the Latvians. He believed his fellow KGB commandants throughout the Soviet Union should follow his example. Many of the other commandants, in his opinion, were becoming too soft. Riga would serve as a role model for the others.

A knock on the office door interrupted Ivan's thoughts. "Come in."

Georgi Pasevs, his Vice Commandant, walked halfway into the room, carrying a report he had just received on the teletype. Stopping, he said, "Boris Yegorov went to Altenburg to meet with Walter Shapnek. He is the American who was in Riga recently."

"Why?"

"I'm not sure." Georgi was always apprehensive whenever he had to meet with the commandant. Ivan was the only person Georgi knew who was more impatient and crueler than himself. "We assume he went to East Germany to make arrangements to defect."

"Did he make any attempt to take money from his Swiss bank account?"

"No. He had a meeting with Shapnek and someone named Shawn Murphy who is a coach with the American bobsled association."

"What did they talk about?" asked Ivan, puzzled about why the three men had met in East Germany.

"Our men were unable to listen to their conversation."

"What do you mean, 'They were unable to listen to their conversation?' Why not?" Ivan was furious and his eyes turned stone cold as he glared at him. Georgi began to sweat and replied warily, "When our men went into the bar they saw the American coach leaving by the back door. Boris went out the front with Shapnek."

"Why weren't they there when the meeting started?"

"They followed the Americans from the border and lost them somewhere in the mountains. It took several hours to relocate them in Altenburg."

"Why wasn't Boris followed?"

"He was, but our agent lost sight of him in the crowds shortly after he got off the train in Warsaw. We suspect he drove to Poznan where he got back on the train and crossed into East Germany. Our men there checked with their agents and learned that Boris's visa allowed him to travel to Altenburg. Our agents located him and questioned him at his hotel in Altenburg after he left the Americans. They interrogated him about his intentions to defect and he denied it. He swears that he met them to obtain sports braces for our athletes."

"He's lying." Ivan was certain Boris was trying to defect. The Americans had to be CIA agents. They were too good at disappearing whenever his men tried to tail them. He would get Boris to confess before his superiors in Moscow became aware of the situation. If Boris defected, his career would be in serious trouble.

"Where is Boris right now?" asked Ivan.

"He's still in Altenburg."

"I want to see him when he returns. Do you understand that?"

"Yes, Commandant," Georgi left quickly, shutting the door behind him. He paused outside the office door and breathed a sigh of relief. Ivan wielded considerable power and Georgi knew he could become an instant victim at Ivan's say-so. The thought produced knee-buckling fear in all of Ivan's subordinates.

Ivan turned in his seat and stared out his fifth floor window. Snow began to accumulate on the sidewalk far below. It was early November and this was the first major snowfall of the season that had any accumulation. The wet snow was frustrating to the Latvians who were having a difficult time trying to stay dry and warm while they stood in the food lines for hours at a time. Although they were frustrated and bitter, they avoided complaining about their situation for fear someone would overhear and report them to the KGB.

Not knowing what Boris was planning to do frustrated Ivan. His superiors in Moscow were pressuring him to retrieve Boris's money hidden in the Swiss bank account and to determine what type of sports technology he sold to the East Germans. He would have to do something drastic to force Boris into disclosing what he had done. He was hesitant to use torture or drugs because of the effects they had on a human brain. Either choice would help him learn if Boris was trying to defect, but the side effects could damage his memory. The technology could be irretrievably lost. He could not take a chance on permanently damaging Boris's brain until he knew what had been sold to the East Germans. Ivan used the phone to call Georgi back into his office. Georgi was there in an instant.

"Yes, Commandant. You wish to see me?" asked a very nervous Gerogi.

"Shut the door, Georgi, and sit down."

Georgi closed the door and sat in the chair across the room and waited for Ivan to speak. He dreaded being called into the commandant's office for fear that he would become a victim just like his predecessor. Once during a private meeting in his office, Ivan had lost his temper and coldly shot the former vice-commandant. Within the circle Ivan claimed the man had snapped and tried to kill him. There were no witnesses and nobody had the nerve to question Ivan. Georgi was next in line and was promoted to vice-commandant, a position he secretly preferred not to take, but he kept his feelings to himself.

"I want you to search Boris Yegorov's laboratory and his home. We need to quickly determine what type of technology he may have sold the East

Germans." Ivan knew the power he had over Georgi and relished it. "I need you to do your best, Georgi. You never fail me and I've never regretted making you my vice-commandant." This was a subtle reminder to Georgi not to mess up or the consequences could be fatal.

"Yes, Commandant. Do you have any idea about what I should specifically look for?"

"No. That's what troubles me the most. What kind of bobsled technology could Boris discover that the East Germans would pay out so much money?"

"Perhaps he discovered something else that can be used other ways besides in bobsledding," suggested Georgi.

Georgi's suggestion surprised him and he thought that Georgi may have something. If the technology was only for bobsledding then it would make sense for an American coach to have an interest. This would explain why he met with Boris in East Germany. The CIA wouldn't be interested in sports technology unless it could be used for something else. "You must be very thorough when you search, especially his laboratory."

"Yes, Commandant." Georgi stood up to leave and said, "I'll call you at once if we find anything."

"Don't let me down," snarled Ivan as he glared at Georgi.

The vice-commandant already knew what he was going to do. He went down the dimly lit-hall to his office. He called two of his best agents and instructed them to bring Anita Yegorov and her parents to the KGB headquarters and hold them for questioning. While they were in custody he would personally search their house for papers that might refer to Boris's technology. This was a rare happening as he normally would not accompany the agents. He was unwilling to be held responsible for any mistakes. Now he had no choice.

He would hold them in custody until he finished searching their apartment. If unsuccessful, he would pressure Anita Yegorov by threatening to put her father back into prison if she did not help him. He would tell her that he knew Boris had papers on secret technology hidden in their home. If she knew nothing about it then he would question her about why Boris had met with the Americans in East Germany.

Georgi was confident that Anita would talk once he threatened to put her father back in prison. She would be reminded of how her father, a concert pianist in his youth, had spent fifteen years in prison because he refused to perform for the Russians. His twisted and deformed fingers were a daily reminder of the physical torture inflicted by the KGB in 1947. He was positive that she would be easy to break and would do or say anything to prevent her father from being harmed or returned to prison. Georgi smiled grimly for the first time in hours. He anticipated his task with pleasure.

It was shortly after two in the morning when Anita and her parents were silently driven to the KGB corner house. This was standard operating procedure. The KGB normally picked up people for questioning during the night hours because the disorientation and confusion of half-awake people added to their terror and susceptibility. Besides, at this late hour, nobody would observe the pick-up.

Georgi left the building a few minutes later with the two agents. The lights were still burning and the front door of the apartment, which was the only way into the former stable, was still ajar. Apparently the other KGB agents forgot to close it in their rush to bring Anita and her parents to headquarters.

Georgi slammed the door shut behind him to keep the bitter cold air outside. He walked around the small-single bedroom house while his agents searched for any papers Boris may have hidden. The only source of heat came from a small wood stove located in the center of the living room, and the three men could see their breath as they first entered. A large bookshelf filled with books also doubled as a china cabinet. Beer glasses and a few coffee cups were carefully placed along the back of the cabinet .

He surmised that Boris was an avid reader and admired the collection. He glanced quickly through some of the books to see if papers had been concealed inside them. Hundreds of books pertaining to science and physics were in the collection, but nothing could be found to link Boris to technology the Americans would want. After an hour, Georgi was bitterly disappointed by the unsuccessful search. He told his men to go to the car and he would join them in a moment. Georgi took one last look through the house before returning to the living room that contained a pullout bed for Boris's in-laws to sleep. His frustration built in him as he looked around the room filled with handmade antique hardwood furniture.

Suddenly, Georgi's rage burst loose and he rushed over and kicked over the wood stove. The coals spilled out onto the meticulously clean floor. He stormed out noisily, slamming the door behind him. The fire burned its way up through the roof before Georgi had time to reach the KGB headquarters only twelve blocks away.

Georgi instructed the driver to let him off at the front entrance of the building before parking the car in the courtyard. He rushed up to his office, still in a rage, frustrated at not being able to locate any type of information regarding Boris's technology. Moments later the sound of fire trucks racing down the street broke the early morning silence. He pulled his curtain back and watched them disappear in the night, leaving dark tracks in the snow It would be a waste of their time, Georgi thought after they had rushed by. He picked up the phone and called the guard in charge of the prisoners and instructed him to bring Anita to his office. Moments later, the guard knocked on the door when he arrived with Anita.

"Come in," Georgi yelled.

The door opened and the guard roughly pushed her into the room, still handcuffed. "Why have you arrested us?" demanded Anita.

Georgi stared at the tall, blonde woman. Her long hair was disheveled and there were dark shadows surrounding her blue eyes. Her short-sleeved blouse revealed bruises on her upper arm where the guards had grabbed her.

"But you have not been arrested," smirked Georgi slyly. "We only brought you here to give you a chance to help your father, otherwise he must go back to prison."

"We have done nothing wrong," she replied heatedly. "The Russians have done enough to my father. I demand that you let us go."

"YOU don't demand anything. Let me remind you that I can put you in prison with your father if you don't help us."

Anita suspected they might have discovered some information about her husband's plan for them to defect to the United States. She surmised that they really didn't know for sure because they would have simply killed Boris if they were certain. She was acutely aware that once they knew the plan and had the money stashed in the Swiss account, they would all be killed. Her only chance for them to stay alive would be to help keep her husband's plan a secret.

"I don't know why you've brought us here," lied Anita. Her thin shoulders slumped forward and her tone of voice was less belligerent.

"Your husband met with some American CIA agents in East Germany yesterday. Why?" Georgi studied Anita's face to catch her reaction.

"He told me that he was working with the Americans to purchase a new type of orthopedic sport brace for the Soviet bobsled athletes."

"You're lying. The Soviet bobsled athletes hate your traitor husband. We know he was secretly hired by the East Germans to train their athletes. We also know he sold them his technology and put 190,000 Deutsch marks in a Swiss account."

"Boris gave his professional help to their athletes, but he would never sell them technology." Anita was visibly nervous and she felt cold and clammy.

"Do you think we are stupid?" Georgi was infuriated that she continued to lie to him. "Perhaps if we put your father back in prison it will help your memory."

"I'm telling you the truth. I don't know what Boris has done. My father has spent enough time in prison. He has never done anything against you Russians."

"You are a stupid woman. Your husband is planning to defect and leave you behind."

Anita's reply was shrill, "My husband would never leave Latvia. This is our home."

"Maybe you will never leave, but your husband is making his own plans for departure, perhaps without you. Maybe he has a lover that you don't know about?" His innuendo was unmistakable but Anita's faith in Boris was unshaken.

"My husband built an Olympic bobsled program that is the envy of the sports world and you people treat him like a criminal. He made the Soviet Union a power in the Winter Olympics Games. Boris has devoted his life to making the Soviet Union a sports power."

"Your husband failed. He misled our government into thinking he could build a better bobsled program than he did. That's another story, perhaps. What I want to know is why he has been meeting with the Americans?"

"I told you everything I know. Boris is trying to obtain special orthopedic sport braces for our athletes, that aren't available in our country or in East Germany." Anita stared at Georgi. She wanted to reach out and rip his face open but refrained from showing any emotion. She knew that if Georgi decided to kill her or her parents he wouldn't hesitate for a moment.

Georgi called the guard and dismissed her abruptly. He called one of his assistants and instructed him to interrogate Anita's parents right away. He sat back in his chair, closing his dark eyes, deep in thought about the fire he started in Boris' home. His failure to located any type of documents to use against Boris distressed him. A short time later he decided that he was too tired. He walked across his office to lie down on the sofa and fell asleep instantly.

Mid-morning the next day Georgi allowed Anita and her parents to leave. They were forced to walk the twelve blocks home since they had no car. They were exhausted and trudging through the deep snow was difficult for them. Anita helped her frail father to prevent him from falling.

She thought about the previous night and hoped that Boris would be home soon with news about when they would be leaving for America. She believed that Georgi was uncertain about their plan or he never would have released them. Time would not be on their side because Georgi would continue his investigation until he got the truth. The pressure would be fierce and she dreaded it.

As they approached their street the acrid smell of smoke was strong and her feeling of dread increased. When they turned the corner Anita saw the remains of their home. The burnt-out structure was still emitting small amounts of smoke into the sky. Their neighbors were noticeably absent from the scene. Anita could not blame them. Everyone feared a KGB threat of arrest for becoming involved.

Her mother wept and sat on the street corner holding her head in her hands. She was pale and drawn. Anita and her father comforted the frail woman who was exhausted from their ordeal and on the verge of fainting. They took one last look at their destroyed home then Anita and her parents walked several blocks to her cousin's home to wait for Boris.

Kassel, West Germany

Walter looked into his rearview mirror and studied the car that had been following them for the past twenty minutes. He turned in a different direction and drove several miles to see if the car tailing them would follow. The other car appeared in his mirror and he made another turn and drove in the direction of the main road that connected Kassel and Marburg. He pulled out on the highway and abruptly pressed the accelerator down. The Porsche instantly picked up speed. The sudden thrust of power woke Shawn who had been sleeping.

"What's going on?" Shawn rubbed his stiff neck and looked at his watch. He was surprised that it was nearly 6 a.m. He had slept soundly since they left the border crossing.

Walter replied tersely, "We have another car following us. I've decided not to go back to Winterberg until we lose them."

"How do we do that?" Shawn was wide awake now.

"I'm not sure. We'll drive down to the Mosel Valley area and try to lose them before we get there. I have some friends who own a vineyard. We can visit them and have lunch." Walter smiled confidently. "This will confuse the hell out of them. If they still follow us, we'll go to Luxembourg for dinner and then go sightseeing in Cologne. These guys will go nuts trying to figure out what we're doing. We'll act like tourists which will help build our cover."

"When do you think I can leave for the States?" Shawn glanced back at the car that was still following them.

"We can stay in Cologne overnight and return to Winterberg in the morning to pick up the things you left in the apartment. I'll drive you to Frankfurt and you can grab the first available flight home."

"Good. I've already missed Thanksgiving and I really don't want to miss my wife's birthday. She must be worried because I didn't tell her what I was doing."

"Will she be upset?" Walter smiled sympathetically, wishing he had a wife at home worried about him.

"Sure. That's normal, but Angela will be all right. Once I get home and she knows I'm okay." Shawn thought about Angela for the first time in several days. His visit to East Germany had completely occupied his mind for the entire trip.

He thought about the unusual snow storm that surprised everyone in Schenectady on October 4th. During a phone call, Angela described to him how the twenty-one inches of wet snow damaged a large number of trees on their property. The trees still had leaves and the heavy snow knocked them down. He was wondering what the upstate New York weather was like at the moment when Walter pulled into a restaurant parking lot.

"Let's get some breakfast and relax for a while before we head down to the Mosel Valley." Walter had been driving since Altenburg and had only taken a short break at the border crossing.

"I don't mind driving if you want to try and get some sleep in the car," volunteered Shawn. He actually wanted to try driving the powerful vehicle. He wondered how it would compare to his Corvette.

"Let's see how I feel when we get finished eating. If I take a short break and eat, I'm good again for another two or three hours of driving. If I get too tired I'll let you drive."

"Where did the two KGB characters disappear to?"

"They pulled off over there," Walter nodded to where they turned onto another street. "They must be around the corner watching what we're doing. In a way they're pretty stupid if they think we didn't notice. Actually, there's no other way to follow someone in the mountains like this." Walter grinned. "It works to our advantage."

They went inside the restaurant and took their time eating breakfast. Walter asked the waitress for directions to the city of Bonn and some other typical tourist questions. Several cups of strong coffee and melt-in-your-mouth rolls covered with home-made jam gave them a second wind. When they got back into the car Walter explained that he was sure the agents would question the waitress before trailing them again.

"She'll tell them we're going sightseeing in Bonn, but we'll actually go to Cologne. They'll never keep up with us after we get on the autobahn. They'll go to Bonn and look around for our car."

Walter drove slowly on the highway to Marburg and the two KGB agents had no problem catching up to them just as Walter predicted. Shortly after they left Marburg, Walter turned onto the autobahn in the direction of Bonn. With no speed limits to worry about, Walter pressed the accelerator to the floor and they watched the two men in the car behind them quickly disappear.

"This should separate us for a while. The highway to the Mosel Valley is about thirty- five miles from here. By the time we arrive there they'll be so far back they won't know we turned off."

They drove parallel to the Mosel River and Walter pointed out places of interest to give Shawn a bit of history about the area. Many of the eighteenth-century stone buildings were damaged during World War II. Many still remained that way but others had been rebuilt to their original design. A closer look would show a slight difference in the color of the stone. Shawn enjoyed the ride and was impressed with Walter's knowledge of history for the area. Years of working in Europe had enabled him to learn a lot about German history which helped him with his work.

It was nearly noon when they reached the small city of Trier in the Mosel Valley near the Luxembourg border. Walter drove slowly through the city so Shawn could look at the stone structures. The stones were dug from area hillsides where commercial vineyards were located. He was fascinated to see farm equipment and cows in buildings attached to houses in small villages. Walter told him that the dairy cows were fed and milked in structures located under or next to their owners home then led back out in the countryside to graze in the fields during the day. The cows had a sleek, yet well-fed look about them. Land in the Mosel Valley was scarce and the Germans did not waste space by building farms. Shawn wondered what it smelled like in the living space located over where the cows slept and were fed. Somehow he just could not visualize himself living that way.

At the edge of the village, Walter turned onto a side street and parked in front of a large stone house. A mammoth stone barn was attached to the sturdy house. Wooden barrels containing different varieties of wine were stacked everywhere.

"This is my friend's house. Her husband died last year and she's been operating the vineyard by herself. We'll eat lunch here and rest up a bit before going to Luxembourg."

They got out of the car and stretched. Shawn was looking around when Walter's friend came out of the barn and greeted him with a hug and a smile. "Walter, you look so thin. Are you taking care of yourself?"

"I'm okay. How've you been?"

"I'm managing. We haven't had a lot of rain and the grapes aren't as good as they should be, but I'll get by." She's an eternal optimist, thought Shawn. He couldn't imagine working this place alone. It was so well kept and Shawn could practically feel all the hours of hard work that had gone into it.

Walter introduced Shawn to Helga whose looks belied her age. He estimated that she was probably in her late sixties. The hard work in the vineyards helped keep her young. Helga was extremely hospitable and was delighted that they were staying for lunch with her. She fed them a meal of fruit salad, and cold cuts on dark German bread. They enjoyed an extraordinary white wine that Helga reserved for special occasions.

They ate in Helga's kitchen which led directly out to the barn. A flight of stairs went down into the cellar where wine-aging barrels were stored. The small kitchen was spotlessly clean but the clutter was remarkable. Pots and pans were scattered over every counter and Shawn was amused at all the wine-making equipment stacked here and there throughout the small room. Storage space was at a premium in this small house.

They left for Luxembourg late that afternoon and stopped to eat a light dinner in an inconspicuous restaurant. Later they drove to Cologne where they spent the night at a hotel. Walter felt confident that the KGB agents had been completely baffled by their change of plans and were totally frustrated at losing them.

The next morning they drove back to Winterberg to pick up Shawn's personal belongings. Shawn felt like he was almost home when they reached the empty apartment. The hotel's entire apartment complex was deserted. Shawn packed the remaining few pieces of clothing he left there and Walter drove him to the airport in Frankfurt. Shawn said good-bye to Walter after he purchased a ticket for a flight to Montreal, Canada. Shawn had a tough time believing that he had been in Europe for seven weeks. He looked forward to seeing Angela again and sleeping in his own bed.

Chapter Nineteen

Schenectady, New York

Shawn rolled onto his side looking at Angela sleeping next to him. He thought about how much he had missed her. It was apparent that Angela had missed him as well because when she had picked him up at the Montreal airport she talked non-stop during the five hour drive to Schenectady. He had been away for nearly eight weeks and she filled him in on all the local news that had taken place during his absence. She told him all about the horrendous job it was to clear the snow out of the driveway. She made it clear that he needed to make arrangements to have someone plow the driveway whenever he was gone in the future. Shawn agreed with her.

His past week in Europe held enough suspense and thrills to last him a long time. Shawn's thoughts drifted to Boris's situation and he began thinking about the technology he had created. Even though nobody had seen any proof to support his claims, the Naval Department was confident that the technology was genuine and a team of specialists from the David Taylor Research Laboratory was convinced as well.

The team included experts who worked with physics, metallurgy, naval ship design, and structural engineers. The Taylor Research facility had worked unsuccessfully for years on the theory that certain metals and alloy composites could be used on ship hulls to reduce friction. The concept of having the ability to reduce friction between any surface while sliding against water or ice was incredible.

Two experts selected to research Boris's information had extensive backgrounds in metallurgy and tribology. They had years of experience working with friction and metal wear. Generally, their research involved bearings, shafts, and sometimes large gun barrels used on naval ships. The possibility of obtaining this metallurgical technology created tremendous excitement at the Taylor facility. Shawn thought about Joe Sweeney's excitement when the CIA agent had briefed him on the case.

Shawn's thoughts returned to his own specific interest. He was fascinated with the possibility that the technology would allow bobsleds to go faster by reducing the ice friction on the runners. He was certain that Boris had fabricated runners made of the secret material and he tried to speculate how much faster bobsleds would go with runners using the new composite. Fractions of seconds would make a major difference in the sport.

Boris must have sold runners to the East Germans in 1986 when he was hired to coach their athletes, he thought, which explained why they protected their runners like a military secret. It was rumored that the East German athletes slept with their runners to make sure nobody had the opportunity to steal them. He wondered if they had been able to analyze the runners to identify the composite so they could duplicate them.

"Well, Mr. Murphy," came a soft voice from the other side of the bed. "What great plans do you have for today?" Angela was awake and immediately cuddled up to him.

"I think I'll just take it easy for a few days." Shawn smiled and smoothed her hair with his fingers. "Between the jet-lag and the excitement I had in

Europe, my body is telling me not to do anything for too soon."

"Now, do you really expect me to believe that?" Angela moved even closer to Shawn. She had really missed him and her eagerness was evident.

"You can believe it. I'm exhausted and don't plan to do anything except rest for the next few days." Shawn pretended indifference to Angela's advances. If this was the result of every trip he'd have to travel more frequently.

Angela wrapped her arms tighter around her husband, saying, "I forgot to tell you last night. Olive called a couple of days ago and wanted to know when you were returning to work."

"What did you tell her?" Shawn really didn't want to hear anything about work.

"I told her that I had no idea when you were coming back from Europe and that I hadn't talked to you in over a week. I'm sure that she didn't believe me. God, what a bitch she is. I don't know how you can stand working for her."

"Deep down I think Olive really likes me," teased Shawn. "But, not a lot," he added with a grin. The talk about work broke the mood and Angela sighed.

"Come on, let's get up and I'll make you breakfast." Angela got out of bed and threw her pillow at Shawn. "Did you miss my cooking?"

"Of course," he replied, getting out of bed and slipping on his bathrobe. "I can't believe the type of food that Jason Pierce and Roger Ferris made arrangements for us to eat."

"Why? What was wrong with it?"

"We had either pork or pork products everyday and sometimes twice a day."

She shook her head in disgust. "What's the matter with them? Any idiot knows that pork isn't good for athletes who are on a vigorous training program."

"You're right, but these idiots don't care about the athletes."

They walked into the kitchen with their arms around each other. Angela laughed when she told Shawn about the excitement the roses created when they were sent to her office each Thursday he was away. Her co-workers at the insurance company in Albany would try to guess each week what color roses would arrive. They became so involved, that each Thursday morning they would keep watch for the florist delivery truck. All work in the office halted whenever the receptionist called to tell Angela her roses had arrived. The office manager would kid her and say he was making arrangements to have Shawn sent home so he could get some work done at his office.

He decided not to call Olive to tell her when he would be back to work. It would be useless for him to try and explain to her that he was exhausted from the trip. She wouldn't care and would expect him to come to the office immediately. He dreaded having to face her. He spent the entire day relaxing and reading old copies of the newspapers Angela saved for him.

Shawn spent the rest of the day working outdoors using his chain-saw to cut up trees and branches damaged by the freak snow storm in early October. He loved the physical exercise the work provided and the peace and quiet of the surrounding countryside. It gave him time to think.

That evening he treated Angela to an Italian dinner at the Roman Villa restaurant. It was their favorite restaurant because the Italian food was outstanding and it was located only ten minutes away from their house. They ran into several people they knew and spent some time visiting with them. They were very interested in Shawn's career as an Olympic coach. The attention was gratifying and Shawn enjoyed being home again.

The drive to the office on Monday was hectic, as usual, with cars racing and switching lanes attempting to reach the downtown General Electric plant in record time. Shawn wondered about what type of projects Olive had going in the public affairs office. He chuckled as he thought about how confused she must have been while he was gone.

The office really shouldn't have had too much work since the fall season is normally quiet. Unfortunately, his boss didn't have the expertise to be a public affairs clerk. Her only help was Bruce Monroe, who shied away from any type of work. Shawn shook his head in amusement. He thought about Bruce and how he would listen to a religious radio station all day long on a headset taking a break only long enough to sneak down the hallway when nobody was around and steal a cup of coffee.

He approached the front gate at the air base and a security guard motioned for him to stop. He asked Shawn to pull over to the side so he could talk to him. Another guard came out of the guard shack and joined in welcoming Shawn back to the base. Both individuals were excited that Shawn had been selected as an Olympic coach. They delightedly filled him in with several bits of information on things that had happened during his absence. They told Shawn not to rush to the office because Olive still hadn't arrived then told him about her meeting with the commander and how Colonel Crosby had advised her to get to work on time and not to take extra time during lunch. Shawn was amazed at how the security police knew everything going on at the base.

The guard telling the story chuckled, "That practice lasted about two weeks and she was back to her normal schedule of coming to work thirty minutes late and using an extra hour during lunch."

Shawn laughed and then said good-bye. He pulled his car into the main parking lot and walked into the building where his office was located. Neither Bruce nor Olive had arrived yet. Shawn blessed the quiet office.

He looked at the clock on the wall. It was seven twenty-five. His desk was over-loaded with papers Olive and Bruce had thrown on it. The mess frustrated him. He picked up his coffee cup and went down the hall stopping at Chief Curley's office. The chief was delighted to see him and said, "I have about one million questions to ask you, Shawn. It's great to have you back."

They went to the break area and poured themselves a cup of coffee. Several other workers greeted Shawn enthusiastically as he and Chief Curley carried their coffee back to the chief's office. Shawn spent nearly thirty minutes inquiring about events that had taken place involving public affairs. He was not surprised when the chief told him some air base gossip about Bruce Monroe and Olive sleeping together. The chief believed the stories were simply fraudulent gossip started by one of hundreds of people at the base that hated Olive and Bruce. When he returned down the hall to his office, Olive and Bruce were just arriving. Both walked in the office ignoring Shawn. He chuckled to himself trying to picture these two having sex together. The thought of it made his stomach turn. He was more disgusted than ever with the mess on his desk as he began the task of cleaning it up.

Olive spoke suddenly, surprising him, "Shawn. Colonel Fowlkes wants a meeting with you and I in his office at ten-thirty." She looked everywhere but straight at him. It was like talking to someone over your shoulder.

"Sure. What's the meeting about?"

"I don't know." Olive feigned ignorance. "He called and said he wants to meet with us at ten-thirty."

Shawn laughed quietly, knowing that Olive must have called Colonel Fowlkes to set up some type of meeting. Her telephone hadn't rung since she arrived at the office. Olive lied so much that it was impossible to know when she was telling the truth. She must have made plans with the colonel to reprimand Shawn for some imaginary offense. This way they could legitimately vent their frustration against him. Shawn was fully aware it was a set up.

At ten-thirty promptly Shawn went to the colonel's office where he and Olive were waiting for him. He shut the door behind him and Fowlkes pointed to a chair for him to sit. Fowlkes was not looking directly at Shawn either.

"We need to review your job evaluation, Shawn," said Colonel Fowlkes nervously. Shawn noticed Olive was sweating profusely and she still avoided looking at him. He stared intently at Fowlkes, a short, very thin individual, who carried around a permanent chip on his shoulder. Shawn was pleased to see that he was rapidly balding.

Shawn asked, "Why?" Shawn's directness took Fowlkes by surprise.

He stammered, "Under the circumstances, Olive asked that I do it for her."

"Under what circumstances?" He knew that Olive was trying to have the colonel do her dirty work.

"She did your job evaluation and we have to review it with you. I must admit that your performance hasn't been up to what it should be."

"I really don't think you should have a problem with my job performance, Colonel Fowlkes. Just before I left for Europe, General Abbott called me at my home to congratulate me on being selected as an Olympic coach. He also told me that he expected you and Olive to do just what you're doing right now. His advice to me was not to argue with either of you and to sign the evaluation. He suggested that I indicate my disagreement on it and send a copy of it to him. He said that he would know how to take care of it."

Colonel Fowlkes and Olive were speechless. Olive's mouth hung open and Shawn could see her gold fillings which disgusted him. Shawn stood up and glared at both of them and said, "Write whatever you want. The two of you operate like eighth grade children." He walked out of the office leaving the door wide open. Olive and Amos sat there stunned, looking at each other blankly. He returned to his office and spent the rest of the day trying to catch up on the large volume of work that accumulated in his absence.

Olive returned to the office twenty minutes later and Shawn noticed that she looked mean enough to kill a bear with her hands. She walked over to Bruce Monroe's desk and told him to get his hat and come with her. Both ignored Shawn completely for which he was grateful.

"What's going on, Olive?" asked Bruce.

"Just get your hat and meet me in the parking lot," replied Olive, impatiently.

They left the office together and went out through a side door of the building to the parking lot. Bruce followed Olive who was almost running to her car. They got into her ten-year-old Ford station wagon and she drove hurriedly off the base.

The two security guards looked at each other, laughing, as Olive's car whizzed past the gate and one said, "Shawn must've really rattled her cage this time!"

Once she drove out onto the highway Olive started venting the frustration that built up during the meeting in Colonel Fowlkes's office. "Murphy is one arrogant son of a bitch who needs to be taught a lesson." Olive was outraged by General Abbott's warning to Shawn. A general in Washington was paying close attention to her and Fowlkes's activities and that wasn't good.

"What can we do to teach the bastard a lesson?" asked Bruce.

"Some time ago you told me you were planning to have your girlfriend call Shawn's wife Angela and tell her that she was having an affair with him." Olive turned her head to look at Bruce and the sound of an approaching car horn warned them that her car had wandered over the center line. She quickly pulled the car back into the proper lane and asked "Can you get her to do it now?"

Bruce stammered, "Ah, right now, that might be a bit of a problem."

"What's the problem?" barked Olive. "I don't want to hear that shit. I take good care of you and don't you forget it." Olive's anger was boiling over. She rudely cut off several cars before pulling into the parking lot at the Skyport restaurant. Getting out of the car, she slammed the door hard and asked again, "What's the problem with having your girlfriend call her? You told me that she'd do anything you asked."

"I know I did, Olive, and at the time I said that she would have." Bruce opened the restaurant's door and they went inside. They sat opposite from each other in a corner booth. Bruce looked around to make sure no one could hear them. "I'm having problems with her. She thinks I'm having an affair with you. Right now is not a good time to ask her."

Olive was outraged and said, "In the two years you've worked for me you only stayed overnight five or six times. That's hardly what I would call an affair."

"I know," comforted Bruce, "but right now she's still upset because of the other night."

"How the hell did she find out?" questioned Olive suspiciously.

The waitress came to their table and took their order for coffee and muffins. Bruce looked at Olive and said, "I just realized that I don't have any money with me."

"What else is new? You never have any money." Olive continued questioning. "I thought you told her that you had to go out of town on military business?"

"I did, but she still found out."

"You lie so much that she probably doesn't believe anything you say." Olive looked at Bruce and laughed. "How can you listen to that religious crap all day and not have some of it rub off on you?"

"Sleeping with you wasn't wrong," replied Bruce sanctimoniously. "I was only trying to help you fulfill your need for sexual gratification."

"I know it and I'm grateful. I really do appreciate having you stay once in a while."

The waitress returned with their order, and after she left, Bruce leaned over the table and quietly said, "I know who we can get to make the call."

"Who?"

"Joyce."

"Joyce Madison?"

"She's very close to me and I'm sure she'll help us."

"I know how close she is to you. I remember the time I overheard you telling her to put her hands in yours and follow you to the Lord. Is there anyone on base you haven't slept with?" asked Olive sarcastically.

"Actually, you and Joyce are the only two women on base with whom I've had sex. You can't believe the gossip that goes around the base."

"I've got you mixed up doll, it's Joyce who's slept with nearly everyone on base," laughed Olive, delighted with her own humor. "I walked in Fowlkes's office once and caught them in a clinch. I thought he'd have a heart attack. Do you really think she'll do it for us?"

"Yeah. She hates Shawn because he always complains about the quality of her work."

"I have to admit that typing isn't one of her fortes." Olive laughed, thinking about some of the problems she had with Joyce's typing. "Talk to her and let me know what she says. She'll have to do it soon because Murphy leaves soon for the Olympics in Canada."

"I'll talk to her this afternoon."

They looked at each other and laughed. She felt much better knowing they would put some misery in Shawn's life. They finished their breakfast and Olive paid the bill. They drove leisurely back to the base. Olive spent the rest of the day in a much better mood.

Riga, Latvia, USSR

Boris Yegorov sat in his car staring at the charred mess that once was his home. He was more determined than ever to sell his discovery to the Americans. He would rather die than give the Russians his secret. He stared at the ruins and vowed to make Georgi Pasevs pay for their suffering.

He was certain that Pasevs and his men had searched his laboratory, located in the VEF factory in Riga. Electronic components made at the factory were used by the Russian Air Force and their navy. His thoughts turned to the Russians and ways he could retaliate for the years of harassment. The time would soon be right and he would enjoy avenging the loss of his home and the disrespectful treatment he suffered since his athletes failed to win a gold medal.

CIA Headquarters, Langley, Virginia

Fred Unser sat at his desk pondering the information he had just received from their agent in Riga. The situation did not look good. The KGB was putting intense pressure on Boris. Fred knew it was because Boris had gone to East Germany to meet Walter and Shawn. He wondered if the KGB was putting on pressure to learn why Boris was meeting the Americans or if they might have stumbled on the real truth. He dismissed the idea. If they discovered that Boris had created the alloy composite, they would have arrested him and put him in custody. Time was becoming even more critical.

Fred called Gary Circe and briefed the CIA's director about the situation in Riga.

"How do we stand on the project right now, Fred?"

"We're about ninety-five percent ready. We still haven't finalized how to get his wife and her parents out."

"You don't have much time, Fred. We're just a few weeks away from Christmas."

"I know, Gary, but we can't just go charging in there. We don't want to alert the Russians. If we get caught in the act it will create one hell of an international embarrassment. The president would have all our heads."

"You're right, Fred. Just keep at it and let me know if there is any change."

Fred hung up the phone and dialed Joe Sweeney's number.

CHAPTER TWENTY

→ *Ice Spy*

Lake Placid, New York

The snow had been accumulating for several hours making the driving conditions extremely hazardous on the winding road that twisted its way from the Adirondack Northway to Lake Placid. Route 73 conditions were often treacherous during the winter months and this trip was no different. Shawn drove with his Blazer engaged in four-wheel drive to help him maintain better traction. He saw several accidents during the two-and-a-half-hour drive from Schenectady and didn't want to chance sliding into a ditch.

He glanced at the clock on the dashboard and the time was approaching 5 a.m., an ungodly hour. The Olympic Bobsled Team was to leave that afternoon by bus for Montreal. From there they would fly to Calgary to prepare for the Olympics. He had to be at the association office at 7 a.m. for an early morning meeting with the coaches and the association officers.

Shawn knew that he should have driven up from Schenectady the night before, but he was reluctant to leave Angela. He would be away at the Olympics for four weeks and there was a strong possibility that he would have to return to Europe and help the CIA get Boris and his family out of the Soviet Union.

His thoughts drifted to the upcoming Olympics and the bobsled association's problems. It still bewildered him that a group of people with connections to the mafia was able to take control of an Olympic association. He was even more amazed at the control that Lester Fetor and Nino Casatelli maintained over its president, Wilbur Hippenbecker.

Shawn hoped the meeting wouldn't be a waste of time, but expected that Lester and Nino would spend the entire time telling everyone how hard they worked on marketing to raise money for the association. They consistently tried to convince everyone that they alone were responsible for the association's success. It rarely worked. The athletes knew the truth.

As Shawn approached the small town of Lake Placid he saw the lights of a snowplow. He was almost there. Shawn thought about the officials in disgust. The storm was letting up, but he realized he was still gripping the steering wheel tightly. His frustration was evident. Lester and Nino had no clue about how to get the attention of sponsors and have them sit down and listen. They were extremely crude and he suspected they really had no interest in sponsors. This was simply an excuse they used for their lavish spending of the association's money. Their real interest was laundering mafia money in Europe and Shawn suspected they received a generous commission for their services.

The association meeting started on time and Shawn's predictions proved correct. Both Lester and Nino used the majority of the time to justify why they were going to the Olympics. Lester claimed his incredible marketing program would attract many sponsors and Nino would replace Jason Pierce as the manager. Nino spoke briefly about the problems they had with Jason in Europe and the importance of having someone of high caliber to manage at the Olympics. Shawn thought he would throw up.

The meeting lasted about two hours and Shawn found it as tedious as he knew it would be. Ron Harrison took Shawn aside and brought him up to date on the investigation of the officials' misuse of funding and money laundering scheme. The FBI was primarily interested in Fetor, Casatelli, Ferris, and John Chapadeau. They were satisfied that Hippenbecker wasn't involved with the money laundering and was only misusing a small amount of funding by taking unnecessary trips. He left when Ron finished to find Jim Bogdan and tell him the news about Nino and Jason. He located him at the bus helping the athletes load their equipment. Jim jokingly assured Shawn that they could manage without him now that Nino was in charge.

Shawn went to the association's main office and was delighted to see Professor Bodyniski there working on some paperwork. Ray told him they would be rooming together in Calgary. The association had rented several apartments and a few available homes in Calgary for the coaches and officials. Shawn filled Ray in on the meeting held earlier that morning.

"No surprise there. I knew that they were going to have the meeting," laughed Ray, highly amused. "I drove up yesterday to get some things ready and Nino stopped me in the hotel and talked to me for about an hour."

"What an idiot!"

"I asked him specific questions about their plan and Nino never gave me a good answer," Ray said in reference to their so called marketing plan. "By the way, I'll be at the Games the entire four weeks."

Shawn was delighted. "I didn't know that! That's terrific news!"

"It was very sudden. Wilbur called me about three weeks ago and asked if I would be interested in the volunteer position as chairman of the association's technical program."

"That's great," Shawn said. "At least someone competent will be involved."

The trip from Lake Placid was long and tiresome. Their plane was scheduled to leave at 3 p.m., but was delayed for nearly an hour loading the massive amount of equipment needed for the competition. They arrived in Calgary late in the evening and then the equipment had to be transferred to a truck and secured.

Ray and Shawn rented a car and left to locate the apartment the association rented for them to use during the Olympics. Roger Ferris had made all the arrangements for the rentals and had given Ray a map to show him how to find the apartment. Shawn thought that this was about the only thing Roger had ever done with any competence.

"It just occurred to me that Roger didn't come with us. Do you know if he's coming later?" asked Shawn.

→ *Ice Spy*

"I don't think he'll be coming up at all," replied Ray with a chuckle. "I was at a meeting with Wilbur a couple of weeks ago and overheard Lester and Nino giving Roger all kinds of hell."

"I thought Roger was in tight with them." Shawn was puzzled and remarked, "He always managed to take good care of both of them."

"I'm not sure what happened between them but it had to do with money. I've got a gut feeling that they were involved with some kind of drug deal together and Roger tried to cheat Nino out of some money."

"I'm not surprised. They both have a reputation for using the crap. They probably deal it as well."

"Well, Roger is on their shit list and I don't think you'll see him here at the Olympics."

Ray handed the map to Shawn and asked him to try and figure out where they were at that moment and where the apartment was located. The drive from the airport took nearly an hour and they eventually found the building. Ray parked the car in the building's private parking lot and they went inside to find the building manager who was waiting for them. He took them up to the apartment on the sixth floor and gave them a quick tour before leaving. There were two large bedrooms, a living room, and a small kitchen with an attached dining area. Shawn was pleased with their accommodations for the next four weeks. He noticed several reproductions on the walls in the living room of the Rocky Mountains west of Calgary.

Shawn offered Ray the larger bedroom because he suspected that Ray's girlfriend might be joining him for the last week. They returned to the car and brought all their luggage up to the apartment. It took two trips and when Shawn finally fell into bed he was asleep in minutes. The long trip had exhausted him.

The next morning Shawn and Ray left the apartment and went to the bobsled track at the Olympic park. Nino held a quick meeting with the athletes and set up a practice schedule for the next day. Once the meeting was over they left to buy groceries for the apartment. They stocked up on food supplies they needed which included: cold cuts, coffee, and most importantly, Molson's.

Later that morning Ray left the apartment to take a short run. Shawn called Angela at work to give her the address and phone number where he was staying. She told him that Joe Sweeney had called her the night before and wanted Shawn to call him. Shawn was curious and wanted to find out what was going on with Boris. When he had finished talking with his wife he called Joe at the CIA headquarters.

Joe asked Shawn where he was staying so he could visit him in Calgary. He needed to discuss the plans to get Boris and his relatives out of the Soviet Union. Shawn gave Joe the address and phone number. Joe told him they had checked the professor's background and gave Shawn permission to brief him on the *IceSpy* project. The CIA had files on Ray dating back to the time he had worked for them at the University of Washington. Joe expected to get there toward the end of the Olympics. He'd brief them about the current status of the project when he arrived.

Ray returned to the apartment after jogging for a half an hour and overheard the latter part of Shawn's conversation with Joe. When Shawn hung up he told Ray the story about Boris and the secret technology he claimed to have developed. Ray was fascinated with the information and was convinced that Boris could be telling the truth.

"I suspected that you were up to something like this when you met with your friends in Winterberg," Ray said seriously. "When you stayed behind I was sure that you were going to East Germany, but I had no idea that you were working on something as big as this."

"I wanted to say something but the CIA agents didn't want anybody to be briefed unless they gave approval. Joe Sweeney told me on the phone that they still have your file and he felt that it's all right to tell you the story." Shawn poured a cup of coffee for both of them and continued. "The plan is to get Boris, his wife, and her parents out of the Soviet Union."

"Why are all of them defecting?"

"Boris won't give us the technology unless they do. He's sure that the Russians will kill the rest of his family unless all of them defect at the same time. If we're successful they'll be hidden through the CIA's protection program in the United States."

"Where does the plan stand right now?"

"I'm not sure. Joe called me during the holidays and said the KGB burned Boris's house while he was meeting with me in East Germany. That's the last bit of news I've received about him."

"He has to be walking a tight rope. The Russians won't waste too much time with him. If they don't get the information they want, they'll kill him out of frustration."

"The CIA knows and they are working overtime to create some way to pull this off."

Shawn and Ray spent the rest of the day relaxing. They finished unpacking. Shawn was surprised and pleased to find a small picture of his wife in his suitcase. A gift from Angela. The morning dawned clear but the winds were warm and unexpected. This could cause major problems with the ice. They drove to the track and helped the athletes get ready for practice. Ray went to the start area to work on the bobsleds with the athletes while Shawn went to the Olympic office to get his coaching instructions.

All the coaches were assigned a seat along the bobsled track about halfway down the bobrun. Shawn was delighted when he discovered that his seat was next to the Soviet Union coach. He left the office and walked back up the track to where his assigned seat was located. The Soviet coach was there and gave a quick nod when Shawn smiled and greeted him warmly. Afterwards, the Soviet coach completely ignored him.

After practice Shawn met Ray in the parking lot and told him about

→ *Ice Spy*

the seating arrangements. Ray warned him not to try too hard to make friends with the Soviet coach because the KGB had to be there observing everything their coaches did during the Olympics.

The rest of the week went by quickly. The odd weather continued and created unexpected problems. The first day of the 1988 Winter Olympics was unusually warm. The two-man bobsled competition on the weekend was a big disappointment for the Americans. One team pulled out of the race because they were doing so poorly and Ron Harrison's team finished seventeenth. Janis Kipurs, a Soviet driver, won the gold medal for his team on Sunday.

Monday morning Shawn and Ray went to the Olympic village to eat breakfast. After they had finished Shawn got up and went to the buffet table for a second cup of coffee. The room was nearly empty since most of the coaches and staff had left for the track to get ready for practice scheduled to start in about thirty minutes.

"Good morning."

Shawn turned around to see who was speaking to him and was shocked to see a rather tall Soviet woman smiling at him.

"Good morning," he replied. I'm Shawn Murphy."

"Pleased to meet you, I'm Irina Bychek."

"I notice you are wearing a Soviet Bobsled jacket. Are you working with the team?"

Shawn was amazed that a Soviet would even talk to him. This was extremely unusual since the KGB never allowed anyone from the Soviet Union to talk with non-Soviets.

"Yes. I work as an interpreter."

"Please join us for coffee." Shawn pointed at Ray sitting alone at the table.

"I'm sorry, but I must sit with the man I work for."

"I hope we may speak again some other day."

"Perhaps we can."

Shawn shook her hand and wished her good luck in the games. He rushed back to the table and quickly told Ray about his brief chat with the Soviet interpreter. They both looked up to see the Soviet woman walking toward their table.

"The man I work for would like you to join him at his table," she smiled and pointed toward her employer.

"We would be honored." Shawn was shocked that this was happening to them.

They followed the woman across the room and when they reached the table she introduced them to her employer. Daumant Znatnajs was the Minister of Sports for the Soviet Union. After the introduction he motioned for them to sit down. Daumant spoke only Russian and Latvian so the interpreter had to translate their conversation.

They talked briefly about the poor weather conditions and how it was affecting the bobsled finish times for everyone. They could only talk for a few minutes since practice would begin shortly. Shawn asked

Daumant if they could meet early the next morning and talk more about bobsledding during breakfast. Daumant agreed and they left the dining room and walked to the track.

They reached the base of the track and separated. Shawn and Ray walked up to the bobrun together discussing the rare meeting. They were surprised and shocked that Daumant, the Soviet Minister of Sports, was willing to meet them again.

Practice was going quite slowly due to the poor weather conditions and Shawn found himself bored. Thirty-six countries with two teams apiece made for a long practice. To keep his mind busy he wrote down the fifty meter start times of each sled on his clipboard as they were announced over the loudspeaker. He waited until he heard the two-hundred meter times and then he would predict the finish time for the sled and write it down. He was amused that his predictions came fairly close to the actual finish times. Shawn noticed that the Soviet coach was writing something on his clipboard each time a sled went down for a practice run and he wondered what he was writing. Later that morning Shawn finally gave in to his curiosity and nudged the Soviet coach. Shawn smiled and pointed to his own clipboard. He showed the Soviet coach the practice times he had jotted down and the estimated finish times with the actual finish time.

The Soviet coach grinned and opened his clipboard and showed Shawn that he had been doing the same thing. They spent the rest of the practice session writing the times and sharing with each other their predictions. Although they never spoke Shawn felt a friendship starting.

Practice was over by noon so Shawn said good-bye to the Soviet coach and went to the storage building where all sleds were worked on and then locked up in small cages. Ray was already there, discussing adjustments needed on the sleds for the next days practice. They helped the athletes make the adjustments, then Shawn and Ray left the bobsled run. They went to the parking lot and got into the rental car. On the way to the apartment in Calgary, Shawn told Ray the story about how he and the Soviet coach had been predicting the finish times of the bobsled teams. Ray was interested in the apparent friendship that Shawn started with the Soviet coach.

"It's because of Glasnost that this is happening, Shawn."

They returned to the apartment and made plans to go out to dinner that evening. They picked a small, intimate Italian restaurant. During dinner, Ray told Shawn he had been examining all the bobsleds in the start area before practice began. He suggested that Shawn bring his camera with the telephoto lens to the run the next morning to take technical photos.

Ray said, "I'll stand near each sled that I want you to photograph. I'll need front, sides, top, and bottom shots of each of the East German and Russian sleds." Ray explained that if Shawn could get clear photos he could scan them and enter the data into a computer. With the results Ray would build scale models one-tenth in size and conduct wind tunnel testing on the miniature bobsleds to determine which foreign bobsled had the best aerodynamic design.

Ray cautioned Shawn to be careful and very discreet because the Soviets and the East Germans would become very hostile if they discovered what he was doing. Shawn assured him that he could get the photos from a distance without them knowing. After dinner they left the restaurant and took a walk around the downtown section. They discussed the poor results of the American 2-man teams.

Calgary was alive with Olympic spectators celebrating throughout the city. Ray noticed a French restaurant across the street and told Shawn he wanted to look at their menu posted on the entrance. He was curious about their prices. They crossed the busy street and walked up to the window. The prices were unbelievably expensive and the least amount someone could spend on dinner alone, without French wine, was nearly one hundred dollars.

They walked past the entrance and glanced into the dinning room. Sitting at a large table were all the bobsled association officials: Lester, Nino, Wilbur, and John Chapadeau.

"Can you believe this shit?" Ray was furious. "These bastards will put this on the association credit card just like they did in Europe."

"Now you know why they don't want anyone to look at the treasurer's reports. John Chapadeau hasn't made the report available to anyone for over two years," Shawn replied.

"How does he get away with it?"

"Nobody can challenge them. At the last annual meeting he stood up to give his report and pulled a piece of paper out of his pocket. He read what the income, expenses, and balance on hand was for the year. Period."

"You mean to tell me that Wilbur and the other officers didn't ask for a written report?" Ray could not believe it.

"The association bylaw's require that a written report be provided to any member asking for a copy. Some of the athletes asked and were told that Chapadeau's accounting firm was preparing the report and it would be available in a day or two." Shawn shook his head and said, "It never arrived."

"It's hard to believe they are so open with their misuse of Olympic funding." Ray was clearly disgusted with the entire group.

They walked back to the apartment enjoying the fresh taste of the early evening air. They discussed what they should talk about with Daumant Znatnajs the next morning. They were very excited about this unusual meeting with the Soviet Minister of Sports.

Shawn woke up early the next morning and decided to go for a short run. He pulled on his jogging outfit and called out to Ray, "I'll be back in about forty minutes." When Shawn returned he met John Chapadeau leaving the apartment building.

"Shawn, you've got to move out of the apartment today," John avoided Shawn's eyes.

"What the hell are you talking about?"

"We have a unexpected guest of the association and need your apartment."

"Where do you expect me to stay?" Shawn was outraged.

"Get a motel room and the association will reimburse you. I've got to go. I've got a lot of other things to get done. I gave the information to Ray, he'll fill you in when you get upstairs." John got into his car and drove away.

Shawn took the elevator up to the sixth floor and went down the hall to their apartment. The door was partially open and he could see the generous backside of a woman standing just inside. Shawn went inside and Ray was standing next to the woman and neither were talking.

"What's going on?" asked Shawn.

"I don't know. John Chapadeau just knocked on the door and told me you had to move out and this woman was going to stay in your bedroom."

"Are you an official with the association?" Shawn asked. He looked at her closely and recalled seeing her some other time, but couldn't remember where.

"Ah, no, I'm not," she replied.

"Well, are you a sponsor or do you work for one of our sponsors?"

"No, not exactly."

Suddenly Shawn recalled who the extremely well endowed woman was. She was Nino Casatelli's mistress. If his wife ever found out she would kill him.

"It just occurred to me who you are." Shawn smiled sarcastically. "You're Nino's mistress. Grab your bags and get your ass out of here. If Nino wants to shack up with you then do it in his bedroom. If you have a problem with that let me know. The press would love to get this. I can see the headlines now, 'Bobsled official pays with Olympic funding to fly his mistress to the Olympics.' I bet his wife would love to read that. Get your ass out of here right now."

"Where do you expect me to go at this hour in the morning?" She asked plaintively. She knew she had no choice.

"I could care less. Call your gigolo, Nino."

The woman picked up her two bags and hustled out of the apartment. Ray and Shawn looked at each other in amazement. They couldn't believe what had just occurred. Shawn quickly took a shower and rushed to get dressed. He didn't want to be late for the breakfast meeting with Daumant.

Daumant and his interpreter were waiting for them when they arrived at the Olympic dining room. Everyone exchanged friendly greetings before crossing the room to the buffet. Their conversation was casual as they ate. Ray asked Daumant about their bobsled technical program and Shawn questioned him about their physical training program.

→ *Ice Spy*

Daumant was very congenial and seemed to be truly interested in sharing information with them. He was about sixty years old and a rather good looking man with black hair streaked with white. Shawn estimated that he was about six feet tall and weighed about two hundred pounds. Daumant told them that he was responsible for arranging the Soviet government's funding for the bobsled program.

It was finally time for all of them to go to the track for the start of practice. They agreed to meet the following morning for breakfast. Shawn and Ray caught a ride to the top of the bobsled track on an equipment truck. Ray left Shawn and went to the start deck where the sleds were stored while the teams waited their turn to go down the track.

Shawn went to the corner of the building where the athletes stayed to keep warm while they were waiting for their turn. He changed the lens on his camera and waited for Ray to identify the first sled he wanted photographed. Ray walked to the front of the East German's number one sled and stopped to take a look. A group of burly men immediately rushed over to block the professor's view and brusquely told him to keep moving.

Shawn knew that this was the first sled to be photographed. He moved down the ramp to the edge of the platform and stood there waiting for the East Germans to relax and move away from the sled. After a few minutes they appeared confident that the professor wasn't coming back and moved away from the sled.

Shawn watched and when they turned their backs he focused his powerful telephoto lens on the sled and quickly took several shots. The sled was upside down and was resting on special braces so work could be done on the bottom without damaging the top. He looked around and noticed that he could go around the other side of the building and get photos from a different angle. From the back of the platform he got some fine shots and when the East Germans turned the sled over to take it to the start of the track he got several more.

Shawn returned to the athlete's warm-up building and waited for the professor to identify another sled. He was certain Ray would go to the Soviet's number one sled and, sure enough, moments later he did just that. Shawn repeated the steps he had taken with the East German sled. The professor identified five more sleds. When Shawn finished the photo shoot, he calculated that he had taken over one hundred photos.

Shawn waited at the athletes warm-up building to see if Ray might have another sled to photograph. He noticed a young woman wearing a Royal Canadian Mounted Police uniform walking up toward him. She stood next to him and looked around for a moment before moving up close to him.

"I think you have taken enough photos for today," she smiled and winked at him. "I have been observing you for the past hour and I finally figured out what you are doing."

"Just trying to learn what the competition has," Shawn replied quietly.

"I understand, but I'm concerned that if they catch you, we'll have an international incident right here. That wouldn't be good."

"I have enough anyway. Thanks for letting me take the ones that I got." Shawn smiled at her again and quickly disappeared into the crowd. The policewoman thought that he had a drop-dead gorgeous smile, and knew it.

Shawn walked down the bobsled track to the coaching section, took his seat next to the Soviet coach and began to record times as he had the previous day. Although they did not speak, they continued to build their friendship by sharing their predictions of the finish times for the sleds as they went down the run.

Shawn smiled at the Soviet coach and waved good-bye when the practice finished. The coach returned the smile and wave. Shawn walked back to the equipment building where Ray was helping the drivers make adjustments on their sleds. It was mid-afternoon before Ray had finished his work so they decided to stop and eat lunch at a nearby restaurant.

Shawn told Ray about the Royal Canadian Mounted policewoman and all the photos he managed to take. Ray was delighted and told Shawn he should have offered to take her to dinner and she might have allowed him to take more in the morning. They agreed that Shawn would take more in the morning unless she stopped him.

"I'm curious, Shawn did you see any of the association officials at the track?"

"The only time I've seen them in Calgary is at the French restaurant and during the race on the weekend." Shawn chuckled. "You won't see them otherwise. Remember how much they came around the track in Germany? Unless there's a reporter or a TV camera you won't see them. Good-God, they won't take a chance on having to work!"

"What a bunch of slime balls. What do you think will happen in the morning when we meet Daumant?"

"Can you imagine what Daumant would think if he ever sat down and talked with Lester or Nino?" Shawn went into a terrific imitation of Lester and Nino's conversation with Daumant, amusing Ray.

They arrived at the apartment and Shawn called Angela at her office to bring her up to date on what he and Ray had been doing. Later they went to a reception at a large hotel in Calgary given by the ABC television network for the Americans involved in the Olympics.

Shawn remarked to Ray sarcastically, "Our beloved association officials look right in place, don't they?"

The next morning Shawn went for a run and when he returned he took a shower. He thought about Nino's mistress and wondered where she went to stay. She wasn't at the ABC party. Ray was waiting for him in the small living room to finish his shower. When Shawn finally got dressed they left to meet with Daumant at the dining room in the Olympic complex.

They arrived in time and Shawn was surprised to see the Soviet coach at the table with Daumant and the interpreter. Shawn and Ray exchanged greetings and Daumant explained that he had asked Hopmahs Polakov, his coach, to join them for breakfast. Daumant explained that Hopmahs could speak some English and could help answer many of the questions Shawn had about the Soviet's physical training program.

Hopmahs was about thirty-five and a rather good-looking man with a medium build. Shawn noticed that Hopmahs was very formal and seemed to have the highest respect for Daumant. Shawn rightly assumed that Daumant must have been very important in the Soviet Union.

They finished breakfast and then Daumant shocked both Shawn and Ray. He suggested that they might want to take Hopmahs back to their apartment after practice so they could talk about the sport of bobsledding in private. This was unbelievable and unprecedented action. Shawn and Ray agreed immediately. They were thrilled that Daumant had made the stunning suggestion. They made plans to meet at the front entrance of the bobsled track at one-thirty. Shawn knew that there would be very few people around at that time to see them leave together. Their meetings each morning in the Olympic complex had already attracted a lot of attention.

The meeting broke up and Shawn went to the start area. Ray took off in a different direction. He spotted the Royal Canadian Mounted policewoman and walked up to where she was stationed.

"Good morning." Shawn smiled cheerfully and reached into his jacket pocket for an American Olympic bobsled pin. "Do you have one of these?"

"No, I don't. It's beautiful," she exclaimed as she took the pin out of the plastic wrapper. She pinned it on her jacket with some others she had collected. "Are you here to take more photos?" she asked quietly.

"I only need a couple," Shawn whispered, giving her his most charming grin. "Just a couple and I'll be out of your hair."

"Come on, do you really think you can bribe me with a simple pin?" She smiled back at Shawn and he knew she would allow him the pictures.

"Of course not. That's why I'm taking you to lunch right after practice."

"I could have lunch with you if we eat at the restaurant here at the bobsled track."

"Good. I'll meet you at noon."

Shawn had all he could do to keep from laughing. He was pleased with himself. Ray was at the top of the run watching Shawn. He wondered how he managed to get the policewoman to let him into the area with his camera and telephoto lens. Ray knew that Shawn would only have a short time to take more pictures so he walked around to identify some other sleds he specifically wanted photographed.

Shawn finished quickly and walked past the policewoman, reminding her to meet him at noon. She looked eager and Shawn almost felt sorry for using her. Although he regretted it he knew that innocent people got used all the time in the espionage business. He went back down the track and took his position next to Hopmahs. The morning practice was busily underway since the four-man sled competition was just two days away.

At noon Shawn walked down the track to the restaurant to meet the policewoman. She arrived a moment later and apologized profusely. She had to leave for another assignment and suggested that perhaps they could have lunch on another day. Shawn was relieved but tried not to let it show too much.

He went to the equipment building where Ray was working on the sleds. Ray walked over to meet him and asked how he managed to get the photos. Shawn laughed and told him about the conversation with the policewoman and the lunch engagement that didn't take place. It was nearly one-thirty that afternoon when Ray finished adjusting the sleds so they had to hurry to meet Hopmahs at the main entrance. When they arrived he was standing off to the side, pacing. Shawn knew that Hopmahs must have been extremely nervous about going with them. He was sure the KGB was watching every move they made.

They exchanged friendly greetings and walked to the rental car in the parking lot. Shawn got into the back seat and Hopmahs sat in the passenger's side. When they drove out of the parking area headed toward the highway, Ray glanced at Shawn in the rearview mirror. They read the clear message in each other's eyes and neither could believe that they were leaving the Olympic area with a Soviet coach in the car. Shawn tried to imagine what their visit would produce.

Chapter Twenty-One

→ *Ice Spy*

Riga, Latvia, USSR

Boris Yegorov glanced at the antique German clock on the mantel. He had moved Anita and her parents into an apartment owned by the Latvian Socialist Slate. Several friends donated spare furniture for them to use after the KGB burned their home in the former stable. It was almost 9 a.m. He put on his heavy jacket and said good-bye to Anita then left the apartment. The temperature outside was nearly zero for the fifth day in a row, but the bitter wind made it feel more like thirty below zero. He walked briskly down the street pulling his coat tight around his neck and then pushed his hands further into his jacket pockets, attempting to keep them warm. He vanished around the corner without seeing the two KGB agents parked across the street.

Pasevs and one of his agents were observing Boris, hoping that his actions might give them some clue about his plans. They were completely stymied with their investigation.

"Shall I follow him?" asked the driver. He was freezing and hoped Pasevs would let him start the car so he could warm up.

"No. Let's sit here and see if his wife leaves with the car. We always follow Boris and he never goes anywhere important. His wife often leaves later so let's see where she goes."

The KGB Vice-Commandant was becoming very frustrated. He felt certain that Boris was planning to defect but had no proof. They knew Boris kept the money he received from the East Germans in a Swiss bank account and had met with Americans on several occasions. Normally, by now, Georgi would have killed someone like Boris, but Ivan Liepinsh, Commandant of the KGB in Riga, was waiting for him to solve the case. He suspected that powerful officials higher up in the agency were also watching very intently. He knew that Ivan was more interested in the money than in justice being served. Pasevs knew that if he didn't solve the case soon his career would be in jeopardy.

It was very difficult during the cold winter weather to follow Boris because he was smart enough to stay away from congested public areas where KGB agents found it much easier to blend in with a large crowd. They were much more noticeable tailing someone on a deserted street. Georgi suspected that Boris was aware of them whenever he was followed. On frequent occasions when they followed him in the past and went into someone's apartment, the KGB agents went into the homes to check on him. Each time he was inside visiting his friends.

Pasevs was aware that Boris could elude them by going into an apartment by the front door and then leaving out a rear door. Typically, the back yards of old Latvian homes faced each other with a large courtyard separating them. The buildings were connected together on each side making it impossible to watch someone leaving by a rear door. Boris could easily have entered the rear door of another home and left by the front. He would be a block away within seconds and the agents would never know he left. It made the surveillance very frustrating for Pasevs.

Late one evening, Pasevs had one of his demolition experts install explosives under Boris' car. He kept the remote switching device in his pocket but had not yet decided when he would blow up the car. He kept thinking about Boris and the money. It tormented him that Boris managed to keep his plan secret making him look incompetent to Ivan and his agents.

Meanwhile, Boris knew that if Ivan requested expert help from headquarters in Moscow his jurisdiction in the case would end. Ivan was very reluctant to do so because if the KGB hierarchy in Moscow solved the case, Ivan and Georgi would be charged with incompetence and the money in the Swiss account would disappear.

He took a bottle of vodka out of his jacket and swallowed a large portion before offering it to his driver. Georgi normally would never have been drinking while he was working but the situation with Boris was pushing him beyond his limits. The vodka slowly warmed his body and helped him relax. Georgi got all the vodka he wanted free of charge. No shop keeper would ever dream of charging the KGB's Vice-Commandant for vodka, or anything else for that matter.

"Look, they're coming out the front door." The driver pointed down the street where Anita and her parents were walking down the front steps. "Should we follow them?"

"It's a waste of time. She won't lead us anyplace if her parents are with her." Georgi swigged from the vodka bottle and generously passed the bottle to his driver. They watched as Anita helped her parents into the small automobile Boris had owned for nearly four years. The Russian government presented him the car as a gift prior to the 1984 Olympics for the prestigious Olympic bobsled program he built. The athletes' eventual failure to win a gold medal started all his problems and Boris was surprised the government never took the car back.

The two KGB agents watched as Anita got into the car and tried to start it. The bitter cold temperatures often made it difficult to start the car and it was no different this time. She sat for a few moments and attempted to start the car once again with no success.

"She'll never start that car without an engine heater," exclaimed Georgi's driver.

"Perhaps I can warm it up for her." Georgi took a generous drink of vodka. "These people are guilty of crimes against the Russian government."

"Do you want me to arrest them and have the van pick them up?"

"No. I'll take care of them myself." Georgi began slurring his words. He took another drink and pulled the remote electronic detonator from his pocket and engaged the switch. The driver's eyes bulged as the car swelled and began to separate. The ear-splitting noise was incredible. Anita and her parents were killed instantly. Heat from the explosion melted all the snow on the street surrounding the car. Windows in the homes nearby shattered blowing glass in every direction. Pieces of metal from the car flew up in the air and landed loudly on the roof of their car. The driver moved toward the steering wheel in total shock. He looked at Georgi who was smiling cockily.

"Take me back to headquarters." Georgi felt much better. His frustration was gone for the time being. "This will force Boris into making a move, and then we will get the evidence we need to arrest him."

Calgary, Canada

Hopmahs watched as Shawn unlocked the front door of the apartment building. Shawn held the door open and Professor Bodynski gestured with his hand for Hopmahs to enter. They walked up a small flight of stairs leading to the elevator and Ray pushed the button to open the door. The men stepped inside and Ray pushed the sixth floor button.

No one spoke. Their conversation in the car had been light and very formal. Hopmahs studied both men and wondered if they might be CIA agents or even worse, undercover KGB. Daumant had called him to his room and suggested that he go with the Americans to converse with them about the Soviet's bobsled physical training program. He assumed Daumant was trying to promote friendship with the Americans by pushing Mikhail Gorbachev's ideas from Glasnost and Perestroika.

The elevator door opened and they walked out into the hallway. The apartment door was just a few feet from the elevator. They went inside and Ray took Hopmah's coat and hung it up in a closet. Hopmahs looked around the apartment and wondered if the two Americans were wealthy. He had never been in an apartment this large and was amazed that only two men were staying there. Two families would live in an apartment this big in the Soviet Union

Shawn went into the kitchen and got out some cold cuts and rye bread to make lunch. He invited Hopmahs to help himself and asked if he would like something to drink.

"Yes, I like to have some Coke." Hopmahs relaxed and smiled as Shawn poured the soda for him. "I like Coke. In Soviet Union we no get Coke." His accent was strong but Ray and Shawn understood him easily.

"Please have a seat, Hopmahs." Shawn pulled out a kitchen chair for him. They joined him at the table. "Ray and I are thrilled that you have come to visit with us."

"Thank you. I'm most happy to come. You live here all the time, yes?"

"No." Shawn shook his head. "Ray and I are only staying here until the Olympics are over and then we will return to our homes in New York. Are you enjoying the Olympics?"

"Yes, very much. Canada is very nice. Like the United States, yes?"

"Yes. It's very much like the United States." Shawn was trying to relax the Soviet coach. "Tell me what it's like where you live in Russia."

"I'm not a Russian." Hopmahs's smile left his face and he became very serious. "I'm a Latvian. Russians invaded my country before I was born. Russians killed many Latvians, including my grandparents, and took everything valuable away from us."

Shawn and Ray were startled by his sudden outburst and were unsure how to proceed. Shawn tried to change the subject and asked Hopmahs how he trained his athletes. They spent the next hour sharing information about training programs for the Olympics. Hopmahs explained to Shawn and Ray how they had trained their drivers on a track in Valmiera.

"That's interesting. I didn't know you had a track in Valmiera. Is it near the bobsled track in Sigulda?" asked Shawn. He wished that Jim Bogdan was there with them to hear the conversation, but unfortunately, Jim was staying at the Olympic Village with the athletes.

"I make mistake. We train drivers in Sigulda."

Hopmahs suddenly froze as he realized the terrible error he made when he told them about the Valmiera bobsled track. No one in the world knew about that secret track except the Soviets. His stomach began to feel queasy. If either of the two men he was with were KGB undercover agents he would be in serious trouble for slipping with the information.

Daumant was the senior KGB officer at the Olympics and Hopmahs assumed that he had sent him to spend time with the Americans because of his Latvian background. He believed that Daumant was forced to work with the KGB to monitor the Latvians. If he had made a mistake, it would cost him his life once he returned to the Soviet Union. Hopmahs suddenly felt very uncomfortable.

"I met a coach once from Riga. His name is Boris Yegorov. Do you know him?"

Hopmahs nodded. "I know him. He is a traitor to the Latvians. He sold Latvian training and equipment technology to East Germans for much money. Some day Latvians will kill him." Shawn and Ray studied Hopmah's reactions very carefully.

"He told me about your track in Sigulda. Did he also build the track in Valmiera?"

"I don't know anything about a track in Valmiera. I make mistake. Yegorov a bad person. Maybe Russians kill him before Latvians." Hopmahs was sweating visibly.

"Soviet bobsled team is all Latvians. Russian athletes are not good enough to make team. Maybe that will change soon." Hopmahs was no longer smiling. "The Russians now know that Latvians want to leave Soviet Union. We won in the International Court. The papers Stalin used to occupy Latvia were illegal."

"Has the Latvian political movement affected your bobsled program?" asked Ray.

"Yes. Now Russians start to take over our bobsled program. They will move all the Latvians out once they have Russian athletes and coaches who manage the program."

Shawn changed the subject because the political tone of the conversation was making Hopmahs visibly upset. He knew the Soviet coach was under a tremendous amount of strain and it would be a waste of time to continue asking him for more information about their program. Ray suggested that they take Hopmahs shopping at one of the large malls in Calgary. Hopmahs was agreeable so they spent the rest of the afternoon showing the Soviet coach all the sights in downtown Calgary.

Later that evening they took him out to dinner at a plush restaurant. When they had finished their meal they drove him back to the Olympic Village where he was staying. On the way back to the apartment, Shawn and Ray discussed their conversation with Hopmahs in depth. Ray confirmed that Hopmahs said he trained his drivers at the Valmiera bobsled track.

They thought it was odd that Hopmahs suddenly denied that he mentioned the Valmiera track. They both agreed it was very clear that he hated the Russians and believed he would rather see the Americans win an Olympic medal than the Russians. Anti-Russian feelings were running strong among the Baltic States.

Shawn and Ray met with Daumant early the next morning for breakfast again and thanked him for allowing Hopmahs to spend time with them. Shawn told Daumant that they were aware of the Latvian political situation within the Soviet bobsled association.

"Yes, this is a very difficult time for the Latvian athletes and coaches." Daumant looked around the room nervously to see if anyone was watching them. "It is very difficult for me to talk here."

"Daumant, is it possible that Ray and I could come to the Soviet Union and spend some time with you?" asked Shawn. "We are very eager to promote the sport of bobsledding between our two countries."

"It is very difficult for you to just visit the Soviet Union without being part of an official tour." Daumant thought for a moment and continued, "Perhaps I can invite both of you to come for a culture exchange."

"That would be great!" Shawn smiled and said, "Glasnost has now become a part of bobsledding."

They laughed at Shawn's comment. Daumant asked his interpreter to take the information necessary to make an official invitation for them to come to the Soviet Union. They made their final visit with the Soviet Minister of Sports last as long as possible. The four-man bobsled race would take place during the next two days which were also the final days of the Olympics. They concluded it might be better if they were not seen together in Calgary and agreed to meet during the cultural exchange in Riga. Shawn looked up at the large clock on the wall and suggested to Ray that they should go to the track and help the athletes.

They said good-bye to Daumant and told him they would look forward to meeting with him in the Soviet Union. Daumant shook their hands vigorously and said their invitation would include a diplomatic visa allowing them to move about freely in the Soviet Union. They walked out of the dining room and once outside the building they looked at each other in amazed disbelief.

"I can't believe he invited us, can you?" asked Shawn.

"I think he really wants to help the Americans beat the Russians." Ray looked at Shawn thoughtfully. "I got the same message yesterday in the apartment."

"Do you really think he'll invite us?"

"I think he's real serious," replied Ray. "Let's keep this to ourselves right now. If the assholes running the association find out, they'll ruin the entire relationship we have created."

"Can you imagine what Lester and Nino would do if they ever went over there?"

"We don't want any of those idiots to find out. We have a golden opportunity to learn about the Soviet's training and technology. If any of them figure out what's going on before we leave, they'll blow the entire deal. Let's keep it to ourselves."

Shawn agreed wholeheartedly. "You've got that right."

They reached the midpoint of the track where Shawn had worked during the previous day's practice. They agreed to meet later in the equipment building and Ray continued his walk to the start of the track. Shawn climbed up to his assigned seat next to Hopmahs. Neither he nor Hopmahs spoke during practice but they continued to share the times as they had been doing in the past.

Another warm, windy day made the track conditions difficult for training. Practice finished early because it was the day before the first two heats of the Olympic four-man bobsled race. Most athletes used the time to rest and prepare for the race. Shawn and Ray spent the entire afternoon helping adjust and prepare the two American sleds for the next day. It was nearly four in the afternoon when they finally left the track.

Ray drove into the parking lot at the apartment house and they saw Joe Sweeney sitting in a car waiting for them. When Joe saw them he got out to greet them.

"I forgot that you were coming up," said Shawn. "I'm glad you're here. Come on up to the apartment. You'll die when I tell what's going on with us."

They went inside and took the elevator up to their apartment. Once they were inside Shawn and Ray told Joe about the meetings with Daumant and Hopmahs. He couldn't believe it when they told him Daumant was planning to send them an invitation with diplomatic visas. Joe was delighted with the unexpected good luck they were having but then he told them what happened to Boris's wife and her parents.

"Where is Boris now?" asked Shawn, concerned.

"He's gone into hiding with our undercover agent in Riga," replied Joe. "He's in a very depressed state right now and is extremely upset that we didn't get his wife and her parents out of the country."

"What are your plans now?" asked Ray.

"We have to wait for Boris to decide if he still wants to defect. He's suicidal and our agent has been trying to help him deal with his situation." At this point, Shawn realized that Joe seemed to be less confident about Boris's successful defection.

"Boris has nothing to live for except the chance to do something big to hurt the Russians. We have to wait and hope he'll come out of his depression."

"If he decides to leave the country, how will the CIA get him out?" asked Shawn.

"I'm really not sure about the plans, but I do know that the navy is working on some sort of a plan with our people down at Langley."

"How soon could they get him out if he decides to go?" Shawn was concerned that the KGB would kill him before they had a chance to get him out.

→ *Ice Spy*

Ray was silent during this exchange. This wasn't really his area of expertise.

"I'm under the impression that the navy is able to put their plan into action within a day's notice," said Joe.

Joe spent the evening with Shawn and Ray, then left to locate a motel on the outskirts of Calgary where he had managed to make a reservation. He was thrilled that Shawn and Ray were able to create the friendship with the Soviets and their invitation from the Minister of Sports to visit the Soviet Union would be perfect cover for *IceSpy*. Joe's excitement over their unexpected fortune made it difficult for him to fall asleep. He could hardly wait until morning to call Fred Unser with the good news.

Shawn and Ray arrived at the track early to help the athletes prepare their sleds for the first two heats of the four-man competition. The media would be out in full force and Shawn knew the association officials would be sticking to them like glue. Shawn dreaded seeing them. He felt sorry for the athletes who suffered from the officials' abuse and understood that they were afraid to speak out. Lester's reputation for revenge would prevent most people from going public.

Ray helped the two American teams make final adjustments to their sleds while Shawn worked with the athletes to help them relax mentally and stretch their muscles to get ready for the first heat. Ray rode to the start of the track with the athletes on the equipment truck and Shawn walked to the coaching area mid-way up the bobsled run.

Hopmahs was already in his assigned seat and smiled broadly when Shawn arrived. Shawn gave him an American Olympic bobsled pin. Hopmahs beamed and returned the favor by presenting Shawn a Soviet bobsled Olympic pin. The first two heats of the four-man bobsled race proved to be very exciting. The Swiss were in first place and the East Germans followed close behind in second; however, the real news of the day was the Americans.

They edged out the Soviet team for third place, the best since '56. That night Shawn prayed mightily that his team could hold on to the bronze position. Everyone in the American equipment area was hustling around in high spirits the next morning. The athletes were ecstatic over their unexpected third place position and were pumped up for the final two heats. Shawn had never seen the team in such a high level of excitement and he felt the exact same way.

Shawn left the equipment building and walked up the track. Hopmahs was waiting for him in the coaching area and greeted him warmly by shaking his hand and patting his back. Shawn was so excited that he wished the race would start immediately. The race finally began after what seemed like an interminable wait and at the end of the third heat the Americans remained in third place just a few hundredths of a second ahead of the Soviets.

The Americans were the fifth sled to go down the run in the final heat. Their run was excellent and it appeared that they would hold on to the bronze medal. Shawn said good-bye to his Soviet friend and left to be with the American athletes at the finish area. Hopmahs would have to wait until the end of the race to leave since the Soviets' number one team was the last sled in the fourth heat.

The American's excitement continued to build as sled after sled came down the bobsled run slower and slower. The crowds began to chant USA! USA! USA! as each sled coming down was eliminated from a medal position. The track conditions continued to erode as the late morning winds blew sand and dust on the ice. Shawn kept thinking it was a blessing that the Americans were the fifth sled to start in a field of forty-three.

Finally, the last sled was at the start of the bobsled run. The crowd quieted as they waited for the Soviet sled to make its final run. Anxiety filled Shawn and the American team standing with him at the finish area. They embraced each other and watched the close-circuit TV showing the Soviet sled preparing to start.

Suddenly, the Soviets began rocking their sled, then pushed it down the start of the run. Shawn quickly turned to look at the start time on the clock and his heart sunk as it flashed a start record time. He prayed that the sandy conditions on the track would slow them down just enough so his team would hold onto the bronze medal. The Soviet sled continued down the run at a record pace although it appeared on television to be in slow motion. The Soviets' sled entered the final turn and shot up the finish ramp. Shawn watched as the clock flashed a record time edging the Americans out of third place by only two one-hundredths of a second. They nearly won a medal, but this fact didn't give them any satisfaction.

Shawn looked at his guys and instantly tears began to run down their cheeks as TV reporters who had been interviewing them suddenly turned and rushed off to the Soviet team. Shawn was devastated and couldn't find the words to help the athletes. He felt an arm encircle him and heard a voice in broken English say, "Do not be sad, be proud of what your team did. They did not win but they made big improvement." Shawn turned to see a sympathetic Hopmahs trying to console him. They hugged and promised to see each other soon when Daumant sent the official invitation. Shawn walked away, feeling much better about the race, but there was still a colossal void in his heart.

Chapter Twenty-Two

→ *Ice Spy*

Montreal, Canada

Shawn and Ray bid each other farewell and Shawn walked down the ramp to catch his flight back to Albany, New York. They had the same flight from Calgary to Montreal giving them more time to discuss the proposed trip to the Soviet Union. Both were hopeful that Daumant would follow through with his invitation for a cultural exchange to promote the sport of bobsledding. This could be the start of something very significant between the two countries.

He walked down the aisle of the plane and slid into his window seat. Angela was planning to meet him at the airport in Albany. He was confident she would want to go out to dinner and spend some time with him since he had been away for the past four weeks. What he really needed was a good night's sleep, but he didn't want to disappoint his wife, either.

It seemed as if the plane had just reached its flight altitude when he felt it descending. It arrived in Albany a few minutes later. Angela was waiting by the exit ramp and excited to see him. She was ecstatic because several of her friends and co-workers had seen Shawn on the TV coverage of the Olympics and would tell her whenever they saw her. They went to the congested luggage area to pick up his suitcases and left in Angela's Thunderbird.

Angela talked non-stop for several minutes attempting to fill Shawn in with all the news. She suggested that they go to eat at the Roman Villa again. It was cozy there and they could catch up with each other's stories and eat dinner at the same time.

During dinner Shawn's mind drifted to Boris and the brutal difficulties he was currently experiencing. Prior to leaving Calgary, Joe called Fred at Langley with the news about Daumant Znatnajs's plans to invite Shawn and the professor to the Soviet Union. A nudge from Angela brought him back to the present. She scolded him for not paying attention to her story about work.

Moscow, USSR

Daumant Znatnajs went to his office on the first day back from the Olympics. He looked through paperwork reading many messages that arrived during his absence. Among them were several congratulating him for the tremendous success the Soviets had in Calgary. He was especially pleased that the Soviets won a gold in the bobsled two-man competition and the bronze in the four-man event.

The bobsled program's success would be looked on very favorably by his superiors. Their poor showing during the 1984 Olympics had haunted him for the past four years. Boris Yegorov nearly ruined his career with his poor results. Daumant called his secretary into his office and gave her instructions to call Gunar Kalgari to his office right away. Gunar was President of the Soviet bobsled club and his office was just down the hall. Gunar arrived within minutes after receiving the call.

"You asked to see me?" inquired Gunar leaning around the corner.

"Come in, Gunar. Thanks for coming so soon." As if he wouldn't. He motioned for Gunar to relax and sit in one of the large chairs next to a conference table in his office.

"You're to be congratulated for your success in Calgary," started Gunar, still slightly nervous. He never enjoyed being called into the Minister of Sports' office.

"I want you to meet with the Latvian Socialist Slate with a proposal. Invite these two men to come over here for a cultural exchange to promote the sport of bobsledding." Daumant leaned forward and handed Gunar a sheet of paper detailing the information he would need to invite Shawn and Ray to the Soviet Union.

"You wish that I go to the Latvian Socialist Slate without seeking permission from Moscow?"

"That's right." He nodded and said, "Let's keep this quiet for now. Catch a train in the morning and go to Riga. Send the Americans a telex after you discuss it with the slate."

Daumant passed Gunar another sheet of instructions. "I want the telex to say the Americans are the guests of the Soviet Union and all their expenses will be paid by us. Do you understand what I want you to do?"

"I understand, but this is highly unusual. Are you sure you want me to do this?"

"Yes. I'll take care of this end in Moscow." Daumant spent the next couple of hours outlining his plan to Gunar. The following morning Gunar got on the train and went to Riga. The trip would give him the opportunity to check in on his mother and father there. He was concerned about their well-being and knew their age made it difficult for them get around the city during the harsh winter months. Gunar and his wife had tried to get his parents to move to Moscow so they could look after them, but they refused to leave Latvia.

He wondered about the future of his parents and his fellow Latvians. The Russians had recently moved into Latvia with the Red Army and several hundred tanks. The political situation was extremely unstable and very volatile. The Latvians were becoming more and more hostile against the Russians. They openly demanded the right to display the Latvian flag and speak their native language, not Russian, as they were forced to do.

Gunar tried to rationalize what Daumant was doing. He couldn't make any sense out of it. One thing for sure, Daumant was committing political suicide and perhaps signing his own death warrant. Once the Russian leaders in Moscow found out what he had done, they would have his head. His own concern right now was how the situation might affect him and his family.

Schenectady, New York

Shawn had just arrived home from work when he heard the telephone ringing in the kitchen. He rushed to pick up the receiver before the caller hung up. Roger Ferris was calling to tell him that he had received a telex from the Latvian Socialist Slate inviting him and Ray to the Soviet Union. Roger said he had faxed a copy of the telex to Shawn's office. The telex gave all the information necessary for them to obtain a special diplomatic visa and the dates they were to visit the Soviet Union. They were to leave the following week.

"I'm curious. Why were you two guys invited to be guests of the Soviet Union for a sports cultural exchange and not the officers of the association?" asked Roger.

"I'm not sure. Why don't you call the Soviets and ask them?"

"Why are you such a pain in the ass whenever I talk to you?"

"I guess it's my basic dislike for thieves, drug users, and people who do nothing but abuse the system, Roger. You and I both know what you're all about, don't we? Don't worry, your time will come. Have a nice day." Shawn hung up the phone and called Ray to tell him the telex had been received by the association and what the dates were. He related to Ray the phone conversation he had with Roger. Ray was delighted to hear it.

Shawn knew Angela would not be thrilled that he was going on another trip so soon after returning from the Olympics, especially since the trip was to the Soviet Union. She had also made it very clear about how she felt about him getting involved again with the CIA. He still felt it was some sort of a dream that he and Ray were going to be guests of the Soviet Union and hoped that Angela could appreciate it as much as he did.

He envisioned in his mind what the trip might be like and what type of information he and Ray might bring back to the United States. Shawn called Joe Sweeney and explained that the telex had arrived and the dates they were to visit the Soviet Union. Joe said he would have the agency make out all the papers required by the Soviets for the trip and would have the Department of Defense make arrangements for him to be away from work.

CIA Headquarters, Langley, Virginia

Fred Unser called Gary Circe, the Director of the CIA, and briefed him on the *IceSpy* situation. They agreed that Fred should contact the State Department to expedite the paperwork for Shawn and Ray. Ray would then contact the Department of Defense to coordinate with them so Shawn would not have a problem with the two people he worked for at the Schenectady Air Base. Fred recalled all the problems Shawn had with Olive Hanson and Colonel Amos Fowlkes. He couldn't imagine working for a pair like them.

He had just gotten off the phone with the Department of Defense when Joe Sweeney rang back. Joe had just read an Associated Press story in the morning paper about the invitation from the Soviets. Fred rushed out into the parking lot and got the *Washington Post*. He flipped through the pages until he found the article. Nino Casatelli and Roger Ferris of the bobsled association took all the credit for setting up the cultural exchange with the Soviets. Nino was quoted in the story that he was sending Shawn Murphy and Professor Ray Bodynski to represent the association. Fred shook his head and thought, "It's no wonder Americans do so poorly in the Olympics when there are jerks like Nino and Roger controlling the associations."

Schenectady, New York

Shawn and Angela were watching the early news on TV when the telephone rang. Shawn went into the kitchen and picked up the phone. The caller identified himself as Vladimir Lipins, an American businessman who was Latvian by birth. He was interested in helping Shawn and the professor when they went to Latvia. Shawn asked how he could help them?

"I read in the paper that you will be going to the Soviet Union to work with the Soviet bobsled athletes in Riga, Latvia. I've been to Riga many times and speak Russian and Latvian fluently which might be a valuable asset for you since most Russians don't speak Latvian. Having an American interpreter who you can trust could benefit you tremendously."

"We don't have the funding available to even pay your expenses, Mr. Lipins."

"Money isn't important," Lipins insisted. "I own a small import-export business and I would simply use this as a business trip and write everything off. I was very excited to read the story in the paper. I thought this would be an excellent way for me to help the American bobsled association. I was very frustrated when the Soviets edged us out of the bronze medal in Calgary."

"I appreciate your offer to help us, but I really don't know what to say."

"It would be important for you to meet with me. Perhaps we could have breakfast together in the morning?"

"I could meet you around seven if we can meet near the air base," replied Shawn. "Meet me at the Skyport restaurant. It's on Freeman's Bridge Road near the airport."

"I know where it is," Vladimir replied excitedly, "and I'll be waiting."

Shawn hung up and walked back into the living room. Angela was reclining on the sofa and asked, "Who was that?"

"He said his name was Vladimir Lipins. He offered to go to the Soviet Union with us and work as our personal interpreter."

"I don't like this at all. He's probably a Russian KGB agent working in this country." Angela was suspicious and her famous temper was rising. "Why did you have to get involved with this stuff all over again? I'll be a nervous wreck until you get home."

"You worry over nothing." Shawn stood up and threw a sofa pillow lightly at his wife. "Come on. Let's run down to the Roman Villa for some ziti and meatballs."

Shawn and Angela took her Thunderbird for the ride to town. The country road wound through farmlands still covered with a blanket of snow. Shawn loved the spectacular view from their small farm. It was early March and darkness fell around five. The city lights illuminated the valley below them. In the distance they could see Albany. The skyscrapers of the capitol were brightly lit and stood out in all their glory.

The Roman Villa was crowded but they found a table for two. Several patrons came up to him during dinner, impressed by the story in the morning's *Schenectady Gazette* and congratulated him. There were seven messages on the answering machine when they arrived home after dinner. Most were from friends who had read the story in the paper. He decided to return Joe Sweeney's call first.

Joe briefed Shawn on the current status with Boris and explained that Fred Unser had taken care of all the paper work for the trip. He explained it was important that Shawn not promote the fact he was in the military. Joe said his diplomatic visa would list him as a public relations director with the bobsled association. This cover would be excellent since he did their public relations work as a volunteer.

Joe finished his briefing and Shawn told him about the phone call he received from Vladimir Lipins. Joe was instantly curious and asked Shawn to get more information about him when they met for breakfast.

"Call me immediately afterward," Joe insisted. He didn't like the idea of Vladimir suddenly surfacing with an offer to help. Another concern he shared was that Znatnajs and the Latvian Socialist Slate might have a political motive for the culture exchange.

He returned the rest of the calls including one from a local TV reporter. Shawn gave her a brief interview over the phone and turned the answering machine on to take calls. He and Angela watched the news at eleven that carried a brief story about the upcoming trip to the Soviet Union.

Shawn met Vladimir at seven the next morning at the Skyport restaurant. Vladimir looked as if he had just stepped off Madison Avenue. He was dressed in a very expensive dark suit and carried a top hat, something businessmen seldom wore in the upstate area.

He told Shawn that he was the son of Latvian parents who were killed in a German concentration camp shortly after World War II. He survived the camp and as an orphan came to the United States after the Americans liberated the Latvians in the camp. He owned a small import-export business and had offices in New York City and Albany. Shawn tried to obtain as much information for Joe as he could without being too rude.

Vladimir's story was convincing to Shawn. He had numerous suggestions about how they should handle themselves once they got to Riga. He claimed that he had been to Riga several times on business and he would also make this a business trip so it wouldn't cost them anything. He now resided in the Kingston area just north of New York city.

Shawn explained that he would fly to Finland then go by ship to Talinn, Estonia where they would be pick up by Soviet athletes. They would drive to Riga, Latvia. He left Vladimir and rushed to get to the base before Olive arrived. He looked at his watch and the time was nearly eight. When he arrived at the main gate he saw that the security guards had pulled Bruce Monroe off to the side and were inspecting his car. One of the guards came over and leaned into Shawn's car window. He explained that the inspection sticker on Bruce's car had expired eight months ago. They had issued a final warning the day before and when they looked at the inspection sticker this morning they couldn't believe their eyes. Bruce had tried to make his own sticker out of a piece of paper, hoping to fool the guards. Shawn laughed delightedly and waved to Bruce as he drove past. Bruce's face read disgust all over it and Shawn could imagine hearing him complaining later to Olive that the security police were always picking on him.

He called Joe as soon as he arrived at his desk and gave him a detailed description of Vladimir Lipins and his Latvian background. Shawn told Joe that he didn't mention anything about Boris to Vladimir, and that they had only discussed the bobsled program in the Soviet Union. Vladimir was confident he could help Shawn with the Latvian athletes because he had connections to the Latvian Socialist Slate.

"Perhaps we can use him but remember, the *IceSpy* project is classified as confidential and we can't take a chance on anyone learning about Boris and his technology." Joe suggested that Shawn go along with whatever Vladimir had to say, in the meantime, he would run a check on him. Joe promised to call back as soon as he had some information on Vladimir.

He hung up the receiver just as Olive and Bruce arrived at the office. Sure enough, Bruce was upset and complaining that the security police were harassing him because they didn't like him. They put their coats away and went down the hall for coffee. Shawn wondered if Olive would have to pay for Bruce's coffee.

Riga, Latvia, USSR

Boris put on his heavy jacket and left the undercover CIA agent's small apartment where he was staying. He knew that he shouldn't leave the apartment and go out on the street when the agent was gone, but he still had a job to do. If it should cost him his life it would be worth it. He now had nothing to lose. He pulled his hat down over his ears to keep the cold out and covered part of his face. He had grown a beard to keep his face warm and change his appearance.

He confidently walked down the street, watching very carefully to be sure he wasn't being followed. He zigzagged through city streets until he reached the VEF plant. VEF was a state-owned factory that manufactured electronic components for the Russian military. His former laboratory was on the second floor of the enormous structure. The Russians took control of the building after the Latvian government began its legal action to become separated from the Soviet Union and the building was now guarded by the Russian army.

During the time he was still working as a physicist at the lab he often noticed that the guards who worked after midnight assumed everyone had left the plant and would drink vodka and sleep. Boris was a rather quiet man and had spent an incredible amount of time working after his normal day had ended. Late at night he worked on bobsleds either in his lab or in the welding shop located on the ground floor below.

Confident that nobody was aware he was in the shadows of the building, Boris quickly darted across the street and entered the dark alley next to VEF. He knew how to enter a side entrance of the building undetected. Looking around one last time to be sure nobody followed, he strained his eyes to study the dark contents in the alley. Certain that he was alone, Boris picked the lock of a side door and slipped into the dark welding shop.

→ *Ice Spy*

He shut the door quietly behind him and stood still to let his eyes adjust. His eyes focused to the darkness and he walked slowly across the room, being careful not to disturb anything that might create noise.

The welding shop was located in the first floor corner of the enormous building that nearly filled the space of a city block. Few people in Riga knew that the majority of all integral parts used in Russian electronic instruments for tanks and airplanes were fabricated inside the three huge floors rising above the welding shop. The plant had been built by the Russians in 1948 and was the largest building in Riga.

Boris walked directly to the enormous acetylene tanks that were stored in a room next to the supply area. He reached into his pocket and took out a key and quickly opened twenty tanks then walked out of the room, leaving the door open. He knew the escaping gas would reach the furnace room down the hall within ten minutes. Even if the guards did smell the gas, it wouldn't matter, it would be too late. The plant not only had a large supply of acetylene tanks but it also stored vast quantities of varnish and paint supplies used to coat electronic components. The wood throughout the inside of the brick building would burn at an enormous speed.

Boris slipped out the side door and ran down the street away from the building. He turned the corner and heard the tremendous blast. Looking back over his shoulder he saw the gigantic flash reflecting off the buildings around him and then he could hear the sharp sound of glass breaking in every direction.

Out of breath, Boris stopped running and walked rapidly toward the apartment. He was four blocks away and could feel the frightening heat from the fire that was now a raging inferno. The streets were brightly lit and new explosions ripped through the night as unopened acetylene tanks exploded throughout the factory. He imagined that tanks stored in other areas blew up along with the flammable material. Fire sirens sounded in the distance and he smiled grimly to himself, knowing they would be useless.

Boris arrived back at the apartment without being discovered. The CIA agent whom he knew only as Standislav had been gone for a couple of days and Boris wasn't sure when he would return. Looking out the front window, he watched the fire's reflection blazing in the night sky. It would become the largest fire in the history of Riga.

Schenectady, New York

Joe Sweeney called Shawn and told him that the Agency had a lot of information on Vladimir and was aware of his business trips to Latvia. The FBI had records of him traveling to Latvia several times during the past couple of years. The Agency assumed he was taking trips for his import-export business, but also suspected Vladimir was involved with a small smuggling operation. They were aware that he smuggled American VCRs and computers into the Soviet Union and sold the electronic equipment on the black market. He used the rubbles to purchase very expensive antique jewelry sold in Latvian co-op stores for a mere percentage of their real value. Latvians were forced to sell their heirlooms to obtain money to purchase food because the Russians were slowly starving them by limiting their supplies. Vladimir would smuggle the jewelry back to the United States and sell them for one hundred times more than he paid. He had once remarked to an undercover FBI agent that he did this to help his poor countrymen.

"Do you think we should consider taking him along with us?"

"Yes," Joe replied. "My instructions are to have you call the bobsled association and have them telex a message to the Soviets requesting permission to allow you and Ray to bring your personal interpreter along with you."

Newark, New Jersey

Shawn, Ray, and Vladimir boarded Continental Airline's flight to London where they would stay overnight, then fly to Helsinki the next morning. Shawn wasn't happy about Vladimir traveling with them to the Soviet Union as their interpreter, but Fred Unser thought it would help to prevent the Soviets thinking the CIA was involved. Fred's plan was to let Vladimir work with them during the cultural exchange and then let him fly back alone from Riga before they left with Boris.

Their flight landed in Helsinki the following day and Shawn was rapidly getting tired of the verbose Vladimir. Ray simply endured him until they arrived downtown at the Hotel Bothnia, where they stayed in separate rooms.

The next morning Shawn left the hotel early, without telling either Ray or Vladimir, to meet with Walter Shapnek. Fred Unser had arranged for Walter to meet him in Helsinki and give him a briefing just before he entered the Soviet Union. Fred had decided that it was too risky for Walter to return to the Soviet Union, but believed it would be safe for him to brief Shawn in Helsinki.

Walter detailed their plan to smuggle Boris out of Riga. Shawn would be met by Standislav Akolous, the CIA's undercover agent who was hiding Boris. Shawn was startled by Walter's admission that the plan was incomplete so far. By the time they were ready to leave Riga with Boris, Standislav would tell them the rest of the plan.

Shawn returned to the hotel and joined Ray and Vladimir who were eating breakfast in the dining room. They had assumed that Shawn had been out jogging. Ray glared at Shawn for a second forcing Shawn to laugh as he realized that Ray was *thanking* him for leaving him alone with Vladimir.

They finished breakfast and checked out of the hotel and took a taxi to the docks where they were to sail on the *George Ott*. The Russian ship was a modern vessel decked out with large red flags featuring the hammer and sickle. Shawn looked at the large ship and was confident it would have no problem sailing the turbulent Baltic Sea. The boat left Helsinki at eleven and Shawn immediately went to the upper deck to take photos. A few minutes later Ray joined him and they watched Finland slowly disappear as the *George Ott* continued its journey in the direction of Estonia.

"I don't know about you, Ray, but this is a strange sight, watching the free world disappear. I really have the feeling that I'm now behind the Iron Curtain."

Ray nodded his agreement and turned to Shawn, asking, "Where did you get this Vladimir character? I get a strange feeling whenever he's around us."

Shawn explained the story about Vladimir and the CIA's suggestion they use him to help them as an interpreter during the cultural exchange and that they would leave him in Riga. He would fly back to the States by himself. Both agreed that Vladimir was nothing more than a slick weasel who would steal the gold out of his mother's teeth if he had the chance.

Shawn confided in Ray what he had been told by Walter in Helsinki. They agreed that they should spend the first week conducting bobsled business. Perhaps they could also obtain more information from Hopmahs. Once they had all the information that they suspected Hopmahs might give them, they hoped Standislav would get them out of the country with Boris, pronto.

"The guy's a royal pain in the ass," commented Ray as he noticed Vladimir walking toward them on the deck. They changed the topic of conversation and chatted with Vladimir about the cultural exchange they would be taking part in while in Riga. Vladimir was full of suggestions about ways he could make their trip more productive and sounded more like a used-car salesman than an import-export businessman.

Five hours later, the *George Ott* slid into the dock area in the Tallinn Harbor. The workers rushed to secure the lines and prepare the ship so the passengers could depart. As Shawn watched the Soviet workers make their final preparations, the excitement in him built. He wondered what was ahead for him and Ray. Their diplomatic visas allowed them to stay four weeks but he suspected they would be leaving much sooner.

Shawn noticed that Vladimir had an incredible amount of luggage and because of the FBI report assumed he had a supply of electronic equipment to sell. He was curious to see how he would get through customs. They took their luggage to the first checkpoint where their papers were carefully scrutinized. They were given a declaration form to fill out to list any valuables they were bringing into the Soviet Union. Ray and Shawn started filling out the long declaration form when Vladimir stopped them and told them not to do it.

"Are you crazy?" asked Shawn. "I'm not going to enter the country without declaring my personal jewelry."

"Shh. Just do what I tell you," whispered Vladimir. "I've been through this many times and I know what I'm doing."

Shawn and Ray looked at each other doubtfully. Both knew what the other was thinking and they didn't trust Vladimir, but they didn't know how to avoid doing what he wanted. They went to the next checkpoint where the guards checked their papers again. The guards looked at Shawn and Ray's diplomatic visas and moved their luggage past without inspecting them. Vladimir put his luggage on the counter along with his passport and visa. One guard looked at his papers and another opened the first suitcase on the counter. Confident that there was nothing but clothing he closed it and started to open a rather large cardboard box Vladimir had placed on the counter with his two suitcases. Vladimir stopped him. "This is Mr. Murphy, the famous American bobsled coach." Vladimir smiled and pointed to Shawn. "He's been invited by your government to help the Soviet bobsled team. This is his equipment and he will be using it to help your athletes."

Vladimir pointed to his own luggage and smiled at the guards who were visibly unsure about what to do. They shrugged their shoulders and told them they were free to continue through the border. Shawn now knew it would be no problem to leave Vladimir behind in Riga when they left with Boris. Shawn was furious with Vladimir's treachery but he realized they were stuck with him, for now.

Gunar Kalgari and his driver, Arthur, were waiting for them on the sidewalk when they left the customs building carrying all their luggage. He introduced himself and told them he was honored to welcome them on behalf of Daumant Znatnajs explaining that he was on a flight from Moscow and would meet them in Riga that evening.

Arthur was a very large man who once had been a bobsled brakeman and now worked full-time for the Latvian bobsled association. He effortlessly picked up all the luggage from the three Americans and loaded it into the van without ever saying a word. Everyone got into the van and Arthur quickly pulled out into the traffic and headed for Latvia.

Vladimir translated all their conversations since Gunar could only speak Russian and Latvian. Gunar explained that they would be staying at the Hotel Riga. Once they arrived at the hotel they would have to hurry and change because they were expected at a state reception and dinner in their honor arranged by Daumant. They were running late and the reception was at another hotel. Vladimir explained in English that the other hotel was the official Communist Party hotel in Riga and only very important people stayed or visited there.

The ride from Tallinn lasted six hours and when they finally arrived at the Hotel Riga they were exhausted and not really looking forward to going out again. Shawn and Ray were thrilled to see Daumant when he met them at the state reception. They talked about the Olympics and Daumant was interested in hearing about their long trip from the United States. The reception and dinner lasted until nearly one in the morning and finally they were taken back to the Hotel Riga.

Shawn had been provided with a large suite on the fifth floor so he and Ray could have meetings there while they were in Riga. Although tired, when he arrived back at his suite he walked around the room looking for bugs the KGB had installed. During his briefing in Helsinki, Walter had cautioned him to never discuss anything in the hotel that he didn't want the KGB to overhear. Walter told him it was guaranteed that their hotel rooms were wired with electronic listening devices. The professor's room was just down the hall from Shawn, and Vladimir was staying on the sixth floor. Vladimir was not far enough away, thought Shawn, but at least he had behaved himself at the dinner party.

Shawn got into bed and turned off the light. Although he was beyond exhaustion, he had trouble falling asleep. Thoughts about Boris, the CIA, and the KGB kept floating around his mind. He tried to envision how they would finally leave with Boris. Shawn was unaware of Olive's plot to have Joyce call his wife and confess she had an affair with him. Joyce was reluctant to lie for Bruce and Olive because of the rumors at the base that Shawn was involved with the Department of Defense. She didn't want to get into a mess like Olive had gotten into by destroying the message.

Chapter Twenty-Three

→ *Ice Spy*

Riga, Latvia, USSR

The morning traffic in the city square below Shawn's room woke him earlier than planned. He climbed out of bed and pulled back the curtains covering the glass doors that led to the small veranda outside his bedroom. He slipped into his robe and went out to watch the traffic and people walking briskly to work. He noticed there was a second veranda suspended outside the other large room in his suite.

Shawn went back inside and walked into the other room looking around at the antique furniture. The only remotely modern piece of furniture was a thirty-year-old black and white television. A sofa and large coffee table were on one end of the room while a kitchen table with four chairs were squeezed into the other. A small refrigerator sat next to the table. He turned on the TV, but nothing was being broadcast. It must be too early, he thought.

He took a moderately warm shower in rust-tinted water and got dressed before calling Ray. Moments later Ray knocked on the door and they walked down the hall together. They turned the corner and passed a desk where a young woman and a man were sitting. The man stood up and walked over and introduced himself in perfect English. He explained that he was their official interpreter and that they were required to turn in their key to whoever was stationed at the desk each time they left their rooms. The young woman at the desk would give them a receipt. He also informed them that he was required to accompany them wherever they went. This was a surprise as they hadn't expected to have someone with them all the time. Ray and Shawn looked at each other questioningly. Shawn turned back to the thin, young man and said, "We assumed that the diplomatic visas allowed us to go anywhere without escort."

He replied sincerely, "I assure you that you are allowed to go wherever you want. I am only here to assist you."

Shawn hesitated for only a second before nodding. They would have to be creative and find ways to get out of the hotel without this guy tagging along all the time. The dining room was located on the main floor just off the lobby. The Russian interpreter followed them and explained that they could eat there anytime they wished and could order anything on the menu. They would not be permitted to pay for anything, reminding them that all their expenses were covered by the Soviet Union and that they had to simply write down their room number on the slip.

A short time later Vladimir joined them and he was visibly uncomfortable about having the young Russian interpreter with them. Shawn enjoyed the food which was a waffle-like pancake covered with strawberries. Strong coffee and juices complimented the meal. He was certain that most Latvians were never treated this well. After breakfast the group left together and went into the hotel lobby where Gunar was waiting for them.

Shawn asked Vladimir why the hotel clerk had taken their passports the night before when they had checked into the hotel. Vladimir explained they were required to keep the passports for several days while the police checked them out. The Russian interpreter confirmed this and added that this was a normal procedure in the Soviet Union. Arthur had the van waiting outside and drove everyone to meet with Daumant in his Riga office. Snow was falling lightly and Shawn assumed the cold and damp weather was normal for March.

Daumant's Riga office was on the third floor of a rather large old government building just down the street from the infamous Corner House. The structure took up most of the block. An extremely large statue of Lenin stood in the park across from the building. It was the tenth statue of Lenin Shawn had seen since arriving in the Soviet Union.

Arthur parked the van and everyone got out except him. Vladimir explained dryly, "Arthur is a peasant and isn't allowed in a government building like the one we are visiting."

They had to climb the three floors up to Daumant's office since elevators were not permitted in Soviet buildings with five floors or less, and this was a five-story building. They walked into the office and the secretary immediately called Daumant and told him the Americans had arrived. Within moments Daumant came out and enthusiastically greeted his guests.

"I trust your rooms are to your liking at the Hotel Riga?" asked Daumant in Russian. Vladimir translated the conversation while their assigned translator listened and smiled.

"They are excellent. I thank you very much for your generosity," replied Shawn.

"Come. Let's go into my office and I will have coffee brought to us." Daumant turned and led them into his office. Shawn was intrigued that a space of four feet with a door on each end separated Daumant's office and his secretaries. He estimated the walls to be about twelve inches thick. He assumed this was old fashioned Russian soundproofing which was so prevalent throughout the Soviet Union.

The office was enormous and had a large conference table positioned with one end located in front of Daumant's desk. A small stand on the left of his desk held an old-style tape recorder. Daumant's room was arranged so he could chair a meeting at the conference table from his desk and record everyone's conversation. There were several people sitting at the table and Daumant introduced his attorney, his personal interpreter, and a third man he introduced as Evalds Kalnins. He said Evalds recently retired as a Colonel from the Soviet Army and was assigned as a coach to the Soviet bobsled association.

Shawn looked at Evalds and instantly disliked the man. He had the dark look of a person who had a vicious, mean personality. Shawn suspected Evalds was really working for the KGB since Daumant said he was assigned as a coach. He instantly felt sympathy for the Latvian bobsled athletes. Looking around the room, Shawn thought the calendar pages must have stopped turning in 1917. The furniture style was similar to the hotel furniture, although it was in remarkably good shape.

Two microphones sat on the conference table with wires leading to Daumant's old style reel-to-reel tape recorder. There was no question about this meeting being taped, thought Shawn, as he watched the reels turning slowly. He turned to look at the professor whose eyes told Shawn he was thinking the same thing. This was not going to be an ordinary welcome briefing. The secretary entered and set a tray of coffee and pastries on the table then

→ *Ice Spy*

left closing the door behind her. Shawn sat back and looked at the gray ceiling and wondered if the KGB had tortured people right here. He tried to get the thought out of his mind. Daumant began the meeting and welcomed them once again.

"I must tell you about a very minor problem that has risen regarding your invitation to the Soviet Union." His relaxed smile was replaced with a very serious expression. "My superiors in Moscow are concerned because they were not consulted by myself about your invitation. This is not a problem for you and I will work it out shortly. I only tell you about it so you will refrain from speaking with the press should they ask you questions." Vladimir quickly translated the conversation preventing the other translators from taking part in the exchange.

"I will respect your request, Daumant. I am sure that Tass is curious about who we are," replied Shawn.

"The Soviet press would never discuss it with you, however, there are several foreign corespondents in Riga, including the American Associated Press. It is with these people I would prefer that you not discuss this very sensitive political situation."

"I believe I can speak for my associates." Shawn looked at Ray and Vladimir before continuing. "We will not discuss anything with them without you being with us."

"Thank you." Daumant smiled and gave a list of places he had chosen for the tours. "You will notice I have arranged for a tour of our bobsled track in Sigulda."

"Yes. I'm looking forward to going there," Shawn said, smiling politely. He asked, "Would it be possible for me to train with one of the Soviet drivers?"

"That can be arranged," replied Daumant. "Who did you have in mind?"

"Janis Kipurs," replied Shawn. "This would be very symbolic. The first time a Soviet and an American ever trained in a bobsled together."

"I will arrange it."

"We have never allowed anyone who was not a Soviet to visit the Sigulda bobsled track," Evalds said, raising his voice and looking straight at Daumant. "Allowing an American to ride with one of our athletes is extremely improper."

"Let me remind you, Evalds," Daumant said sternly, "I'm the Minister of Sports, not you." Daumant stared at the coach then spoke slowly. "You work for me. Mr. Murphy will take the symbolic ride with Janis as he has suggested and we will allow the media to come along. This will be done in the spirit of Glasnost."

Daumant told the group that the symbolic ride would take place within a few days. Shawn noticed that Evalds continued to stare at Daumant and looked extremely upset with his superior. It was obvious that the Latvian political situation was very explosive. Shawn hoped that he and Ray would not become too involved with the sensitive situation.

The meeting with Daumant continued for several hours during which Daumant and the Americans exchanged ideas about how to promote good will between their bobsled associations. Both Shawn and Ray noticed that Daumant continually asserted the Latvian's involvement and not the Soviets.

Neither Shawn nor Ray understood the seriousness of the political situation that was quickly encompassing them, although, Evalds's hostility toward them and Daumant was very evident. Daumant finally stood up and said formally, "We will reconvene in two days and finalize the plans for Sigulda then." The meeting was over.

Gunar and the Americans left the building with the Russian interpreter and went to the van where Arthur was waiting in the driver's seat. He jumped out to open the door for them and quickly drove off once they were inside. Arthur drove to a local restaurant and nobody discussed what took place during the meeting. Vladimir talked continuously about his business, bragging to Gunar and the Russian interpreter about how much he had done for Latvians. Shawn wished he would shut up because it was too obvious that he was grossly exaggerating his story.

They arrived at the restaurant and Gunar instructed Arthur where to park and wait while they were inside having lunch. Shawn wondered how or when Arthur managed to sneak away to eat his own lunch. Maybe he brown-bagged it, thought Shawn, giving Arthur a friendly nod. There was no response from the big silent driver. Shawn studied him and wondered if he worked for the KGB and decided to be careful about what he said whenever riding with him in the van.

Tallinn, Estonia, USSR

Standislav Akolous eased his car into the parking spot next to where his friend, Ivars Baravskis, had parked. He got out and looked at the centuries-old stone building where Ivars had his office. Standislav pulled his coat tight around him, cursing the cold, damp Estonian weather. It was mid-March and the winter air seemed to hang on forever over the Baltic states. The Gulf of Finland, lay behind the building and the icy look of the turbulent water sent chills through him.

Ivars was captain of the *Beriozka*, a Soviet, state-owned commercial fishing vessel. Ivars and his crew fished for cod throughout the Norwegian Sea in the north and as far south as Newfoundland in the North Atlantic. He sailed wherever the cod were running. The shortage of beef and poultry in the Soviet Union had placed tremendous pressure on the Soviet fishing industry. The dramatically increased demands over the past several years made it nearly impossible for the Baltic-based fishermen to meet their quotas. This was extremely frustrating since the Baltic States produced large quantities of beef and dairy products but these products were shipped to Moscow leaving fish as their main source of food.

Standislav went into the stone building and walked up the old wooden stairway leading to Ivars' office. The steps were worn smooth and he could hear the stairs creak under the weight of his body. The paint on the walls had nearly peeled completely off from years of neglect. Ivars was waiting for him and rushed over to embrace Standislav.

"Thanks for taking the time to meet with me," said Standislav gratefully.

"My friend, I was thrilled when you called and asked for a meeting." Ivars sat down in the old chair behind his desk and motioned to Standislav to sit. There was only one other chair in the room. "What brings you to Tallinn?"

"I've come on holiday." Standislav put his finger to his lips and pointed to his ear, a signal to Ivars that he could not tell him the real purpose because the room might be bugged. Ivars understood. "Tallinn is my favorite city for a holiday. Many of the old stone buildings that were built when the city was founded in the eleventh century are still in good repair and are magnificent. I never get tired of looking at them."

"I, too, enjoy looking at these buildings. The Estonian people have worked so hard to keep these old buildings in good condition but, of course, money is becoming harder and harder to find to make much needed repairs."

"Riga is in the same position. The sewers are in such poor condition that sewage pours freely into the streets and rats are everywhere."

"'Tis a shame, I say. Come, my friend, let me give you a tour of my new vessel. We are getting it ready to set sail soon." Ivars led Standislav down to the docks where they could talk quietly without being overheard.

Riga, Latvia, USSR

The telephone rang in Shawn's suite and it was Hopmahs calling from the front desk. Shawn invited him up to his room and hung up. Minutes later Hopmah arrived with a flourish. They embraced warmly and exchanged greetings. Shawn walked down the hall to Ray's room and invited him to join them. Hopmah told them they were being taken to the Sigulda bobsled track so Shawn and Janis could take the symbolic ride together. He said the press would be there as well as a TV reporter with a camera crew from the state-run TV station in Moscow. He suspected that the independent Latvian TV crew from Riga, which produces the TV show *Labvakar* might also be there.

Hopmah explained that the producers of *Labvakar* had been arrested several times for their documentaries about the Russians destroying the environment in the Baltic States and their suppression of Latvians. It was very clear to Shawn that this morning's symbolic bobsled ride had more meaning than its being the first Soviet-American run. Hopmah told them that the Latvian bobsled athletes would have breakfast waiting for them at the track in Sigulda.

The young Russian interpreter was waiting for them in the lobby when they stepped out of the elevator. He followed them out onto the street where the ever-stoic Arthur and Gunar were waiting with the van. Shawn glanced around and noticed that Vladimir wasn't there. He excused himself and took the interpreter back into the hotel and called Vladimir's room. Vladimir explained he had some personal business and wouldn't be going with them. Shawn thought his sudden change in plans was odd, but shrugged it off and left.

The group climbed into the van, but Hopmah insisted that Shawn should ride in his car. They watched Arthur start the van and drive out onto the busy street. Hopmah followed behind him. "I drive my car so we could talk alone." Hopmah's face was very serious. "I have been replaced as an Olympic coach by Evalds Kalnins. He knows nothing about bobsled. KGB did this so he could spy on Latvians for the Russians."

"I suspected that when I met him at Daumant's office yesterday. He looks like a mean son-of-a-bitch."

"He retire from Russian Army where he only learn how to kill and spy on people, that is why KGB hire him. He is no good for sport and athletes hate him."

The trip to Sigulda was fascinating and Shawn was surprised at how much the countryside reminded him of upstate New York. He recalled how air force and Air National Guard pilots often flew simulated attack missions over the Adirondack mountains. The Soviet terrain was very similar but he knew that no American pilots would be flying overhead today. He wanted to share this observation with Hopmah, but knew it was better not to say anything that might associate himself with the military.

The Sigulda bobsled track was very impressive and the start area was built very high off the ground, to create the elevation, needed for the starts, that the local terrain did not provide. While they were enjoying the richly flavored coffee and pastries, they were introduced to Janis Kipurs and several other Soviet bobsled athletes who Shawn knew were Latvian. The track manager explained the history of how the track was built and what was involved in maintaining the facility.

It was nearly 11 a.m. when Shawn and Janis took their first ride together down the bobsled run. Janis and Shawn slid past the finish line and several enthusiastic members of the Soviet bobsled association helped them get out of the sled after Shawn set the brake. The ride was very exciting to Shawn as he thought about its historical significance. He laughed as he recalled Evalds' angered face when they talked about this exact experience in Daumant's office. He noticed that Evalds wasn't at the track. Shawn was convinced that if the American bobsled officials had been there, the entire historical importance of the trip would have gone right over their heads.

"You like our track? Yes?" Janis smiled broadly and shook Shawn's hand. The press took several pictures and the *Labvakar* TV camera crew interviewed Shawn.

"Excuse, please. We must move from the finish area at once," said the Russian interpreter. "Another bobsled is about to come down with Professor Bodynski."

Shawn chuckled to himself. Ray is finally getting a ride in a bobsled and he had to travel all the way to the Soviet Union to get it. The other driver told them later that he drove with his eyes closed.

"I drive by feel when practicing," mimicked the shaken professor. The morning's adventure was thrilling to both men. They were still talking about the excitement after they arrived back at the Hotel Riga late in the afternoon.

It was nearly midnight and Shawn tossed about restlessly in bed so he went out and stood on the small veranda outside his suite. Moments later a car turned the corner and stopped in the square outside the hotel. The driver was a rather young woman wearing an excessive amount of makeup and was only scantily clothed. From his elevated position Shawn could see everything in the glow from the street lights. Vladimir gave the woman some money and then got out of the car and rushed into the hotel. . He was

→ *Ice Spy*

certain she was a prostitute. Shawn was disgusted. He knew it was too late to make changes and they were stuck with Vladimir.

The next week went by rapidly as Gunar and Hopmah kept them busy with sightseeing tours. Several meetings were held with Daumant and Gunar to work out a plan for the Soviet bobsled association to visit America for a cultural exchange. It was agreed that the Soviets would come to the United States to celebrate the tenth anniversary of the 1980 Olympics and the Americans would go to the Soviet Union the following year. Daumant made it very clear that Latvian athletes would represent the Soviet delegation.

Shawn and Ray knew that the Soviets would be upset by having so much emphasis put on the fact that it would be *Latvian* athletes and not *Soviet* athletes.

Their interpreter, stuck to them like glue and Shawn wondered when he slept. He was always in the hotel lobby waiting for them. During the week Shawn found time to walk around the hotel to learn where all the fire escapes were located. He discovered a stairway at the end of the hall, was used by hotel employees. He suspected this particular stairway might be very useful when he needed to leave the hotel undetected.

Evalds Kalnins flashed his credentials at the guard and entered the *Corner House.* Ivan Liepinsh, the Commandant in Riga had called and told him to meet him at his office right away. Evalds walked briskly up the stairs and turned to go down the hallway to Ivan's office. Georgi Pasevs was also entering the Commandant's office.

Evalds wasn't told what the meeting would be about but suspected it would involve the Americans and the Latvians. He entered the room and was greeted unemotionally by Ivan. Georgi nodded but stayed on the other side of the room. Evalds knew Georgi was extremely jealous that he was added to the KGB staff. He thought that perhaps Georgi suspected he had been added to replace the Vice-Commandant in the near future. Ivan directed them to sit at the conference table. He was furious that nobody in the KGB had located Boris.

"Boris had a meeting with two Americans in East Germany last fall," Ivan said, staring at the two men sitting at the table. "I am certain that one of these men is a CIA agent. The other man is now here in Riga working with the Soviet bobsled association. He must also be with the CIA."

"I have been with the Americans nearly every day, Commandant," Evalds said. He enjoyed the chance to brief the KGB Commandant in front of Georgi, who was visibly annoyed that Evalds was becoming so popular. "I suspect that the Americans are too stupid to be involved in any espionage. They seem to be only interested in creating publicity about a cultural exchange with the Latvians."

"Mikhail Gorbachev has created the possibility of a catastrophe in our country with Glasnost and Perestroika." Ivan shocked Evalds and Georgi with such a bold statement about the Soviet president. "Giving Americans this much freedom in our country will create many problems for us. I believe these Americans are with the CIA."

"We may be able to force their interpreter to help us," Evalds smiled.

"How?" asked Ivan.

"He brought a computer, printer, and a VCR with him when he arrived at the border at Tallinn. He entered the country without declaring any of the electronic equipment."

"Why wasn't he arrested immediately?" demanded Georgi.

"It would be stupid to arrest him and not learn what he planned to do with the equipment and who he had planned to sell it to." Evalds chuckled inside because he had made Georgi look stupid. "He told the guards at the border the equipment belonged to Murphy, the bobsled coach. He claimed Murphy brought it to help the Soviet bobsled team."

"Do you believe that?" asked Ivan.

"No," replied Evalds. "We know that the *Labvakar* TV crew met with Vladimir when they were in the United States last summer. I suspected that Vladimir was planning to sell the equipment to them after he arrived in Riga and I was right."

"Do you know this for sure?" asked Georgi.

"Yes, I watched the exchange take place. He was given a briefcase full of rubles and has it hidden in his hotel room."

"What do you suspect he will do with the rubles?" asked Ivan.

"I followed Vladimir the day the Americans went to the track. He went to several co-op jewelry stores and used some of the rubles to purchase several pieces of antique jewelry. I suspect he plans to smuggle the jewelry back to the United States. There he will sell them for many times what he paid for them and will avoid the American tax at the same time."

"Georgi, have your men pick up Vladimir and bring him here."

"Yes, Commandant. I will pick him up right away."

"Georgi."

"Yes, Commandant?"

"Do this very quietly and late at night so the other Americans will not be aware that we have talked to him. Call me at home when you have him."

"Yes, Commandant."

It was nearly 3 a.m. when Georgi and two of his men took the pass key from the woman sitting at the desk in the center of the sixth floor. Georgi unlocked the door and they quietly walked into the room. Georgi quickly placed a piece of cloth soaked with chloroform over Vladimir's face to prevent him from waking up. A short time later Georgi called Ivan and informed him that Vladimir was waiting at the *Corner House*.

Shawn and Ray finished breakfast the next morning and went outside to meet Gunar and Hopmahs in the square in front of the Hotel Riga. On the way out Ivan greeted them good morning and followed them to the van where Arthur was waiting to take them to watch the official Soviet bobsled team trials. Earlier in the week Hopmah confided to Shawn that a lot of tension would be surrounding the event. Latvian athletes had always won in the past and represented the Soviet Union in the international competition. The Russians were making a big effort to prepare their athletes so they could eventually replace the Latvians. The Russian officials were embarrassed that the Latvians were superior.

→ *Ice Spy*

The trials would take place inside a building that had a refrigerated push track. The indoor start track was pitched exactly the same as all bobsled start areas throughout the world, but was only two hundred feet long. The refrigerated track allowed the Soviet athletes to practice their starts as a team all year round. Shawn was amazed at this extravagance and thought about the American officials' lack of comprehension of what was needed to develop Olympic athletes.

Americans were able to practice starts on ice only during the cold weather. It was no wonder these athletes were so much faster Shawn thought. He noticed Evalds staring at him and wondered what he was thinking. Once the trials got started Evalds was kept busy and Shawn began to take photos whenever Evalds wasn't looking. The trials lasted until late in the afternoon and only two Russian athletes were successful in qualifying for the team.

Shawn and Ray asked Gunar if there was a grocery market where they could buy cold cuts, bread, and fruit to eat as snacks in the hotel. Gunar took them to a plush private market where only high officials and their guests were permitted to shop. Shawn again felt great sympathy for the poor people who had to stand in line for hours hoping to purchase a loaf of bread or some milk. Regardless of what the Communist propaganda said, it was very obvious that Soviet people were not treated equally.

They purchased some supplies then Arthur drove the Americans back to the hotel and left with Gunar and Hopmahs. Ivan walked into the hotel with them and sat on a bench in the lobby when Shawn and Ray got on the elevator and went up to their rooms. As the elevator slowly climbed toward the fifth floor Ray asked where Vladimir was?

"I called him this morning and asked him if he wanted to go to the trials with us. He said he was exhausted and needed to sleep," replied Shawn. "He probably stayed up all night with some whore again."

"What a slime ball. The Russians must be having a good laugh at his behavior. When he gets home he'll brag to his wife about how hard he had to work for us."

"Well, so far he has managed to do absolutely nothing for us," replied Shawn. "I hope he catches VD or something and takes it home. That would wake his wife up and let her learn what kind of a disgusting character she married."

Shawn and Ray made plans to meet for dinner at seven and went to their rooms. Shawn looked at his luggage and the personal items he had stored in the closet. He was aware that someone had gone through his possessions because he had purposely left some items in a particular way so he would know if they were moved while he was at the track. He had guessed correctly. All the items had been moved indicating that the KGB had probably been searching for information about him. When he left for dinner he would set the trap again. He looked at his watch and decided to take a quick nap before dinner. He thought about Boris and wondered when the undercover agent in Riga would contact him.

During dinner Shawn told Ray that someone had searched through his possessions. Ray thought someone might have looked through his, too. Shawn suggested that Ray place several items in a particular way and then he would know for sure if it happened again. It was nearly 8 p.m. and they were eating dessert when Vladimir entered the dining room. He sat down at their table acting extremely friendly. He questioned them about their day and asked what their plans were for the next day.

"Where have you been for the past two days, Vladimir?" asked Shawn.

"I've been staying with my relatives. They took me to visit the orphanage I have been helping to support." Vladimir smiled and continued, "I feel so sorry for these poor children who have so little."

This was the most far-fetched excuse that Shawn and Ray had ever heard. Neither believed he was visiting relatives, let alone visiting an orphanage. "They must love you for being so kind," replied Shawn. He restrained himself from laughing at Vladimir's obvious lie.

"These poor children need so much help," Vladimir said piously. "I've spent enough time with them and now I can concentrate on helping you fellows."

"That's wonderful, Vladimir," replied Shawn. "I'm not sure how you can help us. We managed to work out an agreement with Daumant to have a cultural exchange between the two bobsled associations. It would have been nice to have you help us with the interpreting since we were forced to have the Russians translate everything for us."

"Will you have any more meetings with Daumant?"

"I really don't know but I'll tell you if we do," lied Shawn. "Tell me, Vladimir, have you found any great bargains while shopping?"

"Only a few. My poor countrymen have so little to sell. The Russians have taken nearly everything of value from them."

Shawn looked at him and thought that he was no different than the Russians. He was convinced that the FBI report about Vladimir's activities was accurate. Shawn and Ray said good-bye to Vladimir and went upstairs to their rooms. Shawn was addressing a Russian postcard to Angela when the phone rang. It was Hopmahs who asked if he could come up to his room. Shawn agreed and moments later Hopmahs knocked on his door.

"I come to get you. I will take you for a ride to visit my home. Yes?"

"Sure. I'll get Ray so he can go with us."

"No. Only you must come," Hopmahs insisted.

"All right. I want to tell Ray that I'm leaving. Is that okay?"

"Yes, of course. That is okay."

Shawn put on his coat and they went down the hall to Ray's room. Shawn knocked on the door and explained to him that Hopmahs was taking him for a ride to visit his home. Ray looked into Shawn's eyes telling him he was worried about him leaving with Hopmahs.

"I'll let you know when I get back to the hotel."

They left the hotel and got into Hopmahs' car. Shawn noticed that the ever-present Ivan wasn't in the hotel lobby when they left and he wondered why he was gone. Perhaps someone else had replaced him since there were several men sitting on benches in the lobby.

Hopmahs started the car and pulled out onto the street. Soon he realized they were going in the direction of the government sports complex where they watched the bobsled trials earlier in the day. Three blocks away from the complex Hopmahs turned down a side street and parked in the shadows. He sat motionless in the car watching the area around and behind him. Shawn assumed he was waiting to see if someone was following. He put his finger to his lips signaling to Shawn not to make any noise and then motioned with his hand to follow as he got out of the car. When they arrived at the sports complex, Hopmahs stood quietly in the shadows looking around again to see if they were being followed. He nodded with his head for Shawn to follow and he slipped through a section of fence that had been pulled away slightly from the building.

He had to squeeze hard to get through the tight space and went down a few steps to the building. Hopmahs used a pocket knife to pick the lock on the door leading into the basement of the building. Once inside, they moved very slowly being careful not to bump into anything. They went upstairs to the third floor where Hopmahs knelt and carefully unlocked the door to the bobsled office by sliding the latch back with his knife. He crossed the dark room and opened a file cabinet and pulled out several files before closing the drawer. Shawn stepped out into the hallway and Hopmahs quietly pulled the door closed.

They walked down the stairs and when they reached the basement Hopmahs went into the furnace room and opened the small furnace door. The light from the fire enabled Hopmahs to examine the files. He picked out one file and handed it to Shawn before putting the rest into the furnace. When they reached the door leading outside, Hopmahs opened it slowly and looked around to see if anybody was outside. Making a gesture with his hand he signaled for Shawn to follow and once again they slipped through the space between the fence and the building.

Shawn's heart raced as they walked swiftly back to the car being careful to stay in the shadows to reduce the possibility of being seen. Hopmahs started the car and drove for several blocks then parked next to a curb under a street light. Shawn thought this bizarre situation was getting more eerie by the minute because neither of them had spoken a word since they had left the hotel. The thought crossed his mind that he was now in possession of stolen documents and he had absolutely no clue as to the contents.

Hopmahs broke the long silence. "These documents are my personal training files I created for the Soviet bobsled team." Shawn could see the bitterness glowing in Hopmah's eyes as he spoke. "What you have is the current record of all our workouts and training principles I used to prepare our athletes for the Olympics."

"Hopmahs, I don't want to get you into trouble by taking these," replied Shawn nervously. He was no coward but he really didn't want to get caught with them. The thought of a long prison term in Russia wasn't terribly appealing.

"I want you to have these." Hopmahs voice was deadly serious. "I would rather see the Americans win than the Russians. I never give my records to Russians. Soon they will learn Evalds knows nothing about training Olympic athletes." Hopmahs spent the next hour detailing to Shawn how to read the records once he had them translated in the United States. Shawn wrote notes while he explained various items of importance.

Once they were finished, Hopmahs drove Shawn back to the hotel. He cautioned Shawn not to let the documents out of his sight. The consequences could mean death for him and a long prison term in Siberia for Shawn. Shawn thanked him and returned to his room. His stomach was tied up in knots as he thought about the grim warning.

He called Ray as soon as he reached his suite, "I'm back. Come on over."

Ray reached his suite in seconds. Shawn let him in and put his finger to his lips, warning him to silence. Both were keenly aware the rooms were bugged. Ray's eyes swelled when he thumbed through the file. Hopmahs had recorded all his training information in pencil and specified the particulars of his Olympic training program.

"Let's go for a walk and get a bit of fresh air," suggested Ray.

Shawn put the file inside his shirt and they left the hotel. No Ivan this time either, although another man followed them out of the hotel. They walked toward the river and quickly entered the subway entrance and boarded the first train that came along. The man following stayed on the subway platform. They rode in the vacant car and looked through the records once again, still shocked that they were in possession of such secret information.

"You realize that you are taking an incredible risk by keeping them?" Ray stated quietly, looking at Shawn. He waited for his reply.

"I know. Remember, when we were in Calgary we had hoped we could get just a part of this information. Ray, I have it all and I'm not going to give it up now. If you would rather leave now so that you aren't a part of this, I will understand."

"No way." Ray smiled and Shawn grinned back. He knew that would be Ray's answer. "We're in this together and I'll take my chances."

They continued to discuss the file and Vladimir's activities until the subway again reached the stop near the hotel. It was late and he was tired, but as several other times during the trip, Shawn had trouble falling asleep when he returned to his room. His mind could not get rid of the day's chaotic events. He finally fell into a troubled sleep with the files tucked under the sheet below his feet.

Chapter Twenty-Four

→ *Ice Spy*

CIA Headquarters, Langley, Virginia

Fred Unser sat at the conference table looking at the officials who had assembled to make the final arrangements to slip Boris out of the Soviet Union. Sitting across from Fred was Admiral Mark Miller, Commander of the Atlantic Fleet. The president was impressed with the admiral's naval expertise and wisdom during a series of incidents in the Mediterranean Sea with Libya and selected him for this prestigious position. The Admiral's support would be critical to the plan that was about to unfold.

They were waiting for Gary Circe. Within a couple of minutes Circe entered the room through the large wooden doors. Fred immediately shut the glass door of the soundproof enclosure surrounding the conference table. Fred waited for Gary to exchange greetings with the admiral before he started briefing them on the current status of the project. He explained that it was only a matter of a day or two before the KGB would locate Boris and then implicate Murphy and Bodynski as part of the plot to help him defect.

Walter Shapnek had sent word that Standislav Akolous, their undercover agent in Riga, had made arrangements for Boris and the Americans to be smuggled onto a Russian fishing vessel. The ship's captain was Ivars Baravskis, an Estonian who had worked undercover with the CIA for several years. The *Beriozka* was scheduled to leave port in two days. His orders from Moscow were to sail to the North Sea about sixty miles off the coast of Norway where the cod were running.

Standislav would drive Boris and the Americans to Tallinn in a supply van. They would hide in a large wooden crate normally used to store fishing nets. During the night a crane would lift the box onto the rear deck of the ship and stack it with other boxes. This would be done under the watchful eye of the Soviet military which had numerous soldiers patrolling the port. Their timing had to be perfect.

Admiral Miller stood up when Fred finished his briefing and unveiled the navy's plan to have the *Willsboro,* a nuclear submarine, rendezvous with the Russian fishing ship. The rendezvous would take place in the North Sea, eleven hundred miles east of Greenland. The current storms in that area were predicted to move inland and estimated it would be forty-eight hours before another storm arrived. The favorable weather conditions would allow them to transfer the individuals from the *Beriozka* to the *Willsboro* without any difficulty. Once Boris and the Americans were safely on board, the *Willsboro* would return to Norfolk, Virginia where it was scheduled for maintenance. The CIA's plan to put Boris into a witness protection program would be discussed at a later date.

"We are in a very volatile situation that could have grave consequences if we are not successful." Gary's face reflected the seriousness of the situation. The group around the table listened intently. "Should the plan fail, we have made the decision that Boris will be executed."

"Why?" Admiral Miller was horrified at Gary's statement.

"We can't take a chance on the Russians obtaining the technical information."

"The bottom line is, we can't fail," said Fred. "Should the Russians locate Boris, it is very likely that they would be successful with their efforts to obtain the information from him. I don't think it's a secret that they would kill him once they possess this type of technology."

The meeting was adjourned.

Riga, Latvia, USSR

Shawn and Ray finished breakfast and left the hotel to meet Arthur outside who would drive them to Daumant's office to make the final arrangements for an American/Soviet cultural exchange between the two bobsled associations. Vladimir and Arthur were sitting in the van waiting for them. Shawn thought it was interesting that Vladimir suddenly had an interest in their activities. He wondered if Vladimir thought he might get some media attention if he attended the press conference Daumant scheduled for that afternoon at 4 p.m. Vladimir was extremely friendly and greeted them warmly. Shawn was irritated because he knew Vladimir was a phony.

Daumant was pleased with the statement Shawn and Ray had prepared for the press conference that afternoon. They spent the morning ironing out several details for the exchange. It was obvious that Daumant wanted a very strong emphasis placed on the fact that Latvian athletes would be taking part in the program.

Shawn explained it was important that the exchange be promoted as an American/Soviet exchange to encourage American companies to become sponsors. Daumant understood and reluctantly agreed to call it an American/Soviet exchange to promote the sport of bobsledding between the two countries. Finally the agreement was completed and Arthur took them to the Communist Party Hotel where a luncheon was held in the Americans' honor. When lunch was finished Arthur took the group back to their hotel so they could get ready for the press conference at 4 p.m.

They got out of the van and walked across the street to the Hotel Riga and a man standing next to the entrance greeted Shawn as they approached the door. He asked Shawn if he could speak with him for a moment privately. Shawn excused himself and walked down the street with him assuming he might be Walter's undercover contact man in Riga. They went into the park near an opera house and settled on a park bench.

"Mr. Murphy, my name is Standislav Akolous." He glanced nervously around to see if anyone had followed them. "Walter Shapnek asked me to make contact with you."

"Oh, yes. I've been expecting you."

"We need to get Boris out of the country within the next forty-eight hours, otherwise I'm afraid the KGB will locate him. If they do, they will kill him immediately."

"How do you plan to get him out?"

"I've made arrangements to take him and your group to Tallinn, Estonia where you will be smuggled onto a Russian fishing vessel that will sail in two days. The ship's captain has worked for the CIA in the past and is accustomed to this type of assignment."

Shawn explained the details to Standislav about the press conference scheduled that afternoon and the contents of the contract he was signing with Daumant. Standislav agreed that Daumant was taking a big chance by openly promoting the Latvian athletes over the Russian. Shawn opened his attaché case and showed him the stolen file Hopmah had given to him. He warned Shawn not to let it leave his side or the KGB would locate it and there would be tragic consequences.

They spoke for a few more minutes and Standislav gave Shawn a phone number where he could be reached if an emergency developed. He told Shawn to expect a call from him sometime the next day and left. Shawn returned to the hotel to get ready for the press conference which was now only an hour away.

Arthur picked them up at the hotel at three-thirty and drove them to Daumant's office. They arrived twenty minutes before the press conference was scheduled to start. Daumant's attorney was waiting for them at the entrance and led them to the room where the conference would be held. The large room had about thirty chairs set up and the table in front of the room where Daumant and his guests would sit had fresh flowers in a vase. A surprising but nice touch, thought Shawn.

The attorney handed the contract written in English to Shawn to read before the media was permitted to enter the room. He checked it carefully for any errors. Shawn assured him that it appeared okay and Vladimir asked to look at it as well. Reluctantly, Shawn slid the contract across the table to him. He flipped through the papers and handed it back, commenting that he thought it looked okay to sign.

The front door opened and Daumant walked into the room followed by a group of people that Shawn assumed was a mix of media and KGB. He was right.

Daumant waited for everyone to sit before he stood up to introduce Shawn and Ray to the group. He then briefly explained the purpose of the press conference and asked Shawn to read the prepared statement. Shawn read the statement in English, stopping at short intervals so it could be quickly translated in Russian. Daumant and Shawn signed the legal document creating the cultural exchange. Daumant then told the reporters they were permitted to ask questions they might have about the cultural exchange. They were politely curious and asked Shawn and Ray several questions about Olympic sports programs in the United States. They seemed keenly interested in how money was raised for American athletes. They were also curious about American technology and asked Ray many questions about his technical program. Several reporters wanted to know what they thought about the Soviets' bobsled technology and their many training facilities. The questioning went on for an hour.

The press conference was nearly finished when a TV reporter from a state-owned station in Moscow stood up and looked directly at Shawn. He looked down at his note pad one more time before he began to speak. "Mr. Murphy, since 1940 when the Russians occupied Latvia, the Latvian Socialist Slate has not conducted business on its own without first seeking permission from Russian authority in Moscow." He paused for a moment to check his notes before speaking again. "Did it bother you to avoid Moscow and deal directly with the Latvian Socialist Slate?"

Shawn stood up slowly, his mind racing for the proper response. He looked at Ray's eyes and read what he already knew. Choose your words carefully because once you have spoken you cannot change what was said. Shawn carefully determined how to answer and spoke slowly.

"No. It did not bother me and I will explain why." Shawn looked at Daumant and said, "When Professor Bodynski and I first met Mr. Znatnajs at the 1988 Olympics in Calgary, Canada, we spoke at length about how to promote the sport of bobsled. During these discussions, politics between our two countries was never mentioned. All discussions pertained to the sport only and how it might be improved. After the Olympics we continued our talks through the mail and finally, we agreed to meet again to discuss the possibility of creating a cultural exchange between our two countries." Shawn waited to permit the interpreter time to repeat this in Russian.

"In my country it is not necessary for me to seek permission to meet with Mr. Znatnajs, however, I must report all my activities to my government. While I understand and respect your system of government, I left it to Mr. Znatnajs to make the necessary arrangements for our talks."

"Thank you, Mr. Murphy." The reporter repeated the question to Daumant.

Daumant stood up and smiled. "Mr. Murphy has read the statement we prepared together outlining our cultural exchange." His face became very serious. "I personally did not invite the Americans. I consulted with the Latvian Socialist Slate and they discussed the situation together before making the decision to send the invitation."

He continued, "They believed the time has come for Latvians to stand up and start making their own decisions for Latvia. I'm proud that they made the decision without seeking permission from Moscow. This is the last question you will be permitted to ask about that situation."

Shawn thought, that was that! The press conference ended abruptly. Both Shawn and Ray were shocked. It took a few minutes for them to realize that Daumant had chosen the press conference to publicly promote the Latvian's underworld struggle to have the Russians thrown out of Latvia.

Coffee and Russian tea were served in a private room to Daumant's staff and the Americans. Shawn could sense the tension in the room and knew everyone else was feeling the same way. Several members of the KGB were present, adding to the mounting pressure. Shawn and Ray excused themselves as soon as possible and told Daumant they planned to walk back to the hotel. Daumant reminded them that Arthur would pick them up at eight and take them back to the Communist Party Hotel for a state reception and dinner.

They walked slowly discussing the possible effects of Daumant publicly slamming the Russians. Shawn and Ray agreed that the press conference put them in a very sensitive political situation. Resisting any involvement in a political situation was something they had discussed before arriving in the Soviet Union. Suddenly, they were in the middle of the Latvian's political struggle with Russia, a position neither completely understood.

Only the Americans and the Latvians attended the formal affair Daumant scheduled which clearly indicated a serious problem. The reception concluded when the enormous double doors leading to the dining room were opened. The table settings were very plush and flickering candles glowed brightly. Shawn was carrying the illegal papers Hopmah gave him inside his shirt. The papers had not left him since he received them.

Dinner was finally served and during the pause before he started eating Shawn thought about the briefing that Daumant had given them on their second day there. It appeared that he had not worked out his problem with Moscow and, in fact, the situation had escalated. The dinner dragged on and about 10 p.m. Shawn noticed that Vladimir had disappeared from the dining room. He thought, perhaps he had another date with a prostitute.

Shawn and Ray returned to Shawn's suite when the dinner was finally finished. They decided to sneak out the side stairway so they would not be followed by their interpreter and the KGB agents. They quietly walked down the hall to the door leading outside to the fire escape. The hallway was built with an "L" preventing the lady sitting at the desk from seeing them leave. Shawn used a piece of cardboard he took from a box he found in his room and put it in the door frame to prevent the door from closing. He carefully shut the door and they walked down the steel stairway leading to the alley. They waited for a moment to be sure nobody saw them then walked in the direction of the river front and boarded a noisy street trolley that arrived conveniently. They were still worried about the press conference and the fact that the Russians didn't attend the reception or the dinner. The trolley was nearly empty allowing them to speak freely.

Shawn told Ray about his conversation with Standislav. He agreed with Shawn that it was apparent the KGB must be dangerously close to finding Boris. "I think you should get rid of the stolen file," Ray suggested, obviously upset. "If they catch you with it we'll both go to Siberia and they will kill Hopmah; no questions asked."

"I understand the risk, Ray, but I can't let all this information disappear. If I think they might discover the file I'll get rid of it somehow."

"Did the CIA agent say for sure when he would be contacting us?"

"No. He said that he would call me tomorrow. He gave me a phone number so I could contact him if there is a problem. I'll give you the number just in case something happens to me."

They got off the trolley and walked back to the hotel. When they were one block away from the hotel they turned onto the side street and went quietly up the dark alley. Shawn took out his knife and tried unsuccessfully to pry open the side door. The paper had buckled under the pressure of the heavy spring and locked the door. They had no choice but to enter the hotel from the front door. The KGB agents assigned to watch them would spot them coming in and realize that they had been out. This was not a good time to increase their already heightened suspicions.

Shawn cursed to himself for not using a stronger piece of cardboard. There was no excuse for a mistake like this.

The KGB agents were startled and looked at each other in amazement as Shawn and Ray strolled into the lobby and pushed the button for the elevator. The door opened and they stepped inside being careful not to look at the KGB agents.

"Do you think Vladimir is back yet?" asked Ray, thinking about their wayward interpreter.

"Who knows? By the way, the plan is to leave him here in Riga."

"I like your style," laughed Ray.

The elevator reached their floor and they walked out and surprised the lady working at the desk who was unaware that they had left the hotel. Shawn said good-night and watched Ray walk down the hall to his own room. He unlocked the door to his suite and went inside. He looked around the room to see if anyone had been there looking through his belongings. Nothing appeared to have been moved. Exhausted, he went to bed with the file tucked under the bottom sheet.

The ringing telephone woke Shawn abruptly. He leaped out of bed and hastily went into the next room to answer it.

"Hello," he said, still groggy.

"We must come to your room to get statements for Moscow."

"Who's this? What did you say?" asked Shawn.

"We must come to your room to get statements for Moscow."

"Who the hell is this?" demanded Shawn, now wide awake. He looked at his watch. It was three-thirty in the morning.

"Unlock your door. We must get statements from you for Moscow," replied the voice in harsh English.

"Look, asshole, I don't make statements in the middle of the night. Do you understand that? You stupid bastard." Shawn wished he knew how to swear in Russian. He slammed the phone receiver down on the hook and walked back to his bedroom. Before he could reach his bed someone knocked on his door. He turned around and went to the door and asked what they wanted.

"Unlock the door. We need statements for Moscow. Now!" replied the voice.

"If you want statements then go to Room 620 and Mr. Lipins will give you statements. I don't make statements in the middle of the night."

Shawn put his ear to the door and could hear who he suspected were KGB agents walking down the hall in the direction of the elevator. He laughed and wondered what Vladimir would tell them. He probably would have a heart attack thinking they had figured out that he was smuggling jewelry out of the country. If Shawn was lucky they might arrest him but he did not feel lucky right now.

Shawn knew it wouldn't take them long to come back to his suite so he quickly put on sweat pants and a pair of running shoes. He had just tied the second shoe when the phone rang again and he rushed into the other room to answer it.

"We must come to your room now to get statements for Moscow," demanded the harsh voice.

"Look, you asshole, I told you that I don't make statements in the middle of the night." Shawn slammed the receiver down. This was getting ridiculous he thought. He quickly opened the double doors that led outside onto the veranda and pulled the curtains around the glass doors to prevent them from closing.

He quickly slid the table and chairs across the room then rushed to the door. He knew it was crucial to prevent them from unlocking it with a pass key. There was a lever on the inside of the door that was used to either lock or unlock the dead bolt inside the door. Shawn knew that if he held the lever in his hand, the KGB agents couldn't force it open without breaking their key in the lock. He arrived at the door at the same time they knocked on it.

"Unlock the door, we must come in and get statements for Moscow." Again came the harsh, unyielding voice.

"Listen, you stupid son of a bitch. For the last time, I don't give statements in the middle of the night. Now you listen to me, asshole. The first person who comes into this room is going out over the railing on the veranda. Do you understand that?"

"Just unlock the door. We only need to get a short statement and we will leave."

"Fuck you!" screamed Shawn. "You guys decide who is going to be the first person to come in the room because that asshole is going out over the railing. I hope the KGB teaches you jerks how to fly because it's five floors down to the concrete. Do you understand the meaning of fly, asshole?"

Shawn could hear them talking to each other in Russian but couldn't understand what they were talking about. Suddenly the phone started to ring. He assumed that they were trying to get him to go answer the phone so they could then unlock the door.

"Listen," he yelled. "I'm not going to go answer the phone so you can come in. I meant what I said about the first person coming in here going out over the railing."

"We only need to get a statement for Moscow and we will leave you alone."

"If you want a statement from me then come back in the morning at nine and I will give you a statement. You can go back and tell your flunky leaders that I don't make statements in the middle of the night."

Shawn put his ear against the door and he could hear them walking away toward the front desk. He suddenly realized that the phone was still ringing. Slowly he turned and walked backwards toward the phone. He continued to watch the lever on the door to make sure they didn't return and unlock the door. The thought occurred to him that they might have waited to see if he would answer the phone. This would get him away from the door long enough for them to rush back and unlock it.

"What do you want?" He yelled into the receiver while he stared at the lever.

"What's going on over there?" asked Ray. Shawn was relieved to hear his voice.

"For the past twenty minutes the KGB has been trying to get into my room and have me make some kind of a statement for their people in Moscow. Sit next to your door and keep your eye on the dead bolt lever so they don't force their way into your room. I'll call you back later."

He hung up and rushed back to the door and sat down on the floor. His eyes focused on the small lever that provided his only hope for keeping the KGB agents out of the room.

He retrieved a razor-sharp fiber composite knife from his luggage that Walter had given him in Helsinki and was clutching it in his hand. He was determined to kill the first person who came into the room. Suddenly, he thought about the possibility of KGB agents climbing over the railing from the veranda next door. He decided to leave the veranda doors open just in case they muscled their way in through the front door. There was no question in his mind that one of them would end up on the street five floors below.

His heart was racing and he thought about Angela, wondering if he would ever see her again. He leaned at an angle to look at his watch in the street light shining into the room through the open doors. It was only 3:50 a.m. It suddenly occurred to him that there was absolutely nobody, other than Ray or Vladimir, within five-hundred miles who he could call for help. Not even an American Consulate.

Slowly the room brightened as the sun rose in the eastern sky. Shawn checked his watch again and saw that it was only a few minutes before six. He stood up, stretched his cramped muscles and walked over to the veranda. He peeked out from behind the curtain to see if anyone was in the street below. He knew that the KGB had some of their agents in the lobby around the clock so he could not go downstairs.

He put on a jacket and ripped a piece of cardboard from a small box and went to the door. He carefully opened the door and looked out into the hallway. No one was there so he stepped outside and closed the door. He put the knife in his jacket pocket and quietly walked to the end of the hall. He opened the fire-door, placed extra cardboard in the door jam so it wouldn't lock and rushed down the back stairway two steps at a time. He never made the same mistake twice.

He walked down the alley that led into the street behind the hotel. Nobody was in sight and there were no cars parked on the street so he walked to a phone booth he had seen near the book store. His hands were shaking as he pulled out the paper with Standislav's phone number.

"*Dohbrayi ootra,*"

"Is this Standislav?"

"Yes. Is that you Shawn?"

"Yes. I think the KGB has decided to make their move."

"What happened?"

"A couple of thugs came to my room about three hours ago and demanded that I let them in and give them statements for Moscow."

"What did you tell them?"

Shawn told him about their argument and that they finally left when he told them he would give them a statement at nine in the morning. He explained how he had gone out the rear door without anyone seeing him.

"Good. Go back and tell Ray and Vladimir to pack just their bare essentials and leave the rest of their belongings in the rooms. If you leave most of your luggage behind it will take them several hours to figure out that you left. Go to their rooms and tell them. Don't call them on your phone because it will be bugged. Make sure you speak very quietly. I want the three of you to meet me in front of the Rossiya Hotel on Shirimyetiva street. Do you know where it is?"

"Yes. Why are we taking Vladimir? I was told that the plan was to leave him here."

"We can't take a chance on him talking to the KGB," replied Standislav. "If he doesn't want to come and gives you a problem, kill him. Do you have a problem with that?"

"None at all. When do you want us to meet you in front of the hotel?"

"Be there at exactly seven-thirty. Don't leave your hotel until twenty after. That should give you enough time. I won't be picking you up. A red van will come up the street slowly and will stop and pick you up. Get in as quickly as you can, don't waste time. Make sure you leave by the rear door again."

Shawn hung up and rushed back to the hotel. He slipped into the rear door and removed the piece of cardboard he used to prevent the door's latch from locking. He put the small piece of cardboard into his pocket so nobody would see it. He opened the door to the hall slowly, checking to make sure nobody was there.

He knocked quietly on Ray's door and asked him to let him inside. He told Ray what to do and when he finished he went to the sixth floor and woke up Vladimir. Vladimir was shocked that the KGB had been harassing Shawn and said that he would pack his bags at once. Shawn took out his knife and cut the wires to his phone. He told Vladimir to take only minimal luggage then looked at his watch and told him he had only fifteen minutes.

It only took Shawn a few minutes to pack his large bag. He decided to leave most of his clothing to lighten up his load. Vladimir was late so Shawn rushed up to his room to get him. He had packed four bags and Shawn suspected that one of them contained the jewelry.

"You idiot! Take only what you really need because your life might be riding on your ability to travel light. I left more than half of my own stuff behind so decide what you really need because we're leaving now, period. With or without you."

Vladimir grabbed the large suitcase and the small leather bag that Shawn assumed had the jewelry and followed him out the door and down the hallway leading to the stairs. They arrived at the Rossiya Hotel minutes before the van arrived. The van pulled to a stop and someone inside slid open the side door. They climbed inside with their luggage.

The driver never spoke and drove them out of the city to a farm just north of Riga. Vladimir was visibly upset that they were leaving so soon. He complained that he still had business to finish.

"Just be thankful that we are taking you," said Shawn. "If we left you behind the Russians would catch you at the border with your black-market jewelry."

I don't know what you're talking about!" Vladimir protested defensively. "Why would you make such a statement?"

"Have you forgotten that you used me to get the computer and the VCR over the border by telling the officials they were part of my equipment?"

Shawn was furious at Vladimir's attempt to cover up his actions. "We are well aware that you sold the equipment to the Latvian television station and have been using the money to buy jewelry from the co-op stores."

"There's nothing wrong with what I've done," replied Vladimir heatedly. "I've done this to help my fellow Latvians."

"Bull shit! Look, slime ball, you've done nothing to help the Latvians. You're only interested in filling your own pockets with money," Shawn said, glaring at him.

"It's a wonder that the KGB hasn't picked you up," interjected Ray, "because most everyone we talked with knew what you were doing."

"The KGB wouldn't be interested in what I do," lied Vladimir. Talking about the KGB suddenly gave him the chills. Georgi put the fear of God in him when the KGB agents took him to the *Corner House*. "They are only interested in larger, worthier cases."

"By the way, we know about the prostitutes you've been seeing. What would your wife think?" laughed Shawn. "I'll remind you that Ray and I have diplomatic visa's, you don't. If you give us any more shit, I'll turn you into the KGB myself."

Nobody spoke the rest of the way to the farm house. Vladimir sat silently and thought about the threats the KGB had made to him the night he was taken to the *Corner House*. Shawn's reminder was more on target than anyone in the van realized.

It was nearly 9 a.m. when they arrived at the old stone farm house. The driver opened the side door and pointed to the front indicating that they should go inside. They carried their luggage and went inside to wait for Standislav and Boris. It was cold inside the old house and the cob-webbed rooms indicated that it had been deserted for a long time.

"Why are we waiting here?" asked Vladimir curiously.

"Someone is going to meet us here shortly and help us get out of the country without crossing the border," replied Shawn. "Just relax and shut up. I'm tired of your bullshit."

"So who put you in charge?" demanded Vladimir.

"Just shut up. You've caused us enough embarrassment and problems," Ray said, also tired of listening to Vladimir complain. "We're tired and frankly, I'm fed up with you myself."

Moments later Standislav arrived with Boris. The driver of the van left the house and drove away with the car Standislav arrived in. Vladimir was shocked when Standislav introduced the defecting coach. This was very unsettling to the chicken-hearted Vladimir.

Vladimir suddenly turned cunning. This could be a break if he could get to a phone and tell Georgi where Boris was hiding. On second thought if Georgi found Boris he might shoot everyone, including him. He was in a worse predicament now than before.

"I want everyone to just relax," said Standislav. "We'll leave here around six tonight when it gets dark."

"Where are we going?" asked Vladimir.

"We're going for a ride. That's all you need to know right now," answered

Standislav. "If you try to leave or signal anybody, I will kill you. Do you understand?"

"I understand. I was only trying to learn what I'm going to be doing. This is a rather strange situation that you have put me into."

"You put yourself in this strange situation, Mr. Lipins," Standislav replied, staring at him coldly. "Why don't you tell us about your little trip down to the *Corner House* the other night?"

"I don't know what you're talking about," he lied. Cold chills ran down his back.

"Oh, really?" replied Standislav. "For your information you were seen being carried out of the hotel and later my informant watched you taken back to the hotel by the KGB. Don't be cute with me or I'll kill you right now." He pulled a pistol with a silencer out of his jacket and pointed it at Vladimir.

Sweat started rolling down Vladimir's posterior. He walked across the room and plopped down on an old sofa, continuing to stare at Standislav. He was normally a confident man, but now he was uncertain about the future. The bag of jewels lay on the sofa next to him. He wasn't going to let the heavy bag out of his sight.

Vladimir grew increasingly upset as he watched Shawn and Ray whispering with Standislav. He was certain that they were planning to kill him. His stomach growled and he looked at his watch. It was nearly three in the afternoon and he had not eaten anything since he got up. "Do you have any food for us?" asked Vladimir tentatively.

"There is some bread and cold cuts in the kitchen," replied Standislav. "I'll get it for you. The door behind you leads to the bathroom if you need it."

Vladimir got up with his small but heavy bag and walked into the bathroom. He shut the door and looked around the room. It was empty except for a few towels and a bar of soap. He checked the window and discovered it was nailed shut. He relieved himself and went back to rest on the sofa. Standislav brought in the bread with cold cuts and placed them on some old newspapers laying on an old table.

The old farm house had no heat and everyone was shivering in the cold air. All of them kept their hands in their pockets in an attempt to keep warm. Shawn was relieved to see the sun drop because it meant they would be leaving soon. He looked forward to getting in the van and turning the heat on. Standislav waited another hour to be sure it would be safe to travel.

"It's time for us to leave," said Standislav. "Pick up your bags and let's get out of here. Vladimir, if you try to run or pass a signal to anyone I'll shoot you instantly."

Boris had remained strangely quiet all this time. Shawn felt real sympathy for the man, knowing the tragedy he had endured and the changes he faced. Shawn understood Boris's agony over leaving his native country. Although his wife and family were murdered here, he still felt uncomfortable leaving their graves behind. It was like leaving a great part of himself.

They got into the van and Standislav started the motor and drove out onto the highway. The heat felt pleasant to everyone. It was a five hour ride to Tallinn, Estonia and Shawn thought it was a perfect hiding place because the

KGB wouldn't suspect that they left Riga. Standislav made the right decision to leave most of their luggage behind.

The dock area would be empty late at night making it easier to put the group on the ship without the Soviet Army guards realizing what they were doing, thought Standislav. He glanced in the rearview mirror and noticed that Vladimir was sleeping. He had to agree with Shawn that Vladimir was a real slime ball. They had been on the road for nearly two hours when Standislav spotted a police car behind him, flashing the lights. He pulled the van to the side of the road and the action brought everyone to full attention. Fear grabbed each and every one of them.

The middle-aged Russian policeman stepped up right outside the driver's side window and asked Standislav for his license. He said he had been speeding with the van. The policeman glanced in the back seat at Shawn and Boris but said nothing. Standislav and the policeman spoke back and forth for a few minutes in Russian. Standislav suddenly reached into his pant's back pocket and pulled out his leather wallet. He passed an unknown amount of Russian rubles over to him and they were soon on their way.

Standislav told them that it was very common for local policemen to stop drivers for speeding and openly accepted money to pay for the fines. They did this to earn more money since their state wages were too low to raise a family. Shawn never learned how much this cost Standislav but he would always remember the fear he had experienced.

It was nearly twelve-thirty when Standislav pulled into the parking lot next to the building where his contact had told him to park. He shut off the van and waited for a few minutes. The side door of the stone building opened and Ivars, the captain of the fishing vessel, *Beriozka* motioned for the group to come inside. The suspense in Shawn built even higher as they waited inside the building. Without saying a word, he knew Ray shared his feelings.

Chapter Twenty-Five

→ *Ice Spy*

North Atlantic

Captain Harris Young read the coded message just handed to him. He had been commander of the *Willsboro* for nearly two years and had spent the majority of this tour patrolling the North Atlantic. The ballistic-missile nuclear submarine Young was assigned to was one of the navy's newest and was outfitted with the latest technology.

Captain Young was looking forward to returning to Norfolk to be with his wife while his submarine was being serviced and prepared for another tour. The captain and his crew had been to sea for nearly four months. Young was in his mid-fifties with black hair beginning to gray. He read the message once again and wondered if the emergency assignment might delay their scheduled trip to Norfolk.

The captain went up to the watch and checked the weather forecast for the North Sea to the west of Norway. High winds were currently in that area, making the sea very rough. The forecast predicted that the winds would be reduced to about five knots by late morning. He looked at his watch. The time was 07:20 a.m. He walked into the chart room and gave the message to the navigator and instructed him to change course.

Tallinn, Estonia, USSR

Ivars looked at his watch and told Standislav it was time to get the group ready for the trip. They quietly led the men down into the storage area in the basement of the large stone building. Shawn noticed several very large wooden crates that were neatly stacked in the center of the large room. It was obvious that this room was used to prepare supplies for the fishing vessels.

Ivars explained that they would be placed inside one of the wooden crates and a forklift truck would carry the box out onto the dock. A large crane would lift the crate onto the rear deck and place it alongside other wooden boxes that stored fishing nets. They would remain in these cramped quarters until after the ship had departed and was safely out in the Baltic. He estimated that they would be in the crate for approximately eight hours.

The cover of the wooden crate had several places where air could get inside, but they would have no food or water until they were released. Ivars warned them that a Russian political officer could possibly be placed on board and would be constantly observing everything taking place. Ivars would not know for sure if the political officer would sail with them until they were ready to leave the port. He suggested that they try to sleep during their cramped seclusion and to avoid any sounds, even whispering during this time.

Shawn thought about the next several hours and the conditions they would have to endure. He hated being crowded or confined in any way. However, the alternative was much worse. He could handle the time in the crate, but he was not at all confident about Vladimir. Shawn knew that this jackass wasn't accustomed to difficult living conditions or hard work. He belonged on Fifth Avenue. Shawn placed his knife in his shirt pocket so it would be readily available if Vladimir attempted to make any noise. Shawn nudged him and showed him the knife to make him aware of what would happen if he attempted to signal anybody.

One by one they climbed into the crate. Shawn noticed that Boris never changed his facial expression. He always looked like he was mad at the world. Shawn empathized with the man. Boris had every reason to feel this way after the problems he had with the Russians. Ray entered the crate last. The tall man had to shrink his large frame down to squeeze his body inside the small space.

Standislav and Ivars wished them luck and repeated their warning to remain quiet. The rectangular wooden top was put in place and Shawn could hear them tapping down the nails on the cover. He fervently hoped the truck would pick up the crate properly and not accidentally push its forks through the side. He'd seen that happen all too often. He closed his eyes and thought of Angela and wondered what she was doing right now. He could imagine what she would think if she knew what he was involved with at that moment.

CIA Headquarters, Langley, Virginia

Fred Unser called Gary Circe at home and told the director that Boris and the group were in Tallinn, Estonia. He explained that they were in the process of being placed onto the *Beriozka* and were scheduled to sail at daybreak. He anticipated the *Beriozka* would have no problem keeping its rendezvous with the *Willsboro*.

"Call me as soon as you get some more information," said Gary. He added, "I don't care what time it is."

"I will, sir. We're still concerned over the weather. The front is supposed to move out during the next few hours and we hope the sea will calm down. It's very rough right now."

"Well, call me if anything comes up."

Fred hung up and checked the time again. It was nearly midnight and he quickly calculated it to be nearly 8 a.m. in Tallinn. He thought that Boris and the rest must be on the ship by now and on their way to the Baltic Sea.

North Atlantic

Captain Young and his navigator, Lieutenant John Gochenaur, studied the recent weather update intently. The winds were calming as the front continued to move northeast.

"What are we going to be doing when we reach our destination, sir?" asked Gochenaur, a short, stocky man with light brown hair. His German ancestry was evident in his straight jaw and compact build.

"We're meeting a Russian fishing boat and will be picking up four passengers."

"May I ask who they are, sir?" The navigator was professionally curious.

"I don't know, Lieutenant," he replied. "This is a top secret mission that came directly from the Pentagon. I assume the CIA has put this together. I have no additional information and our orders are to meet the *Beriozka* at the location I showed you, at 0230 zulu time and to maintain strict radio silence."

"They really don't give us much to go on, sir," commented Gochenaur seriously.

"No, they don't," Young shook his head and said wryly, "Guaranteed this is a CIA covert operation. I'm going below to my cabin. Call me immediately if any more messages are received or if there is any change in the weather."

"Yes, Sir."

The *Beriozka*

The stale air surrounding Shawn was nauseating him and the cramped quarters were driving him crazy. He thought that the terrible conditions might be worth it since Vladimir was forced to keep his mouth shut.

To keep his mind busy he tried to calculate how long they had been in the crate. He guessed that the crate had been sitting on the upper deck for about two hours before they felt the ship move. It seemed as if they had been at sea for nearly four hours but it was difficult to tell from the dark interior. He tried to remember what Standislav had told them. He couldn't remember when Ivars would take them out of the crate, his mind was blank.

He lost track of time and fell asleep. Someone moving about outside the crate woke him and he pressed his ear to the wall. It sounded like someone had climbed onto the top of the crate. His heart raced as he wondered if it might be Ivars—or had someone else discovered them? Moments later someone began to pry the crate's lid open.

To Shawn's intense relief it was Ivars. The captain opened the lid and they climbed out one after the other. Shawn's legs were screaming and he wasn't alone. Ray and the ever-stoic Boris were wobbling around the deck that was shifting violently from the rough sea. It was difficult to keep their balance as the ship rolled back and forth but it was enjoyable to be out of their temporary prison.

Ivars let them stretch for a minute before leading them to a cabin near the stern deck where they could relax. On the way he informed them that nobody had questioned him at the port and a political officer had not been assigned to the ship. Ivars gave them hot, steaming coffee and a loaf of dark rye bread with cold cuts. They ate ravenously. They were still extremely stiff and had to hold on to the walls to prevent themselves from falling while the ship rocked and rolled.

Ivars explained that the crew was aware they were on board and were more than willing to help them escape from the Russians. He informed them that it was safe to walk around on the deck but not to go below. He left them and returned to the lower deck to check on the ship's progress.

Boris walked over to a small cot next to the wall and laid down on his side while he continued to watch the other three men warily. Shawn nudged Ray and motioned with his head for Ray to join him outside on the deck. They looked at Vladimir who was sitting on another cot and still clutching his small bag of jewels.

The air outside the cabin was cold and damp but they didn't care. The fresh air felt good after the long hours spent in the crate. Shawn knew they were still on the Baltic Sea but had no idea of their true location. The sea was still rough and the ship continued to toss and turn. The wind had died down so he assumed that the sea would soon follow suit and calm down as well.

Ray and Shawn walked around the upper deck studying the equipment stored on the Russian fishing vessel. Neither of them had ever been on an American commercial fishing vessel so they had no idea if the equipment was unusual or not.

They had been told to stay on the upper deck and they followed these instructions carefully. Their observations went on without a hassle for the next couple of hours. Ray was more curious about the ship's workings than Shawn. The time went by swiftly and when they finally realized that they were chilled to the bone they headed back to the cabin. As Shawn opened the door, the warmth jumped out at him and he was startled to hear Vladimir arguing heatedly in Russian with Boris.

"What's the problem?" asked Shawn, dismayed. The tension in the small cabin was so thick Shawn could almost touch it. "Back off, Vladimir. Get the hell away from him."

Vladimir instantly moved away and replied, "We're just having a simple disagreement about his loyalty to the government."

What a bastard, thought Shawn and then said, "You've got to be kidding. You have no loyalty to anyone but yourself! Your only interest in people is whether they can put something in your pocket or turn their head while you steal."

"Perhaps we should examine the bag that's joined to your hip," said Ray dryly. "We know, Vladimir. The bag's filled with jewels you bought on the black market with the rubles you got from selling the computer and VCR. What a weasel! We should've left you in the Soviet Union to rot."

Boris sat stiffly on his bunk staring fiercely at Vladimir. Shawn wished he had a better handle on the Russian language so he could find out exactly what Vladimir was arguing about with him. Ray and Shawn agreed to stay in the cabin to prevent Vladimir from disturbing Boris. Ray sat down on one of the vacant bunks while Shawn walked across the small cabin and sat on the floor, leaning his back against the cold wall.

The time moved very slowly as they waited. Conversation was at a standstill. Shawn noticed that the ship was rolling much less than it had several hours earlier. He was encouraged that their pick-up would not be delayed.

Later Ivars returned to the cabin with more food and told them the sky was clearing and the sun was setting. He suggested that they go out on deck and watch the sunset. Shawn and Ray followed him out of the cabin. Neither had any intention of leaving Vladimir alone with Boris for more than a few minutes. They were delighted at the incredible view of the sunset. It appeared that the sun was actually dropping into the sea.

They walked to the front section of the deck and watched the sun as it appeared to slip into the sea. It was a beautiful sight to witness and it kept Shawn and Ray on deck much longer than they had intended. They remained on the deck breathing the fresh sea air until it was nearly dark. Shawn grew anxious about their prolonged absence so they decided to go back and check on Boris.

They were about fifty feet from the cabin when they heard glass shatter and Boris scream. They ran down the deck and rushed into the cabin. Vladimir turned as they entered and looked at them with shock. His right hand held a large piece of glass and was bleeding profusely. Boris was holding his stomach and they could see blood oozing out of his clothing through his fingers.

"He attacked me," stammered Vladimir, dropping the broken glass. It shattered as it hit the cabin floor and the bloody pieces scattered everywhere. "I had to protect myself. He's crazy! He was going to kill me!"

"He should have killed you," yelled Shawn as he rushed past him to help Boris. "Get out of here, you son-of-a-bitch."

Vladimir turned and ran out of the cabin. Ray rushed over to the wounded man and ripped open his shirt to get at the wound. Ray helped Boris lay back on the now blood-covered cot. He reached under the cot and grabbed a T-shirt out of his luggage and quickly, but carefully wiped the blood from the wound. He wanted to stem the flow of blood so he could determine how badly Boris was cut.

"He has a very deep laceration," said Ray. Shawn watched in horror as Ray pulled a small piece of broken glass from the wound. "About the only thing I can do now is stuff some cloth into the wound and apply pressure to slow the bleeding. Find Ivars so he can contact the sub. We need to get him to a doctor right away or he'll die."

Shawn left the cabin and ran toward the stairway door. Vladimir was waiting nearby and rushed up to him, stammering, "He tried to kill me."

"You lousy bastard," yelled Shawn, pushing him out of the way.

Vladimir refused to be moved and stepped back directly in front of Shawn. His hand was bound with a white handkerchief. He pleaded, "Listen to me! I had to kill him. The KGB threatened to kill my wife and children if I didn't help them. I was supposed to tell them where Boris was hiding when we were in Riga but you forced me to leave before I found out where he was. They would kill my family for sure if I didn't do something to help them."

"You're about the lowest slime ball I've ever had to work with," interrupted Shawn angrily. "You lousy bastard! You did nothing to help me and Ray on this trip like you agreed. In fact, you only used us to help yourself make money by smuggling the computer and VCR into the Soviet Union. You nearly got my ass in a sling with the Russians by telling them that your equipment belonged to me."

He grabbed Vladimir by the jacket and punched him in the face with his right fist. The two men struggled and fell to the deck when the ship rolled slightly. Vladimir was nearly as big as Shawn, but much weaker. Shawn easily got to his feet and pulled Vladimir up with him. He continued to punch Vladimir's face until blood began to pour from his nose and mouth. Vladimir clutched Shawn and hung on in an effort to prevent Shawn from punching him.

In a rage Shawn broke loose, spinning Vladimir around so he could hit him again. Blood splattered on Shawn's face as he grabbed Vladimir by the jacket and the crotch. He picked him up and threw him over the ship's railing.

Vladimir's screams were lost in the buffeting sound of the wind and the waves slapping against the side of *Beriozka*. His body slipped into the Baltic without anyone witnessing what had happened.

Shawn turned and rushed up the stairs leading to the bridge. He quickly told Ivars what had happened to Boris. Ivars tersely instructed his assistant to take over and grabbed his jacket off the wall rack. They ran back to the cabin where Ray was applying pressure to the wound and trying to comfort Boris. "I can't stop the bleeding. I think an artery was cut."

"I'll get the ship's doctor to look at him." The captain immediately left the cabin to get help.

"You'd better keep an eye on Vladimir," said Ray.

"He's gone."

"What the hell do you mean 'He's gone'?" asked Ray, looking directly up at Shawn for the first time since he re-entered the cabin.

"The son-of-a-bitch jumped over board and is swimming back to the coast."

"That's crazy. He'll never make it. If he doesn't drown he'll die from exposure within minutes. The water temperature is in the thirties."

"I know," replied Shawn. "He got just what he deserved. I should've helped him overboard as soon as we got out of the crate."

A smile slowly appeared on Ray's face as he finally understood what Shawn was saying. At that moment, Ivars returned with the ship's doctor. The Estonian doctor removed the towel Ray had used to slow the bleeding. He started to give Boris an injection, but Shawn stopped him, unsure of what was in the syringe. Ivars translated that the injection was a pain-killer, but Shawn still would not permit it.

The doctor shrugged and went back to treating the wounded Boris. He finally managed to stop the bleeding and removed several other pieces of glass as he cleaned the wound. He applied a dressing and walked over to Ivars. They spoke for several minutes in Russian and then he left. Boris lay on the cot, his skin was pale white, but he was calm. His eyes stared at the ceiling.

"The bleeding has stopped, but he still needs additional medical attention we can't give him," Ivars told them. "He has lost so much blood that his blood pressure is very low. This is certainly very serious."

"Contact the sub. Tell them we have an emergency and we need to meet sooner then planned to get medical help or Boris will die."

"That would be impossible," replied Ivars, shaking his head. "My instructions were to be at a precise spot at a certain time. Standislav said the sub would find us. I cannot take a chance and risk everyone's life by sending a radio message. I have no idea if there are other Russian ships near-by. You can be certain that the Russians would hear any transmission we made from this ship."

"When are you supposed to meet with the sub?" asked Ray.

"Soon. We have to be in place only a couple of hours away," Ivars replied after looking at his watch. "We are close to the location and have reduced our speed so that we don't have to stop and wait for your sub. That would surely attract attention from the Russians."

"You're right, Captain," replied Shawn. "The Russians have several boats

→ *Ice Spy*

located in the Atlantic equipped with electronic gear similar to what we have on our AWACS planes."

"That's right," replied Ivars. "What most Americans don't realize is the Russians spy on their own people with the same intensity as they spy on other countries."

"I'm not surprised," replied Ray. "This trip was an eye opener for me. The Russians have spies who spy on their own spies and probably have more spies spying on them."

"Perhaps you are right," replied Ivars, smiling at Ray's humor. "We live this way because we have no choice. Now you understand why the Latvians and the Estonians hate the Russians." He looked back at Shawn, and said, "Excuse me. I must return to the bridge. Come and get me if Boris needs help. I will tell you when the sub contacts us."

The *Willsboro*

The *Willsboro* continued on its northeast course to rendezvous with the *Beriozka*. Captain Harris Young had served in the US Navy for nearly 30 years but had never before taken part in any type of a CIA covert operation. The secrecy and the mystery attached to this mission were exciting to him. He was thrilled to be a part of a CIA operation.

Captain Young and his navigator, Lt. John Gochenaur, continued to study the charts while keeping a watchful eye on the radar screen. The ship's position had to be perfect when it surfaced, otherwise Russian ships that were monitoring ship movement in the northeast Atlantic would be alerted in advance. It was impossible to prevent them from knowing the two ships had met, but it would be too late for them to interfere with the rendezvous.

"What'll happen to the *Beriozka's* crew after we pick up these people?" asked the Lieutenant.

"No one really knows for sure," replied Captain Young. "The plan is for us to surface near the *Beriozka*. They'll stop and we'll pull along side them. It'll appear to the Russians that we are checking their papers. I was told that their captain will tell his superiors we were questioning their right to be in these waters. There are two other Soviet ships in this area."

"How many people are we picking up, sir?"

"I was told four," replied Captain Young. "How far are we from the coordinates?"

Gochenaur told him they were six miles away and none of the other Soviet ships had changed course.

"Reduce speed by ten knots. I don't want to get any closer until it's time. I'm sure they are now puzzled as to why we are this close to one of their ships."

The *Beriozka*

Boris had lost so much blood he could barely stay awake. His condition worsened by the hour. Shawn and Ray knew they were racing against time and if the defecting coach did not get a blood transfusion soon he would never make it to the States alive. If Boris died, his research would be irretrievably lost. Shawn assumed that the American sub would have a small supply of blood if Boris could only hang on long enough. It was one-thirty. Only another hour before the sub would arrive. The minutes seemed to last an eternity while he and Ray waited helplessly.

"I'm going to the bridge to find out if Ivars had any contact with the sub," said Shawn, pacing nervously. He was worried about Boris's condition and couldn't stay still.

"Okay. If there has been no word, encourage Ivars to try and make contact now," replied Ray. "Boris's condition is getting worse. His pulse is down to fifty-six."

Shawn went up to the bridge and updated Ivars on Boris' condition. Shawn pleaded with the captain to attempt a radio contact with the sub. Ivars insisted it was much too risky to attempt because he was worried that a Russian ship might arrive before the sub. He reminded Shawn that he was not sure which sub would be their contact. Standislav had simply given him a precise location of where to be at 0230 zulu time and said a sub would meet them. He assured Shawn he would tell him the moment he had contact with the sub and would send the ship's doctor back to stay with them until the transfer was made.

The *Willsboro*

The phone rang and Captain Young picked up the receiver. It was Lieutenant Gochenaur. "Sir, the Soviet sub, *Krahsnays*, has changed course and is now heading in our direction. They also increased their speed, sir."

"Keep a close watch on the other ship and tell me if it changes course," ordered Captain Young. He hung up the receiver and went back up to the bridge where Lieutenant Gochenaur was studying the radar screen.

"How far away is the *Beriozka*, John?"

"They just came within two miles of us, Sir."

The phone rang and Lt. Gochenaur picked up the receiver and took a message for the captain who was studying the weather conditions.

"Sir, there is radio communication between the two Russian ships. The *Krahsnays* just ordered the Russian cruiser, *Veenstan*, to change course and proceed to the *Beriozka*."

"Check the computer. I want to know exactly how far away they are right now."

Gochenaur entered the data into the computer and studied the screen. "The *Krahsnays* is thirty-three miles out and the *Veenstan* is forty-one, sir."

"And the *Beriozka*?"

"A mile and a half, sir."

The captain glanced at his watch. It was six minutes after two. He rapidly calculated how long it would take the *Willsboro* to surface and reach the *Beriozka*.

"Let's do it. Prepare to surface," the captain barked into the microphone. "It's ten minutes too early but I want to pick up the four passengers and submerge again before either the *Veenstan* or the *Krahsnays* can reach us.

The *Beriozka*

Ray and the ship's doctor watched Boris intently while they waited for the submarine to surface. Boris spoke softly through cracked lips to the doctor. The doctor got up and gave him a glass of water and several pieces of an orange Ray had just peeled. Boris's face was pale and he was now getting weaker by the minute, thought Ray. The Doctor took his blood pressure and pulse again and copied the numbers in his notebook. Ray looked at the figures. They were lower than the readings taken ten minutes earlier. Shawn went to the bridge to check on the location of the sub.

"Something just surfaced on the radar screen," Ivars pointed to the small screen. "That must be them. They are less than one kilometer from us."

"Can we see them?" asked Shawn. His heart was racing. What if this is a Russian sub? he thought. They would all be killed.

"No, I do not think so yet. It is much too dark. I will put on the deck lights to help them see us."

Shawn hurried down the short flight of stairs leading from the bridge and ran toward the cabin where Ray was staying with Boris. He opened the door so fast he startled both Ray and the doctor. They relaxed simultaneously when they saw him.

"A sub has just surfaced and is about a half mile from us," said Shawn. "Let's hope it's ours and not a Russian sub."

"Does the captain know whose sub it is?" asked Ray.

"No. He has radar and the only ships he can monitor are those on the surface. He really doesn't know for sure who they are," replied Shawn. "I hope this one is ours, otherwise we're in deep shit."

"What time is it?" asked Ray.

"Two-eighteen," replied Shawn.

"That has got to be ours," replied Ray confidently. "I'm relieved that they're a little early because Boris's condition is worsening. His blood pressure and pulse keep dropping."

"Stay with him, Ray. I'll go back to the bridge in case there's radio contact with the sub."

Shawn ran back toward the bridge and when he was amidships he suddenly noticed a huge dark shape lurking on the starboard side of the *Beriozka*. His heart raced as he hurried to the bulwark and strained to identify it. It was a sub, but he still could not figure out in the darkness if it was American.

Hearing footsteps, Shawn leaned back from the bulwark and saw Ivars running toward him. "This is your sub," he said, as soon as he reached him.

"How do you know for sure?" asked Shawn.

"They just asked permission to board. Go get your friends."

"I don't want to move Boris until the sub's doctor tells us it's okay," said Shawn. "Ray and your doctor are still with him."

"Stay here. I have to go below to get my crew to come up and help us."

Shawn watched as three rafts were inflated and placed in the water next to the sub's port side. His eyes had adjusted to the darkness and he realized the huge shape he had seen was the sub's main hatch. The sea was still agitated and Shawn assumed this is why the sub had not come closer to the *Beriozka*. It was about two hundred feet to the starboard side of the fishing vessel. The small inflatable rafts tossed and turned on the massive waves, but continued to approach their ship.

The first raft pulled up next to the *Beriozka* and the crew lowered a rope for them to grab to prevent the raft from drifting. Ivars yelled to the sailors in the raft that his crew would swing a derrick out to lift up their raft. The raft was on the *Beriozka's* lee side which meant they were away from the wind that was still blowing steady at five knots.

The derrick hoisted the raft up and lowered it on the deck. Shawn rushed over to the four sailors and told them that Boris had been stabbed and needed immediate medical attention before they could move him. One of the sailors, who said he was a corpsman, followed Shawn to the bulkhead in the stern to check on Boris's condition. The corpsman immediately checked Boris' blood pressure and pulse then pulled out a small two-way radio. He called the sub and asked to talk with the doctor.

Doctor Angerosa, the sub's doctor, listened very intently and gave the corpsman instructions to make a determination of the extent of the internal bleeding. Doctor Angerosa suspected that Vladimir may have pierced Boris's spleen when he stabbed him with the glass.

"His blood pressure is eighty-six over forty-five and his pulse is forty-six," spoke the corpsman over the radio. "His breathing is slow, Doc. He's not in good shape."

"There's no time to explain about that now, sailor," snapped Shawn. "Let's get him on the sub so the doctor can look at him or we'll lose him."

"Start an IV and then wrap him in a thermal blanket before you put him on the raft," ordered the doctor. "We need to get him on board as soon as possible." Doctor Angerosa decided to move Boris to the sub's operating room at once so he could stop the internal bleeding, otherwise the defecting coach would surely die.

The corpsman started an IV, then Shawn and Ray helped him put Boris on a litter and carried him out onto the deck. A large group of Estonian sailors had gathered on the deck and began cheering when they saw Boris being brought out onto the litter. Shawn knew the cheers were because Boris was getting away from the Russians.

Boris was gently placed into the raft that had been lifted onto the deck. The corpsman and two sailors got in with them then Ivars gave instructions to have the *Beriozka's* derrick lower them back to the water. Everyone watched as the raft began to cross the space between them and the *Willsboro*. A second raft rode next to the first, ready to give assistance if needed.

Shawn and Ray quickly said farewell to Ivars and were lowered by the derrick to the last raft still moored to the lee side of the *Beriozka*. The American sailors helped Ray and Shawn into the large rubber raft then pushed off the side of the *Beriozka*. The crossing only took about six minutes. The slapping waves sprayed the frigid salt water on everyone making the short ride seem to last much longer.

The crew on the *Willsboro* waited anxiously for the rafts to reach the sub.

→ *Ice Spy*

When they arrived, the sailors quickly tossed heavy, thick ropes to them. One of the sailors in Boris's raft caught a rope and secured it to the raft. The ship's medical crew immediately carried Boris below to the scrubbed operating room.

Shawn climbed onto the sub and two sailors reached for him and guided him across the unstable deck. They went below and the sailor behind them secured the hatch. It seemed to be only seconds and Shawn could feel the submarine shift position and begin to descend. Intense activity surrounded Ray and Shawn as the ship returned to the comfort of the sea's depth.

"I can't believe we've made it this far, can you?" asked Shawn, looking at Ray. He noticed the professor looked as exhausted as he, himself, felt.

"It'll be a miracle if that doctor can keep Boris alive," remarked Ray sadly. "And after all we've been through."

"There's a lot riding on keeping him alive," replied Shawn. "I wish we could have gotten Boris to write the information down for us when he was well."

"Let's face it, he probably wouldn't be alive now if he had written it down because no one would have needed him then."

"You're right," nodded Shawn, as he thought about what they had gone through the past several days.

Captain Young walked into the room and introduced himself. He took them to the sub's guest quarters and suggested that they try to get some sleep, unless they were hungry. Both were famished since they only had a small amount of bread and cold cuts while on the *Beriozka*. Young called the galley and requested that something light be brought up to them. They quickly finished the meal and took the captain's suggestion and went to bed.

The sub reached the cruising depth Captain Young had selected, then changed course and headed toward the United States.

Chapter Twenty-Six

→ *Ice Spy*

CIA Headquarters, Langley, Virginia

Gary Circe sat at his desk looking at the *IceSpy* file. He still had some small details to work out before Boris's anticipated arrival. Moments later his secretary buzzed him on the intercom and said Admiral Mark Miller from the Atlantic Fleet was calling. Gary thanked her and pushed the flashing red button.

"Good afternoon, Mark. Any word yet from the *Willsboro*?"

"Yes, and it's not good news, Gary," replied the admiral. "We just received a cryptic message from the *Willsboro* and Boris was stabbed while he was on the *Beriozka*. Apparently the Russians had a double agent on the fishing vessel and no one knew it."

"Where's Boris now?"

"They got him onto the sub and the doctor is operating on him right now."

"How serious is he?" asked Gary thinking, all of this will be for nothing if Boris dies.

"The doctor said Boris's spleen ruptured. He needs to be transferred to a medical facility right away if we want to keep him alive."

"How can you do that?"

"There's an Air National Guard Medical Evacuation unit in upstate New York just outside of Albany," replied the Admiral. "The 109th Tactical Airlift Group has C-130 cargo planes that can be used to air-transport patients."

"That's a long way from the polar ice cap. Don't you have military planes any closer than upstate New York?"

"No. They're the closest with a plane that can do air evacuation and they'll have enough time to get there."

"How the hell do you plan to get Boris from the sub to the 130?"

"Their C-130s are equipped with skis and can land on ice," replied the admiral. "My staff alerted the base immediately after I received the message from the *Willsboro*. The code-one priority message clearly indicated Boris could not survive the six days it'll take the sub to reach the States."

"Where on earth can they pick him up?"

Admiral Miller paused for a second and then replied, "They're working out the best place for a transfer. I'm not sure exactly where, but it will happen on the polar ice cap. We have no choice, Gary. Boris is running out of time."

"What do you need from me?"

"Nothing at the moment. We just need to pray that Boris can stay alive until we can get him to Albany. The Albany Medical Center is the nearest American hospital capable of performing the surgery he needs and it's one of the best in the States."

"I'm really worried about transferring him from the sub onto a C-130 that has to land and take off on the ice cap," said Gary. He implored, "Please call me back when you have more information."

"I will," agreed the Admiral.

"I don't understand how this huge cargo plane can land on anything other than a paved runway."

"The Air National Guard has several C-130 cargo planes that have two landing gear systems. During a normal landing on paved runways, the skis are kept tight to the bottom of the plane in their normal flight position. When they are ready to land on snow or ice, the landing gear is let down and then the skis are lowered just a bit below the tires."

"Someday I'd like to watch them land on snow, but I'm not sure I want to be on the plane," remarked Gary.

"If anybody can pull this mission off, the people in that air guard unit can. They are the best in the world at landing and taking off on ice and snow. They have the attitude that if a mission needs to be done they can do it. This will be just another assignment for them. I'll call you as soon as I hear something."

Schenectady, New York

Major Kathy Barnes parked her Saab and pulled the heavy garage door down. Just as the rolling door came to a stop her husband entered the garage through the kitchen door and said the Air National Guard base wanted her to return immediately.

"I just left there," she replied, exasperated. "What did they want?"

"I don't know. They just said it was 'Top Secret' and an emergency."

"Well, there goes supper," Kathy sighed resignedly. "I'll call you if I'll be late."

Major Barnes drove back to the base located only a few miles from her home. She strode into base operations and asked for the officer on duty who had called. The Operation's officer told her Colonel Crosby was waiting for her in the flight briefing room.

Major Barnes entered the briefing room and immediately realized something very big was happening. Waiting in the room with Colonel Crosby were several pilots and other flight crew members from the base.

"Come in and shut the door, Major," said Colonel Crosby. He briefed them that the unit received an emergency assignment from the Pentagon to pick up three people for the CIA who were on an American sub. One person was injured and in serious condition. They would transport them to the Albany Airport. He then added that Shawn Murphy was one of the three people.

When Crosby said Shawn Murphy's name, Kathy looked around the room and noticed others were doing the same thing. She was confident that they were as shocked as she was that Shawn was working on an assignment with the CIA.

Everyone had assumed he was in Europe working as a coach for the bobsled association. Kathy was amused and laughed to herself when she thought about how pissed Murphy's supervisor, Olive Hanson would be when she found out. Good. Murphy put one over on the bitch.

The briefing lasted twenty minutes. Two C-130 planes were being prepared for the mission. Both planes would leave within the hour and the final instructions would be given when they landed at Sondrestrom Air Base, Greenland. The plan was for one plane to land on the ice cap and the second plane would be used only in the event the first plane had problems. It would circle overhead observing the mission and would be prepared to land and assist if an emergency developed.

The briefing ended and Major Barnes rushed back to her office to pick up her flight gear and medical equipment. She served part-time in the Air National Guard as the commander of the air evacuation unit. Kathy was a physician's assistance and worked full-time in a hospital near Schenectady. She was the best qualified person to handle the medical emergency that Crosby had described to them.

She walked around the corner into her office and was greeted by a flight medical technician who handed her a crew list. "These people will be here within the next fifteen minutes, Major. What's going on?".

"We can't discuss it with anyone," she replied. "All I can say is we're going to Greenland to air-evac some injured person for the CIA."

He looked at his list that contained the names of three nurses and six medical technicians to make up two medical crews. Kathy wrote up a request for the medical equipment she needed for the mission and gave it to the supply clerk. His instructions were for half of the equipment to be placed on the first plane and the other half on the second plane. Kathy picked up the phone and called her husband to tell him that she would be gone for at least two days. He was a retired medical officer and understood her situation.

She made out the paperwork required prior to the flight and went to the Air Evac briefing room. She was surprised that everyone in the medical crew had already arrived. Major Barnes gave a quick mission briefing to the two flight medical crews. They left the building and walked out to the planes.

Colonel Crosby was already on the first plane waiting for Major Barnes and the medical crew. There was little conversation as the flight engineer and the loadmaster prepared the huge, gray and orange C-130 for take off. The second plane was scheduled to leave ten minutes behind them and would catch up during the flight.

Major Barnes sat in her seat and tried to imagine what Shawn Murphy was doing that would involve the CIA. She knew that Shawn spent a lot of time in Europe but still didn't have a clue as to why the CIA was involved or what was he doing on the Greenland ice cap. She gave up and leaned back in her webbed seat. Despite the tremendous noise inside the plane, Major Barnes closed her eyes in an attempt to rest as the plane warmed up.

North Atlantic

Shawn and Ray walked down the narrow hallway and knocked on Doctor Angerosa's office door. They had been checking in on Boris every fifteen or twenty minutes trying to obtain information about his condition.

"Come in," called Dr. Angerosa patiently.

"Sorry to keep bothering you so often, Doctor," Shawn replied, ducking his head as he stepped into the small room.

"That's okay," laughed Angerosa. "You two guys are more nervous than a young man who's wife is delivering their first child."

"Probably so, but we have a lot at stake here, Doctor," said Ray, worried.

"Boris is somewhat stable, but he's still in very serious condition," replied the doctor. "However, his blood pressure has picked up a bit and that's a good sign."

"What are his chances?" asked Shawn.

"It's really much too early to make an accurate prediction." Doctor Angerosa ran his fingers through his hair as he thought about Boris's condition. "I've temporarily repaired his spleen, removed several slivers of glass, and sutured the severed artery."

"Will this hold him until we can get him to a medical center in the States?" asked Ray.

"I can't answer that," replied the doctor. "He needs a splenectomy and I can't perform it here because we don't have the necessary equipment on the sub."

"We have to do something. We can't let this guy die." Shawn was anxious and upset.

"There's another problem," said the doctor. "The longer we wait to remove his spleen, the greater the chances are it will get infected. I started an IV to give him antibiotics but he needs to have his spleen removed. If you wait too long he'll either die from the infection or the spleen will rupture and kill him."

"What the hell can we do?" asked Shawn.

"I've asked Captain Young to contact Admiral Miller who is the Commander of the Atlantic Fleet and brief him on Boris's condition. Captain Young and Admiral Miller have been in contact with each other and I got the impression that they're working on an air evacuation plan. Why don't you go to the bridge and talk to the captain?"

"Do you think Boris is stable enough for an air evacuation?" asked Shawn.

"I don't think you have a choice," replied the doctor. "He has to get to a medical center soon or he'll die and I don't think this sub will get there quick enough."

Shawn and Ray thanked the doctor and went to the bridge where Captain Young was working. The captain filled them in on the plan to airlift Boris on a C-130. The sub would surface through the ice four hundred miles south of the North Pole. A ski-equipped C-130 would land on the ice cap and pick up Boris then airlift him to Albany.

The captain told them the C-130 could transport Boris to Albany in about thirteen hours compared to six days in the sub. He was confident after conferring with Doctor Angerosa that the risk of air transporting Boris was worth it.

Schenectady, New York

Colonel Crosby and his co-pilot completed their checklist and taxied the C-130 onto the ramp leading to the airport's runway. They stopped just short of the runway to test the brakes once more and checked the engine rpm's. Satisfied everything was ready for takeoff, the colonel slowly eased the huge plane toward the runway.

"Schenectady tower, this is three-niner-seven requesting clearance for takeoff," the colonel spoke into his mike.

"Three-niner-seven, you are clear," replied the voice from the control tower. "Have a safe flight north."

"Roger," responded the colonel.

Colonel Crosby lined the plane up on the runway, locked the brakes and increased the rpm's on the four huge turbo props. He released the brakes and pushed all four throttles forward to their maximum position and the plane moved forward picking up speed rapidly. Within seconds their ground speed reached one hundred and five knots and the colonel set the flaps into the take-off position forcing the plane to lift away from the runway.

Major Barnes held onto the web seat straps as she felt the plane lifting under her. The thrust from the turboprops pushed the C-130 higher and higher. The plane banked and continued to gain elevation as it headed north. The C-130 finally reached a flight altitude of thirty-three thousand feet and leveled off. A short time later Colonel Crosby received a call on the radio from Major Hudson, the pilot of the second C-130 that left ten minutes behind them. He informed Colonel Crosby that the Pentagon had sent another message ordering a third C-130 be sent north to assist them.

North Atlantic

Captain Young looked at the message that the radioman had given him. The Soviet sub, *Krahsnays*, had changed course again and was following less than one mile behind them, well within striking distance. The Soviet cruiser, *Veenstan* had reached the *Beriozka* and was alongside the fishing vessel.

"What is the current position of the *Charmer?*" asked the Captain without looking up. He wanted the Destroyer moved closer to the *Willsboro*.

"She's about thirty-two miles southwest of us, sir," Gochenaur pointed to the location on the screen.

"John, I want the *Charmer* in a position so she will intersect our path if we continue in a straight line."

Lieutenant Gochenaur picked up a pencil and drew a line on the chart sitting on the table. He marked an X on the map and punched several figures into the computer and a mark appeared on the screen. "She'll intersect with us in two hours and fifteen minutes if we both maintain our speeds, sir."

"Send this code one priority message to her, " ordered the captain. "Proceed to sixty-one degrees north, zero one-thirty west...stop...*Krahsnays* within striking distance... further orders will follow."

"Yes, sir."

The captain turned to John, saying, "Give me another position that will put us about four hundred miles from the North Pole where we can safely rendezvous with the C-130. I want a straight line. Doc Angerosa said we don't have a moment to waste because this guy is fading fast. His only hope of staying alive lies with us and the med-evac people getting him to a hospital in time."

Gochenaur picked up the pencil and ruler and drew a straight line on the chart from their location to the North Pole then placed another X on the map. He entered the information into the computer and instantly, several figures appeared on the screen. "Here's the best position, sir," Gochenaur pointed to the X on the map. "Eighty-three degrees north, zero zero three degrees east. It's eight-hundred and forty nautical miles from our present position and four-hundred and twenty nautical miles from the North Pole."

"What's the depth of the ice there?"

"Nine feet, sir."

"Perfect!"

"Is that thick enough for the C-130 to land?"

"Yes. They need at least seven feet and we can't break up through more than ten feet," replied the captain. "How much time will it take us to get there?"

"Thirty hours at twenty-eight knots, sir."

The captain picked up the phone and called the radioman and told him to come back to the bridge. Within a minute he walked into the room with a note pad and pen.

"I want to send a coded message. Send it code-one priority to Captain Miller at Atlantic Fleet Headquarters," said the captain. "*Krahsnays* sub trailing *Willsboro* within striking distance...request permission for *Charmer* to intersect and challenge...stop...request permission for *Willsboro* to rendezvous with C-130 at eighty-three degrees north, zero zero three degrees east, zero two zero zero...stop...request confirmation...stop. Get that out immediately and let me know the moment you have a confirmation."

"Yes, sir," The radioman turned and left the room, shutting the door behind him.

"I want the *Charmer* to run interference with the *Krahsnays* so we can rendezvous on time with the C-130," said the captain, looking at Gochenaur. "I hope to hell this doesn't create an international incident."

The Pentagon

Admiral Miller's secretary called and told him that Commander Craig Talarico had a code-one priority message to deliver to him personally.

"Tell him to come in, please."

Commander Talarico opened the door and briskly walked across the large office and handed the sealed envelope to the admiral. He immediately opened it and pulled out the message. He read it several times before he spoke. "Send back a confirmation for both requests at once. Be sure to send it code-one priority," reminded the admiral.

"Yes, sir," replied Talarico.

Admiral Miller waited until he left and then called the White House on a safe line. He informed the Chief of Staff of the current situation in the North Atlantic and the present medical condition of Boris. He hung up and called Gary Circe at CIA Headquarters and brought him up to date on the situation. He finished the phone call and sat back in his large chair thinking about Boris and hoping they would get him to the medical center in time.

Sondrestrom Air Force Base, Greenland

Colonel David Crosby eased the C-130 toward the runway at the Sondrestrom Air Force Base. The tower had just given him permission to land and the huge plane touched down on the runway. The colonel put the flaps in the down position while his co-pilot changed the pitch of the enormous propellers to help slow the plane. Crosby applied pressure to the brakes and the C-130 instantly decreased speed.

The C-130 rolled to the taxi strip and the colonel headed the plane for the

→ *Ice Spy*

parking ramp located in front of the Base Operations building. The crew completed the final items on the checklist then everyone left the aircraft and walked to the operations building. Crosby separated himself from the crew and went to the desk to file his flight papers. He identified himself to the operations officer and asked if there were any messages for him. The operations officer handed him a sealed envelope with *Top Secret* inscribed on it in several places. Crosby signed for the message and opened the envelope. The message directed both C-130s to rendezvous with the *Willsboro* the next morning at zero six five zero zulu at eighty-three degrees north, zero zero three degrees east. 0650 zulu time meant 0750 at the ice cap so they should take off at 0600 in the morning.

Crosby walked across the room where the crew was waiting for him. He briefed them, then suggested they get some rest and be at the plane at 0500 for a 0600 take off. The co-pilot handed the colonel a key for his room and the crew left to get some well needed rest. The ten hour flight had tired everyone and they knew the next day would be a long one.

Colonel Crosby opened the door to his small room and went inside, tossing his jacket on the chair. He opened the side compartment to his flight bag and pulled out a fifth of scotch. He guzzled a large portion then looked at the bottle and thought, "This is about the only thing I can enjoy anymore. At least you let me relax." Crosby was a lonely man, not an alcoholic. He finished the rest of the scotch and turned off the light.

North Atlantic

The subs radioman's computer deciphered and printed out the code-one priority message just received from the Pentagon. He rushed out of the radio room and went to the bridge to deliver the message to Captain Young. The captain took the message and read the directive.

"Admiral Miller just sent us confirmation on both my requests," stated the Captain. "I want to send a message to the *Charmer*."

"Permission received...stop... you are directed to intercept and challenge the *Krahsnays*," dictated the Captain. "Send it code-one priority."

"Yes, sir," He left and returned to the radio room.

"What's our position now, Lieutenant?" asked Captain Young.

"Seventy degrees north, zero one six zero east." He put the information into the computer and pointed to their position on the screen. "Right here, sir. We should pass the *Charmer* within the hour."

The *Krahsnays* had slowed slightly and was now following two miles behind them. The *Charmer* was still on course and Captain Young assumed the *Krahsnays* was hesitant about challenging two American ships. He studied the chart for several minutes and then he walked over to his table and began to write his report, complaining to himself that everything had to be documented.

Sondrestrom Air Base, Greenland

Colonel Crosby and his crew went down through the checklist while at the same time the second C-130 crew did the same. A third C-130 with two extra crews had arrived during the night. Crosby was annoyed, thinking the third plane was a waste of money that would come out of his flying budget at the base. He wasn't happy since he was already in trouble for authorizing too many missions. He would try to have the Pentagon pick up the expenses for this mission since they had directed it.

"Checklist complete, Colonel," said the co-pilot.

"What's our heading?" asked the navigator.

"Put in zero eighty-three degrees north, zero zero three degrees east," replied Crosby.

"Roger," replied the navigator, thinking uneasily that the colonel's breath reeked heavily of booze. "What time is our rendezvous?"

"Zero six fifty zulu time," replied Crosby. "Exactly."

"We need to maintain an air speed of two hundred and five knots. That will put us there a couple of minutes early," said the navigator.

"Good. We'll have to make a couple of low level approaches to survey the ice conditions before we can attempt to land," replied the colonel. "Cobra two, this is Cobra one. Fix your heading for zero eighty-three degrees north, zero zero three degrees east. Maintain radio silence until we reach the target. Do you read me?"

"Zero eighty-three degrees north, zero zero three degrees east," came the reply. "We'll be at your back door all the way. Good luck."

Colonel Crosby eased the plane out onto the taxi strip and prepared the C-130 for take-off after the crew completed their final checklist. Moments later the plane sped down the runway and climbed quickly up into the early morning darkness and disappeared in the sky. The second C-130 left three minutes later and the two planes flew together in the direction of the polar ice cap.

North Atlantic

Captain Young looked at his watch. It was zulu one thirty, just thirty minutes till they were scheduled to rendezvous with the C-130. Doctor Angerosa had just given him an update on Boris's condition and it wasn't good. They would have to get him on the C-130 soon or the defecting coach would die.

"John, get the radioman in here," ordered the captain. "We need to make contact with the C-130 before we break through the ice. I want to make sure that they are ready."

Lieutenant Gochenaur called and told him to come to the bridge. The captain walked over to the large radar screen where Gochenaur was working and looked over the navigator's shoulder. Moments later the radioman entered the room and waited for the captain to give him instructions.

"Where are the *Charmer* and the *Krahsnays* right now?" asked Captain Young.

"Right here, sir," Gochenaur pointed to two spots on the large screen. "This is the *Krahsnays* and the *Charmer* is about three miles behind. The *Krahsnays* changed course when the *Charmer* began to follow her. She has been on a straight course in the direction of Norway ever since and may be headed for the *Beriozka*."

"Where is the C-130?"

"These two bleeps are the 130s, sir," replied Gochenaur. I would estimate that they are about a hundred and twenty miles out."

"What's our exact position right now?"

"I just checked the figures with the global position on the satellite and it indicates that we are eighty-three degrees north, zero zero three one degrees east."

"Try to contact the C-130," instructed the Captain. "Her call sign is Cobra one."

The radioman sat down at the radio and picked up the mike. "Cobra one, this is Icebreaker two, do you read me?"

"Icebreaker two, this is Cobra one," came the reply. "Authenticate zulu alfa, repeat, authenticate zulu alfa."

"Authenticate zulu alfa, X-ray," replied the radioman. Authenticate zulu alfa was a special code request for the *Willsboro* to verify that she was an American submarine. The code for all American military ships and planes that day was 'X-ray.' The C-130 was thirty minutes away from the target area so Captain Young gave the order to surface. It would take the sub nearly that long to ram up through the nine foot ice ceiling and the submarine's black hatch would give the C-130's navigator a visible point to use for landing.

The submarine would rise up slowly until it made contact with the ice. It would apply pressure to the ice to weaken it and then descend fifty feet and rise up again slightly faster ramming the ice on the second attempt. The *Willsboro* would ram the ice four or five times before it could break through to the surface.

The flight crew was apprehensive because they were aware just how difficult and extremely dangerous the polar ice cap was to land on in a C-130 with skis. The white snow made it nearly impossible for the crew to clearly see what the ice conditions were below on the snow's surface. The two C-130 crews had their eyes focused on the ice cap below when suddenly they spotted the *Willsboro*'s main hatch break through the ice.

"Icebreaker two, this is Cobra one," said Colonel Crosby. "We have visual contact with you. Repeat, we have visual contact."

"Cobra one. Make your low level approaches now but don't attempt a landing until we instruct you to do so," came the reply. "We'll put some flags in the snow to outline a safe place for you to land."

"Affirmative," replied Colonel Crosby.

The two low level passes would permit the crew to inspect the ice for any obvious obstructions such as broken sections of ice or large snow drifts. The C-130 circled and made the first pass at five hundred feet without any problems. The C-130 crew watched the hatch open and several sailors came out and climbed down to the ice on the sub's surface. Several members from the sub ran out onto the ice and quickly inserted bright orange flags into the snow to show the C-130 where to land. When the snow-covered ice runway was marked out the sailors stood off to the side.

The winds appeared to be calm and the aircraft stayed on course during the simulated approach. Crosby circled again and dropped down to two hundred feet. The second attempt went without any problem so Colonel Crosby radioed the submarine that they were ready to land. The sub's crew felt the wind created by the huge plane as it passed directly over them.

"Cobra one, you are cleared to land," replied the sub. "Be advised there are low level high wind gusts. Repeat, you are cleared to land, be advised, we are experiencing low level high wind gusts."

"Cobra two, this is Cobra one. Stand by, we are going in, do you read me?"

"We read you, Cobra one," came the reply. "We are overhead at one thousand and Cobra three is flying a pattern two miles west. Good luck and be careful."

Crosby instructed the co-pilot to lower and lock the skis into place. The crew went through the checklist and the colonel eased the huge plane down to the right side of the sub and her crew. The orange flags outlined the runway perfectly against the snow giving the colonel an excellent target. The C-130 had dropped to within a hundred feet of the packed snow when a powerful gust blew the plane thirty feet to the left.

A sailor standing next to the runway with large orange flags ready to direct and marshall the plane to the runway instantly waved the flags desperately trying to warn Crosby to abort the landing attempt.

"Cobra one, pull up, Cobra one, pull up," yelled the voice frantically on the radio. "Cobra one, pull up. Oh, shit! They're going to crash."

The plane's skis made contact on the surface and slid along the ice. Crosby and his co-pilot were horror-struck when two hundred feet away and directly in front of the plane appeared a six-foot snow drift. The plane had missed the emergency runway completely and was sliding toward the snow mound.

"I can miss it," yelled Crosby as he attempted to guide the plane to the right of the huge snow drift. Suddenly, he realized the plane's ground speed was too fast. The indicator showed one hundred and twenty miles an hour. The heavy plane refused to respond to his attempts to maneuver the plane back on course and plowed through the huge snow drift. It continued on its course for a few hundred feet before the plane stopped, throwing maps, papers, books, and anything not fastened down. During the impact, the right wing dipped sharply and the number four turbo prop engine slammed into the ice, shattering the four large propellers. One propeller flew off and rammed into the number three engine, destroying it.

"Kill the power," yelled Crosby. He and the co-pilot frantically began to hit switches.

"Cobra one. This is Cobra two, do you read me?" asked the voice on the radio.

"We read you, Cobra two," replied the colonel.

"What's your situation? Is anyone injured?"

"We're checking the crew right now for injuries," replied Crosby. "We shut down power and it appears that our skis and both number three and four engines are destroyed. We haven't spotted any fires yet."

Major Raymond Hudson eased his C-130 lower and circled the crash site while his crew looked for signs of fire or smoke. They could see the sub's crew running toward the immobile plane laying about a thousand feet from the submarine. Moments later the two crew doors opened and Hudson could see the crew exit the plane.

"Cobra three, this is Cobra two, do you read me?" asked Major Hudson.

"Affirmative Cobra two," replied the voice on the radio.

"We need back up," instructed Major Hudson. "Cobra one had a mishap on landing and we're going in to pick up the crew, do you read me?"

"Affirmative, Cobra two," replied the voice. "We're to your south right now and have visual sight of you. For Christ's sake, be careful. Don't be stupid like Crosby. Pull up if they wave you off."

"Affirmative," replied Hudson. "Okay, guys, let's go through the checklist."

The major and his crew rushed through the list and after the skis were locked into place they made two low level approaches. On the third approach the major eased the plane onto the snow and immediately began to reverse the turboprops. This was the only way to stop a ski-equipped plane on the Arctic ice. Something, thought Hudson, that Crosby forgot. An enormous blanket of snow blew in all directions as the plane slid along the ice runway marked with bright orange flags.

Major Hudson successfully stopped the plane several thousand feet from his touchdown point. He turned it around and slowly headed back toward the sub and the crash site. He pulled the C-130 to within fifty feet of the disabled C-130 and stopped, leaving the turbo props running to make certain the plane had power for take off. The aero-medical team rushed off the plane and helped the crew from the wrecked plane get on board. There were no major injuries among the crew, although most were visibly shaken. The last crew member climbed on and Major Hudson eased the plane toward the submarine.

Chapter Twenty-Seven

→ *Ice Spy*

Polar Ice Cap

Doctor Angerosa and his medical team strapped Boris into a litter with a make-shift brace holding his IV bag in place. The moment Major Barnes and the air-evac team arrived the doctor briefed them on Boris's current condition.. He finished the medical briefing and the team picked up the litter and transported the defecting Soviet coach to the C-130. Shawn and the professor followed them across the snow covered ice cap and walked up the rear ramp into the plane.

The third C-130 continued to fly overhead in a narrow, circular pattern prepared to give support if needed by the two crews on the ground. The air-evac medical crew secured Boris's litter in place and advised Major Hudson they were ready to take off. He moved the C-130 to the end of the make-shift runway and slowly turned the huge cargo plane around. The crew quickly went through the take-off checklist and then the loud rumble from the engines vibrated off the ice cap as Hudson pushed the throttles forward. The four turbo prop engines roared and the plane started moving forward.

Major Barnes made a last minute adjustment to Boris's litter then rushed to secure herself in a web seat. The submarine crew covered their ears with their hands to protect themselves against the extraordinary noise and watched the plane rapidly accelerate across the snow. The combination of soft snow under the skis and extra passengers on board made the plane respond sluggishly. It reached ground speed of sixty-five knots and the co-pilot set the flaps in the takeoff position.

"Prepare the JATO rockets for blast off," ordered Major Hudson.

The flight engineer instantly reached up and held his hand on the JATO rocket assist switch waiting for Hudson to give him the command to engage the rockets.

"JATO now."

The engineer hit the JATO assist rocket switch and four rockets on each side of the plane instantly fired. An incredible force from the JATO rockets thrust the plane forward reaching one hundred knots. The JATO assist lasted for only eight seconds, long enough for the plane to separate from the ice-covered runway and start climbing into the sky. Hudson banked and pointed the plane south in the direction of the States.

The Pentagon

Commander Craig Talarico scanned the top secret coded message then immediately took it down the hall to Admiral Mark Miller. The admiral thanked him and called Gary Circe at CIA headquarters in Langley, Virginia.

"Circe, here, may I help you?"

"Gary, this is Mark Miller."

"Good morning, Mark. What's up?"

"I'd like to update you on Boris Yegorov's condition."

" I was just thinking about him."

Mark immediately informed the CIA chief on Boris's situation and then told him about the accident. He hung up and called General Abbott at Air National Guard Headquarters.

"General Abbott, can I help you?"

"Good morning, Howard. Mark Miller here." The admiral knew General Abbott would not be happy with the information he was about to impart. "They had a slight mishap with one of the C-130's on the Polar ice cap. I wanted to brief you about it personally before the damn media gets wind of it and starts hounding you."

"What happened?"

"The first C-130 crashed when it attempted to land next to the *Willsboro*."

"Oh, my God! Were there any casualties?"

"No, thank God. In fact, there were no serious injuries," replied the admiral with relief. "Unfortunately, the plane was seriously damaged."

"I was afraid you were going to say that." Abbott closed his eyes and the plane's price tag flashed in his mind. "The plane is worth over twenty-eight million. I hope the guy they're smuggling out of the Soviet Union is worth it."

"We never want to have problems like this, Howard. It's tough to place a dollar value on his technical information but some of the brightest people in this country believe it's worth it."

Abbott was silent for a minute and then asked, "What caused the crash?"

"The official investigation hasn't begun yet, but Captain Young from the *Willsboro* indicated it was pilot error," answered the Admiral.

"Who was the aircraft commander?"

"Colonel Crosby," replied Miller, shuffling papers. "The initial report indicates that Crosby refused to abort his first attempt to land after a crosswind blew the plane off course during its landing attempt. The sub's crew waved him off and ordered him on the radio to abort, but he ignored them and attempted the landing anyway."

"I'm upset that this happened, but frankly, Mark, we've been expecting it for some time," replied Abbott. "Crosby marches to his own drum roll and he thinks he's infallible. This mistake will take some of the starch out of his damn arrogance. I'll personally see to it that he gets assigned to a desk job in a closet somewhere when this is over."

Admiral Miller briefed the general on the rest of the mission and hung up. He sat at his desk and thought about the accident. I'll never understand why some individuals refuse to take advice. Their cocky and arrogant attitude often put so many people in such risky positions just like this one on the ice cap.

Albany, New York

Doctor Albert Hayes studied the information he had just received from the navy's Atlantic Fleet Headquarters in Washington. Boris Yegorov needed an emergency splenectomy. The medical information was no longer pertinent to Doctor Hayes since Boris's condition may have deteriorated immensely from when the report was made eleven hours earlier. One of the first things they would have to do the moment Boris arrived would be to start a blood transfusion, so he ordered an ample supply that matched Boris's blood type on the sheet. The doctor made arrangements to have an operating room available with the special medical equipment he would need for the operation.

The Albany Medical Center dispatched their ambulance to the Albany County Airport to meet the C-130 due to land within the hour. Major Ray Hudson made arrangements with the airport to keep the runway open and give immediate clearance to their plane when they were within fifty miles. The air-evac plane would be directed to a taxi strip where the ambulance would be waiting. To save time, the huge plane's turbo-props would continue running while Boris was transferred to the waiting ambulance.

Joe Sweeney sat near the runway in a New York State Police car waiting for the plane to arrive with the injured, defecting Soviet coach. He looked over the list of security requests he had given the State Police Commissioner. He was taking every precaution to protect Boris once he was on American soil.

Joe knew that it would be quite easy for a Soviet agent to kill Boris and make it look accidental. He had made arrangements to have three different ambulances meet the plane to confuse any effort to murder Boris. His concern was that a Soviet agent would attempt to launch a rocket or a small bomb if they could identify the ambulance. Each ambulance would then go to a different hospital to make it difficult for anyone to know which ambulance Boris was placed in or which hospital he was admitted as a patient. All three hospitals would list on their record a fictitious name. The Albany Medical Center had been instructed not to list Boris as a patient and if any inquires were made they were to notify the CIA immediately.

Cobra Two

Shawn and Ray watched Major Kathy Barnes brush some loose hairs away from Boris's forehead. She gently massaged his hand in an effort to help relax the semi-conscious man. The loadmaster signaled, thumbs down, to Kathy indicating that the plane was descending and would land shortly. She nodded her understanding and began to prepare the Soviet coach for the landing. The medical technicians helped her secure the litter straps snugly and she checked the IV bag to be sure it wouldn't break loose when the plane reversed its turbo-props to slow the C-130 once they landed on the runway. Confident that Boris was protected in the litter, she took his vital signals once more before returning to her seat.

"Albany tower, this is Cobra two requesting immediate military clearance to land?" Major Hudson turned the page in his checklist while he waited for a response from the tower.

"Cobra two, you are clear for landing on runway two-two," replied the voice on the radio. "Winds are north-west at six knots and ground temperature is thirty-eight degrees. Take your aircraft to the last exit once you have landed and turn off onto the taxi strip. Make the turn and stop. Your party is prepared to receive your passenger at that location."

"That's affirmative, Albany tower," replied Hudson. "We're approximately seven minutes away."

"We have you on radar," replied the voice on the radio. "You are cleared to land."

Joe Sweeney was glad trooper Hoyt finally turned the heat up in the cruiser. The temperature was only thirty-eight degrees, normal for a mid-March evening. He wasn't dressed properly and had gotten chilled while they waited for the plane to arrive. The car was running but the heater was turned down. Hoyt wasn't a very talkative man and seemed content to just sit and think while he waited.

Their silence was interrupted when the police cruiser's radio informed them that the C-130 was on final approach and would be on the ground within five or six minutes. The aircraft approached the runway in a straight line from the north and continued to descend rapidly. They watched the plane disappear for a moment as the trees at the end of the runway blocked their view. Seconds later the huge cargo plane rolled into sight again. The noise created when the C-130 ski-plane reversed its turbo-props prompted them to hold their hands over their ears for protection.

Inside the plane, Major Barnes stood up and pointed to the medical technicians who were waiting to get on the two extra litters. They had volunteered to be carried out to the two extra ambulances and be transported to neighboring hospitals as decoys.

Major Hudson turned the steering wheel and guided the plane toward the exit ramp where police and ambulances were now waiting. He told his co-pilot to lock the parking brakes and then he instructed the loadmaster, to open the large cargo door in the rear of the plane. The door opened and the loadmaster quickly put the walk ramps in place so the air-evac medical crew could carry the litters to the waiting ambulances. Boris was brought out on the second litter and placed into the ambulance waiting to transfer him to the Albany Medical Center. Major Barnes climbed in and rode with him to the hospital.

Trooper Hoyt rushed over to Shawn and Ray and led them back to the police cruiser waiting with Sweeney. They watched the ambulance with Boris pull away from the plane and then the trooper immediately followed it with the police cruiser. A state police car followed each ambulance out of the airport.

Several fire trucks were parked on the edge of the taxi strip as part of the plan. Joe wanted it to look as if the plane was having problems with its landing gear. This also gave the ambulances an excuse for being there. He knew the media wouldn't be fooled for long once they saw the ambulances rush out with their lights flashing.

Shawn was amused as he watched Hoyt skillfully maneuver the cruiser through the Friday night traffic staying close to the ambulance. They arrived at the hospital in eight minutes and the ambulance quickly backed up to the emergency room entrance. The hospital doors swung open and Fred Unser rushed out with the medical crew. He stood watch while they whisked Boris into the hospital on the stretcher with a blanket over his face. Shawn and Ray followed Fred into the emergency room that had been closed off to the public by state police troopers and several CIA agents.

Boris was taken to the fifth floor where Doctor Hayes and his team were waiting to prep the defecting coach for the operation. Two members of the hospital's medical staff took blood samples in the elevator to save time and continued to check Boris's vital signs on the way up to the operating room. Joe Sweeney had made arrangements to have a CIA agent scrubbed and dressed in a hospital gown. The agent would stay in the operating room with Boris during the procedure.

Fred entered the small waiting room at the end of the hall where Shawn and Ray were waiting with Joe. "You guys did one hell of a job," said Fred as he reached out to shake Shawn and Ray's hands. "I said in the beginning that it would be a miracle if we could pull this off, and by God, it *was* a miracle."

"If I had known what was going to happen, I would have hung up on Joe when he first called me," replied Shawn laughing. "Man, this has been a rough few weeks."

"Don't think it's over yet, Shawn," said Ray. "Wait till you call Angela. You haven't called her for nearly three weeks. She'll snag you by the ear when she sees you."

"Before you call your wife, I want to set up a time for all of us to debrief the mission tomorrow," said Fred.

"How about one in the afternoon at the air base where we can have some privacy?" asked Shawn. "Ray can stay overnight at my house. We can sleep late and get some well-deserved rest."

"That's fine," replied Fred. "You guys get out of here and try to relax. I'll see you both tomorrow afternoon at the base."

Shawn went over to the desk and asked to use the telephone. He called Angela and asked her to meet him and Ray at the Roman Villa restaurant in an hour. He hung up and walked over to Ray and told him of the plan to meet Angela for dinner at the restaurant. They took the elevator to the first floor and left the hospital unnoticed by a side door. Outside they hailed a waiting taxi and the driver slowly drove the cab around the mass of police cars and two TV mobile broadcast vehicles that were in the hospital parking lot.

The taxi pulled out onto New Scotland Avenue and Shawn looked back at the scene in the parking lot. Red lights were still flashing on police cars throughout the lot and the TV news teams had erected portable towers so they could broadcast live from the hospital.

Shawn nudged Ray and pointed to the mass of confusion in the lot.

"Why are the TV crews here?" asked Ray. "How would the media know so quickly that something was happening at the hospital?"

"They monitor police radio bands, but I'll bet they don't know what is really going on right now," laughed Shawn.

Ray smiled and looked at Shawn. "No one will ever believe us. *No one.*"